PARADISE
JUNCTION

Also by Phillip Finch

The Reckoning
In a Place Dark and Secret
Trespass
Sugarland
Fatal Flaw

PHILLIP FINCH

PARADISE JUNCTION

ST. MARTIN'S PRESS   NEW YORK

This novel is a work of fiction. All of the events, characters, names, and places depicted in this novel are entirely fictitious or are used fictitiously. No representation that any statement made in this novel is true or that any incident depicted in this novel actually occurred is intended or should be inferred by the reader.

PARADISE JUNCTION. Copyright © 1993 by Phillip Finch. All rights reserved. Printed in the United States of America. No part of this book may be used or reproduced in any manner whatsoever without written permission except in the case of brief quotations embodied in critical articles or reviews. For information, address St. Martin's Press, 175 Fifth Avenue, New York, N.Y. 10010.

Editor: Jared Kieling
Design by Dawn Niles

Library of Congress Cataloging-in-Publication Data

Finch, Phillip.
    Paradise junction / Phillip Finch.
      p. cm.
    ISBN 0-312-08869-8
    I. Title.
    PS3556.I456P37   1993
    813'.54—dc20   92-40823
                           CIP

First Edition: February 1993
10 9 8 7 6 5 4 3 2 1

To my darling Dahlia
Who brought gifts
Of light
And love
And life

PARADISE JUNCTION

Out to the edge.

Into the abyss.

Caitlin Hames had this notion. Life was boring, life had no meaning, if you stuck to what was safe and acceptable. You had to free yourself from middle-ground mediocrity. Break away, maybe break some rules to do it. Journey out to the extremes. Get out to the rim of existence, lean out, and stare into blankness.

It was the kind of idea that could sprout in the head of someone who achieved her lifelong ambition of having too much money and not enough to do.

Or maybe she was born slightly kinked, with this germ of wickedness that she had cultivated all these years, until finally it flourished.

Out to the edge.

At first Hays Teale blamed it on the burbs. Caitlin grew up in New Rochelle, Westchester County, an only child in a four-bedroom Tudor, couple of cars, a wheaten Scottie. Her father was in advertising, took the train into Manhattan every morning. New Rochelle was nice, not some collection of cookie-cutter subdivisions, not Levittown by a wide stretch. But garnish it any way you wanted, if Daddy trooped off in the morning and joined the gray throngs on the station platform, then you were a suburban brat, forever stamped by shopping mall and station wagon.

In the first few months of their marriage Hays believed that New Rochelle had created Caitlin. Certainly it explained her disdain for the settled and predictable. It would also explain her taste for the ultrafine. Not that she had grown up with it—New Rochelle was hardly ultra—but she had been close enough to realize what she was missing, to sense the polished dimensions of fineness, to know it and to feel deserving and deprived: a special hunger that even the hungry never knew. The hungry least of all.

Hays himself grew up in Scottsdale, son of a man who managed half a dozen supermarkets in Tucson and Phoenix. Hays too sensed the depressing rut of the so-called good life, a huge notch or two shy of what was really worth having. Wasn't this the goad that pushed him into top-bracket achievement, ninety-ninth-percentile earnings?

But Caitlin had something else. Caitlin knew how to live free. Not that she gave up the good things. Far from it: she took them as her due, and went on from there. She explored. She knew how to color outside the lines. Caitlin was ever ready to tweak the tiger's nose, and it was exhilarating. Scary, and addictive.

After a while Hays realized that you did not explain Caitlin, not really. You either walked away from her, fast, or you hung on and let her take you where she would.

Into the abyss.

Still, even knowing all this, Hays never really expected her to go the limit. He figured it was like a good ride at an amusement park. It thrilled you, it raced your pulse, but you were never in jeopardy.

Later, Hays realized that when Caitlin acted out of control . . . she really was out of control.

Even then, up to the end, he could have gotten off. But he didn't. She was going where he wanted to go, doing what he wanted to do. She went out there to the edge, and beyond, and he did, too.

1

Merle Welcome watched the gas dump blow.

It was underground. Underground, air didn't reach it all at once. The explosion blossomed, in stages maybe half a second apart. First the earth was jolted. Big slabs of concrete lifted above the bunker, levitating for an instant. Gouts of flame burst through the seams between the slabs, and then it was all flame, a sooty orange fireball that bloomed and bloomed and bloomed, sucking air and spending it and sucking some more.

It was still burning hard when Welcome turned away and crawled back to Oliver, his battle buddy from the Recon squad.

"This is one strange war," Welcome said.

"They're all strange," Oliver said.

Welcome couldn't disagree with that. Maybe it was just him.

But he did feel different.

It started a couple of months before, a little after New Year's, when he picked an envelope out of the mail pile for "Any Soldier." It was a third-grade girl. *In my class we are writing to soljers. is it hot in the desert? Do you have Water to drink? Are you Afriad?*

Welcome read all the way to the end before he realized that the letter was from Coffeyville, Kansas. Welcome grew up outside Coffeyville. The school was his old grade school.

Spooky. He thought about the girl sitting in the same classroom where he had sat, maybe even in the same desk. And he ends up with the letter. What were the odds?

He didn't even think of the place as home anymore. His parents died; his brother and sister got married and moved away. It was seventeen years since he left, joined the Marines on his eighteenth birthday. He had seldom been back.

Now he read this letter in the mottled shade of a camouflage tent. All around him were heat and sand and the bare desert, and what he saw was Kansas. It came back to him hard, the memory of storms marching across the prairie, purple veils of rain falling off the edge of a distant thunderhead. Of driving his father's tractor, the old red Model M International pulling a plow, smoke blowing from the upright muffler and brown loam furrowing behind.

He could see it. Oh man, and he didn't want to. Welcome got superstitious when the time to fight got near. These memories felt too much like the home movies that are supposed to play in the mind at the moment of death. He crumpled the letter, but for weeks afterward the memories kept coming.

Then he was catapulted into the war. He was back in the here-and-now. He didn't have time to remember what he had done the day before, much less years.

For Welcome the fighting started about two days sooner than for almost everybody else. Midnight chopper ride, sixty miles over the wrong side of the lines, him and Oliver. The helicopter flew along a wadi, slowed and dumped them and their equipment, and was gone. Welcome and Oliver had a job list that involved the various command posts and hidden supply dumps of the enemy division—say, fifteen thousand men—that surrounded them.

Recon, this was how you lived.

For forty-eight hours they did the jobs, and then they hid and waited for the fighting to come to them. And it did. The front swept by like one of those prairie thunderheads. You watched it come, you felt its fury, you watched it go. When it was gone they called on the radio, and within a few hours they were in a Humvee on the way to the rear.

In war you cannot discount the little bastard in a hole. You can starve him, you can bomb and shell him, you can bring hell down around him, but sooner or later if he stays alive he may stand up and fight. Welcome knew this very well, having been in the hole more than once.

This time Welcome actually saw him stand up. It was at night. Welcome was sprawled in the Humvee. He was grimy and tired and fought out, but he had that good blessed feeling of having been spared. Every few seconds the northern skyline would brighten with the dull light of bomb blasts. It brightened once again, a whole string of eruptions, and

4

in that light Welcome saw him stand up about fifty meters away, chest high in the earth, a little bastard in a hole with a rocket tube on his shoulder.

Welcome actually had time to imagine him crouching there while the battle swirled around him. Too scared to move—if he was the hero type he'd be history by now. Welcome wondered how many tanks had churned past him, this close or even closer, real targets. While he crouched, scared. Hating himself for being scared. Then the fight moves on and in the darkness he thinks what a coward he has been. Until he hears a motor coming his way, getting louder, and with an effort of will and self-loathing he gathers himself and pops up.

In a breath Welcome could see how it must have happened. He could see it all. He saw the burp of fire from the tube, a yellow streak zipping toward the Hummer. He saw the white flash when it hit, felt the jolt and the sudden furnace blast. He was not aware of any sound, but he knew it must be loud. He felt the Hummer lift off the ground, turning over, exposing flame underneath, cartwheeling. He felt his legs burn. He was not at all surprised to find himself thrust back through the years, back to the dark rain and the brown fresh furrows. He heard quail beating out of a soybean field, touched frost rimed on the window, lifted a hay bale as chaff fell down the front of his shirt. Coffeyville, Montgomery County, Kansas, U.S.A. He was there. These were the real home movies, he knew it, and he knew he was about to die.

2

Little things added up when it came to murder. Annoyances, random incidents, crazy notions—they all went into the mix. They were intricate pieces. Take away just one, the whole mess would collapse.

Though it could also be said that once Caitlin got killing in her head, somebody was bound to die.

After the idea got a life of its own, moments that first appeared insignificant took on a whole new luster.

This was before she married Hays, who was Ruark's business partner. She was dating Ruark, overnighting with him once or twice a week. Ruark was a case. Worth at least five million dollars, he kept his hair in a ponytail and had a closet full of second-hand Hawaiian shirts that he wore with rumpled khakis. Today he might fast on distilled water. Tomorrow it would be whole greasy duck, roasted twenty minutes at five hundred degrees.

True, this *was* Marin County, California, marvelous Marin, mellow Marin of whim and fancy and honeysuckle fantasy. In Marin a superficial kink or two was expected. But with Ruark, the deeper you went, the more strangeness you found. In fact he was stranger than strange—Ruark was scary. Caitlin once watched him hold his hand in the flame of a candle, hold it steady while the sweat burst on his forehead and streamed into his eyes. This was supposed to be a favorite recreation of G. Gordon Liddy, one of the original Watergate spooks. But not even Liddy held it in the flame until the skin blistered on his palm.

That kind of stunt kept Caitlin interested. With Ruark she never knew what might happen.

Ruark was also an iron man in the sack. Hard body, good wind. He would go at it with her for two or three hours, tireless, wringing every bit of need and tension out of her. She realized this was probably a variant of the hand-in-the-candle trick, but she didn't complain.

Usually she slept hard after those marathons. One night, though, she woke and found herself alone in his bed. (Always his—he didn't like being on unfamiliar turf.) She waited for him, and waited. Ruark lived in an old farmhouse, in the middle of twenty acres in the rural north of the county, and night was strictly moonbeams and cricket chirps. She waited. A light was on downstairs, and she decided to find him.

She went down to the main room. There was nobody, just Ruark's cheap, bland furniture that looked like surplus Motel 6. A fuzzy TV light came from the downstairs bedroom. Three video monitors from the security system—even on his own turf Ruark didn't feel all that secure. But when she went into the room she found nobody. The monitors were playing to an empty seat.

The kitchen was dark, but some light came up from the cellar. Caitlin went down to the basement. She didn't say anything. It was just an instinct. The steps made a ninety-degree around a wall, and she stopped and looked around the corner.

Ruark was hunched, bare-ass, at the far side of the concrete floor. His back was turned to her. The basement was dim and dingy, exposed pipes and furnace and water heater, lit by a single bare bulb. Ruark was over by the washing machine and dryer, and she noticed that the washer had been shoved aside. Ruark was squatting where the washer should have been. He was looking down, something on the floor.

Not once did she consider calling his name. Ruark was not someone you wanted to surprise.

She couldn't see what was in front of him. But now he was making some movements with his arms, and in a second she heard a clunk like a manhole cover dropping into place.

Ruark stood. She saw that it was a strongbox, a combination safe set flush into the concrete of the floor. She got a good look at the door, bright burnished steel.

She ducked back up the stairs as Ruark started shoving the washer back where it belonged. Right on top of the safe. She beat him upstairs and pretended to be asleep when he came to bed.

She split with Ruark not long afterward, aggravated to find him such a flagrant tightwad. He was constantly doing things on the cheap. Except for a few personal extravagances, Ruark lived like a steam fitter. It was wearying, to be that close to big money and yet so distant.

His partner, Hays, was in the middle of a divorce, and interested. Ruark and Hays were sole and equal holders in a going company; therefore (she reasoned) were equally prosperous. Hays was slick and good-looking, if slightly bland in aftertaste. He knew what to do with his money. He knew how to spend it.

She married him a few weeks after his final decree came through. Ruark came to the wedding and wished them well. He gave them a Lalique bowl. She wondered how much agony that had put him through.

What she saw in the basement that night, she filed away and kept to herself. She certainly wouldn't tell Ruark: *By the way, did you know I spied on you?* No, no, no. She didn't tell Hays, either. Because then it wouldn't be hers anymore. It would be diminished.

She just tucked it away, out of mind but never quite out of memory. It was an esoteric found object that you didn't discard because you knew that one day you would learn its true value. One of Ruark's indulgences was his car, which was a restored '65 Shelby Mustang, showroom fresh. It appeared to be just another Mustang. Actually it was a very valuable car, a classic. But the value of it didn't just leap out at you. Like so much else about Ruark, you had to know what to look for.

And where.

*   *   *

Hays knew Ruark for almost ten years before he realized that he really didn't know him at all.

They met at biz school, Stanford. This was the start of the Eighties, the fast-moving, high-leverage Eighties. Ruark had a chem degree. Hays was a marketing whiz. They were a couple of sharp kids hurdling the credits to an MBA, in a hurry to get out and bite off a chunk of the world's ripe ass. Ruark had whipped up a line of aloe vera skin- and hair-care products. For his thesis Hays was lining out a multilevel marketing plan that would avoid the legal problems of pyramid-sales scams.

They put Ruark's line of aloe together with Hays's marketing scheme. Between them they tapped relatives for $160,000 in start-up money, and they incorporated during Christmas break before their last semester. EvHaTek they called the company. In March they posted their first monthly profit. They paid back the loans the day before graduation. Their first year, they showed sales of three and a half million dollars, profit of four hundred thousand, and the trends were all on the rise.

For years Hays would brag: "Before my twenty-fifth birthday I had thirty individuals in my top tier showing downlines of a hundred K or more."

They made money and kept making it. They built a headquarters in San Rafael. They expanded into gourmet foods, travel accessories, consumer electronics. They got into telemarketing, mail order, even retail outlets in upscale shopping malls around the Bay Area.

The corporation consisted of one thousand shares, of which they each owned five hundred. They swapped corporate titles like kids trading baseball cards, and had been known to settle decisions with dice cups in a cocktail lounge. It was easy, when everything they planted came up blooming. They had salaries, fifteen thousand a month, but the real money was in the profit that they took in dividends at the end of every fiscal year. Once business took off, the dividend ran at least half a million apiece, once as high as two million four. Just like that, lump sum. Nice little nugget to find in your mailbox.

Hays came to count on the dividend. He thought it was automatic, that they couldn't avoid making money. Ruark tried to warn him that he shouldn't confuse genius with a bull market.

Hays put his money into income property and stocks and a knockout home that he built in the hills above Tiburon, in Marin County. He loved

8

the house. When he divorced he wanted to keep the place. His property settlement to his first wife was a check for $4.6 million, much of which he covered by selling stock positions and mortgaging the investment property. But he kept the place.

Hays and Caitlin were married in June. This was the same year that EvHaTek started to seep profits. Hays and Caitlin honeymooned for the month on a rented yacht off Cap d'Antibes, and then lived in Hays's home. In July, the company's annual report came through. The dividend was down to somewhat under two hundred thousand.

And Caitlin could go through the bucks—could she ever. Galleries, mail order, department stores, jewelers, restaurants. They put it on plastic and paid off the balances before the end of each billing cycle. One afternoon before their first anniversary Hays toted up the statements and found that in the past year they had run $166,700 through the cards. Like a few quarters in a pinball machine. Bing bing bing.

At least she was happy, he thought. Ever the live wire, snapping and sizzling, throwing off sparks.

She could always get him to do things. She knew him better than he knew himself. When she wanted something, she almost always wanted it more than he wanted to fight her on it. Before long he just surrendered. When she got restless, he did, too. When she said, *Life's so hollow,* he agreed. When she told him that they would have to step beyond boundaries to find something real, he stepped right along. If it came to force of will, she won every time.

The summer of their first anniversary she decided they needed a second home, a weekend retreat. She found an unpretentious little A-frame on a bluff just south of Point Sur, with the ocean in front and the high hills of the Coast Range behind. A mere $800 K. To make the down payment Hays sold off some T-bills and unloaded his interest in a Medical Arts building in Daly City.

Their first night in the A-frame, the ocean was so loud that he had trouble sleeping. The morning was warm and clear. They ate raspberries and drank a bottle of Dom. The surf pounded. A light breeze carried sea mist over the top of the cliffs.

He poured her the last of the bottle and said, "Mornings like this, you know you're doing something right. To be here, in this place, at this moment, you know you're on track to something great."

He didn't actually feel this way. But he thought he should.

She said, "Let's not get carried away."

9

"Come on," he said. "This is great. It doesn't get any better than this."

"I hope that's not true."

"You don't think this is great?"

"I'm not knocking it."

"That's it? You're not knocking it—that's the best you can do?"

"Sorry. It's lovely, it's wonderful, it's idyllic, I'm transported. You want more? I mean, I can lie and lie if it makes you happy. But the truth, you want to know the truth, morning's morning, ocean's the ocean, any dumb shit with money could be sitting here right now. Not to sound ungrateful—God knows—but really, is this as good as it gets? Not to come off like some cut-rate Peggy Lee or anything, but is this all there is?"

Not long afterward the annual report came through. Hays's dividend was down to ninety thousand. This put his income at less than three hundred thousand a year.

He was indignant. He might have made more money if he'd gone to law school.

At about this same time, Hays and Caitlin started dabbling in mischief. That Christmas they hooked up with Sonny Naull and got serious about crime. EvHaTek by now was hemorrhaging. That summer Hays looked at the new annual report and discovered that he was, effectively, broke.

It all came together, Caitlin's restiveness and her hold on Hays and his stark terror of insolvency. So it might have been money, it might have been perversity—you couldn't separate the two.

All that mattered, the upshot of it, was that when Caitlin started talking about murder, Hays didn't say that killing was wrong or tell her that she was nuts.

Instead he said, "You have no idea what's involved. You have no concept. You don't even know where to start."

Caitlin, with the image in her mind of that bright door under the washing machine in Evan Ruark's basement, said, "Oh yes I do."

3

Several times Welcome woke in a dull fog, with a dull ache below his hips. Ahead of him through the fog was a bright, unwavering light. Behind him was oblivion. He could retreat from the light or keep going to it. The first few times he gave himself back to sleep and darkness. Eventually, though, something drew him forward. Maybe it was the ache, which was sharper now. Welcome found himself plummeting forward. The fog dissolved, the light showed itself to be a white fluorescent tube in a fixture overhead. The dull ache became a searing roaring pain. Welcome could close his eyes to the light, but against the pain he could do nothing.

He was in bed. Somebody was standing over him, a nurse in whites so bright they hurt his eyes, making notes on a chart.

"Where am I?" he said.

"Army field hospital, Riyadh."

"Alive."

She looked over the top of her clipboard.

"You think dead feels like this?" she said.

He went in and out. Time passed: hours or days or more, he didn't know. Strangers would stand over him, then he would be alone. Always there was pain: sometimes dull, sometimes piercing, but always there.

He became aware of being trundled outside, lifted to an ambulance. Then he was in an airplane, a cargo plane, strapped on a stretcher. He wondered where he was going, and why. Someone was beside him, an orderly maybe, but when Welcome tried to speak he found his tongue was thick, his mouth dry. Too much trouble to talk; he went out again.

His mouth worked better next time. Now he was off the plane, in a hospital. That much he knew. He asked one of them, who answered, "Frankfurt. Germany. U.S. Air Force Hospital, the burn unit."

Here time resolved itself into parcels again. Night and day, hours and minutes. When he slept he wasn't drugged to a stupor. He was just sleeping. When he was awake he was really awake. He could talk and think. He was aware. Excruciatingly aware.

His legs were burned. They were pink and raw, and for his treatment they were covered every day by tissue-thin sheets of damp pigskin. Once a day, in the morning, he would get a Demerol. Half an hour later, two nurses would pull off the old pigskin. By then it would have started to bond, and to have it pulled off was like having his own skin pulled away. The Demerol was supposed to take the edge off his pain, but when the old tissue came off he had to grab the bed rails and clamp his mouth shut to keep from screaming.

And then in the last stage of treatment they actually did strip his own skin off his back and his sides, to graft onto his legs.

That came toward the end of his month in Frankfurt. It was a dreary, grinding time. Welcome couldn't move. His right leg also had a compound fracture—"a nasty fib-tib," one doctor said—that couldn't be set until the burns healed. Also, a big chunk of his right calf muscle was gone. It looked as if an animal had taken a bite. This was in addition to more contusions and small shrapnel wounds than the doctors would bother to count.

A couple of weeks after the skin graft, one of the ranking doctors on the ward came to Welcome's bed, pulled out his chart, made a few notations. Welcome saw him only about once a week, for a minute or two at a time, so this was an occasion.

The honcho said, "How'd you like to get stateside?"

"I can handle that," Welcome said.

"We've just about done our thing. We'll hand you off for the orthopedic work."

"Get my butt out of bed."

"Sooner or later."

"Back with the boys."

"Marine," the doctor said. He was scanning the front page of the chart.

"Marine Recon," Welcome said. Bragging, but what the hell: he had earned it.

"Tough guys." Now the doctor was noticing the tattoo on Welcome's right bicep. It was a grinning death's head with a Ka-Bar knife clenched in its teeth. KILL 'EM ALL, it said above the head. LET GOD SORT 'EM OUT, it said underneath.

Tattoo parlor outside Camp Lejeune. It was the kind of thing you did when you were twenty and full of yourself. He had hated it for years.

"Baddest of the bad," the doctor said.

"Reputations get inflated, you know how it is."

"Jumping out of airplanes, humping ninety-pound packs, scuba-certified—is that the picture?"

"Something like that."

"I wouldn't count on it," the doctor said.

"Got to," Welcome said.

"Your leg—did anybody show you the X rays?—above the ankle there's a gap in the bones. Roughly six centimeters across, pulverized, where there ought to be fibula and tibia. These days they hand people the ticket for a lot less than that."

The ticket. Out of the service. He was talking about being cashiered.

"Come on now," Welcome said.

"You'll be looking at some disability. Not that you won't be walking. But within limits. Maybe forty percent loss on that leg."

"No way," Welcome said.

"You realize, it's not my call. I'm no orthopod. Stateside, people who put your leg together, they'll say the word. But I've seen my share, and I have to say, I don't miss many."

"No," Welcome said.

"They know what they're doing," the doctor said. Welcome barely heard him. He kept thinking: the ticket. "Fine bunch of the boys and girls, top facility. Letterman Hospital. San Francisco. Ever been there?"

Welcome shook his head numbly. The ticket.

"Great town," the doctor said. "Lots of action. San Francisco, get you on your feet, you'll have a hell of a good time."

At Letterman they pinned Welcome's leg together with a couple of stainless-steel rods. It was early June before he was able to put any weight on it. In the meantime he did isometrics with the one good leg. He talked one of the nurses into letting him have a set of traction weights, so he could keep up the tone in his arms and his upper body. He did a thousand sit-ups a day, in sets of one hundred.

His first steps, completely unofficial, were from his bed to the toilet. Liberation from the bedpan.

The doctors started him on physical therapy, three times a day, to restore strength and flexibility. Welcome began his own rehab program. What you did with legs was walk, he thought. So he walked. He was on the eighth floor, orthopedic. He would take an elevator down one floor, to the seventh—cardiovascular—away from the doctors and the ward nurses who knew better.

Letterman was a big hospital. He paced off the main wing of the seventh floor, and calculated that a full lap was one-seventh of a mile.

Took him a week to get up to one full lap at a time. Next day it was two laps. He began to think that maybe the corps had changed its mind, would let him stay. He was getting stronger. His body never failed him.

In June the ticket came through. EFFECTIVE DATE 02 JULY, his papers said. The doctor told him he should be ready for release by then.

Shortly afterward a VA counselor visited him. *To help you through the period of reacclimation,* were the words she used. She filled out a biodata sheet, to be used in preparing a job application that would be sent to appropriate employers throughout the state.

Welcome got irked with her, without reason. It wasn't her fault that he was applying for jobs that he had never wanted.

She asked him about his military training, something that might transfer into the civilian market.

"Pretty specialized," he said. "I doubt that it would be worth much out in the world. What it comes down to, I spent seventeen years killing people and blowing things up. You think there's much demand for that out there?"

About a week after Thanksgiving, Albuquerque lost twenty thousand units of EvHaTek's Skin So Smooth Variety Pak, staple of the company's direct-sales line. Height of the Christmas season, the entire Mountain States Region's allotment disappears.

Where? Hays wondered. Into a desert sinkhole somewhere.

He spent half a morning talking to warehouses and shipping brokers. Worked through lunch, had his secretary bring him yogurt and mint iced tea.

It was not a bad place to be, if you had to be bolted to the phone. The company offices in San Rafael resembled those California community colleges that the state built by the dozens in the late Fifties, the Sixties, back when money ranked on a list of priorities somewhere behind pleasant good taste and utter charm. Long low buildings, airy rooms, skylights and white walls and exposed beams and hardwood floors, plenty of windows with views of the landscaped grounds.

Hays kept talking to the Southwest. Two in the afternoon, through his half-opened door, he saw Ruark heading toward the front door with that gone-for-the-day blitheness.

He yelled, and Ruark ducked his head in.

"Where are you going?"

"Home," Ruark said. As if it's any of your business, he seemed to say.

"Fucking Albuquerque misplaced twenty thousand Paks."

"Yeah?"

"Twenty thousand Paks," Hays said.

"Why are you screwing with it?" Ruark said.

"Twenty thousand Paks, Evan."

"We pay people to deal with these problems," Ruark said.

"As if our distributors aren't pissed enough already."

"That's business," Ruark said impatiently. He seemed a lot more perturbed about being detained than about losing twenty thousand Paks.

"It's okay, I've got it under control," Hays said.

"You're doing grunt work."

"Go ahead, you can go."

"Right," Ruark said.

He turned and left. Hays swiveled in his chair and watched him stride down the walk to his Shelby at the head of the executive row in the parking lot. Unconcerned, you could tell from the way he walked. Absolutely unconcerned.

How did he do it? Like this was just his night gig, and he had another day job.

Once Hays admired Ruark's detachment. Cool head in a crisis.

The Shelby's engine turned over, throbbed, and rapped loud as Ruark backed it out of the space and through the lot.

Now, though, Hays thought, it was an attitude that could seriously get under your skin.

They just dropped into Sonny Naull's life. He was at home with his five-year-old son on a Saturday morning. Naull and his wife Marie and Roy Boy lived in a shotgun cottage in San Pablo, behind some oil storage tanks. Naull did handyman stuff, painting and carpentry, small-engine repair. Good with his hands. He advertised with hand-written index cards that he posted on bulletin boards in supermarkets and laundromats. He hadn't had a regular job in seven months. Marie was waiting tables in the Paddock Club at Golden Gate Fields.

Saturday morning, the phone rang. It was a guy who called himself Harry. Naull had never heard the voice, a sharp voice, direct. Said he knew that Naull was looking for a job, maybe they could do business.

"What kind of job would this be?" Naull said.

"What you do best."

After a few seconds of silence Naull said, "I'm finished with that line of work."

"We'll talk about it," Harry said.

"Nothing to talk about. I don't want to waste your time."

"I don't mind."

"Then let's not waste mine," Naull said. "If you want to put it that way."

"It's worth five hundred to discuss. Easiest money you ever made. I'll give you five hundred for half an hour of your time."

"Sure you will," Naull said.

"The city, Ghirardelli Square, by the fountain, seven," Harry said, and hung up before Naull could say any more.

All day Naull told himself that he wasn't going. He was out of the life. Nobody was going to pay him five hundred to talk.

He kept thinking about Marie, though, working for two-twenty a week plus tips. On a good week they brought home about four hundred dollars between them. It barely covered rent and groceries, gas and insurance for the van. They bought Roy Boy's clothes at second-hand stores.

This was now the second week of December. Christmas music on the radio, there was no getting away from it. Naull had to count his pocket change if he wanted to make a quick pass through Burger King. Now here somebody was offering five hundred for half an hour, all he had to do was talk.

Marie got home at five, Naull changed his shirt, took the Econoline van. He told her he'd be home by eight.

Ghirardelli Square is a pricey shopping arcade on the bayside in San Francisco, at the foot of the Powell Street cable line—tourist heaven. Naull stood beside the fountain in the middle of the plaza, surrounded by three floors of shops. Ghirardelli made him edgy, the sheen of it. Men and women sauntered the brick courtyard and drifted along corridors, walking the easy walk of people with cash in their pockets and money in their checkbooks.

A solo guitar version of "Oh Tannenbaum" lilted down from one of the upper levels. It sounded cool and austere. Naull knew exactly how out of place he was, standing beside the Ghirardelli fountain in his flannel shirt and twill pants and steel-toed Wellington boots.

He watched the faces, looking for a Harry who was looking for a thief.

He noticed the man and the woman on the other side of the fountain. They were in their thirties, him maybe a few years older than her. They were fair, fresh and attractive, the way you can be when you can afford to make everything just right. Great haircuts, spotless skin, perfect teeth. He wore gray slacks and Gucci loafers and a cranberry-colored pullover that had to be cashmere. She wrapped herself in a long suede coat, a Hermes scarf loose around her neck, diamond tennis bracelet on one wrist.

They stood apart from everybody else, insolent and airy, like they were enjoying a private joke. To Naull they looked like a matched set of smirky little dolls. Not once did he connect them with the phone call. They were so far out of his world, they were visitors from another galaxy.

A few minutes went by. Naull began to feel silly, real dumb, standing around waiting for somebody to pay him five hundred dollars for a few minutes' chat.

The golden kids were watching him. He wished they wouldn't.

Naull felt upset at himself for being here, for blowing the time and the parking money, the gas and the bridge toll. They were still watching him. Naull stared down at the plaza's red brickwork, and when he glanced up they were walking his way, the two of them, him first and her about a step behind, walking straight toward Naull and stopping in front of him.

"You have to be Ralph," the guy said. Naull recognized the voice on the phone.

"Maybe," Naull said.

"Maybe. I want Ralph Artis Naull, born 1949 in Sapulpa, Oklahoma, lives on Holman Avenue in San Pablo. Would that be you?"

"Keep talking. You called me."

"Ralph, I'll be direct and to the point. We want to do a little B and E."

"Breaking and entering," the woman said.

"I know what the fuck it means," Naull said. "But I don't know who you are; I don't know what this is all about."

"I'm Harry; call her Connie. Say we're looking for an individual with some credentials. Two convictions for possession of stolen goods, one for B and E, served four years of a six-to-ten on that one. Vacaville, wasn't it? I would imagine those are the credentials we want."

He knew Naull's record. Didn't know his face, didn't know that nobody called him Ralph, but knew his record.

"What for?" Naull was irritated, some stranger on the street knowing he did time.

"We have our reasons," Harry said.

"Giggles," Connie said.

Giggles, Naull thought. *Giggles.* He said, "I'm out of here."

"There is substantial money to be made," Harry said.

That reminded Naull. He said, "By the way. This was supposed to rate five bills."

Naull didn't expect to get the money. He wanted it known, though, that he didn't forget what he was promised.

Harry gave a level little smile, reached into the pocket of his slacks, took out a slim packet of greenbacks. He put the money in Naull's hand.

It felt solid there, delicious. Naull peeked at it. In his palm was Ben Franklin, looking amused. Ben Franklin five times. Naull quickly put the money in his pants.

"That buys half an hour," Harry said.

"Fair enough," Naull said. "You want to do this some place more private?" He felt naked, standing around the fountain at Ghirardelli Square, talking about a felony.

"Why?" Harry said. "Somebody follow you?"

"No. I've been straight since I got out, almost a year."

"Nobody followed us," Harry said. "Nobody knows what we're into."

"We're avid amateurs," Connie said. She still had the smirk, also an eagerness that Naull found disconcerting. She was all lit up.

"Okay," Naull said. "B and E. What, a one-shot deal? Speaking theoretically, I mean."

"No, it'll be an ongoing thing," Harry said. "We want to do it, you know how."

"Hold on. I'm talking theoretically," Naull said.

"You do the jobs, we go along for the ride. You show us the ropes. So we can learn."

Naull wanted to ask, What the hell for? Then he remembered. Giggles.

Harry said, "We supply you the names of individuals, addresses and phone numbers, planning to be out of town a minimum of one week. Upper-bracket demographics, excellent neighborhood—the A List. I won't guarantee they'll all be empty. Once in a while there might be somebody hanging around. So you have to check it out. But eight, nine times out of ten, they'll be vacant at least a week."

"Sure they will," Naull said.

"Bank on it. You hit as many as you want to hit. We go with you when we choose. Any you do alone, you give us twenty percent of the proceeds. I assume you know a fence. Any we do together, we split it down the middle. This is for real. It's platinum. You can look all your life without finding a deal like this."

People were walking past, glancing in store windows. Nobody was paying attention. Naull thought it was bizarre. Standing beside the fountain at Ghirardelli Square, discussing burglary while people strolled past.

"I don't know," he said.

"Indecision bums the hell out of me," Connie said. "It's a bad sign. I consider it the mark of a poorly evolved psyche."

"Go to hell," Naull said.

"It's okay," Harry said. "The man's entitled to be cautious. He's a professional; it comes with the package."

"Next fall I take won't be four years. It'll be closer to fifteen."

"I know that," Harry said. "That's why we called you. You have something to lose."

"Jeopardy concentrates the mind," Connie said. "Do a handstand on the edge of a cliff, that's when you know you're really alive."

"How'd you find me?" Naull said. "Somebody recommend me, somebody I know?"

"I think it's a safe assumption that we have no acquaintances in common," Harry said.

"This is what makes me nervous," Naull said. "You come out of nowhere, you know my name, my background, but I ain't got clue one about you. You could be setting me up. You could be with the authorities."

Right away he wished he hadn't said it. There was never a cop who looked and talked like these two. Not to mention that he wasn't important enough, all this trouble to set him up. Nobody cared.

"You think we're cops?" Connie said.

"Not really—"

"*Cops!*"

"It was a poor choice of words," Naull said.

"No, you think we're cops, we'll have to do something about that."

She made a quick scan around the plaza. Her eyes lit on an art gallery on the other side of the fountain, and she started toward it. Harry followed her across the bricks. When Naull didn't move she turned and said, "Hey, this is for you, you don't want to miss this. Command performance."

Naull followed them to the gallery. They stood outside, by the smoked-glass window. Naull could see that it was about what he expected, a single large room with vanilla walls and a hardwood floor. Indecipherable modern paintings were spotlit from track lights on the ceiling, and pieces of modern sculpture stood on white pedestals. Eight browsing customers and two clerks struck poses in the precious hush.

"What do you think?" Harry said to Connie.

"Got it," she said.

"You want me to take it?"

"No, no, I got it," she said. "Just do your thing."

Harry took out his wallet, gave it to her, and went into the gallery. Connie put the wallet in her purse. She turned to Naull and said, "Stay here. Watch. You think we're cops—you watch."

She went in too.

Harry was drifting down to the far end of the room. Connie wandered over to a large square canvas hung near the front door. The painting showed washed-out streaks of brown and mustard on a field of beige. She got in close and then started backing up, as if taking it in. She kept backing until she was abreast of one of the waist-high pedestals. It held four near-identical pieces of sculpture that looked to Naull like shafts of black rock, each maybe eighteen inches high. He knew this was supposed to be art, and probably went for a K and a half or more.

One of the clerks, the one closest to Harry, was mildly watchful as she looked around the room. Everyone else seemed to be sleepwalking.

But now Harry was moving. He reached around to pat his back pockets. His face registered surprise.

He said something. Naull couldn't hear him, but the clerk near Harry did. She looked at him. Harry spoke again. Naull still couldn't hear through the glass, but he could make out the words on Harry's lips.

My wallet, Harry was saying.

Now a few more people turned toward Harry, and he said it again, this time loud enough that it carried outside.

'My wallet,' he said. "Somebody stole my wallet."

Now everybody was looking at Harry. Everybody but Connie, who kept studying the canvas. Naull kept his eyes on her as she opened the suede coat, took a side step to the pedestal, and closed the coat again. When she moved away, one of the four black shafts was missing from the pedestal.

It was a slick move, Naull had to admit. Everybody in the room was watching Harry, now frantically searching his pockets.

Connie didn't leave right away. She kept the coat wrapped around her as she stared at the big painting for a couple seconds more. Then she went out the door, not in any big hurry. She came out, kept walking, and over her shoulder said to Naull, "Come on. He'll be out."

Naull followed her across the courtyard, past the fountain, to the stairwell of the underground garage. They stopped there. Harry was out of the gallery and coming their way. Connie waited until he caught up, and then they went down the concrete stairs.

They stopped on the first landing, and Connie took the black rock out from under the duster. She held it up. Under the base Naull could see two stickers that read "Obelisk XXII" and "$1,800."

Connie said, "Would cops do that?"

"I wasn't saying you're cops," Naull said. "Just that you might be, for all I know about you."

Connie swung the sculpture. It smashed against the concrete corner post and exploded into shards. She was left holding a jagged black stub.

"Would cops do *that*?" she said.

"No," Naull said.

"Then can we finally tune out this static?"

"Yes," Naull said.

Quickly, Harry said, "Good. Got something here for you." He held out a slip of paper. "Three addresses. A Napa, a San Mateo, a Potrero Hill. All yours. Show you what I've got to offer. Take a few days, look 'em over, see if I'm lying. Go ahead and hit one if you want, it's on me."

"Pop," Naull said. "Not hit." He took the slip. "You pop a place, you crack a place, you take a place, you do a place. But you don't hit it. That's cop-show stuff."

"Pop," Harry said. "Terminology of the trade, huh? Pop. Crack. Learning already."

"We learn fast," Connie said.

Naull put the paper in his pocket. His hand brushed the bills, and he held them.

"I'll have a look," Naull said. "Let you know. Give me your number."

"We'll call you," Harry said.

"I got to be able to find you."

"No you don't. I'm Harry, she's Connie, that's all you need to know. I give you the prospects, you do your thing, we'll tell you when we want to go along."

"I can't work like that."

"You'll find a way. The money starts coming in, believe me, you'll adjust."

"This is too far out," Naull said. "This is weird."

"That's the whole idea," Connie said. "Conventional pursuits bring conventional satisfactions. The real payoffs are out on the fringes."

"You want to try it or not?" Harry said. "Otherwise we find somebody else. It's not like you're a one-of-a-kind talent."

Naull knew that was true, but he didn't like hearing it out loud.

"I'll have a look," he said. "You call me, huh, a few days?"

"Sure, six, seven days, take your time."

"I make no promises," Naull said.

But he knew he was kidding himself. It was all over. His fingers rubbed the bills. They had that good, tacky, real-money touch. Harry and Connie, they had him. He was ashamed to admit how good the money felt. He was ashamed to admit how easy he was.

"So what do you think?" Hays said when they were alone in the car.

"Made to order," Caitlin said. "Perfect."

"We're going to do it," Hays said. At this point he was talking about burglary.

"Oh, yeah," Caitlin said. "We're doing it, all right. It's a Goddamn karmic imperative."

"Did you hear him? 'This is too far out.'"

"'This is weird.'"

"You have to admit," Hays said. "He does have a point."

"Did you see that shirt?" Caitlin said. "Those pants? Those *boots*!"

"A blue-collar guy for a blue-collar job."

"The ultimate barney," she said.

"How's that?"

"Like in the cartoons. Barney Rubble, best friend of Fred Flintstone. Mister Blah."

"Dumb as a stack of firewood," Hays said.

"Not that dumb," she said. "Just half a step slow. That's what you're looking for. Somebody smart enough to do the job, but not quite up to speed. No aspirations, no imagination. I don't care how hard he tries, he'll always be behind the curve."

They were on Lombard Street, near the south end of the Golden Gate Bridge. They were on the way home. They had a BMW, a new Bimmer, an 850i, top of the line. It moved through traffic like a tiger loping through trees.

"That's what we wanted," Hays said.

"That's what we got," she said. "Our barney."

Naull hid the five hundred under a can of Pennzoil in his garage. He didn't tell his wife about Harry and Connie. Before he got out of Vacaville he promised her that he was never going back to the life, and he didn't want to disappoint her until he was sure.

With Roy Boy in the seat beside him, he spent four days checking out the three addresses. He burned a lot of gas. He wanted to drive past each of the houses at different times over several days, looking for cars that came and went from driveways, windows that didn't stay shut from one time to the next.

The Napa address was a big split-level in a new subdivision of half-million-dollar homes. The Potrero Hill was a restored Victorian, freshly painted, gleaming gingerbread. The San Mateo was a Dutch colonial in a suburban neighborhood that probably went back to the Fifties, decent but nothing special.

He didn't see anybody in any of them. Empty driveways stayed empty. Closed windows stayed closed. He tried the phones, too, and got only answering machines.

Finally he decided to do the Potrero Hill. The Napa looked like a place where alarms might come standard. The San Mateo was a shade too modest. He could see himself walking out with a Polaroid camera and a three-year-old Goldstar TV.

They were all vacant, though. He was impressed. He wondered how Harry did it.

On Thursday Naull made a couple of calls. Then he put Roy Boy beside him in the van.

"Where we going?" Roy Boy wanted to know.

"See a man."

"Man who?"

"You don't know him," Naull said.

"Man *who*?"

"Andy is his name. Andy Pops. You call him Sir."

"Pops goes the weasel."

"Something like that."

Naull took the Nimitz freeway past the Oakland-Alameda Coliseum and down to the city of Fremont at the south end of the bay. He drove through an aging industrial park, to a warehouse that was surrounded by a high chain-link fence and topped with a V of barbed wire. It had no windows, and sat apart from other buildings at the edge of the industrial complex. Beyond the warehouse were mud flats and the dull flat line of the bay.

Naull parked in front of a sliding gate. A sign on the fence said:

CURIOSITIES UNLIMITED
Wholesaling Antiques and Fine Objects
To the World

A uniformed guard came out of a small white shack inside the gate. He was carrying a clipboard. The embroidered patch on his shoulder read

"Olympus Security." You would not find it in the phone book. His nickle-plated badge said "Special Deputy." You could buy it in any pawn shop, two or three dollars.

"I'm expected," Naull said. "Mr. Holmes." For security, Andy Pops assigned names to his clients and customers on the gray side of the business. He appreciated nineteenth-century Americans.

The guard checked a list on the clipboard. He leaned into the shack and pushed a button inside. Hum and snap of a magnetic lock, and the gate began to clank aside on rollers. Prison gates were exactly like that.

Naull parked the van in the asphalt lot in front of the building.

"In the back," the guard said, "the office, straight along the side wall—"

"I've been there. Thanks," Naull said.

He and Roy Boy went through the doorway beside the loading dock. The warehouse had the look and feel of a huge attic. Boxes, packing crates, intricate jumbles of chairs and tables. A lot of it was in shadows—the only light was from six weak bulbs, three on each side, up high near the rafters.

Naull and Roy Boy picked their way toward the back. A loft ran the width of the back side of the building. Up in the loft were more furniture and packing crates. Tucked underneath was an office where big panes of glass reached from knee-high partitions to the ceiling. The office had a single metal desk, three chairs, and a green metal filing cabinet. Beside the desk was a gooseneck quartz halogen lamp that splashed garish brightness into this corner of the warehouse.

Andy Pops was at his desk. He had a pencil mustache, salt-and-pepper fringes above his ears, rheumy eyes behind thick lenses. He was mostly bald. About eight or ten hairs lay stiff across his skull, like they were lacquered.

Naull and Roy Boy went in.

Andy Pops extended his hand and said hello. A breath of an accent. Andy Pops was Greek. Naull once heard his true name. And-something Papa-something.

"Long time, good to see you," Andy Pops said. He sounded at least half sincere. "Who is this?"

"My son," Naull said. "Roy."

"You didn't have him last time you were here."

"That would have been about six months before he showed up."

"Ah." A sympathetic grimace came and went on Andy Pops's face. Born while you sat in a cell. Bad break.

25

To Roy Boy he said, "You want a sucker?" He took a handful of Tootsie Roll Pops out of his shirt pocket. "A Pop from Andy Pops. My trademark. Every business needs a hook."

"Go ahead," Naull said, and Roy Boy took an orange one.

"Thank you," Roy Boy said. "Sir."

"Hey. Good boy," Andy Pops said.

"I think I got something going," Naull said.

"I'm sorry to hear that. I always liked you."

"I need a receiver who stays clean."

"And I deal with sources who do not get dirty."

"I never mentioned your name," Naull said. "Yours, nobody's. It would have been worth months. But I don't give up the people who treat me right."

"I didn't know that. I lost a lot of sleep over you, waiting for the knock on the door." It wasn't an act. His voice had some real spine in it. He looked like a wreck, but something was always going on behind those liquid old-horse eyes.

He said, "I don't need this. I have a legitimate business—you know this end of it is less than ten percent of my volume? And ninety-nine percent of the trouble. I don't even know why I bother."

"I do," Naull said. "What thieves steal tends to be a lot more interesting than what people sell."

"You have a point," Andy Pops said.

"I'm into something sweet. I have a line on some premium addresses. No telling what kind of items I'll be into." Roy Boy was unwrapping the sucker, swinging his legs from the chair, oblivious. "You recognize quality. Anybody but you, I'm taking a chance they won't even know what they're looking at."

"This is quality?"

"I never know till I get in, do I? But seeing these places, I can imagine."

Andy Pops took off his glasses. He rubbed his eyes. He exhaled a quiet sigh that sounded like surrender.

"You get something unusual, bring it by," he said.

"Now as to consumer goods."

"Take them somewhere else!" Andy Pops said. "What do I want with a used VCR? I am not a fence."

"Sure you are," Naull said. "A hell of a picky fence. But you are a fence."

"I do not need these problems," Andy Pops said.

"I wouldn't think you'd want me dealing anywhere else," Naull said. "With some squirrely amateur that may point a finger at me the minute he looks at a fall. It was hard enough to be noble when I was looking at six to eight. Make it fifteen to twenty, who knows whether I'd have to name names?"

The old wreck got hard and silent. His eyes got clear, and he fastened them on Naull.

Roy Boy stopped swinging his legs on the chair. Naull waited for Andy Pops to speak. Wondering if he had pushed too far.

Andy Pops said, "I'll get rid of it for you. Nothing with an I.D., though. I don't care if it's a new Hasselblad. If it has a name or a number engraved on it, you might as well take it fishing and use it for a boat anchor. I won't give you ten cents for it."

"My feelings exactly," Naull said.

Andy Pops walked them out of the office and through the warehouse. At the front door he said, "You're working alone, I hope."

"More or less," Naull said.

"We're only as safe as the people around us. You should remember that. Myself, personally, my partner can only be someone I trust completely."

"I didn't know you had a partner," Naull said.

"I don't," said Andy Pops.

Next day, Friday, Naull hired a sitter for his son and took the van to Potrero Hill around one in the afternoon. Once a neighborhood of the poor, in the past ten years it had been set upon by the working affluent, who admired its bay views and its location in the lee of the ocean fog. Homes on the Hill now ran upwards of three hundred thousand.

Naull backed the van up to the garage door. The street was quiet. Lord love the yupsters, Naull thought. Working fools. The middle of a weekday, their neighborhoods were as empty as Deadwood.

He went around back, down a couple of stairs to the basement door. He had a gym bag with a pry bar and a few screwdrivers, a glass cutter, some duct tape, and a small flashlight. He put on a pair of cotton gloves, took out the pry bar, and shoved the blade end between the door and the jamb. The lock plate would be held by a couple of one-inch wood screws, he thought. The bolt would be mortised into about half an inch of fir. He pulled the bar toward him, let it take a little of his weight, and the door popped open.

He climbed the basement steps to a hallway. At the top of the stairs he stopped to catch his breath. Oh man. The air got thin when you were standing in the middle of a fifteen-to-twenty.

He started carrying things out. Bang and Olufsen sound system, pair of Barcelona chairs from a white-on-white living room. Dozen Baccarat goblets and a disappointing Mikasa china service from the dining room. Also a set of Oneida silver plate, even more disappointing.

In the hall was a mirror-back display case with fifty to sixty pieces of antique netsuke. He wrapped them individually in paper towels and took them out in a pillow case that he found in the hall linen closet.

The main bedroom was burgundy and tan, a rosewood bed and a couple of rosewood bureaus. Naull wished he had room. Hanging at the head of the bed was a big Hockney litho, a hunky sunbather under a turquoise sky. In Naull's opinion, it clashed with the rest of the decor. He took it off the wall and down into the van, and it didn't clash anymore.

The bedroom had two closets. One of them held a couple of dozen Armani and Gianni Versace suits that looked like thirty-eight smalls. To any other fence they'd be worth at least ten dollars apiece, but Andy Pops would give him only grief. The second closet was full of Cable Car Clothiers stuff, tweed suits and blazers, forty-four long. This was Naull's size, and he picked himself a pair of charcoal slacks and a herringbone jacket with leather patches at the elbows.

Each of the other two bedrooms was outfitted for a home office. One Mac, one 386, H-P laser printer, Murata fax, and Canon desktop copier. Naull carried them all down. The van was filling up now. Naull checked his watch and saw that he had been in for twelve minutes. He put his gym bag in the back, covered the goods with a canvas tarp, closed the doors, and drove away.

Down to Fremont was an hour. Naull was in no hurry. The guard at the gate was waiting for Mr. Holmes. Naull backed up to the loading dock, and Andy Pops came out from the warehouse.

Andy Pops stuck his head in the back of the van, pulled away the tarp and looked around, picked through the netsuke, and said, "Three-one."

Three thousand one hundred. In the gray trade Andy Pops usually paid twenty to thirty percent of wholesale.

28

Naull said, "That's a Hockney. Signed and numbered."

"Express ticket to jail, signed and numbered. Anyway, Hockney's cooled off. Oversaturated the market."

"The netsuke isn't signed and numbered."

"Yesterday's fad. You've been out of circulation too long."

Naull followed Andy Pops into the office while somebody else unloaded the van. He took it in hundreds and fifties, and Andy Pops gave him a couple of suckers for Roy Boy. Before the start of rush hour Naull was headed back to San Pablo with $3,100 in cash, wondering if he had been lowballed on the netsuke. He'd have to get current again on values.

He thought about taking Marie out to a nice restaurant. Call a baby-sitter. Wear the slacks and the herringbone. A couple of blocks from home, he stopped and stuffed the clothes into a Goodwill bin. Tweed jacket with leather patches, not in a million years. He picked up Marie and Roy Boy, took them to dinner at a Sizzler, then to Baskin-Robbins for sundaes.

To pay for the ice cream he took out the roll and peeled off a fifty. He knew she would notice. It was one way to break the news.

They ate the ice cream. Naull watched Marie with sidelong glances and waited for her to say something.

She was a good-looking woman. Her skin was smooth and clear. Big eyes, milk chocolate brown. Good strong cheekbones that fit with the definite angles of her brows and her chin. She was thirty-six, and was showing just faint lines at the corners of her mouth. Even that you could blame on worry. She married Naull when she was twenty, and had been through a lot with him.

He was scraping the last of the hot fudge out of the dish when she said, "I see you've had a pretty good week."

"Not bad."

"Working hard?" she said.

Great full lips, too, but right now she had them set tight and narrow.

"I think I found myself a situation," he said.

"Oh Sonny."

"This looks like a good one."

"There is no such thing."

"I'm tired of scraping by."

"I would a damn sight rather scrape by and not have to worry about bringing up my son alone."

"I'll do my best not to let that happen," he said.

Roy Boy stopped eating his ice cream. His eyes shuttled back and forth between Naull and Marie. He was a surprise child conceived long after they had stopped hoping. He tended to be clingy. Naull wondered whether that had anything to do with never touching your father until you were four years old.

Naull reached out and held his hand.

"Not much to count on," she said.

"That's all I can do, do my best."

"Don't expect me to wait for you," she said. "I don't want to be a penitentiary widow anymore. You go again, I'm getting me a life."

She took Roy Boy's other hand. Then she said, "Oh hell, that's a lie."

"I know," he said.

"Be careful. Will you promise me that? Don't get greedy. Pick your spots. All right?"

"That's the only way."

"What are we talking about this time? Six, eight years? There won't be much of me left when you get out."

"Think positive."

"Or more. Ten? Twelve? You can stop me anytime. More than twelve years?"

"Hard to say exactly."

"More than twelve years. My Lord. There won't be *nothing* of me left."

"I won't let it happen."

"You wasn't going to let it happen last time."

"I don't suppose it would do any good to mention that the money is great, the setup is a dream."

"Don't even try," she said. She clamped her big eyes on him, hard.

Roy Boy squirmed. He looked at them both, and he started to whine. Naull said, "Let's go," and gathered his son up in his arms, and the three of them walked out together.

Next day Harry called. Naull told him yeah, he was in.

"Your source is right on," Naull said. "I never saw anything like it. Ducks on the pond."

"Knew you'd appreciate it," Hays said.

"The people're gone on a trip, on vacation."

"Think so?"

"Got to be."

"You might be right."

"I'm thinking it's some kind of travel agency deal," Naull said. "Pipeline into a travel agency, you'd know when people were taking a trip."

"Don't worry about it."

"It's not a bad idea on principle. The problem is, you're relying on somebody else, your contact in the agency. You're only good as long as they're happy."

"It isn't that."

"I wonder what, then."

"Don't wear yourself out," Hays said. "You'll never guess. Nobody will. This is a lock, a mortal lock; this is good for the next ten years if we don't get bored first."

Next week the three of them together popped a ranch-style in Los Altos, and a few days later Naull did one more on his own, another San Francisco Victorian, Noe Valley. Naull's share of the two ran just over five thousand dollars. Harry and Connie took him on his word when he gave them their cut. Naull didn't short them, but he knew he could. They didn't care. Clearly they weren't in it for the money. Giggles, she'd said, and once he saw the two of them in action Naull could believe it. They were like sixth-graders on a field trip, pumped up, too loud, full of dumb questions, laughing.

It made Naull uneasy. He thought you weren't supposed to enjoy crime this much.

One night, in another rancher near Corte Madera, Connie started whooping when they saw the Navajo wall hangings and the Pueblo pottery. They liked that. In the excitement, jabbering, arguing—the Bobbsey Twins on angel dust, Naull thought—they let their real names slip. Hays and Caitlin. Not that it brought Naull any closer to knowing who they were or what they were about.

The weeks went on, Hays kept coming up with addresses. Naull kept pulling in the money. Plenty of things about Hays and Caitlin either offended Naull or made him nervous—almost everything, in fact—but they did have this endless supply of sweet plums, ripe, ready to fall.

In Vietnam Naull knew a man who kept a monkey. Naull hadn't thought about it for years, but it came back to him when he watched Hays and Caitlin in action. The monkey bit, screeched, and refused to be housebroken. Naull never could see the attraction. On the other hand, suppose the monkey shit golden turds. That would be different. In that case you would put up with a lot.

Gerald Moon drove toward a bank of fog that sat like a wall across the road. This was about thirteen miles after he turned off Highway 101 in north Marin. He was headed west, on a two-lane county road twisting toward the ocean through redwood hills.

TOMALES ROAD, the occasional sign said. It was gloomy, even in the middle of the day. The redwoods were tall and stood close together. A few narrow spears of sunlight would jut through the maze of branches, that was all.

And now here was this curtain of fog draped across the road. Gerald slowed down and turned on the lights of his Isuzu sedan.

He assumed it was his. Mr. Ruark told him where to pick it up. Parking garage on Geary, 10:30. Gerald wasn't surprised to find it there. The man definitely had his act together. Finding his name on the registration, though, that was unexpected.

The man had a way of keeping you off balance.

Gerald drove into the fog. It was like driving through milk. Gerald let off the gas, and the car slowed down. Twenty-five miles an hour. Twenty. Gerald peered out the windshield, trying to keep track of the white line that marked the edge of the road. The Isuzu had no power steering, but Gerald moved the steering wheel back and forth without effort. He was twenty-two years old, six feet six and nearly as wide as he was tall. His fists were the size of cantaloupes. They made the steering wheel look like a piece of licorice rope. He got his size from his mother, who was Samoan. His father was Korean, smart and quiet but prone to snap. From the neck up, Gerald was his father's boy.

Gerald kept driving. He wanted to glance at his wristwatch, but he couldn't take his eyes off the road. Mr. Ruark wanted him at noon, and Gerald wasn't going to be late.

No other traffic. At least he had that going for him. And he memorized the directions, so he didn't have to look at a paper. Fourteen and a half miles from the freeway would be an intersection, Larkspur Road, and a sign for The Blue Goose Inn . . . there.

Now four-tenths of a mile more on Tomales. He checked the odometer. Two-tenths. Three. Four. Gravel driveway, left side. He was past it. He put the Isuzu into reverse, backed up, and turned into the gravel.

It dropped down from the road. Some kind of thick brush grew up to the sides of the narrow road. Gerald had noticed very few houses in the last five or six miles. He was definitely in the boonies.

The gravel crunched under his tires. He looked down at his watch— five to twelve—and when he looked up, the black steel shafts of a high gate stood in front of him.

He hit the brakes. The Isuzu skidded and stopped maybe three inches short of the gate.

Outside the car came a noise. Gargling sound. Like gargling with sand. Gerald put down his window. The sound was coming from a black speaker mounted on one gatepost.

"Let me see your face," said Ruark's voice from the speaker.

On top of the gatepost was a TV camera. Gerald stuck his head out the window and looked up at the lens. *Click, buzz,* the black gate swung back. Gerald drove through.

Mr. Ruark, he was something. You never knew what you were going to get. Every Thursday afternoon, the past three weeks, he had given Gerald six hundred dollars. Stone-cold cash, asking nothing in return. This was on top of miscellaneous fifties and hundreds that he had dropped on Gerald over the past few months, Gerald telling him he wanted to earn the money and Mr. Ruark promising to give him the chance.

The gravel went on through a field and stopped outside a two-story frame house with a Toyota Tercel parked out front. Gerald pulled up beside the Tercel. When he was out of the car he shifted his shoulders inside the jacket of his blue serge suit, checking the fit. He bought it at a Big & Tall shop. It was the first suit he ever owned, and it cost him the better part of one week's salary—if that was the word. But he sensed that Mr. Ruark, raggedy as he might appear, would appreciate a businesslike approach.

Gerald pulled at the hem of the jacket and went up to the porch. Ruark was at the door before Gerald could knock, and he told Gerald to come in.

Inside it was what you would expect of somebody who seemed to buy his clothes at thrift shops. In fact it reminded Gerald of the apartment that he shared with his mother and his sister in the Mission District, San Francisco. The man had money, and lived like Gerald's mother.

Not to put him down, though. If Mr. Ruark wanted to give it away in cars and cash, instead of putting it into furniture, that was fine with Gerald.

A third party slouched in a brocade armchair in the corner. Guy a little older than Gerald. Bee-stung lips, black hair combed straight back in a greasy d.a., like his night job was doing Elvis at a Ramada lounge.

"Gerald, this is Harmon," Ruark said. "Harmon, Gerald."

Harmon just gave Gerald a pouty nod, and Gerald gave him one back. It would have to be Elvis with muscles, Gerald thought. Harmon was wearing a tight Ban-Lon shirt, and Gerald could see that he was in shape. Big knotty arms and shoulders, solid pecs that tapered down to a slim waist. Unlike Gerald, who was huge all over.

"You work out," Gerald said.

"Pump it up, max it out," Harmon said. "Got to do it."

"Harmon is a competitive body-builder," Ruark said. He had a needle in his tone. "He was last year's fourth runner-up in the heavyweight division at the Golden State Hardbody regionals."

"*Third* runner-up. And my lats were weak then." Harmon didn't even know that the man was jerking his chain. "I got my lats *shaped* now."

"How's the car?" Ruark said.

"Fine," Gerald said. "Great."

"I want you and Harmon to run an errand. Can you handle that?"

"No problem," Gerald said.

Ruark reached beside the couch. He had a bag, a crumpled brown Albertson's grocery sack, looked about half full.

"Deliver what's inside here," Ruark said. "Harmon knows the place. A man there is going to give you a package. Bring it back to me this afternoon. Don't make any other stops. Straight down and straight back."

"All right," Gerald said. He took the bag.

"Open it," Ruark said. "I want you to know what you're dealing with."

Gerald looked in the bag. It was bundles of money, wrapped in rubber bands. Gerald never saw so much money.

"That's eighty-five thousand," Ruark said. "U.S. dollars."

"Okay," Gerald said.

"The man at the other end will count it after you leave. I trust him. He says it's short, I'll believe him. You understand what I'm getting at?"

"I believe I do," Gerald said.

"You want to count the money, so there's no confusion?"

"If you wouldn't mind."

"I don't mind."

Harmon snorted like it was the craziest thing he ever heard. He said he'd wait outside, and he left.

"Sit down," Ruark said to Gerald. He pointed to the sofa, which was covered in a worn blue velveteen. There was a coffee table in front of the sofa. Gerald sat on the sofa and shook the money onto the table.

Each bundle had a hand-written slip of paper stuck under the rubber band. If it was twenties it would be "20 X 50—1000." Fifties would be "50 X 50—2500." Gerald started working through the first bundle.

Ruark said, "You see how it works?"

"Yeah. I think I've got it."

"Harmon's been running these errands at least twice a month for nine months. He never asked to count it."

"He's lucky," Gerald said. "He could've got his balls caught in a drill press. All it would take is one mistake in putting the package together."

"I put it together," Ruark said.

"No offense, but everybody makes a mistake."

"That's right."

Ruark sat and watched him. Gerald kept counting. He worked through all the bundles. He was careful. He thought maybe Mr. Ruark was testing him, slip an extra fifty in there. But all the bundles counted right.

He put the money in the bag and cradled the bag in one hand as he stood. He decided that if Mr. Ruark asked him to run any more errands, he was going to buy himself a nice briefcase. Leather. This was embarrassing.

"Give this to the individual at the other end, bring back what he gives me, is that all?"

"Do it right, that's enough."

"I'll do it right," Gerald said.

"You never asked if it's illegal," Ruark said.

"I assume it is. Otherwise you'd use a cashier's check, send it by Speedy Messenger. Be a lot cheaper."

35

"That's good thinking," Ruark said. "It is illegal. Not dangerous, though. Unless somebody tried to take it away from you."

"Nobody ever took anything away from me before," Gerald said. "I don't know why they'd start today."

Gerald knew he should be going. Something bothered him, though. He had to get something straight.

He said, "Mr. Ruark, I know I owe you more than this."

"I like that," Ruark said. "You're loyal. It's an Asian concept. Be good to those who are good to you. Over here we've got it all wrong. We're good to those who we want to impress or persuade, but we neglect our benefactors. Asians grasp the priorities. That probably came from your father."

"Could be," Gerald said. "I know this trip is worth maybe a bag of burgers. It doesn't pay you back. All you've done for me."

"That's an investment," Ruark said. "You have possibilities."

"I owe you."

"Take care of this one, there's always more. I operate in many spheres."

"I believe you do," Gerald said.

"The blood of warriors runs through your veins," Ruark said. "Do you believe that, too?"

"If you say so," Gerald said.

They took the Isuzu. Gerald drove through the fog and then out of it again, back to Highway 101. For a while Harmon squeezed spring grips. Then he took a snapshot out of his wallet and showed it to Gerald.

It was him, Harmon, at a body-builder's contest. Striking one of these goofy body-builder poses, biceps ballooned, stomach rippled like a washboard. He was wearing a G-string, and was slicked down with sweat—or didn't they use oil, mineral oil?

The disgusting thing about the picture was that Harmon didn't have a single hair on him, except what was on his head. His chest, hairless. His legs, hairless. One of his hairless arms was raised—no hair in his pit, either. Gerald wasn't exactly a fur ball, but as an Asian, he wasn't supposed to be. It was different for white men. The picture of Hairless Harmon posing in his G-string made Gerald think of a big, wet, sculpted slab of tofu.

"You could do it too," Harmon said. "You got a good built. The raw material is there. After that it's hard work. You work hard enough, you can make your body whatever you want it to be."

"I have no problems with my body."

"You meet a lot of interesting people in gyms," Harmon said. "That's how I met Evan."

It took Gerald a couple of seconds to realize that Harmon was talking about Ruark.

"He's in it more for the exercise," Harmon said. "He has the discipline, though. The cat is a fool on discipline."

Gerald himself met Ruark in a dojo, a karate studio. They were in the same class. Gerald noticed Ruark; seldom did you see anyone fight so focused and furious. Ruark, naturally, noticed Gerald. Everyone noticed Gerald.

They would talk. Ruark seemed interested in him. What he liked and didn't like, what he wanted to do with his life, the fact that Gerald had a probation officer from whom he concealed his karate and tae kwan do classes. With two assault counts as a juvenile and another when he was twenty, Gerald did not qualify as someone who needed to learn more about manual mayhem.

When Ruark started to lay money on him, Gerald had to wonder whether Ruark was infatuated. Rich bachelor hanging around with a big good-looking kid, sure wouldn't be the first time. Gerald asked himself what he would do if the price got better. But it wasn't that way. Ruark was just friendly. He even went home with Gerald a couple of times to meet his mother.

Brought his mother flowers. At that point Gerald would have done anything for Ruark, and his mother would've blessed it.

"I hope you and me get along better than the last guy," Harmon said.

"What last guy?" Gerald said.

"You don't know? You're a replacement, my man. Black dude named Oscar. Big, mean, and ug-*lee*. He hated my ass on principle. I said so to Evan, and he says to me, 'You don't think that's how I want it? You two driving around with my money, why do I want you to be pals?' I never thought of it that way."

"Checks and balances," Gerald said. "The man is quick."

"I guess."

"What happened to Oscar?"

"Don't ask me. Last week it's him, today it's you."

But, Gerald thought, was the man really so smart? Harmon was supposed to keep him, Gerald, from getting any ideas. But Gerald knew he could take out Harmon in the space between heartbeats. Leaving him, Gerald, with three years' worth of six-hundred-dollar-a-week handouts and a car in his own name.

What was to stop him?

Then it came to Gerald. Mr. Ruark had been to his apartment. The man knew where his mother lived.

Would he hurt somebody's mother? Gerald had seen how intense Ruark would get doing a simple karate exercise in the dojo. The look in his eyes. Imagine if he was ripped off and made to look like a fool.

"You seem to be an easy-going type," Harmon said. "Not like Oscar."

Gerald looked over at him. Harmon's eyes were half closed, and he had this off-balance grin. Trying to look sly.

"I can't work with hostility," Harmon said. "But I think you and me could get along. Cut us a deal sometime. He don't just have us do deliveries. We do pickups, too. I've known days when there was almost two hundred thou in the bag."

Gerald braked the Isuzu hard and pulled over to the shoulder of the highway. He put his hands around Harmon's neck. Harmon thrashed his hairless arms. He made gagging sounds and started to turn red before Gerald relaxed his grip.

"Don't even *think* about it," Gerald said.

"Are we gonna do something kicky tonight?" Caitlin said.

"Kind of short notice," Hays said.

"Honey, babycakes, please." She put her arms around his neck. She was like a little girl with Daddy, playing to him.

"It isn't a good idea, spur-of-the-moment. It's chancy."

"That's the part I like best." She leaned in close and kissed his ear. She bit the fleshy bottom of the lobe, not too hard, just so he'd notice.

"I can call the barney," he said. "Have him scope out the Piedmont."

"Something kicky, huh?"

"Kicky, sure."

"A kicky something. Kicky-kinky. A kicky-kinky-stinky something."

"If that's what you want."

"Me?" she said. "Like you don't get off on it too."

"Yeah," he said. "I do. I do."

"Got one for you," Hays said to Naull on the phone, and gave him the address and number.

Naull breathed a soft grunt over the line. Piedmont. Nice.

"Now the fine print," Hays said. "We do it tonight."

"No way," Naull said.

"Tonight," Hays repeated.

"I need at least two days to make sure," Naull said. "Two days minimum, couple drive-bys each day."

"Tonight or never," Hays said.

"I'm ready to say no," Naull said.

"Are you ready to queer the whole deal?" Hays said. "You are definitely replaceable."

There was a short unhappy silence before Naull said, "I can drive over, have a look."

"You do that," Hays said. "Then let's say midnight, huh? Grand Avenue, across from the theater, entrance to Lakeside Park."

"I'll see what it looks like."

"Be there," Hays said.

It was June now. By this time Naull had been hooked up with them for about six months. Strangest six months of his life. And the most profitable. Their bills were paid, and the last time he peeked in Marie's savings book she had a balance of twenty-two thousand.

He didn't like to take a place without a couple of days' prep. But he knew it would probably be empty. They almost always were.

He got in the Econoline and drove to Piedmont, up in the hills above Oakland.

The Piedmont address was a wood-shingled bungalow. It was set

39

close to the street, but flowering bushes grew in front of some windows. A six-foot privacy fence enclosed the back end of the lot and blocked the view from around back, where an alley ran.

As usual it was a great neighborhood. But in Piedmont they all were.

Naull drove past twice. He didn't see anybody. A light shone in the front room, and the back-porch bulb burned. Otherwise the place was dark. The evening was warm, but the house was buttoned up. The grass was getting long. He drove down the hill, had steak and eggs at a Denny's on Grand Avenue, went down the street to a bar where the lights were dim and Merle Haggard played on the jukebox. He sat at the bar, smoked half a dozen cigarettes and drank a couple of Olys and ate salted peanuts. About every half hour he tried the number of the bungalow. No answer.

It was half past eleven when he left the bar. He got in the van, drove past the house again. Maybe he was overly cautious, but he had to make sure. It made him nervous, one sweet address after another, prime neighborhoods, empty houses, easy, easy, easy. Nothing this good ever happened to Naull.

But it kept happening. It was happening again tonight. The bungalow was still shut up, still dark except for the front-room lamp and the back-porch light. Almost midnight. Nobody was home.

He drove down from Piedmont, back to Grand, past Lake Merritt. Hays and Caitlin were already there, outside the entrance to Lakeside Park, holding identical overnight bags. Hays wore slacks and a leather Ike jacket. Caitlin had on a silk blouse, a nappy silk jacket, and hundred-dollar denims over lizard cowboy boots.

Naull pulled over to the curb. They got in behind Naull, and he pulled away.

"Probably thought I wasn't coming," Naull said.

"I wasn't worried," Hays said.

"You wouldn't let us down, would you, Ralph?" Caitlin said.

"What are we looking at?" Hays said.

"Older bungalow, no big problems far as I can see," Naull said. "Back door's got some glass, I'd say we probably go in through there."

"Just tell me we're doing it," Caitlin said.

"I guess we are."

"Bitchin'."

They started putting on black jumpsuits from the overnight bags. Black knit caps, black leather gloves, black Air Jordans. Simple

40

burglary, they acted like it was a SWAT raid. Naull wore what he usually wore, work pants, a flannel shirt.

He drove up the hill and pointed out the bungalow as they drove past. He parked about a block away, and made them take off the hats and gloves while they walked along the street and down the alley. The high gate was latched from the inside, but Naull boosted Caitlin over and she opened it. They went into the backyard and up on the porch.

Naull put on his gloves and backed the bulb out of the socket. A row of four small panes, each a few inches square, extended across the top of the back door.

"You going to do the tape thing?" Caitlin said. "I want to try."

Naull said fine. He didn't want to argue. She took a roll of duct tape out of his tool bag, tore off several strips, and pressed them over one pane. With the butt end of a screwdriver she broke the glass under the tape. It made a crunching sound, nothing else. She gave a little grunt that sounded to Naull like something she might do in bed, in the act.

"Pop," said Hays.

"Pop that cherry," she said. "Yow!"

She pulled the tape away, and pulled away the broken glass that stuck to it.

"We're doing it," Caitlin said. She was buzzing. "*Doing* it. Yeah, oh yeah, we're *doing* it, huh?"

"Quiet," Naull said. He cleared out the small shards, reached inside, found a bolt and pulled it back, and turned the button on the door lock.

The door opened on a utility room: boxes, canning jars on a shelf, garden tools, a row of paint cans, stacks of old *Chronicles*. There was another locked door into the kitchen. Naull pried it in about two seconds and stepped inside. He felt tight and alert.

They walked up the long center hall, toward the pale light in the front room. The bungalow had that fussed-over, settled-in-place feel of a house where an older woman lived alone. Twin rows of annual Yule plates hung on both sides of the long hall, some going back to the early fifties. Beige carpet stretched wall to wall across the front room, with a six-by-eight Oriental rug laid over the beige. Baby grand in one corner, big brocade couch with matching armchairs and love seat, grouping of family photos on the wall, fireplace topped by a fox hunt engraving in a gilt frame.

"Menopause Manor," Caitlin said. "Some little old biddy's gonna have a shitty homecoming."

Hays and Naull went to the dining room, the mahogany breakfront. Up top in the china cabinet were a silver platter, silver gravy boat, couple of silver covered dishes. The china was Limoges, a flowery pattern. Naull opened the doors below, and there was more silver: two boxes of place settings, three more big platters, three more covered dishes, and a tea service. Sterling. Naull didn't have to look at the marks. An older woman's house, place this nice, it had to be sterling.

"Kitsch City," Caitlin said from the front room. She was looking at a row of figurehead mugs on the mantel, couple dozen.

"Yeah, that's Royal Doulton," Naull said over his shoulder. "We'll take that."

"Somebody actually wants this?"

"My receiver will handle all he can get, twelve bucks apiece. Wrap 'em up in newspapers. The plates, too, Christmas plates in the hall."

"Christmas plates!"

"Delft. They're collectible. Seven apiece for the newer years, probably fifteen, twenty for some of the old ones."

"Hallelujah America. Land of the free and banal."

"I don't have to like it to steal it," Naull said. Actually he didn't know what she had against them. He imagined it would be nice one day to have a home with a long row of Yule plates, scenes of sleigh rides and decorated trees on blue porcelain. He would have to buy them, though. Marie would never allow stolen goods on the wall.

Naull took out a couple of big cloth sacks and told Hays to load the silver, then box up the china. He got a couple of empty cardboard boxes and a stack of newspapers from the rear room. When he got back Caitlin was hooting at the figurines in one of the display cases. He told her yeah, they go too.

"You must be kidding."

"Good money."

"Spare me!"

"Wrap 'em up good," he said.

He went down the hall again. It was an old-fashioned layout, separate bath and water closet. Third door down was a guest bedroom. Fourth one, the main bedroom. Naull knew something about older people. Those who had lived through the Depression tended to want their goodies at hand. He went into the main bedroom, turned on his flashlight, poked the beam around.

It was furnished with a Forties-style suite. Most of the jewelry was gone from the glass case on the dressing table. What was left wasn't worth taking. He dumped out all the dresser drawers, looked at the undersides, good place to tape envelopes full of cash. Same with the bedside table. But there was nothing. He crouched beside the bed, pulled up the dust ruffle, looked underneath. He pushed the mattress off. Old women, you never knew. But nothing. He went around the room and tried all the electric receptacles, plugging in a night light that he found. You could buy fake outlets that covered a little hideaway box in the baseboard. These were all real, though.

One wall was covered with built-in bookcases. Naull scanned the titles. *National Geographics*, Harlequin paperbacks, Reader's Digest Condensed Books. He was ready to turn away when he noticed *Practical Manual of Homesteading* up on the top shelf.

Uh-huh.

He pulled it out. It was lighter than it ought to be.

He took it to the door and looked up the hall to the front room. Hays was rolling up the rug. Caitlin was putting the plates into a box, yelling about sentimental junk.

"Keep it down," Naull hissed. He took a couple of steps back into the room, and opened the book.

The pages were cut away inside. The edges of the sheets were intact, so the book looked right if it was closed, but inside was a neat hollow that held a Ziploc bag with a stack of greenbacks.

Naull held the flashlight between his teeth. His heart was tripping hard and fast. The packet of cash was almost an inch thick, and when he riffled through he saw it was all hundreds. He zipped up the bag and stuck it inside his shirt, in his waistband.

He wasn't surprised to find a treasure like this. Nothing that people did with their riches, dumb as it might be, surprised him anymore.

He went back into the hall, trying to act normal.

Hays had the silverware stacked, the china in a box, the rug rolled up. He said, "Ralph, we like the carpet. It might be a Tabriz. We'll just take that if it's all right with you, leave you the rest. Call it even?"

"I guess," Naull said. He didn't want to talk about it. He wanted to leave fast, get out with what he had on him. But he told himself no. A thief should never run like a thief. He said, "If that's a Tabriz, you're cutting yourself a pretty sweet deal. What would that go, couple of thousand retail?"

"Who pays retail?" Hays said.

Caitlin came up the hall with a box and yelled, "All right, I did the plates, but I'm not diddling around with any schlocky figurines."

"They're Hummel," Naull said.

"They're crap. You like it so much, you can wrap it up and carry it out."

"The Doultons, anyway."

"Hey, all yours, Ralph."

"You want the carpet, you can crate up the Doultons." The thought came to him, What a way to spend my time. Haggling with a couple of rich brats.

"I'll do it," Hays said.

"Somebody knows a bargain," Naull said. He got some newsprint and started wrapping the Hummels.

"Did it occur to you that we're artists?" Caitlin said. She was in the living room, near the family pictures on the wall. Naull wasn't paying much attention—he was working fast. She said, "This is alternate reality. This is performance. We could sell tickets. People would pay good money to watch this."

Something in her voice made Naull look up. She was holding one of the framed pictures, an old black-and-white of a boy on a tricycle. She flipped it underhand, and it flew across the room and smashed in the fireplace.

"Don't do that," Naull said.

"What? Don't do what? This?" She had another picture and she threw it. It turned end over end in the air and broke against the far wall.

"Don't," Naull said.

"Wrap up your crap. You get your jollies, I'll get mine."

"You're dangerous," Hays said, making like a joke but not pulling it off. He knew it was true.

"That's right," Caitlin said. She knew it, too.

She had another one. Naull didn't move. He couldn't see getting into it with her here, but it took an effort to stand and watch. He didn't know why he should care. He did care, though. She threw the picture across the room, and it sailed and kept sailing into a front window. The pane shattered. To Naull the sound seemed very loud and endless, glass exploding, splinters of glass flying and tinkling, tinkling, outside as they fell.

"That's it," Naull said. He was tight and angry. "Time to cut and run."

"We're just getting started," Hays said.

"I'm not even warmed up yet," Caitlin said.

Naull didn't answer. He picked up his tools and the two sacks of sterling and started out the back door. From the hall he said, "I'm getting the van. Meet you around back. Don't forget my breakables. You want the rug, you better bring that too."

"Don't be such a pussy," Caitlin said. "We just got here."

"I want you waiting for me. Unless you'd rather walk back to Grand Avenue."

Naull forgot and let the back door slam behind him, he was that upset. Then he got upset for letting her get to him that way. He left the sacks of silver behind the high fence, by the gate, and went out into the alley, walking quickly out to the sidewalk, around the block to the van.

When he was inside the van he put the cash under his seat. Tucking it away gave him a quiet thrill and helped simmer him. Then he drove up the alley to the back of the bungalow. Nobody was there.

He left the motor idling. Once he was out of the truck he could hear Caitlin inside, laughing, shrieking. The silver was beside the gate. Nothing else. Naull didn't want to leave the van in sight, but he didn't see that he had a choice. He went in the back door, strode through the kitchen. Food was everywhere, jars broken on the floor, mustard and ketchup splattered on the cabinets. Flour powdered at his heels as he walked. He started boiling again. Striding up the hall, figuring that a little more noise wouldn't make any difference, he yelled, "Goddamn. What the hell you doing?"

He smelled it as he came up the hall, fresh paint. Then bright color jolted him as he walked into the room. Emerald green flowed together with yellow on beige carpet. Spats of dark blue exploded up one wall and across the ceiling. Deep red gashed across the brocade of the couch and the love seat. Caitlin was standing in the middle of the room, holding a quart can of paint, with three or four empty cans around her feet, the paint from the back room.

"Redecorating," she said. She threw the can. A white cascade flowed through the air and slopped heavily across the baby grand. "Yow!"

"Goddamn," Naull said.

"I am cranked," she said. She was chattering. "*Cranked.* How 'bout you, sweetie, you cranked too?"

"Cranked," Hays said. He was beside her, working the top off another can. He gave it to her.

45

"We're going," Naull said.

"Hang on, Ralph," she said. She tossed the can. Thick ivory clots splashed across the fox hunt scene, and she squealed. "Aw right. *Yow!*"

Hays heaved a wave of blue across the dining room table.

"Uh-*huh*," she said.

"This is pathetic," Naull said. He picked up the boxes of Hummels and Doultons. "I'm taking these out, I'm coming back for the china, I'm getting my ass down the hill."

"You do that, Ralph," she said.

He picked up the boxes and started out.

"With or without you."

Hays said, "Ralph, don't kid yourself. You're not doing anything without us."

Naull heard paint splash behind him.

"Yes!" Caitlin yelled.

Naull put the boxes in the back of the van. He put in the bags of silver. Glass crashed out front, and crashed again as he ran back into the house. Caitlin had the fireplace poker. When Naull got to the living room she was bashing out the front windows one by one. Hays was grinning. To Naull he said, "Do you believe this shit?"

Caitlin swung and a window exploded.

"*Yes!*" she said, and she laughed a giddy laugh.

She moved to the baby grand and bashed the keyboard. Broken keys flew, and the piano rang.

"*Yes!*"

Through an empty window Naull could see lights coming on in a house across the street.

The piano rang again.

"*Yes!*"

She moved to the dining room. Naull saw more lights coming on across the street, and he started toward her. She whacked the dining table.

"*Yes!*"

She swung at the doors of the china cabinet, and they came apart in a shower of glass and mahogany trim.

"*Yes!*" she yelled, and Naull grabbed her and put her over his shoulder.

"Have I gone overboard?" she said. "I have. Oh, I know I have. I've gone overboard, I've done it again."

"Shut up," Naull said. He was carrying her to the back door.

"Oh my. I guess we're leaving," she said. "Oh my." She didn't seem to mind Naull carrying her. Hays didn't mind. They both thought it was a damn joke. It made Naull hold her tighter, his arm around her thin waist. Squeeze some of the laugh out of her.

"Done it again. Oh my oh my."

He carried her out the back door, through the yard and the gate. Lights were coming on in houses along both sides of the alley. Naull put her in the backseat, told Hays to stay back there with her. He got up front and drove. Heads were popping up in windows as he went down the alley. For moments like this Naull never cleaned the grime off his license plates or replaced the dead bulb in the plate light. He drove out onto the street, down the hill to Oakland. Going down Moraga Avenue, they met a Piedmont Police cruiser headed up, fast. It kept going, and in a couple of minutes the van was back in thoroughfare traffic again.

"Are you using?" Naull said when they turned on Grand.

"You mean drugs?" she said. She was calm now. They were both taking off the jumpsuits. "Of course not."

"Because if you are it's the dumbest thing you can do. Get loaded before you do a job."

"Do we look like a couple of druggies?" Hays said.

"You act like it."

"We're just high on crime," Hays said. "Don't let it throw you."

"We're *real* sorry about that," Caitlin said. "Something about that place. I hated it right away. It was offensive, you know? I don't mind out of date. Unconscious retro, I can live with it. But sappy—no way. It set me off. And Ralph, let's be realistic. What's the point of being criminals if we have to behave ourselves?"

"That's right," Hays said. "Play by the rules when you rip off an old lady's prized possessions. What a crock."

"That silver," Caitlin said. "Her wedding gifts, no doubt. Tad bit hypocritical, aren't you, Ralph?"

Naull was pulling up to the park.

"I should've left you up there," he said. He turned into the curb at the spot where he picked them up.

"And kissed off the best deal you ever had," Hays said.

"Leave you up there for the cops to find."

"Ralph, you never would," Hays said. "You realize, we get caught, we're giving you up in about ten seconds. You do realize that. Right?"

"I go, you go," Naull said.

47

They stepped out on the curb.

"I don't think so," Hays said. "Look at us, Ralph. Ralph, I want you to look at us."

Naull looked. All the commando stuff was in the bags. There was Hays in his suede Guccis and leather Ike jacket. There was Caitlin in her silk blouse and lizard boots and hundred-dollar jeans. They were the smirky golden kids again, Flopsy and Mopsy with a wicked slant.

Hays said, "Do we look like the kind of people who go to jail? I think not. We are not the type. People like us do not go to jail. People like us can get away with anything."

They watched Naull turn the corner off Grand. Then they walked down the block to where the Bimmer was parked, and got in. Hays put the key in the ignition but didn't turn it. They were across from the Grand Lake Theater, right under a streetlight.

He waited. He expected something: thanks, enthusiasm, pleasure. She didn't move.

He said, "Some night, huh?"

She said, "It's a long way home."

Naull took the van around the block. Three right turns brought him back to Grand Avenue. He stopped at a blinking red and watched Hays and Caitlin get into the BMW.

He pulled over to the curb and waited. The lights came on, the BMW pulled out. Naull accelerated to follow.

They turned north on the Nimitz. Hays drove too fast. It made Naull nervous; he imagined being stopped for speeding, a Highway Patrol officer pointing his flashlight inside.

But he didn't know when he'd get a better chance.

He followed them up the east side of the bay, across the Richmond–San Rafael Bridge. Marin. Traffic was light, and he was able to drop back a few hundred yards without losing them. He wasn't worried that they'd notice him. They were not the type. They had never been burned. It was dangerous, he thought, when life treated you too gently. It made you cocky and dull, a bad combination.

The BMW crossed two lanes to leap up the Tiburon exit ramp. They took a left off the stop sign at the top of the interchange, and Naull followed, clipping along Tiburon Boulevard. The road ran beside an estuary. Through breaks in the stands of eucalyptus Naull could see Angel Island in close, and beyond it the bay and the lights of San Francisco. A tall ridge stood up along the other side of the road. About a mile short of Tiburon the BMW turned left on a street that wriggled steeply up the ridge in a series of sharp turns.

Naull checked the sign as he made the turn. Altamonte Drive. He kept driving. Every now and then he could see them, three or four switchbacks ahead of him.

He noticed that going up Altamonte was like climbing through levels of money. Every couple of turns, you could tack on another hundred thousand or so to the price of a house. At the bottom of the hill was the realm of $180,000 condos. Above the condos, town houses kicked in, then duplexes and three-bedrooms, $350,000 ranchers stamped out on fifty-by-one-hundred-foot lots. It went that way. As you climbed, the homes got bigger and nicer and farther apart, and much more expensive.

Near the top of the ridge Naull started to wonder if they had spotted him after all. According to the signs, the road dead-ended up here at the top of the hill. Maybe they were leading him into the cul-de-sac. Have some yuks at his expense, remind him how smart they were.

Up ahead the BMW was slipping into a driveway. Naull quickly pulled the van over to the curb, and cut the lights and engine.

The BMW was out of sight. Therefore they could not see the van. Naull got out and started walking up the road. He was almost at the top of the ridge. No houses were in sight, only rolling fields and a speckling of oak trees.

Naull climbed through another switchback, and there was the BMW at the top of the driveway, under a four-bay carport with a Mercedes coupe, a Land Rover wagon, a Corvette convertible. Hays and Caitlin were climbing a set of stone steps up to an octagon house at the top of the ridge. They stopped at the front door. Hays got out some keys, unlocked the door, and they went in.

Lights went on inside as Naull stood looking at the house. It straddled the crest of the ridge. Five thousand, six thousand square feet. Maybe more—it looked like some lower levels might be notched into the east side of the hill.

Naull knew construction. This place was super solid. The redwood rafters under the eaves were as big as the timbers of a railroad bridge. The house seemed to grow out of the ridge. To move the house you would have to move the mountain.

Naull got in his van again and turned down the hill. In his mind he kept seeing the octagon, riding the crest of the hill like a battleship plowing through the ocean. At the same time he thought of Hays and Caitlin in the living room of the Piedmont bungalow, the paint splashing and the broken glass flying.

It took some effort to bring it all together. Naull knew that life was strange, that life certainly was not fair. But damn. He couldn't get over it.

People like them. In a house like that.

Caitlin said nothing on the drive home. She said nothing as they got ready for bed. She could drive you crazy with chatter, but Hays thought her silence was worse.

They got into bed and turned out the lights.

Hays said, "I'm sorry you didn't enjoy it."

"I had a good time."

"I mean, all the trouble that's involved. Why bother if you don't enjoy it?"

"I had a good time. Do you hear me complaining? No. I'm not complaining. I had a good time, all right?"

"*I* had a good time," Hays said.

"You would," she said.

In Carmel, Carmel-by-the-Sea, they first sampled the sublime voltage of crime. It was, maybe, by accident.

One Sunday evening, on the way home from the Big Sur cabin, they stopped for dinner at a *shabu-shabu* restaurant on San Carlos Street in Carmel. They ate, they drank some sake. When they were ready to go, Hays left the check with Caitlin and stopped by the men's room. Then he went out front. Caitlin was there, waiting on the sidewalk.

She said, "What did it come to? The tab?"

"I left it with you," he said.

"Bullshit, you took it."

"The hell I did. I left it on the table."

"You didn't."

"On the table, Cait."

"Did I forget it? Oh my God. I did. I forgot it."

She acted surprised, as if she really did forget. When he started to go back, though, she grabbed his arm.

"Don't," she said.

"I have to get the check," he said.

"Why?"

"We just walked out on an eighty-dollar dinner tab."

"Yeah," she said.

"I think we can afford to pay the bill," Hays said.

"Sweetie, I realize that, but do we want to?"

Right here he began to wonder whether she really had forgotten it. He was never sure, and he never bothered to ask.

"Maybe we ought to scoot," she said.

They started down the sidewalk. The car was about a block away. It was a chilly night, and the fog was in, curling around their legs. Hays kept waiting for the maître d' or the manager to come out of the restaurant, waving the check, shouting threats. She told him walk, don't run. It was a good feeling, letting the fog swallow them up, knowing what they had done.

At the car she put her arms around him and held him tight.

"Goddamn," Hays said. "We did it. We actually did it." He drew the air in deep. It was cool and rich and moist. It had the tang of pine and the musk of sea salt. He couldn't remember the last time he actually tasted the air he breathed.

"Were you scared?" Caitlin said. "I wasn't. It was a heightened experience. Almost an out-of-body kind of thing."

"The adrenaline," Hays said.

"The rush."

"Yeah, the rush."

They didn't say much on the way home. Hays knew they were going to do it again, though. And they did. Twice more in the next three nights, at restaurants in the city. Taking the Reebok discount, Caitlin called it.

It turned out to be so easy. People like them, nobody expected them to steal anything.

And right away, being so easy, it got stale.

Zero risk, zero payoff, Caitlin said.

That was the night she walked into a liquor store in Mill Valley, stuck a bottle of '68 Robert Mondavi cabernet under her coat, and walked out. Now *that* was something, she yelled at Hays as they drove off in the BMW, *that* was kicky. She was high, she was drawing energy out of the ozone that night.

So they were into shoplifting for a while. In no way could it be called zero-risk. You gave yourself no wiggle room when you left a store with a $220 bottle of wine—or a set of Villeroy & Boch candlesticks, or a carved Inuit fetish—clutched under your Burberry.

They kept at it for a few weeks. By the end of that time it was still a thrill; but an old thrill, and a small one. She started to get that cat-on-the-prowl edginess. Hays wondered what was next.

They were at a dinner party in San Francisco, business acquaintances, when table talk turned to burglary. Two of the women had recently come home to broken windows, forced doors, missing valuables.

The sense of being violated, one of the women said. The invasion. Knowing that some asshole has been going through your dresser.

Makes you feel like you've been raped, the other agreed.

Caitlin listened, quiet and thoughtful. She looked like La Gioconda remembering a good roll in the hay. And he knew what was next.

Back home, before she could mention it, he said, "I want you to know, you have to realize, burglary, breaking and entering, is not some bullshit petty crime. People go to jail, they do serious time. People get shot sometimes. You could be facing guns and dogs. This is dangerous."

She said, "If you're trying to make it sound unattractive, you're taking the wrong approach."

Back-pedaling fast, he said, "There are specific ways to do it, things we know nothing about. This is the point I'm trying to make."

"Like a craft," she said. "You've got your masters, your journeymen, your apprentices."

"Exactly," he said. "And I know you, you do something, you don't want to blunder around like some ignorant doofus."

"I was thinking about that."

"Good."

She said, "We find a professional. A journeyman. We apprentice to a journeyman, that's easy."

"I guess we just go out and hire one. Is that what you had in mind? Get serious. Criminals don't fill out job applications, you know."

"Don't they?" she said.

EvHaTek employed nearly six hundred in direct sales, telemarketing, mail order, and retail. Its personnel department at the headquarters in San Rafael received more than a thousand job applications a quarter. Caitlin made Hays go through all of them for the past six months.

He couldn't believe that anyone asking for a job would be stupid enough to admit being a convicted felon. But there he was. Ralph Artis Naull, San Pablo, looking for work in maintenance or custodial. One misdemeanor conviction and two felony, for possession of stolen goods and breaking and entering.

For the past few months the company had been using ad inserts to promote a line of Brazilian leather luggage. It came in colors. Black leather, the business look, was moving fine. But the tan, the red, the blue—resort luggage, vacation luggage—were backing up in warehouses. Hays came up with a hook: buy a set of luggage, qualify for a vacation rain-out insurance policy. Now the tan, the red, the blue were starting to move.

This angle cost the company just a few dollars per policy. To get it the customer had to fill out a form showing dates of travel. The company parceled out the policies to several underwriters, but all forms were funneled through the San Rafael office. At the touch of a key Hays could call up the names, addresses, and phone numbers of holders whose policies were about to go into effect. He could sort out Bay Area addresses by zip code, prime neighborhoods.

The scheme was all but undiscoverable, spread out that way around the area, a string of unlucky travelers whose sole connection was the trademark on their luggage.

It was not 100 percent. People changed plans without canceling policies. Not 100 percent, but close enough for an out-of-work convict, for a barney like Naull.

"What do you want?" Hays said in their bed. "That's as much excitement as I can handle."

"You want to know the truth, I'll tell you; it doesn't ring my bell anymore. Anything gets old after a while."

"You looked like you were having a good time."

"Is that what you thought? Sorry about that—I was forcing it. Yell a little bit, try to shake things up. But it wasn't happening."

Hays lay in the darkness and tried to think what this could mean. He said, "Damn. Where do we go from here?"

"I don't know," she said. Her voice was brighter now. "I suppose we'll just have to use our imaginations."

Naull drove home, parked out front, cut the engine. He reached under his seat for the stack of hundreds.

He started to count. He took his time. Curling these beautiful bills under his fingers.

When he got to fifty he'd hardly made a dent in the stack.

At one hundred he had a long way to go.

One-fifty, and he was still counting.

Toward the end he could guess how it was going to turn out. One ninety-eight. One ninety-nine. Two hundred. He had twenty thousand dollars in his hands.

He wanted to wake up Marie, fling it into the air and let it blizzard down around them, a storm of hundreds in their bedroom. But he let her sleep.

She kept a jar in the kitchen, an old Sanka jar where Naull would put his money. They had been doing it that way for years. She never asked what was in it, or how it got there. If there was money in the jar, she used it. That was how she dealt with the fruits of crime. That was how Naull put the fruits into circulation.

But this was way too big for that. Reach into the jar and fill her hand with hundreds, she might go into shock.

He didn't mention it at breakfast. He kept it in his pocket, this delicious humongous doubled-over wad of Franklins. He told Marie he'd need the Econoline, so he and Roy Boy took her to the track. She wouldn't look at the pile of goods in the back. After he dropped her off, Naull brought the silver and the rest down to Andy Pops. Two seven. He got that in hundreds, too.

Now the wad was getting conspicuous. Once it reached a certain size, critical mass, you had to deal with it. He knew he was going to do something extravagant, even a little stupid, but that it wouldn't matter. He had a margin. Their bills were paid for the month, Marie was putting money in the bank. He could do something reckless and it wouldn't hurt. They wouldn't even feel it.

That was the great part. Having this cushion against your own foolishness.

He got off the freeway in Berkeley and started north. At least a dozen used-car lots lined San Pablo Avenue between Berkeley and Richmond.

"We need some wheels," Naull said.

"A car?"

"Damn straight, a car. Don't you think we need a car?"

"Uh-huh."

"That's right. Damn straight."

"What about the van?" Roy Boy said.

"We'll keep the van, naturally. Got to have the van."

"All right," Roy Boy said.

"A second set of wheels. Some Dee-troit iron. A big Goddamn V-eight."

"All *right*," Roy Boy said.

Naull drove slow past each lot. Strings of flapping plastic banners, prices whitewashed on windshields, Day-Glo placards that said LO MILES and FACTORY AIR and CHECK OUT THIS HONEY. Rows and rows of bright chrome and buffed paint. Mama, yes, yes, yes!

Naull pulled over. He got out in front of Smilin' Jim's Pre-Owned Classics. Roy Boy got out, too, and followed him without saying anything—he knew the look. In the back of the lot was a blue Camaro with A REAL RUNNER shoved under one wiper and 4-SPEED under the other. Naull started to look it over. Good tires. No rust underneath. The odometer said 78,554, for what that was worth.

Naull was in the front seat when the salesman came over. Middle-age guy with a comfortable pot belly under his short-sleeve shirt and the last faint licks of a twang in his voice when he leaned in the window and said, "She's a runner, all right."

"Yeah, that's what the sign says. This is what, a 'seventy-seven or 'seventy-eight?"

"This is a 'seventy-seven. This here's a collector's item."

"What's this collector's item gonna set me back?"

"We'll figure sumpin' out."

Naull said, "What's your name?"

"Call me Ed."

Naull knew the accent. He knew exactly how to talk to Ed. He said, "Ed, I'm Sonny. And I'll tell you what. You and me gonna get along a whole lot better if you don't try to rag my ass. Now I know the car has a price on it. Why don't you tell me what you're askin' for it, we can go from there."

Ed stepped back, looking front to back at the Camaro, as if he were seeing it for the first time.

"I imagine we could let this sweetheart go for three thousand and a half."

"Kind of steep."

"Sonny, you'll never know till you roll some rubber on the road."

He had the key. He got in beside Naull, and Roy Boy sat in the back. Naull turned it over. Caught right away. That lovely V-8 burble. It moved out nice, too.

"Brakes're a little spongy," Naull said when they stopped at a light.

"Find you a good mechanic, it won't set you back much."

"I'll do it myself, it'll set me back even less."

"Work on cars, do you?" Ed said.

"I work on just about anything."

Naull took it back to the lot and checked the compression on the cylinders. He had a gauge—he came prepared. Compression was good. He argued Ed down to three thousand. They went into the office, which was a house trailer on blocks. Naull paid him the cash and spent a few minutes filling out forms.

"You'd be from Oklahoma," Ed said while Naull wrote.

"Me and you both."

"Okmulgee's where I come home," Ed said. "You?"

"Little town called Lenapah, up near the Kansas border," Naull said. "Born in Sapulpa, but we moved when I was a kid. Been gone a long time?"

"Twenty-three years."

"Fourteen for me," Naull said. "Sometimes it seems like a hunnerd and fourteen."

"I know what you mean. I ain't had a decent chicken-fried steak since I got here. Ain't—that felt good. *Ain't*. I miss saying ain't and cain't."

"Oh yeah. And *git* for get. I know how to talk right, but I fall into Okie now and then, just to get under people's skin. I don't know, folks around here, walking around like they got a burr up their butt. I want to tell 'em to ease up some."

"I got news for you," Ed said. "Them *are* us. The way this place pulls you in. Once you been here a year or so, you're automatically part of the crowd."

"Speak for yourself," Naull said.

He finished the last form, signed them all, and handed them to Ed.

"Pretty country up there," Ed said, "up around the state line."

"It can be, when it gets some moisture."

"You ever think about going back?"

"Naw."

"I do," Ed said. "Every Goddamn day."

Naull left the van at the curb out front. He could pick it up later. He buckled up Roy Boy and drove the Camaro up San Pablo Avenue, toward home. He felt a little down. It was crazy, he thought; he ought to feel high. A new car. A Z-28 Camaro. But something was dragging him, and he knew what it was. Ed. Homesick Ed, bringing him down.

He stopped, waited for a light, and at the green he dumped the clutch and fed in plenty of gas. The tires screamed, then chirped again as he worked up through the gears . . . *brat, brat, brat* . . . fast as Naull could work the shifter.

Wow. That was better—it was like being eighteen all over again.

"She is a runner," Naull said.

"Yes sir," Roy Boy said. He was hanging on to the seat.

"Moves right out."

"Yes *sir.*"

"Your mama has a big surprise coming her way."

"Damn straight," Roy Boy said.

The Marin County offices were in San Rafael. Roy Boy dangled his legs from a bench while Naull found the lot number from the Tiburon plat maps. Last lot at the top of Altamonte Drive.

The place was assessed at $1.2 million. No liens, and they were up to date on the property tax. Hays Tilton Teale was the name on the tax rolls. Joint tenant with Caitlin Hames.

Naull looked at the names and thought of splashing paint, broken glass, crazy laughter.

There was a public phone next to the bench where Roy Boy sat. And a phone book. Naull paged through it. Boom. Hays had his listing, Caitlin had hers. Both at 771 Altamonte.

The numbers were right there under his finger. He could drop a quarter, give them a ring. Hey guys, guess who.

Gotcha.

But he put away the idea. What would a crank call get him? Only trouble, he thought. Clue them in that maybe the dumb Okie wasn't so dumb after all. Naull didn't know when, or how, but he was sure that he could do a whole lot better than that.

They were on the road to Lodi when Hairless Harmon told Gerald about his career as a porn-film star. Not features, but ten-minute loops, the ones they run in peep-show arcades. Two hundred a pop to do what you'd do for free anyway.

"You want to get into it, I can arrange it," Harmon said. "You got a good bod on you. You could use some definition, but the basic bulk is sure there."

Gerald wondered if this could be a proposition, a low-rent version of the casting couch. You oughta be in stag films.

"Boy or girl stuff?" Gerald said. They were in Harmon's Tercel. All of a sudden Gerald was aware of how close they were, jammed together in the front seats.

"You get a girl gig once in a while," Harmon said. "But mostly it's solo. Whacking. The fruits go in for that. Watching a well-built guy choke his chicken. What the hell. It pays the rent."

"I have no trouble paying my rent," Gerald said.

Ruark's job was a pickup this time. Gerald and Harmon were supposed to meet a certain Booger in the parking lot of a produce stand on Route 12, three miles from Lodi. This was out of the Bay Area, inland toward the valley.

Mister Ruark told him to pick up a paper bag containing ninety-five thousand dollars. Booger was going to hand it over.

They'd done at least one pickup a month since Gerald started working for Ruark. Harmon said Booger was a biker. Harmon said a lot that wasn't worth listening to, but Gerald was inclined to believe him on that one. True, Booger drove four wheels and dressed like a normal human being. But Gerald knew a scum bucket when he saw one. You could pull a biker off his chopper, you could cut away his colors and even give him a bath and a haircut, but there was no getting away from that bowlegged walk and the broken nose and the scar along his jaw and—above all—those Charlie Manson eyes, like cracked marbles.

Gerald figured that Booger was either a biker or a rodeo cowboy with a serious LSD history. Take your pick.

Booger's vehicle was in the dusty lot behind the vegetable stand. It was a small Winnebago camper—a mini-Winnie, it was called. Booger was inside with his seat pushed back and his boots propped on the dash. The windows were up. An air-conditioning unit hummed and buzzed on the roof.

Harmon pulled in beside him. A western mural, sunset on a mesa, was airbrushed on the side of the camper. It showed the silhouetted figure of an Indian and his weary pony, the Indian with his head bowed and his lance lowered.

Gerald got out and thumped on the window. Booger turned around, slid the window down, and passed three paper bags out the window.

"Your sweet corn," he said. "Your tomatoes. And your leafy greens."

Gerald opened the bags one by one. Corn. Tomatoes. The cash.

"You want me to count it in the car?" Gerald said. "Or do you want to watch while I do it?"

"I want to get the fuck home." Booger wore a Fu Manchu. He was holding a can of Coors and wearing a red nylon 49ers' windbreaker. From a distance he could pass, say, as a mill hand or a flag man on a road crew, pulling down twenty-eight five a year and in hock for this land-bound cabin cruiser.

"As soon as I count the money," Gerald said. Harmon was out of the car now, and Gerald handed him the first two bags.

"Not again. I don't *believe* you, man."

"In the car? Or you want to watch?"

"I'm leaving."

"The problem is, suppose you leave and the count comes up short. It wouldn't look good for you."

"Don't fight him on it," Harmon said to Booger. "You ought to know by now. He just wears you down."

"Might as well do it in there," Gerald said. He tried the side door, and Booger unlocked it.

"They got cherry cider," Harmon said. "You want some?"

"Cherry cider, sounds good," Gerald said, and he got in the van.

Inside it was carpeted with long blue shag. A double mattress under a blue velour bedspread fit wall to wall across the back. There was a small refrigerator and a set of built-in shelves for a VCR and a small TV. It had adjustable blinds on the windows. Gerald closed the blinds.

On the TV a man in a hockey goaltender's mask was slashing away with a cleaver.

The bed sloshed under Gerald when he sat on it. Waterbed mattress. Gerald put the bag at his feet and started taking out money. When he finished counting one packet, he would put it beside him on the bedspread.

When he finished, the guy with the mask and the cleaver was chasing a girl in bra and panties across what looked like a college campus.

"Okay," Gerald said. "All there."

"It's always all there. When you gonna learn?"

"Everybody makes mistakes," Gerald said.

He stepped out onto the gravel. Harmon handed him a plastic cup of cherry cider. Gerald drank it down.

"Asshole," Booger said. He had the Winnebago started now.

"Don't get him pissed," Harmon said. "He's a terror."

"I doubt it," Booger said. "Charlie Chan. Just another rice burner." Gerald looked up.

"One way to find out," he said.

Booger thought about it for a couple of seconds. Then the window went up. The camper raised dust as it left.

Harmon drove. Gerald opened his leather Samsonite attaché case and began filling it with cash from the bag. Just about filled it up.

Who knew why a scum bucket was giving the man all that money, cash? Harmon wondered out loud about it all the time. Gerald thought he could guess, the same way he could guess what the money bought. But he didn't see the point of idle speculation. Ruark by now had bumped him up to eight hundred a week. Since he was living at home, his expenses were zip. He was socking it away.

He fastened the snaps on the attaché case.

"You see him?" Harmon said. "You give him one bad look, he's out of here. You have a future in this line of work."

"I hope not," Gerald said.

"You got another idea?"

"I want to open up a restaurant," Gerald said. "Samoan. It hasn't been tried. San Francisco, you got Italian and Mexican, you got Thai and Cuban and about fifty different kinds of Chinese. Not one Samoan."

"A Samoan restaurant," Harmon said.

"Something a little different. Break away from the competition, create your niche. That's what the books say. Business books."

"What, you're going to run some restaurant? That's it?"

"Yeah," Gerald said.

"Get up every morning, go into the same place every day? Get married, have a couple rug rats that sit around playing Nintendo? My blue heaven, white picket fence? You see that happening?"

"If I'm lucky," Gerald said.

12

Marie never saw them. She stood at the employee gate outside the grandstand. He was parked no more than fifty feet away. But she was looking for the Econoline.

Roy Boy had to yell, "Mommy."

She walked up to the Camaro.

"Sonny," she said. Naull opened the door for her and she got in.

"I know it's an extravagance," he said.

"The things we need, bills next month . . ."

"Hey," he said gently, and he put the wad in her hands. Even after sales tax, it was still more than nineteen thousand.

For a second he wasn't sure what she'd do with it. He thought she might throw it in his face. Walk over to a trash can and toss it. But finally she stuck it in her purse and held the purse with both arms.

"I'm on a hot streak," he said.

"I know."

"This's something I been really wanting, drive around in a real car instead of an Econoline."

"I have something like that," she said. "That I been wanting."

"Really? Well, hey. We'll have to go buy her. Right now."

She opened the purse. She took out a folded-up copy of a real estate booklet. You found them near the front doors of all the supermarkets and convenience stores, listings of houses and property for sale.

Naull had never known Marie to pick up one of them, though.

She opened it. New Homes North Bay, it said on the cover. She went right to the page.

"It's a drive," she said. "Other side of Suisun City."

Naull knew Suisun City. It was on the way to Vacaville, up Interstate 80.

"Sit back and relax," Naull said. "We're going for a ride."

The Camaro thundered through the parking lot.

"She's a runner," Roy Boy said from the backseat.

They were on the interstate for about thirty minutes. When they got to the exit, Marie started reading directions out of the booklet. Four or five miles along a series of state highways and county roads, through farm fields scattered with small clumps of homes and roadside businesses.

The Bay Area, these days, you had to drive halfway to hell-and-gone to find a grazing Holstein.

It was July. Naull turned on the air-conditioning. In San Francisco you would probably want to wear a sweater. But here summer was summer, a few miles away from the ocean and the fog. Here the grass was brown. Cows and horses were wilting under the sun.

Marie called out one more right, and they stopped at the brick portals of Edgewood Manor. Three and four bedrooms starting at $189,500, said the billboard out front.

Naull did a quick rough count and thought that there had to be a hundred ranchers on maybe fifteen acres. Some of the houses were finished, others were just slabs in the ground.

"Go ahead," she said. "You wanted to drive. So drive."

Naull idled the Camaro down fresh black paved streets. Stacks of lumber, boxes of roofing tiles, rolls of sod, saplings with their roots balled in burlap—it looked like someone was erecting suburbia, every nail and leaf of it, in the middle of a pasture.

Naull thought about it for a minute and realized that this was exactly true.

Everyone wanted to be part of the action, was the problem. You considered yourself a sweepstakes winner if you lived within an hour of the first traffic jam on the freeway. You were, by definition, enjoying the good life.

"It's a drive to the city," Marie said, on his wavelength again. "But you don't commute."

"I certainly don't," Naull said.

"I never thought about owning a house, Sonny. I never figured it was in the cards. But the way you're going . . . It makes me consider. I want a place of our own. No more landlords, huh? I want it so much, I don't care anymore where it comes from."

The soil was almost black in the gashes that the bulldozers left. The sky was perfect blue. You could see soft, mounded, wheaten hills in the background. In the fall, after a good rain, they would turn the color of felt on a billiard table. He wondered how long it would be before somebody decided to erect suburbia on the hills.

"I had Oklahoma on the brain today," Naull said. "I was trying to think why we left."

"You don't remember? We wanted to feast on milk and honey. The Golden Gate Bridge was solid gold. We was gonna knock off a chunk and live on it for the rest of our lives."

"Oh yeah, that's right," Naull said. "I forget sometimes."

The pavement ended. They were looking at an empty fenced field with the gate open at the other end. Naull saw that the ground was staked out, markers and plastic ribbons lining out more lots and a longer street.

"So what do you think?" Marie said.

Naull turned the Camaro around in the dry grass, and started back up the way he had come.

He said, "I think I'm still a little short, and I better git to work if I want to make up the difference."

Andy Pops couldn't believe it. He looked up from his desk to see a hype, a drug addict, standing in front of him with an armload of stolen junk.

That the guy was a hype was obvious at a glance. And a hype with his arms full of a clock radio, a guitar, a car CD player with the wires dangling . . . Andy Pops drew his own conclusions about their provenance.

"Are you the buyer, man?" the hype said.

Andy Pops didn't answer at first. He reached for the transmit button of the intercom box on his desk.

"Where is my security?" he said. "Give me security back here now."

"I wanta talk to a buyer," the hype said. He was sallow and cadaverous. The bones stuck out in the backs of his hands. Andy Pops thought he would be in his deathbed, except that a habit gives you a powerful reason to be up and about.

"There's no buyer," Andy Pops said. "How'd you get in here?"

"Truck was coming in, gate was open, I walked in. Look here, man, I got some fine stuff."

He was walking into the office. Before Andy Pops could stop him, he was dumping his load on top of the desk.

"I want security," Andy Pops yelled at the intercom.

"Take a look," the hype said.

"I don't want to look. It's junk. I don't want you here. You're making a mistake. We don't buy stolen property."

"It ain't stolen, man."

"Don't insult me. Pick it up. Get it out of here."

"Take a look," the hype said. He was digging in a pocket of his baggy pants. Taking out a shiny piece of something, placing it on the desk.

Two security guards were coming from the front. Andy Pops could see them hustling through the dark warehouse. He was also aware of what the hype had put on the desk. It was a Thirties-vintage jeweled butterfly in Deco style, gold and precious stones, a wingspread of three inches or more.

Andy Pops gave it that quick glance and looked up again. The real thing, when it came along, you didn't have to pore over it. It jumped right out at you.

"Look at it," the hype said.

Andy Pops kept his eyes on the hype. He could still see the piece in his mind. The body of the butterfly, which was wide in the middle and narrower at the top and bottom, consisted of round diamonds, perfectly matched to the tapered gold frame of the setting. The largest diamonds ran close to two carets. In the wings, flowing rows of baguette emeralds in channel settings alternated with rows of round diamonds. It made an impression.

"*Look*," the hype said.

Andy Pops obliged, with great weariness. He flipped the butterfly over.

His eyes worked a lot better than they seemed. He could make out the thin line stamped in the gold. Tiffany & Co.

He tossed it back across the desk.

"More junk," he said.

"Oh, man, that's primo, man."

The two guards were at the door. They took the hype by the elbows.

"Fifty dollars for the lot," Andy Pops said. "Because I pity you. On condition that I never see you again, you forget you were ever here."

"Fifty—that thing is beautiful."

"Fine." He slid the butterfly across the desk. "Forty, you keep your junk. All the same to me. Call the police is what I ought to do."

The hype picked up his butterfly. Indecision. Andy Pops was reaching for his wallet. In his desk he had nothing smaller than fifties. There. Two twenties and a ten. He spread them on the desk. Force him to actually leave the ten, that was the idea.

Did hypes examine the markings on jewelry?

No, Andy Pops told himself. They had other things on the mind.

"Hell," the hype said. He put the butterfly down on the desk and scooped up the three bills.

Right away the guards had him by the elbow, taking him away.

Less than a minute later one of them was back. By then the butterfly was out of sight.

"Get this out of here," Andy Pops said. The junk on the desk. "I don't want it on the premises—get it out."

"Yes sir," the guard said. "Sorry. The gate wasn't open ten seconds, we must've missed him."

"You certainly did," Andy Pops said.

"I don't know how. This is bad."

"Ah, don't let it eat at you," Andy Pops said. "Worse things have happened."

Hays got the bad news over coffee and croissants. He was on the back deck of the big octagon, where he usually had breakfast when the weather was right.

He spent a lot of time out there, that exact spot, at a table near the edge of the deck. Caitlin thought he was inordinately fond of the deck. Mostly of the view. It was a great view; it took in most of the bay from north to south, the entire Bay Bridge, with Oakland and San Francisco at either end of it.

A great view, but Caitlin thought it was dangerous. Sitting out on the deck, admiring his view, was the kind of thing that allowed Hays to think he was happy. He tended to get complacent.

Caitlin put on a leotard and went out on the deck to do t'ai chi. He didn't turn to look at her—too moony over his view, she guessed—so she went over to him and stood behind his chair. Beside the breakfast tray he had a portable phone and a portable computer, his Compaq laptop. That wasn't unusual. He liked to check his E-mail, overnight messages, from the office.

"That is not decaf," she said.

"Not today."

"Agh. You'll be climbing the walls. Don't expect me to bring you down."

He said nothing.

"Croissants and jam. Butter. Cream. Agh. Waistline, darling, waistline. And the cholesterol, the fats, my God, the *lipids,* you're eating yourself into an early grave."

"It's my grave," he said.

Ignore him if he gets rebellious. This was the key with Hays. She walked a few feet away and started her stretching routine. When you meet resistance, disengage. It never lasted long. Now and then you had to indulge him.

But she wondered what was getting to him. He was edgy, she could tell.

He pushed the breakfast to one side and pulled the Compaq in front of him. He plugged the modem cord into a phone jack on the railing post, and he powered up the computer.

With a few keystrokes—she knew the drill—he was into the company's system. Checking his electronic mailbox. She watched the screen. He paged past memos, through a couple of long documents. Now something with columns of figures.

He stopped. This was what he wanted. He studied it and paged down once more. End of the figures. The legendary bottom line.

He didn't like what he saw. She knew him, she could tell.

"Problem, sweetie?" she said.

If he heard her, he didn't show it. He reached for the portable phone, and his fingers stabbed the buttons.

Evan Ruark was driving toward San Rafael when the telephone chirped beside the driver's seat of his Shelby. It was the rapid squeak of an electronic cricket.

He was in the middle of a turn. The phone chirped again, and he picked it up when the road straightened out.

"Evan." It was Hays. "Got to talk."

He was ruffled.

"Okay, talk."

"I'm looking at the annual statement. Seen it yet?"

"Can't say that I have."

"It is bad."

"I'm not surprised," Ruark said. He had to yell. The engine was rapping; wind was streaming through the window.

"Evan, we have no dividend."

67

"I'm not surprised," Ruark yelled again.

"I am."

"You shouldn't be. Trends are down across the board. Anything we make is getting eaten up by retail." The chain of retail stores was Hays's idea. He had insisted on it.

"This is not acceptable."

"I don't know what to tell you, pal. The numbers don't care if you accept them or not. They're still there."

"I need the dividend."

"Out of what? You want dividends, you have to earn money. We're not earning much. I wouldn't be surprised if you told me we took a loss."

"Hundred and forty thousand."

"I'm not surprised."

"That's it?" Hays said. "That's all you have to say?"

"You shouldn't have let this sneak up on you."

"We always get a dividend."

"Nothing is always. Especially in business."

"I need the money." Ruark came up on a Volvo station wagon, too slow through a curve. Ruark held the Mustang tight on the Volvo's rear bumper. When the road opened up he downshifted to third, swung out, and passed.

"I need the money," Hays said again. He was shouting too, now.

"You've still got your salary. Hundred and eighty thousand a year is not bad for a captain who just ran his ship up on a reef."

"I'm not the only captain. We are not on a reef. A hundred and eighty thousand will not do it."

"Fifteen K a month."

"Do you hear what you're saying? That's five hundred dollars a day. Dentists do better."

"You live high," Ruark said. "It always worried me. I never mentioned it; it was not for me to comment on. But I wondered what would happen when fat times got lean. It had to come, you know. Whenever you've got ups, you've got downs on the way. Good times are the ultimate predictor of bad times. You have to be prepared to ride 'em out."

Ruark heard nothing. With the wind, the noise, he couldn't tell if the line was still live.

Then Hays finally spoke.

He said, "Gee, Evan, thanks for the input."

And then the line went dead for sure.

Hays put down the telephone.

"Something *is* wrong," Caitlin said. "I can tell."

Hays turned.

"You really think so?" he said.

"I know so."

"You're fucking clairvoyant."

"Don't be rude. Tell me what's the problem."

"We have no money."

"That's absurd. I can show you checking balances. I can show you T-bills and rental receipts. We own apartment buildings—"

"What comes in goes out. And that doesn't cover half of it. We're living on mortgages."

"You should look for positive aspects."

"I'm positive that we have no money."

"I won't put up with this attitude," she said. "I banish your negativity from my presence."

"You want me to leave?" Hays said. "Is that what you're telling me?"

"I'm not going to let you drain my shining essence."

"You want me to leave?" he said.

"Yes."

"Thank you," he said.

Naull sat at a picnic table in a rec park beside Tiburon Boulevard. Directly across the street was the intersection of Altamonte Drive.

He was eating a cinnamon roll and drinking coffee from a Styrofoam cup. Roy Boy, beside him, was shuffling baseball cards.

"Let's go, son," Naull said.

They were in the Camaro, with the engine running, when Hays rolled through the stop sign at the bottom of the hill. He turned west, toward 101.

"Seat belt?" Naull said. The boy was buckled up. Naull waited a few seconds and turned after the black BMW. Naull had the Camaro up to sixty, but the BMW was pulling away. Naull gave it more gas, and he stayed even. Seventy.

Naull wanted to know more about Hays and Caitlin. He had a free day, and he thought there were worse ways to spend it.

"In a hurry!" Roy Boy said.

"That's right."

"Racing!"

"Chasing," Naull said.

"Catch him, Daddy."

"Not that kind of chasing," Naull said. "This is close enough."

They were about a quarter of a mile apart, nothing but pavement between them. If Hays looked back, even if he noticed the Camaro, it would mean nothing to him. This was another good reason for buying the car.

The BMW drove past the northbound entrance to the freeway. Up on the overpass, left on the southbound cloverleaf. Toward the Golden Gate Bridge. Naull followed.

He was looking for an edge on them. Stubbornness, contrariness, entered into it, too: they refused to tell him anything, therefore he wanted to know everything he could.

The BMW flew past the last exit before the Golden Gate. He was going to San Francisco. Off the south end of the bridge you had two choices. The Lombard Street ramp bore left, toward the heart of the city. Straight ahead, Park Presidio Drive shot through the residential Richmond District, into Golden Gate Park.

The BMW stayed left over the bridge. Naull pulled in closer, mixing with traffic. Out of the toll plaza, onto Lombard Street.

Lombard was stop and go. A mile or more to Van Ness Avenue, right, up Van Ness and over the hump, and a right on Jackson Street.

It was mixed residential here, the back side of the Pacific Heights neighborhood. Pacific Heights, the north side of the slope, was prime of prime. Old town houses, stacks of flats, small apartment buildings. The street was narrow, and everything hedged in close. Buildings were shoulder to shoulder, back to back. Some of them stood right up against the sidewalk. Others had pitiful patches of front lawns, three or four feet deep.

San Francisco always made Naull slightly nervous. He'd been raised in country where you could fire a rifle blind and be confident of hitting nothing but grass and dirt. San Francisco was hemmed by water on three sides, and you were always aware of it, the desperate economy of space.

The BMW turned into the driveway of an apartment garage, and stopped. Hays got out.

Naull pulled over to let traffic pass. The building was four stories, narrow and not very deep. Naull guessed four units per floor, two in the front and two in the rear. A little garden in the back. The rear units would look out on the garden, the front ones out into the street.

Hays chugged up the front steps of the building and let himself in with a key.

It looked to be turn-of-the-century. In 1906, with the city in flames after the earthquake, they dynamited along Van Ness to form a firebreak. So from Van Ness, on east to the city center, almost everything was post-'06. Here on the east side of Van Ness you still found plenty that predated The Big One.

Each of the front units had a big, wide window that faced the street. One of the ground-floor windows was open now. The rattan blinds were rolled up. Through wrought-iron bars Naull got a good look inside, at high ceilings and hanging plants and a couple of framed posters on the walls. Bouncy music came through the window.

It was a woman's apartment, Naull thought. And then he saw her. Oh yes. A woman.

She was young, twenties. Gorgeous. She wore a purple leotard, pink tights. Slight, but with a figure. Yellow hair in a sprightly ponytail.

She was crossing the room. Over to the front door. Naull got no more than a second or two of her, walking to the door. But he liked her. Even aside from the obvious attractions.

It sounded ridiculous, see a stranger for a second or two and form an opinion. But Naull trusted his instincts. Maybe crime tuned you in. How many strangers had he come to know, just looking through their homes and touching their belongings? This was her place, he could see that. He saw that she took care of it. She worked at things, she worked at herself. Even a young woman had to work, keep looking like that. That music, the leotard—she had to be in the middle of an exercise tape.

Anyway, she crossed the room. Light, quick steps. She kept the chain on and looked through the peephole. Good for you. Slipped the chain and opened it all the way.

Hays walked through. He put his arms out and she went to him, and they kissed.

Naull angled the Camaro into a space on the corner, fire hydrant. He told Roy Boy to wait, and he went up to the building.

It had a glass front door. He could see a short hall with the front doors of the four downstairs units. He could see the numbers of the first two doors. 1-B was hers. Two rows of metal mailboxes were set into the wall outside. G. GIBBS was the name on 1-B.

71

The blinds were down when he looked again. Naull didn't want to wait.

On the way home he thought about her. G. Gibbs. What would it stand for, the G.? Gloria? Ginny? It didn't matter, he thought. Neither did she.

But he couldn't help it. G. Gibbs—he saw her, he liked her. He felt sorry for her.

"You didn't call," Grace Gibbs said when she pulled away from Hays. He still held her. He was running his hands up and down her back.

"Spur of the moment," he said.

"I happen to know you have a phone in your car."

"So I didn't call. What's the problem?"

His hands stopped moving.

"I could have been anywhere. I want to be here for you, that's all. So you don't waste your time."

"I was willing to take my chances. It's my time, my car phone, it's my Goddamn apartment."

His grip got tight around her waist.

"You don't trust me," she said.

He said, "If I have to eat one more ration of shit—"

"Don't," she said softly, and she kissed him on the lips.

She had left home when she was eighteen. Chase County, Kansas, in the Flint Hills northeast of Wichita. Of course nobody in California had ever heard of Chase County, where homes and farms nestle in the grassy hills like babies in a mother's bosom. What most knew about Kansas was *The Wizard of Oz* and the Dust Bowl, and maybe the endless wheat fields that stretch along both sides of the interstate when you're barreling along I-70 from Denver to Kansas City.

After a while she didn't mention Chase County or the Flint Hills. She didn't mention Kansas unless she had to. Let them think that it was flat and dusty. What did she care? She was out of there.

For as long as she could remember, that was what she wanted: out. She had a friend, couple of years older, a management trainee in the Hyatt chain. The friend got a placement at the Regency in San Francisco. If Grace came to visit, she had a place to sleep and a job as a room maid.

Two weeks after she graduated, she got on a Trailways bus in Emporia. They saw her off, friends and family, believing that she'd be back in a month or two. It amazed her, they really did expect her to use that return ticket. Couldn't they look around them, and look at her? Couldn't they see?

She was sure of two things. She would never come back unless she could do it in style. And she would not be cleaning hotel rooms for long.

Because she also knew that she had the looks. *Pretty* was not the word. You could find pretty anywhere. Even beautiful, beautiful was not so unusual. But to go one level further, to whatever it was that made people look at you the way they look at a bride coming up the aisle—that was something special.

She knew that she had it. And she knew that whatever it was, it had to be just as powerful in California as in Chase County.

And she was right.

What astonished Grace, what she never would have dreamed, was that to have it might not be enough. It got you chased, it got you attention, but it did not anoint you. You could dazzle the world and still find yourself spinning your wheels.

The first time she saw Hays she was working a trade show in the Civic Center basement, housewares and small appliances. Three days, seven hours a day, standing at a booth and demonstrating a pasta machine and an espresso maker while she wore spike heels, fishnet stockings, and a sort of modified serving-wench costume with a bodice scooped almost to her nipples.

Oh, the boys kept her busy scalding milk and churning out spinach fettucine.

Hays was one of the boys. He looked, all right, he chatted. But nothing else. Three weeks later—it was her next job, this was always the problem, too much time between paychecks—she was in a studio on Folsom Street when he walked in.

It was a catalog shoot. Swimwear, the kind that never gets wet. At the moment she was wearing a gold lamé number, the top a couple of little triangles on a string top, the bottom a scrap of cloth with a thong back. And she was on spike heels again.

He seemed to know the photographer. Little jokes and asides as he stood around, not looking at her, avoiding her, being very cool. Uh-huh.

The photographer shot a few more frames, and told her to get into the next two-piece. She walked off, past Hays, and he looked up, looked surprised, like he was noticing her for the first time. Right. Like what a coincidence. *Right.*

"Hey," he said. "You!"

"I keep thinking it shouldn't bother me," she said. "But it does."

"What's that?"

"Getting geeked by miscellaneous perverts," she said.

"I should think you'd be used to being stared at. The day they stop looking, you're out of a job."

"In a job, that's one thing. What bugs me is the ones that sneak in the tent. They get their jollies, it's worth nothing to me. It's like they're copping a feel in a crowded elevator, do you get my drift? Like they're getting something for free."

"I wouldn't call it free," Hays said. "I'm the boss, I know what this is costing."

He asked her to go out to dinner. She refused.

He stuck around through a few more changes. Lunch, he said, and she refused.

He stuck around for most of the afternoon. Coffee, he said again, and this time she said yes.

He took her to the dining room at the Palace. His wedding ring was right out there, she had to give him that. No pink stripe on a tan finger, no hiding his hand in his pocket. After a while, after enough evasions, you came to appreciate the straightforward. His wedding ring was worth points, a few points anyway.

Before his cup was warm she said, "I want to tell you where I stand. You're the boss, that's great for you, but I've been hustled by bosses till I'm sick of it. My situation, I started in this business six years ago. My first month, I did an Emporium print ad, I did a Sea Ranch brochure and a Sharper Image catalog, I did a L'eggs national TV spot. One month."

"Nothing like a few face."

"I thought every month would be like that. What did I know? Now I'm doing bikini shots. The next stop after that is lingerie, and you're in the business, you know, that's the end of the line. Nobody will touch you for anything else after you've done lingerie."

"True," he said.

"I'm two months behind on my rent, my roommate is ready to throw my clothes out on the sidewalk. My car, the rear differential's in pieces. I've got people lined up for the money I'm making on this shoot. Six years I've been sitting at tables like this getting job titles thrown at me like they're supposed to make me roll over and beg. I've been presidented and CEO'd up to my ears. I don't want to fly to Palm Springs on your jet, I don't want to spend the weekend on your sailboat. There's nothing you can tell me that I haven't heard, and I've got plenty to worry about anyway, besides getting smooth-talked out of my shorts. Just so you'll know."

This usually chased them off, fast. It was all true, the money problems and the rest, but it was nothing new. It had been true almost from the start.

Hays watched her. For some reason he did not look like he had been chased.

"What's the boyfriend situation?" he said.

"No situation. I'm on the wagon, nine weeks and counting. I get the offers. But the ones I like, I never yet had one that was good for me."

"Meaning what? Hearts and flowers?"

"A little devotion, some consideration, is that asking so much? But if they can't pull that off, at least some support. Moral or otherwise. It's a tough world out here. You get so, you'll take it where you can find it."

He said, "The world supply of devotion is extremely limited these days."

"Tell me about it."

"But the bit about support—that should be a snap for you. I mean real support. The kind that puts clothes in the closet and pays the rent."

"There's a word for that."

"Are you going to get hung up on words?"

"No," she said. "I've thought about it. It's not like I'd be the first."

He said, "The car, no problem. We can fix you up with a lease vehicle anytime. The apartment, I have some places. I own a stack of flats on Jackson Street, near Fillmore, fully furnished, nice. I believe we've got a vacancy right now on a one-bedroom."

The normal thing would be to laugh it off. Bluff called.

Instead she said, "The apartment. Would it come with a lease? Paid?"

75

"I don't know why not," Hays said. "Six-month lease."

"Twelve."

"Nine. And oh, you want work, we do catalogs all the time. The camera likes you, I can tell. I have no trouble guaranteeing you all the catalog work you can use."

"I can use plenty," she said.

"You've got it."

He was not joking.

"The car, the apartment, nine-month lease, catalog work," she said. "Does that cover it?"

"Best I can do."

That was five months ago. The car was a Ford Tempo. She didn't complain. The apartment—her own place, finally, after six years of roommates—was clean and quiet and safe, exactly what she'd had in mind the day she got on the bus. She bought a couple of gallery posters, a Judy Chicago rose and an Ansel Adams view of El Capitan. From Pier 1, brass candlesticks, a white ceramic elephant, and batik fabric to throw across the sofa.

Hays was almost an afterthought. It was strange. If you went by the book, rated him against the standard checklist, he would grade out near the top. Looks and money and brains and smoothness.

But she was unmoved. He reminded her of certain restaurants where she had been CEO'd. Order the lamb chops, you got a wafer of meat, a dab of sauce, a few thimblefuls of scented rice, and a couple of pea pods, all fanned out across a white plate as big as a sombrero. It was fine, it was tasty, but nothing you could sink your teeth into.

And unhappy—he was miserable most of the time. She thought he came to her as much for refuge as for sex.

This was not a complaint, though. None of it. By no means a deal-killer. She wanted him to want her, for whatever reason. Because she sure wanted, she needed, what he had for her.

She dozed, afterward. Hays was wide awake. He thought it must be great, have so little on your mind, an easy boff and you just drop away like that.

She was delectable, though, an out-and-out confection. Spun sugar, melt in your mouth. He saw her, he had to have her. Caitlin was not much of an obstacle: the financial arrangement was buried under about four layers of figures in electronic ledgers, beyond her interest. And, modern creature that she was, Caitlin asked no accounting of his time and movements, and gave none of her own. Hays could almost go so far as to say that his wife didn't care whether he had a little something on the side, but that wasn't exactly true. It was more precise to say that if she ever decided to go for his throat, she wouldn't need a reason. Whether he had nibbled on a sweet bonbon, or not, would be beside the point.

Grace woke up and found him staring up at the ceiling.

"You okay?" she said.

"Do we have a problem?" Hays said. "Is there something I should be worrying about?"

"Of course not."

"Because I walk in, the first thing I get is, 'You don't trust me.'"

"Forget I said it."

"You sure? I can relax, I don't have to worry that there's some fly in the ointment, some wrinkle I have to iron out? No crisis that's going to blow up in my face?"

"Relax," she said. "Everything's fine."

"Thank God for small favors," he said.

Andreas Papazouglou, Andy Pops, locked the door of his office and pulled down on the blinds on the window partitions. He took his 12-gauge pump gun out of a closet and leaned it against the desk.

With a pocket knife he levered up one of the floorboards along one wall. The warehouse had a floor like an old saloon, rough planks. He reached into the cavity and pulled out a tin box that originally contained five pounds of Danish butter cookies. It was an old dodge, maybe, a cache under the floor. But it was still effective here. Nearly all the floorboards in the warehouse were loose. You could spend all night looking for the right one.

And even if you found it, Andy Pops wasn't going to let you get away that easy.

He put the tin on the desk. Several quarter-inch holes had been drilled in the sides of the box. He opened it.

Down in the box a coiled snake raised its head. The snake hissed. It waggled its black tongue. It had tiny black eyes and grainy brown skin overlaid with a black diamondback pattern. It lunged at Andy Pops.

"Hello, Paulie," said Andy Pops.

The snake hissed and struck again.

Feeling cranky.

Paulie was a bull snake of the genus *Pituophis*, intended for the pleasure of anyone who got where he wasn't supposed to be. A cordial fuck-you from the management. Being nonvenomous, a bull snake lacks a viper's spade head and deep pit cheeks. Andy Pops sincerely doubted that any midnight skulker would note the difference.

Andy Pops reached around the snake and pulled out a glass jar with a Peter Pan Peanut Butter label. Inside the jar was a conglomeration of rings, bracelets, necklaces, charms, and pendants, a bright layer of gold and gemstones about two inches deep.

Andy Pops opened the bottom drawer of his file cabinet. He took out a paper carton printed with the name of a pet store and the words *My Furry Little Friend*. Something scrabbled inside. Andy Pops flipped a white rat out of the carton and into the cookie box. He clapped the tin lid on the box and put it back in the floor, and he replaced the board.

He snapped on the quartz gooseneck lamp. In the cabinet drawer he found a small ultrasound cleaning tank, then filled the tank with water from the cooler and dumped in the jewelry.

He gave the cleaner about a minute. In the meantime he removed from the drawer a set of jeweler's tools, a small precision scale in a padded case, and a magnifying lens on a stand. He arranged all this in front of him on the desk. Lastly he took out a stack of tiny Ziploc bags, about an inch square.

He turned off the ultrasound, reached into the tank, and came out with a diamond solitaire, marquise cut. Maybe three-quarters of a carat, he guessed. Not a bad way to start. He pried up the prongs on the setting and extracted the stone. On the scale's digital readout it was eighty points. Under the lens it showed fair yellow color and a couple of small occluded flecks.

He dropped the diamond into one of the bags, marked the bag with the numeral 1, and sealed it. On a legal pad he wrote:

1: marquise dimd.—.80 ct. VS2—$450.

The grading was conservative and the price was right, even for a stolen stone. Andy Pops believed that you take care of your good customers. Mr. Emerson was one of his best.

2: cherry opal—28.33 ct.—color & clarity good—$335.

He had known Emerson for four years now. For the first two and a half years Emerson bought estate jewelry, a piece now and then. He would return the empty settings for the value of the gold. Loose stones was what Emerson wanted.

All of it was legal. Never, never would Andy Pops offer gray goods to a stranger. But after two and a half years, he knew Emerson could be trusted. Andy Pops remarked to him that destroying heirloom pieces for their gemstones was a common practice on the illegitimate market.

You know something about the illegitimate market? Emerson asked. From the way he said it, Andy Pops knew he'd been waiting all that time to ask the question.

3: rnd. dimd.—1.15 ct. VS1—$1,100.

Emerson preferred diamonds. He was definitely into carbon. But he bought almost everything that Andy Pops offered, in any size, from decent quality to the finest. Anything but junk, was the standing order. Andy Pops consigned him a shipment about every six weeks.

Emerson paid cash, of course. Stacks of cash. He no longer bought in person. Andy Pops would call a number and get a man's voice on an answering machine. Andy Pops would state the total of the shipment. Sixty, seventy thousand was about average. Later that day, two gentlemen appropriate to the task would bring the money to the warehouse, take the stones.

Rarely did Emerson reject a stone. Never did he quibble over price.

4: asst. rnd. dimd.—.10 ct. ea.—14 @ $35—total $490.

The gems were not for resale in North America. This was the only stipulation Andy Pops made. Larger stones could be identified, traced. Even a half-carat diamond might be matched to an X-ray record someplace. Emerson told him the stones would not be resold anywhere. Andy Pops tended to believe someone who could wait two and a half years to ask the pertinent question.

Now Andy Pops plucked out the Tiffany butterfly. He held it under the light. He knew what he ought to do with it. What he did with all gray items: pull out the stones, melt the setting. This one especially, distinctive as it was. This one could put a man in the penitentiary.

Andy Pops tilted it back and forth, letting the facets catch the lamp's glare. It was gorgeous. He thought of some long-dead craftsman bent over his creation. It was that kind of piece.

5: 19th Cent. Tiffany—an extraordinary example, probably 1 of a kind—$35,000.

Emerson would realize that the stones weren't worth that much, not gray market. He would either keep the piece intact or return it. Andy Pops decided that if it was returned it would go back in the box with Paulie. He would take it out once in a while and admire it. Andy Pops was a sucker for beautiful objects, and he didn't fight it. He knew that in this life one of the quickest ways to stub your toe was to stop being true to what you are.

Gerald and Harmon took the Bayshore south. They were jammed into the Isuzu again.

It was lunchtime, but they didn't stop. Ruark's orders, go direct. Gerald usually packed a lunch for the trip, but this morning he'd been in a hurry. Harmon had a body-building concoction that he drank while he drove. A steroid shake, something like that.

They took the Dumbarton straight across to Fremont, to the industrial park and the front gate of Curiosities Unlimited.

"Welcome to the fucking gulag," Gerald said.

"Stalag Nineteen," said Harmon, who had seen every episode of "Hogan's Heroes" at least twice. He blatted a few half-notes on the horn. "Sergeant Schultz, vhere the hell are you? Ve vant to see Colonel Klink."

The guard came out holding a crumpled Subway bag and wiping his mouth with a napkin.

"Longfellow and Sherman," Gerald said, and the guard reached into the white shack.

The high gate clanked open. Harmon pulled in and parked beside the gate. He grabbed the briefcase between the front seats. Harmon liked to carry the briefcase. This big pink hairless chunk of bean curd, stuffed into a poly-blend shirt and flea market Gitanos, carrying a black leather Samsonite briefcase. Be my guest, Gerald thought.

"In the back," the guard said.

The blinds were up on the windows. The Greek was on the phone. Gerald stopped Harmon outside the door, until the Greek put the phone down and waved them in. The package was on his desk, wrapped in brown kraft paper like a couple of kielbasas from the butcher.

Harmon opened the briefcase. He took out a second package. This one was about the same size, but neatly wrapped in white-and-silver gift paper, a wedding motif. Inside were fifteen packets of fifty-dollar bills, one hundred bills to the packet. Five stacks of three packets each. Gerald knew exactly.

The Greek took it from Harmon gently, with both hands.

"Very nice," he said. "Is this your work?"

"Mine," Gerald said.

"Delightful!"

"It was that or an old *Examiner.*"

"A good choice."

Harmon put the brown package in the briefcase and closed the latches.

"Gotta run," he said.

"A pleasure, as always," the Greek said.

"Short but sweet," Harmon said, and they went out to the car.

Gerald put the briefcase between them and drove out of the gate. But when they were back over the Dumbarton, passing through Redwood City, Harmon put the briefcase in his lap and opened it.

He took out the package and shook it near his ear. It didn't make a sound.

"You ever wonder what's inside?" he said.

Gerald said, "The man doesn't pay me to wonder."

"We bring a shitload of money and leave with something that'll fit in my shoe, I wonder."

"I assume it's something valuable," Gerald said. "Small and valuable."

Harmon kneaded the package. His big right hand nearly swallowed it up.

"Drugs," Harmon said.

"Coals to Newcastle."

"Say what?"

"Forget it," Gerald said.

Harmon was feeling around one end of the package. One flap wasn't completely taped down.

"Don't do that," Gerald said.

"Sure would like to know," Harmon said. He looked like a gorilla picking fleas, the way his thick fingers explored the package.

"Jewels," Gerald said. "Now put it away."

"Jewels?"

"Name me something else, that small and expensive."

"Huh. How 'bout that," Harmon said.

"It would make sense."

"What does he want with jewels?"

"I *assume* the man wants to do something with his cash," Gerald said. "But I don't think too hard about it, because personally it doesn't concern me."

"Huh." Harmon worked his index finger under the loose flap. The paper made a short, distinct ripping sound as it tore away from the tape.

"Oh shit," Harmon said.

The flap was in half. Gerald could see a layer of bubble wrap through the rip.

"Oh, *man,*" Gerald said.

"No problem, no problem, we'll stop and get some tape. Fix it right up."

"No," Gerald said. "The man will know."

"He won't know."

"The man will know," Gerald said. "Believe me."

"I can see 'em," Harmon said. "Through the bubble shit."

"Put the package away," Gerald said, using a low, end-of-my-rope tone that sometimes worked on his three-year-old niece.

Harmon put the package in the briefcase.

"You were right," he said. He put the briefcase between the seats. "I could see 'em. Jewels. A hell of a lot of jewels."

Gerald drove north, though the city and across the Golden Gate. He stopped being hungry. He kept wondering about the torn package, how to handle it with Ruark.

He thought he had it by the time he drove through Ruark's gate. He parked and told Harmon to wait in the car. But Harmon wouldn't wait, didn't trust him. Harmon and Gerald walked up to the front porch, where Ruark was standing, waiting.

Gerald put the briefcase in Ruark's hands.

"He tore the package," Gerald said to Ruark, first thing. "He was farting around, he was curious. I thought you ought to know."

Ruark looked sour. He took the briefcase inside without a word. The door was open, and Gerald decided to follow him in. Harmon started to go in, too, but Ruark told him to stay out, sit down and shut up.

Ruark sat at the couch. He opened the briefcase, held the package, looked at the torn flap.

"He didn't get any farther than that," Gerald said. "He had to see, that's all. He's got a mind like, I don't know—like a dog. An idea gets stuck in there, it won't go away. Not to be bad-mouthing anybody. He just got it into his head that he had to see."

"He saw?"

"Yes sir, he did."

"What about you?"

"I was driving," Gerald said. That didn't sound exactly right. He said, "I didn't care to see what's in there, I really didn't."

"That's funny," Ruark said. "I would have thought you'd be the one was curious."

"A person could figure it out without opening the package," Gerald said. "That's the difference between him and me."

Ruark gave a sharp bark. Almost a laugh. Then he pulled off the brown paper. Gerald could see the glint and colors of the jewels through bubble wrap. He started to leave.

"Just hang around," Ruark said.

"It's all there," Gerald said.

"You better hope to kiss your ass, it's all there."

Gerald watched him open the bundle on the coffee table and unfold a yellow piece of paper that was tucked inside. There were dozens of these small bags. Ruark was checking them against a list on the paper. Finding one, taking a good look at the gem inside before he put it in a separate pile.

"What's the state of the world?" Ruark said. "Your opinion. Since you're the smart guy."

What kind of question is that? Gerald wondered.

"About the same as always," he said. Playing it safe.

"Meaning what?"

"You get your good, you get your bad, but the big wheel keeps turning. The sun keeps rising in the east." He chose his words carefully. You had to watch the man.

"Stable," Ruark said.

"I guess that's it." *What the hell is he getting at?*

"Let me tell you about stability," Ruark said. He was very interested in one bag now. It was not a jewel, but a whole piece. A bird. No, a butterfly. "Stability is an illusion. We pretend stability, because it's convenient. But the illusion has to be by consensus. If a few malcontents stop pretending—end of consensus. End of illusion."

"Are we talking about the package?" Gerald said. The man could make you nervous without even looking at you.

Ruark put the butterfly down in the pile.

"Don't you get it?" he said. "Look, what do we have? Corruption. Erosion of values. The cities are ready to blow. At. Any. Minute. We're a ten-ton load of garbage hanging by a thread. I'm surprised it hasn't broken already." He was getting revved up. "I can see mobs in the street. It's happening. I can see police stations burning. And there won't be any fire engines to put them out. Hence the stones."

Hence the stones? Gerald thought.

"We'll have chaos. It'll be hell, but it won't last long. We'll go running back to illusion, since chaos is such a pain in the ass. We'll rebuild, but it'll be a shambles for quite a few years. This is what you might call the transition period, while we figure out who's on top for the next go-round. Paper won't mean a damn. Records'll be destroyed or incomplete. Currency, deeds, land titles—trash. Tangibles will be the only thing we can count on. Something you can hold in your hand, that has always had value, and always will."

Hence the stones, Gerald thought. He watched Ruark examine the small plastic bags. He wondered how long it took him to come up with this theory. How many years without a reality check.

"Good enough," Ruark said. He put the last bag in the pile.

"Thank you," Gerald said.

"Don't let it happen again."

"No sir. No way."

Gerald went out. It was green and quiet here in the country. Did rural life bend a man's head so bad? No, couldn't be. Otherwise the world would be full of nutty farmers.

He decided the problem was never having anybody talk back to you, or yell at you, or tell you that you were off the wall. It wasn't healthy.

Harmon was standing by the Isuzu.

"So?" Harmon said.

"I finessed it," Gerald said. "But don't mess with his things again. It's a bad idea. Take my word for it."

Ruark watched them leave up the driveway. He went in and then buzzed them out the gate. Then he got a bowl from the kitchen. He sat at the coffee table and shook each of the gems into the bowl, and he carried them down into his cellar. He turned on all the lights downstairs. He went to the washer and pushed it aside.

He put down the bowl, knelt at the safe, and turned the dial.

The last tumbler fell with a thunk. Ruark lifted the door up and swung it open. It was heavy, but not as heavy as it might have been. You would need a winch to open a top-of-the-line Mosler set in the floor. He was mostly worried about fire, earthquakes, and the stray vandal.

From inside the safe he removed a roll of black velvet, tied with a black ribbon. He loosened the ribbon, laid the velvet out flat on the floor, and unzipped the pouch at one end. Diamonds spilled out—hundreds— and he pushed out the rest. Many hundreds.

He added the new stones to the others in the pile. He put in the butterfly, too. Maybe somebody on the other side of chaos would appreciate it. Then he just sat and took in the sight. *Takes your breath away,* people would say about this or that. But how many really knew what it felt like, that supreme jolt?

He thought about it all the time. Miles away, he could think about the safe, the stones, the thrill of unrolling black velvet. At night he sometimes lay awake thinking of the stones. There in his house, under his bedroom, pulsing with energy and power.

Let it come, he would think. Come what may. He had the goods.

17

Twice a year EvHaTek brought in its regional sales managers. Two days of meetings, conferences, pep talks. Usually, the last night, they rented a banquet room at a restaurant. This time, to save money, Hays said they'd do it at his place, hire some caterers.

The house would be an inspiration. Remind them what was possible.

Nineteen regional managers, their spouses and others, and Hays and Caitlin and Ruark, gathered out on the deck. It was a nice night, warm and clear. The house had plenty of room inside; they could handle fifty. But with the deck, the view, everybody would be looking out the windows anyway.

Cocktails before dinner. Ruark came over to where Caitlin was chatting with the manager from South Bend. She was perfect, the ultimate corporate spouse. She could play the game when she wanted to.

South Bend went away, it was just Ruark and Caitlin. Wide as the view was, you still couldn't see the hill beneath it. Being on the deck was like hovering silently above the bay, unsupported.

He had been to the house before, a couple of times with Caitlin when they were dating. This was the first time since then.

"Best view for a hundred miles," Ruark said.

"That's what Hays thinks. I never heard anybody argue with him."

"You did all right," he said.

"You bet your ass."

"Hit the jackpot."

"The mother lode."

"Every lode plays out," he said.

"Go play yourself out," she said.

"People never think it'll happen, but it always does. And it's worse when you don't expect it. You start to wonder, you ask yourself what you might have done different. Where you went wrong. And what next? These are the questions. I would say, right now, these are the questions before us."

"Be a warrior!" Ruark shouted.

After dinner he insisted on addressing them. Nineteen regional managers, their spouses and otherwise, full of crêpes and sole Veronique, half tanked or more on red wine and vodka, swirling Drambuie in their snifters. Slouching in their chairs while Ruark in his Hawaiian shirt and khakis, Ruark with his salt-and-pepper ponytail, stood in front of them at the edge of the deck. The edge of the world.

"Do not avoid obstacles—attack them. Embrace them. They are your path to true strength. Without challenge there is no greatness. A true warrior knows this!"

What a load of crap, Hays thought. And the others, he could see them thinking the same. Guarded, worried glances back and forth. They fly in for the weekend from Omaha and Mobile, worried about shrinking commissions and wondering how to move more shampoo, and they get . . . your path to true strength.

"The Japanese," Ruark said, "the Japanese are kicking our collective national ass. They are handing us our balls on a platter. Removed with surgical precision. How can they do this?"

Here it comes, Hays thought.

"They cheat," somebody said.

"Because they share a cultural mentality," Ruark said—as he chopped the air with each syllable, short and furious karate punches— "that is informed by the code of Bushido, by the ineffable example of the samurai."

Directly in front of him, the rep from Salt Lake City flinched in his chair.

"And the way of the samurai, my friends, is the resolute acceptance of death. Think about it."

Now he was off. He had a whole rap along this vein, the samurai and *Also Sprach Zarathustra* and Carlos Castaneda's bit about death sitting on your shoulder, whispering in your ear.

Ruark was nuts. It came to Hays suddenly, with instant clarity. He should have known it all along. But success does lull you, he thought. Ruark had that right. Disaster, though, will give you a fresh perspective.

Now—watching the crazy bastard stomp around the deck, seeing him as Hartford and Tucson saw him—Hays understood what baggage the company had been carrying all these years. Of course they were hurting now. A drag like that on the operation, it had to bring you down eventually.

Hays knew, now, what a weight he had been fighting all along. And he had prospered in spite of it. By desire and work and talent he had made millions.

And he had to wonder what he might have done, what might have been possible, if he hadn't had to fight the drag.

"Warriors!" Ruark cried.

After everybody left, and the caterers packed up, Hays got the laptop and sat out on the deck, under the floodlights. He had the annual statement on disk now. He kept scrolling through the figures, reminding himself that since cash flow had reversed, half of every dollar the company spent was cutting into profits, coming out of pocket. This had always been true, but he had never felt it so keenly.

His head hurt. He said, "Shit, shit," and got up, walked around.

Caitlin was watching from inside. Now she came out. Her nose for trouble was unerring.

She went to the computer, studied the screen, tapped a key to page down through the numbers. She was no airhead. When Ruark met her she was the sales rep for EvHaTek's software vendor. She understood these things when she wanted to.

Hays, standing in the kitchen doorway, watched the lines roll up on the screen.

"Don't lose my place," he said.

"Looking for cuts, is that the story?"

"Pretty much."

"You have to be careful. Watch out for false economy. It's real easy to cut in the wrong place."

"I appreciate the advice," he said.

"Maybe we ought to pop a place every night. Two a night. Get Naull off his butt. That's the problem with a barney, no ambition."

"It isn't that kind of money," he said. "We aren't talking thousands. We're talking hundreds of thousands. Losses will run close to a million for the year. Assuming we can level out the rate of increase. That is by no means a given."

"Ought to be some fat in here," she said, and she hit the button to page down again.

She peered. She said, "This corporate outlay, insurance. Almost nine hundred a month. What's that?"

Hays wanted to be left alone. But this was not something you said to Caitlin, leave me alone. He went over to her. He looked where the cursor was blinking.

"That," he said, "that's life insurance. Key man insurance. Ruark and me."

"I thought you had some already."

"Mine, personal. Two million term coverage. That's different, that's in your name," he said. "This here, this is three million term."

"For who?"

"I told you. On Ruark and me."

"I mean, who's the beneficiary?"

"Company pays the premium, company would get the payoff. When the business entity would suffer if certain individuals should die—key men—that's how the company covers itself. They do it all the time in big corporations. We've had it for years."

"Lot of money," she said.

"Nine hundred a month—not so bad."

"I mean three million," she said.

"Oh. Yeah. Course somebody would have to die." He said it without even thinking. He was tired, and his head hurt. He said, "Can I sit down, please?"

She let him have the chair. She stood behind him and said, "Three million just like that."

Hays was looking at the numbers, trying to tune her out.

She said, "Cover your million in losses. It would still leave you two million for capital investment. Or declare yourself a dividend. Or liquidate—you could do that. Get out. Sell off the assets, the land and the building alone, prime property in San Rafael, who knows what it'd bring? It would only be half yours. I mean, I assume. Is that the arrangement, shares pass down to the estate? Or is there some kind of a provision, the surviving shareholder gets some kind of sweetheart deal on the decedent's shares?"

He caught the last part of it. He said, "No. No provision. If I die, my shares go to you, whole and entire."

"Not you. Ruark. If something happened to Ruark, his shares would pass on to his heirs. Whoever. I think his mother's alive, back in Indiana. Just as well. You make *too* much, somebody might notice. She can have half. That's all right. It would still be a million for you, free and clear."

He was catching on now.

"I don't believe what I'm hearing," he said.

"I don't believe *you*," she said. "You simp. Sitting here like some Ebenezer with a green eye shade, trying to squeeze a few dollars out of the numbers. You awful simp. Wringing your hands about losses. With three million in term sitting right under your nose. A million free and clear. You *simp*. You awful, pitiful simp."

18

Hays kept an office at home, in one of the extra rooms. He had a desktop Compaq, a fax machine, and a printer. He had a couple of phone lines.

After he left the next morning, she sat at the computer. She knew her way around the EvHaTek internal system. She had all of Hays's passwords. She got into the job apps files, and started working her way through.

One of them, a new submission, she noticed the name first. It wasn't one you saw very often. A common word, but interesting when you used it for a name.

She looked at the rest. It was a submission from the Veterans Administration; every so often the VA transmitted a mass of apps and résumés, to EvHaTek and hundreds of other companies.

This one, under "Previous Experience," the entries were short. But compelling.

She touched a key, the printer started humming. It zipped out the app in the time that it took her to walk three steps and tear it off.

WELCOME, the name was. And the rest . . .

Oh yes, she thought. Oh *yes*.

Hays worked all day and through the evening. Ruark was gone, never even called in. Hays reminded himself that this was just as well.

He got home after dark. He opened the door and found inside . . . a horse's skull. In stainless steel. About ten times life size.

"Like it?" Caitlin said.

"What is it?"

"Sculpture."

"What did it cost?"

"The sculptress, she's very hot. She's slaying Soho even as we speak."

"How much?"

"Sixteen, cheap at twice the price."

"Sixteen hundred," Hays said.

"Thousand, sweet."

He started waving his arms, shouting.

"I want it out! I want my money back. We are broke. Does this mean nothing to you? Are you totally dense, is it possible?"

He went out on the deck. Minute or two later, she came and stood beside him. Hays waited for the fire. Nobody shouted at Caitlin.

But she touched him on the arm. Her voice was benevolent.

She said, "I've been thinking about Ruark."

The world was spread out in front of them. There were the city and the bay, there were Alcatraz and Angel Island, there were the Bay Bridge and the Richmond–San Rafael, there were Oakland and Berkeley.

"What about him?" Hays said.

"I want to go the distance on him," she said. "Void him. Off him. Punch his ticket. I think we ought to kill the son of a bitch—do you have a problem with that?"

He looked at the universe of lights below them.

"You have no idea what's involved," he said. "You have no concept. You don't even know where to start."

"Oh yes I do."

"He's my partner. I've known him almost ten years."

"Meaning what?" she said. "Are you telling me you give a rip about Ruark? I don't buy it. You really care about him? You're really close to him? Uh-uh. You aren't that close to anybody."

"To you," he said.

"Oh, lover, please. Just 'cause you can't put any distance on me doesn't mean we're close."

She almost—almost—sounded wistful.

Hays, looking north, became aware of a complex of faint lights in the distance, rows of lights forming rectangles within a rectangle, at the west end of the Richmond–San Rafael Bridge. The rows of lights were the walls and cell decks of San Quentin prison.

"There's something else to consider," he said. "A minor catch. If he gets killed, they'll look for a motive. They'll want to see who stands to gain. That's me."

"Oh, I figured that out," she said. "Ruark gets killed in a burglary. He surprises the intruders, they kill him—who looks for the motive? Yeah, yeah, the barney won't go for it. He doesn't have to know. We pop the place, we drop the hammer on Ruark, what's he going to do about it? Go to the police? Tell them, 'Yeah, I broke into the place last night, a guy happened to get killed, but I didn't have anything to do with it.' Sure he is. With three priors already. Uh-huh."

For some long moments he stared at the patterns of lights in the darkness. His mind was racing to find angles and possibilities. He realized that she was way, way ahead of him. He thought, Why am I surprised?

"It would have to be a serious burglary," he said. Discussing it as if it were real. "Some phony break-in, they'll see through it. Which means there has to be something worth taking. And you know how Ruark lives."

"Please," she said. "Give me some credit. You think I'm a feeb? Down in the basement, he's got a safe. He doesn't know I know. But I do. Okay, we don't know anything about safe-cracking. I doubt if the barney does either. But we don't care if we actually get in it, do we? As long as we give it a try. Make it look good. That's all."

"What does he keep in it?" Hays said.

"Who cares? It's there; it's a reason somebody would break in. That's all we need."

He didn't look at her. He knew if he met her eyes, it would be all over.

"I want to do this," she said. He refused to look at her.

But she didn't need to see his face.

"You do, too," she said.

And she was right.

The last angle came to Hays around three in the morning. Looking up into the darkness, tossing it around. It hit him.

He got up, walked to the window. It looked toward the south. Off to the right was the Golden Gate Bridge, parallel lines of lights that followed the sagging curves of the suspension cables.

He walked to the bed and back to the window again.

In the darkness Caitlin said, "You're pacing."

He said, "If Ralph doesn't know safes, and we don't, how do we get him to do it? What's in it for him, popping the place, if he can't get in the safe?"

She turned on the light beside the bed.

"Why can't he get into it?" she said. "We'll blow the door off. Or at least try, that's what counts."

"You still need some background. I don't know much about safes. But I do know, throwing a stick of dynamite at it won't even come close. And Ralph will know that too. Any way you look at it, we still need somebody who knows safes."

She got up out of bed, walked to the closet.

"You're thinking safes," she said. "I want you to think explosives. I want you to think *destruction.*"

She was taking a slip of paper from the pocket of a pair of slacks. She held it out to him.

"The job bank comes through again," she said.

He went over and took it.

"Another journeyman?" he said.

"No, baby, not a journeyman. This is a master. You want to talk destruction, this is as good as it gets. The United States Goddamn Marines, can you top that?"

Welcome checked every day with the VA job counselor. He was sharing a room at Letterman with a reservist named Wilmer, whose foot had been run over by a truck in a training accident.

Wilmer was an accountant. Welcome asked about opportunities in accounting—the VA would help with his schooling. Wilmer told him to forget it, accounting was not his line.

"What have you got?" Wilmer said.

"I can sell cars," Welcome said. "No experience necessary, if I'm genial and hardworking. That's what it says."

He was looking at the classifieds in the early edition of the *Chronicle*. Less than two weeks from discharge, he had no idea how he was going to spend the rest of his life.

"Not your line," Wilmer said.

"Something has to be my line."

"You're a bad-ass," Wilmer said. "That's your niche."

"Don't remind me," Welcome said.

19

"Ma, I'm out of here," Gerald Moon said.

"Come here," Hannah Moon said from the armchair in front of the TV. She was watching "General Hospital." Gerald went over and stood beside her. It was a big chair, and she filled it.

"Look at you," she said.

"What do you think?" Gerald said. He had a new outfit, a short-sleeve button-down shirt, poplin pants, deck shoes—no socks. Mr. Ruark said they were going on a houseboat, and he wanted to look right.

"Very snappy," she said.

"So Gerald," said a female voice from the kitchen, "do we set a place for dinner, or what?"

This was his sister Jinky. She came to the kitchen door. Jinky was eighteen and weighed ninety-nine pounds. Samoan sisters were nymphs. Samoan mothers, and their sons, were as solid as boulders.

"I don't think so," Gerald said. "Don't wait for me, that's for sure."

"Hey, looking good," Jinky said.

"Thank you."

"Will you get something to eat?" Hannah said.

"Is this a party you're going to?" Jinky said.

"Kind of an outing," Gerald said. "I think there'll be some food."

"Get something to eat," Jinky said.

"Mr. Ruark will take care of him," Hannah said.

"That's right," Gerald said. His mother made a come-here gesture, and he bent down to her. She kissed him on the lips. Jinky came over, and she kissed him, too.

"Don't be too late," Hannah said.

"Don't get into trouble," Jinky said.

"Give my regards to Mr. Ruark," Hannah said.

"Eat," Jinky said.

"*Eat!*" Hannah said.

The ice chests, Mr. Ruark said. Bring the ice chests. Both of them.

Gerald lugged them out of Ruark's kitchen, onto the backseat of the Isuzu. They were heavy, *heavy,* even for Gerald. What was the man bringing to the houseboat? Cannonballs?

He let Gerald drive. They picked up Harmon in Berkeley. Then through Contra Costa County. Walnut Creek, Concord, Antioch. An hour out of the city, two hours since they left Ruark's, more than three since Gerald left home. It was getting into dinnertime. Ruark had Harmon pull some drinks from one of the chests. Gerald had a Coke, Harmon drank a couple of Coors, Ruark had an Evian. That was all Gerald could see when he glanced back, bottles and cans stuck in heaps of ice. Had to be more than that, heavy as it was.

His stomach was rumbling something fierce.

Out here the country was arid and not very appealing. Flat, featureless, not much color. It didn't feel like California. Maybe the Midwest, Gerald thought. Texas. Though he had never seen either place, never been east of Reno.

They called this the Delta. Here the Sacramento River broadened and flowed into the bay. You could see river from the highway once you got out of Antioch, driving east. In some places it was a broad sluggish ribbon. Farther on it was brown water flowing around low islands and sloughs.

There were houseboats, fishermen in dinghies, powerboats towing skiers. Ruark told Gerald to turn off the highway, and they took a dirt road north toward the river, into the parking lot of a scruffy marina. It had two piers, maybe thirty berths. A big sturgeon hung from a hook at the foot of one of the piers. The place needed paint. Across the gravel road was a fish-and-fries shack, equally shabby.

Four Harley choppers were parked in echelon beside the shack. Four bikers in black leather and dirty denim sat at a picnic table, drinking beer by the pitcher.

Booger was one of them. Yo, Booger, Gerald thought. Score one for Harmon.

The colors, embroidered patches on the backs of their jackets, said SCORPIONS M.C.

Ruark told Gerald to park at the far pier, ignore the bikers. Take the ice chests down to the end of the pier. Gerald carried one. Harmon got the other, grunting when he picked it up. For once he had no comment.

They passed beside the sturgeon. It was gathering flies. Gerald smelled old fish and creosote and diesel fuel. They put the ice chests down at the end of the pier. Ruark sat on one and Harmon took the other. There was no shade, but the sun was getting lower. Ruark, who wore no watch, kept asking Gerald the time. Past dinner now, and a big rat was gnawing inside Gerald's belly. Besides all the other smells, the aroma of fried food was wafting over to him. What he would give to walk across the road and put twenty bucks on the counter. Oh, fries, onion rings, chicken, filet of cod, maybe a mess of gizzards . . . he could drop twenty easy.

But Gerald knew without asking that the answer had to be no. The bikers were ignoring them, and they were ignoring the bikers, and Gerald figured that was how it was supposed to be. Couldn't be an accident, they drive out to the Delta and run into a scum bucket who gives Ruark a fortune once a month. Had to be some arrangement. Mr. Ruark would make it clear when the time came.

Twenty, forty minutes, an hour. They drank more from one of the ice chests, and this time Gerald glimpsed something big and dark, plastic wrapped, under the ice. But he closed the chest before Mr. Ruark could accuse him of prying. Gerald watched the rainbow oil slicks on the water

95

and the minnows that darted around the pilings. It was close to dusk now, and Gerald was getting up the nerve to ask if they could please break out the eats, when a houseboat drifted off the river and up toward the marina.

It was glass-walled cabana stuck on a small barge. Up top was a sheltered deck where somebody was turning a wheel, shifting gears, backing the houseboat up to the pier.

He stopped the engine, went down, and threw off a line that Ruark tied to a piling. The boat had a powerful odor. Some smells turned your stomach, others were so sharp they seemed to lance your sinuses. This one did both. It wasn't like anything Gerald had ever smelled before.

But Harmon had. He said, "Mr. Ruark. Hold on. Somebody's been cooking crank on this tub."

"Methamphetamines," Ruark said. "I certainly hope so."

How about that, Gerald thought. Mr. Ruark was into the nasty.

"Hey, Evan," said the guy on the boat. "How they hangin'?"

It was the tone of somebody trying too hard to be friendly. That was one of the things that hit Gerald, the plastic sound of his voice. The other was the guy himself. He looked like the skinny half of Laurel and Hardy, young Stanley Laurel on the Delta—so close it was eerie, not just the long face and the jug-handle ears but the general deadhead air he had about him.

"You're late," Ruark said, sharp and unhappy. The hey-buddy look vanished off Stan's face.

Stan started to go for one of the ice chests, but Ruark said, "Get 'em on," in a way that made Gerald and Harmon grab for the chests and carry them aboard, set them down on the front deck.

And now the bikers were tromping down the pier, heavy boots banging on the planks. Booger was slightly ahead of the others, swaggering, a pit bull leading three monster warthogs. A scene out of the Saturday-night Creature Features.

Everybody met everybody else at the end of the pier.

Evan said, "Booger. It was supposed to be just you."

Booger said, "Evan. It was supposed to be just you."

"I don't travel alone," Ruark said.

"Neither do I," Booger said. "How we going to work this out?"

"Gerald comes," Ruark said.

"Gerald comes, Cleotis comes," Booger said.

Ruark told Harmon to get off the houseboat, wait in the car. Cleotis was the biggest of the warthogs, thick arms and this huge belly spreading under a leather vest. He climbed aboard, behind Booger.

Stan Laurel freed up the line, threw it back, and climbed on. He went up and gunned the houseboat out of the marina, into the river. Ruark opened the ice chest, and it was beers for everybody. But this was not the picnic on the water that Gerald had imagined. Mr. Ruark and Booger were going to have serious words. Stan figured in it, too.

Maybe it was the way they were all standing around on the deck, tense and aware, the spring inside winding tighter. Because all of a sudden, Gerald knew somebody was going to get hurt this evening.

Almost sunset. Gerald went up to the front rail and watched the sun and felt the breeze. Whatever was going to happen was a ways off yet. He knew that, too. It was the kind of thing that usually waits for dark.

Mr. Ruark came up beside him and pretended to watch the sun. He said, "You'll be alone out here with the big fucker. I want you to fix it so he's not a factor for a while, can you do that?"

"Sure," Gerald said. The drumming of the motor and the splash of the boat through the river smothered their words.

"I'm going to tell you to come in the cabin. You come in. Act natural, but don't sit down. Work your way behind Booger. When you can, grab him so he can't move."

"So he can't move," Gerald said. "Sure. Is that all?"

"This is for a thousand," Ruark said. "When we get out of here."

Mr. Ruark moved away from him, along the rail. It doesn't have to be a thousand, Gerald wanted to tell him. The man was owed, didn't he know that? Gerald watched the sun and the river, the sun dropping out of sight, the river purple and then black. Out here it was wide. They were in the middle of the channel. The skiers and most of the fishermen were gone, and lights were coming on along the banks.

It was getting dark.

Ruark yelled something at Stan Laurel, and Stan cut the engine off. He came down and threw out an anchor.

"Inside," Ruark said, and he and Stan and Booger went toward the sliding glass door.

"Don't rock the boat, boys," Stan said. "Fucking Godzilla and Megalon."

Nobody laughed. They went in, and Ruark slid the door shut. He pulled all the drapes.

It left Gerald and Cleotis. Gerald looked over at him. Six-two, maybe two-seventy, but a lot of it jiggled when he walked. Cleotis reached into a cooler and got out two cans of Coors, and he popped the tab on both of them. He came over and handed one to Gerald.

Gerald wished he hadn't. Gerald wanted to work up a good head of steam, and here the big tub was bringing him a can of beer.

"I been trying to figure you," Cleotis said. "What you are. Booger says Chinese, but you're no Chinaman."

"No," Gerald said.

"You're built like a gaw damn sumo wrestler, but you're no Jap neither."

"No," Gerald said. "That's pretty good. Most people don't get past Chinese and Japanese."

In his mind Gerald was imagining Cleotis with Jinky. Cleotis grabbing Jinky. Cleotis putting his dirty hands up Jinky's T-shirt.

"Somewhere on the other side of the big water," Cleotis said. "Wherever it is, a man with your size, all the dinks in that part of the world, you'd be king shit if you went back home."

Gerald grabbed the leather vest with his left hand. He rammed his right fist into the huge belly, in deep, almost up to his elbow.

Cleotis honked a wounded walrus grunt. He doubled over. Gerald pulled his fist out and brought his forearm up, hard, into Cleotis's bent-over face. *Through* his face, it felt like.

Gerald had to grab him to keep Cleotis from hitting the deck. Cleotis didn't move. Gerald lowered him carefully to the deck. His nose was pushed off to one side, and his lips were starting to swell. He didn't look like he was going anywhere for a while, but just the same Gerald used one of the docking lines to hog-tie him.

They were yelling inside the cabin. Mr. Ruark was saying he'd been cheated, his good will had been abused. Stan Laurel and Booger were saying no, no, he was wrong. But this didn't help. Mr. Ruark was seriously put out. Somebody playing him for a fool—Gerald could only imagine.

Gerald stood and listened to the shouting for a couple of minutes. Then Mr. Ruark was yelling his name.

"Gerald," he was saying. "Gerald. Come in here a minute."

Gerald slid open the glass door and pushed aside the drapes. It was cool inside the cabin, air-conditioned. Ruark was in a chair on the far side of the room, away from Gerald. Booger and Stan were at opposite ends of a couch that faced Ruark's chair, looking over their shoulders at Gerald as he came in.

Booger tried to look around Gerald, trying to see Cleotis. But Gerald let the curtain fall, cutting off the view outside.

"I'm trying to tell my associates something about loyalty," Ruark said.

"Loyalty is important," Gerald said.

"What should be our attitude toward those who treat us well?"

"Be good to those who are good to you," Gerald said. "It's an Asian concept."

Booger was still looking over his shoulder. Gerald made him nervous, standing behind him.

"That's exactly right," Ruark said, but he stopped. He said, "Booger. Booger. Look at me when I talk to you, Booger."

Booger looked over at Ruark.

"Over here we've got it all wrong," Ruark said. "We're always trying to impress those who *might* do us some good down the road. Instead of taking care of those who already treat us well."

Gerald grabbed Booger from behind. One big hand on each bicep. He squeezed, Booger yelled with pain, and Gerald pulled his arms back.

Booger groaned.

Ruark got up from his chair. He put his right hand in the pocket of his baggy pants and came out with a dagger. It was thin, narrow—almost a long spike, a wicked long spike. He stepped up and sank the dagger into Booger's chest, to the hilt, so deep the bloody tip poked out of Booger's back.

Gerald knew it had to be the heart, the way Booger sagged, all of the life going out of him at once. Ruark took out the knife and Gerald let Booger collapse on the sofa. Booger tried to take one breath, but when he exhaled it was blood that gushed from his mouth and his nose.

Stanley jumped off the couch and stood against the drapes.

"He's dead," Stanley said.

"No shit," Ruark said. Gerald watched him wipe the knife on Booger's pants and put it back in his pocket.

The man was *cold*.

"Let's get him out before he bleeds all over," Ruark said. Gerald took him under the shoulders and lifted Booger up off the couch. He thought of his new clothes, and held the body at arm's length.

He took Booger out to the front deck. Cleotis was slowly wagging his head, blinking his eyes. Ruark overturned one ice chest. Cans and bottles and ice flowed out onto the deck, and then something else thumped down hard. The big, dark, plastic-wrapped package. Ruark tore it open. Inside were four barbell weights, fifty pounds each, Gerald saw. And lengths of quarter-inch cable.

Gerald didn't catch on at first. Not until Ruark started stacking the weights beside Booger's body, saying to Gerald, "Come on, let's get him out of here. Over the side."

Mr. Ruark knew all along what he was going to do. He came prepared.

Gerald wound the cable three or four times around Booger's torso, and threaded the end through four of the weights. The ends of the cable were fitted with snap hooks that Gerald fastened together.

He looked around and saw nobody except Ruark, Stan Laurel, and wide-eyed Cleotis. The sun was down, the moon wasn't up yet. Gerald dragged the body and the weights over to the edge, and he lifted them all together and dropped them over the rail.

Gerald thought about the fish in the river, the sturgeon hanging at the dock, big mothers.

"Oh," said Cleotis. *"Oh!"* The first one sounded like pain, the second like anger. Ruark turned on him fast.

"You're taking over," Ruark said to Cleotis. "Everything from your end. Don't fuck with me, I'll do you, too. I'll do you all one by one until I find somebody that shows me some respect."

They went back into the cabin. Stan was cleaning the floor with a wet rag and a mop. Mr. Ruark sat in his same chair. He looked tired.

"It's a great idea, foolproof, can't miss, everybody wins," he said. He didn't seem to be talking to anyone in particular. Just talking. "Meth, it's incredible, it's like baking a cake. All you need is the ingredients. You don't have to smuggle it in, you don't have to deal with the Mafia or Colombians, you just follow the recipe. Distribution, outlaw bikers have been running meth for years. The stink is what shoots most people down. Follow the smell to the lab. But I figure, I put the lab on a houseboat, I get my cook to cruise up and down the river. Where'd the stink come from? Where did it go? Nobody knows. 'It was there, officer, I smelled it. But now it's gone.'"

He seemed to shift gears. He looked straight at Stanley now.

"The thing is, it's chemistry. It's high school science. Dumb fuck, two molecules of hydrogen will bond with one molecule of oxygen the same way every time. Today, tomorrow, on the river, in Czechoslovakia, it always works out the same. I supply you a thirty-gallon drum of ether, I know I'm getting X number ounces of product. You tell me you're not getting X, you're getting Y, I know it's a lie. It was his idea, I realize. Skim it, sell the skim for yourselves. But *fuck.* You're stealing from me. I pay you good, you run the river, you have nothing to do but cook up a batch a week. It is not a bad deal."

He stopped. He asked Gerald, "You want to live on a houseboat for a while? Cruise the river, nothing to it."

Gerald knew what would happen if he said yes. Ruark must have another set of weights and cables in the other ice chest. Stanley could bend down and kiss his butt good-bye. One more for the sturgeon.

"I'd rather not," Gerald said. "If it's all the same with you. I was planning to enroll at San Francisco State next semester, did I mention it?"

"No," Ruark said. "Congratulations."

"A food service degree."

"That's commendable," Ruark said. He seemed to forget about Stanley for a few seconds. Then told him to get up to the wheel, take them back to the dock. Stanley left, rapidly.

Mr. Ruark said nothing on the way in, except when Gerald started to clean the blood. Ruark told him no, let Hal do it. Hal was his name, not Stanley. It dries, he can get on his hands and knees and scrub it. Maybe it'll make an impression on him.

When they were within sight of the marina, Ruark told Gerald to cut Cleotis loose. Gerald did. Cleotis had nothing to say. Harmon and the other two warthogs were together at the end of the pier when the houseboat slipped in. They looked for Booger. Ruark, climbing off the boat, said, "Forget it. The former Number Two is the new Number One. The former Number One gets remanded to the bottom of the food chain. That's how it goes."

20

Welcome assumed, when they came through the door, that they had the wrong room. He knew nobody in San Francisco. And if he did, they wouldn't be Prince Charming and Miss April.

The girl—woman; she was somewhere in there—was a knockout. Put clothes on a centerfold, a black jersey dress, and this was what you would get. Funny, she wasn't trying hard. Not much makeup, simple flat heels, hair straight down her back. The dress was nothing outrageous, couple of inches above the knee. But it fit.

"Sergeant Welcome?" the prince said. "Merle Welcome?"

"Here," Welcome said. He was alone in the room. Wilmer was out for therapy.

The prince was carrying his huge, ridiculous gift basket, wrapped in yellow cellophane. He set it down on Wilmer's bed and put out his hand for Welcome. He was slick, Welcome thought. And rich. He looked like he walked out of a liquor ad. You would know, seeing his picture in the ad, that the whiskey he drank was likewise smooth and rich. It kept your pants pressed and your teeth white, it put Rolex on your wrist, it cleared up your complexion. It made you slim, it made you suave and confident, it let you walk into a hospital room like you were royalty gone slumming.

He was about Welcome's age. As far as Welcome could tell, this was all they had in common.

Welcome reached to shake his hand. But the prince pulled his back.

"No," he said. "First. Before we get our hopes up. Do you have a job yet?"

"No," Welcome said.

The prince put his hand out again.

"You do now," he said.

In all it had to be the strangest half hour Welcome had ever spent. And he could remember some strange ones.

Prince Hays owned a company in the Bay Area. Merchandising. He was a patriot who wanted to do something good for one of the nation's heroes. He wanted to give Welcome a job. Not labor—get him on the management track, $650 a week to start.

He also owned apartments. He was offering Welcome the use of one of them, nice place in San Francisco. Welcome could have it rent free for the first couple of months.

After all, Hays said, Welcome would need an apartment when he was discharged. And when would that be?

Saturday, Welcome said. This was Wednesday.

Great, Hays said; I'll pick you up.

Oh, and by the way. The building was the same one where Grace lived. So you'll know somebody who knows her way around the city.

Grace Gibbs was the centerfold. Welcome almost wished that she weren't there. He was trying to concentrate on what Hays was telling him, the unbelievable words that kept coming out of Hays's mouth—*six-fifty a week . . . management track . . . rent-free apartment*—but she kept distracting him.

She said almost nothing. But she was certainly there. She had a sweet little smile. She seemed to be slightly embarrassed. At Hays, maybe, laying it on the way he did.

She was from Kansas. Chase County, the Flint Hills. The few times she did speak, he thought he could hear some country in her voice, a little of it still left in certain words. But she was trying to get rid of it. *Thang,* she said once, and she caught herself. She said it again. *Thing,* she said, carefully.

He wondered what she was doing with Hays. Hays was married, there was the ring, but Grace was not his wife. *My friend Grace Gibbs,* he had introduced her. Meaning nothing, or everything.

So what was Grace to him? It was probably a stupid question, Welcome thought, but he didn't want to jump to conclusions. Here was Hays, after all, putting him in the same building with her, inviting him to knock on her door.

If, Welcome thought. If it is all for real. It was about as unreal a proposal as he could imagine.

He kept trying to tell Hays that he knew nothing about management or merchandising. Nothing about business. His training was specialized, it didn't have many applications in civilian life.

Hard as Welcome tried, Hays kept pushing the job on him. Every time Welcome tried to tell him he had the wrong man, Hays insisted that Welcome was exactly what he had in mind. He kept asking Welcome questions about himself, about his training, what he had planned to do after his discharge.

Then he said they had to go. He gave Welcome a business card: Hays T. Teale, Executive Director of Marketing, EvHaTek Sales, Inc. He wrote a couple of phone numbers on the back. His home number, his cellular number, a third number. Grace's. Call anytime.

"A pleasure," he said, and he pumped Welcome's hand.

"Thank you."

"Saturday morning, I'll be here."

"If you want."

"Looking forward to working with you."

Welcome realized that he had never said yes. He hadn't said no, either.

"This is very sudden," Welcome said.

"Some of the best things in life are."

"You don't mind if I think about it."

The way Hays looked at him, Welcome knew he had said the wrong thing.

"Not that it doesn't sound great," Welcome said. "I mean, *great.*"

"It is," Hays said. "It is great."

"I more or less need a little while to get used to the idea."

"I can understand that," Hays said. He didn't sound understanding. "Day or two."

"We'll talk on Saturday," Hays said.

"Right, terrific," Welcome said.

Hays and Grace—ah, Grace!—went out together. Hays lightly touching her elbow.

Welcome swung his legs over the edge of the bed. He walked a couple of steps over to Wilmer's side, picked up the gift basket, and carried it back to his own bed. He purposely did it without the cane.

The leg hurt, but he did it.

The gift card was a reproduction of the famous recruiting poster, stern Uncle Sam pointing his finger.

EvHaTek Wants You! somebody had written inside.

Welcome tore off the cellophane. Fresh fruit, candy, a small canned Westphalian ham, smoked salmon, chocolate-dipped strawberries, five or six different kinds of cheese in foil-wrapped rounds . . .

Some magazines were stuck along the side. *Playboy, Penthouse, Esquire, Soldier of Fortune.* And a catalog, a slim mail-order catalog of twenty or thirty pages. *American Surf and Sun* was the company. Welcome riffled through it, swimsuits and beach accessories. He didn't get the point, until on the order page he noticed the line "A division of EvHaTek Sales."

He was going to put it down when he noticed the model splashing through the breakers on the opposite page.

You couldn't see much of her, for all the froth and water. But it was Grace, for sure. He looked through again, paying attention this time, and saw that she was all over the catalog.

Welcome was going through it, picking her out on one page after another, in tank suits and bikinis, cutoffs and halter tops, when an orderly wheeled in Wilmer and lifted him to the bed.

Welcome carried the basket over to Wilmer. Wilmer picked out an apple and a round of Camembert and a can of roasted almonds and *Playboy.*

"You ever have anything happen to you," Welcome said, "that was so good, you thought there had to be something wrong? Something put in front of you, so great, you wondered if you should turn it down?"

"No," Wilmer said. "Nothing that good ever happens. Not in this life."

"That's what I used to think," Welcome said.

"Go see him tomorrow," Hays said to Grace.

"I don't like hospitals," she said. "Why me?"

"He likes you. You can talk to him, you're both from the same place."

"The same state," she said. "And it's a big state. Coffeyville's a hundred-some miles from Chase County. It's practically in Oklahoma."

"I'm asking you," he said.

"If that's what you want."

"It definitely is."

"What's the big deal with him?" she said.

"I want to hire him."

"He doesn't seem to be your type."

"He is," Hays said. "Take my word for it."

21

Next day, Grace was listening to her "French for Beginners" tapes when Hays called, late afternoon.

It was broadening, she thought, to have a second language. It was a necessary improvement. As a bonus, she also heard English properly pronounced. Six years, she still hadn't gotten eastern Kansas out of her tongue and off her lips.

The instructors spoke both languages precisely. You not only got "*merveilleux*," but also a perfect "marvelous."

Marvelous. It sounded light and rounded when the instructor said it.

In Chase County it would sound like . . . well, she wasn't sure anyone in Chase County had ever used the word.

She was practicing it—"mar-ve-lous," slightly breathy on the first syllable—when Hays called from the office.

She stopped the Walkman and pulled off the headphones.

"Did you see him?" Hays said. Meaning the Marine.

"No," she said. "I didn't."

"I wanted you to stop by and see him."

"I ran out of time."

"You're resisting me on this," he said. "I wish I knew why."

You don't know? she thought. You really don't?

"He called," she said.

"Good." This picked him up. "How did he sound?"

At first he sounded like a fifteen-year-old kid, she thought, tongue-tied and awkward, how about that? Then, when he got warmed up, he sounded funny, he sounded happy, he sounded gentle. How about that? We talked for about an hour, I didn't mean to but the time ran away from me, how about that?

"He sounded all right."

"What did he have to say?"

He said he never met anybody like me, and it wasn't a hustle. He wished he could see me again. I told him no.

"You know, things are up in the air with him right now," she said.

"Go see the guy."

"Are you sure?"

"What is this, three times now I've asked you?"

"If I knew what the purpose was—"

"I want him to come to work for me. I want him to like me, understand?"

"I don't get it, me visiting him is going to make him like you?"

"One simple request, I get a ton of backchat."

"Okay," she said, "I'll do it, I'll see him."

If you insist, she thought.

Welcome did five laps of the seventh floor. Not a step without some pain. But he was covering the distance, this was what counted. Every bit of pain, he told himself, was like money in the bank. The injury was a huge debt to his body. It had to be repaid, one step after another.

Instead of the elevator he took the flight of stairs back up to eight, and this was tough. But it gave him the idea. Start repaying the debt in slightly larger increments. He took the stairs all the way to the basement, and then climbed them, nine sets in all, twelve steps per set. Hundred and eight steps closer to being right again.

The last couple of flights almost did him in, though. He felt queasy, and his skin was clammy. He knew he must look bad. The nurses at the central station didn't notice, but one of the aides did. She stared as he passed on the way to his room.

He made it to the bed. Wilmer said, "You know a Grace?"

"I sure do."

"She said she was coming by to see you."

"When?"

"She's on her way," Wilmer said.

He was a mess. Sweaty, though clammy cold. In the bathroom mirror his face was pale; his eyes looked hollow. His hair was a joke. He wanted to grow it to civilian length. But he was finding that if you start with a bad haircut, adding an inch or two all around does not improve it.

He brought a pair of shorts and a clean T-shirt when he went to shower, down the hall. Good thing, too, because when he came back she was already there.

She was talking with Wilmer. A trace of a soft smile came over her when she saw Welcome enter the room. Nothing overboard, but Welcome knew she was glad to see him.

Later he couldn't recall much of what they talked about. He remembered mostly being nervous. It was bad at first, but he got it under control. She wore a blouse and shorts that came almost to the knee, both in a soft, thin fabric the color of vanilla ice cream. It was a modest outfit that wasn't designed to be spectacular. But it was. She was.

They had a good time together, Welcome thought later. It wasn't just him; she was enjoying it too, being there. She helped to put him at ease. Funny, ten years younger, she was more comfortable than he was. She had poise to spare.

Toward the end she said, "You're thinking of going to work for Hays?"

"It's an opportunity."

"That depends," she said.

"I try to be realistic. I don't want to be in over my head, a job I can't do."

"You wouldn't," she said.

"You know something about the job?"

"About you," she said.

She sounded flirty and serious at the same time.

"What would that be?"

"You're smart," she said. "You've been places. You know things. Everything else would be a joke, after what you've done."

"You're guessing," Welcome said.

"I have this feeling," she said.

She stayed more than two hours that night, Thursday. Next day, Friday, she came before lunch and left a few minutes before dinner. It was true, she didn't like hospitals or the infirm. But she liked being with Welcome, who didn't act sick. He was impatient to get out.

Welcome was interesting. The soldier part of him was tough and confident. He didn't boast; actually he kept that part of him pretty close, but you still had no doubt about what he was and what he had done. The flip side of the soldier was almost a virgin, the super-straight way he looked at life and the world. He didn't know about her and Hays, not for sure. It would shake him some, when he learned.

At first she didn't understand how someone could have seen and done so much, yet know so little. But what he had seen and done was actually narrow. Think about it, he had spent the last half of his life eating what he was fed, sleeping where he was told to sleep, doing what he was told to do.

No wonder he was a virgin. No wonder he seemed aimless now.

She herself could pull off the world-weary act. It was a defense against sharks in the water. But she had to tone it down with Welcome. He didn't understand it. When she was with him she didn't need it, anyway.

In the end, with men, what mattered most was not what they were, but how they made you feel. With Welcome she felt tended to. She felt observed, but not stalked. She felt wanted, but not preyed upon.

She felt calm. Welcome carried this stillness around with him, and it was contagious. He believed, he *knew,* that he could take care of himself and do what had to be done, that somehow he would find a way. For himself. For anybody who stayed close to him.

She tended to get attached. Most of the time she considered it an affliction. Wanting it or not was immaterial, though. That was how she was made, she knew it, and she could feel it starting now.

22

"Watch the ball," Naull said. "Here comes now. Watch the ball."

He gave the Wiffle ball an underhand toss. Roy Boy waved his plastic bat at it and missed it by about a foot and a half.

"Keep your eye on the ball, son," Naull said.

They were in the park across from Altamonte. It was a sunny morning. A couple of kids flipped a Frisbee over the grass. Joggers in shorts or spandex tights would trot past on the running path, swinging hand weights, Walkman headphones snugged over their ears.

Roy Boy retrieved the ball and heaved it back. It bounced a few times and stopped at Naull's feet. Before Naull picked it up, he looked over his shoulder at the road clinging to the hillside.

"Your *eye* on the *ball*," Naull said. He tossed it again, and this time Roy Boy hit a little fly that lifted over Naull's head. Naull went back a couple of steps for it and reached. It bounced off his fingers.

"Home run!" Roy Boy said.

"Just about," Naull said. He bent to get it, and when he looked up the black BMW was tracking through a curve near the top of the hill.

"You win," Naull said.

"That's all?"

"For a while."

Roy Boy looked up and saw it, too.

"We gonna chase him again?" he said.

"Uh huh."

"Like he's a rabbit," Roy Boy said.

"Like he's a rabbit. And we was hounds from hell."

Welcome collected all his miscellaneous stuff in a plastic trash bag that one of the nurses gave him. He dressed in a T-shirt and Levi's. He sat on the edge of the bed. He thought about Grace. He thought of how she looked in the white shorts, walking down the corridor. Three times he picked up the phone, punched her number, but hung up before the first ring. The fourth time he let it ring, and got her voice on an answering machine.

He wondered what she was doing on a Saturday morning. He tried to see himself with her. It was hard to do, get that image. He tried to see her with Hays. That came much easier.

He was still sitting on the edge of the bed when Hays came in.

"Ready?" Hays said. He was dressed in khaki slacks and a polo shirt the color of sloe gin. A pair of black Ray-Bans hung from a cord around his neck. He didn't look like he belonged in an Army hospital. A catered picnic was more like it.

"I guess I am," Welcome said.

"Car's out front, let's boogie on out of here."

An orderly was supposed to take Welcome to the front door in a wheelchair. Regulations. He was also supposed to take the cane. But he decided to leave it. He didn't want Hays to think he was some kind of gimp. Anyway, for the first time in his adult life, military regulations meant nothing to him. He picked up the duffel and the plastic bag, and nobody stopped him when they went past the nurses' station, down the hall to the elevators. The leg hurt some, but Welcome tried not to limp.

They went out the front door. Hays said wait, he'd get the car. Welcome watched him stroll over to this hunkering BMW, low and black and mean, double-parked in the turnaround drive. Traffic was backing up behind it. An MP was waving cars around the snarl, and when he noticed Hays at the BMW, he came over, first talking, then getting louder.

Hays ignored him. He just let himself into the BMW. He put on the sunglasses, started the engine, and drove away from the MP. He pulled up in front of Welcome.

Welcome levered the leg in first. Then he lowered the rest of himself inside. The MP was striding over, waving his arms and yelling. He didn't like being ignored. Hays looked straight ahead and said, "Close the door, Merle."

Welcome did. It made a muffled thump. All at once they were in a private world, dark and quiet. The upholstery had the smell and soft touch of new leather. The driver's instruments reminded Welcome of a helicopter's control panel. Now the MP was truly pissed, bending down at

Welcome's window, shouting. Little bits of spittle flew from his lips. From in here it was like watching TV with the sound turned down.

Son of a bitch, he was saying. Motherfucker. Welcome could barely make out the words. He couldn't even hear the engine running. But the car leaped away when Hays put his right foot down.

Welcome looked back. For a moment he could see the MP's face, his mouth twisted and unhappy. The BMW ripped out toward the front gate, and the MP was out of sight before Welcome realized that it was his last official glimpse of the Army, this look of complete loathing on the MP's face as he watched the big black car disappear.

Naull stayed close over the Golden Gate. Otherwise he never would have followed him off Lombard Street to the Presidio and Letterman. An Army base, a military hospital, was the last place he'd expect Hays to be.

The Presidio is an open base, no sentries at the gates. Naull drove in after Hays and watched him double-park the BMW near the front entrance of the hospital. There were plenty of spaces in the lot. Naull found one right away, maybe a half-minute walk to the front door, but obviously it was half a minute too much for Hays.

What an asshole, Naull thought.

He was wondering how Hays connected with Letterman when Hays appeared again at the front door. Naull watched him walk over to the car, drive up to the front door. Snub the MP—might as well flip the guy your middle finger.

Not just an asshole, Naull thought. A smug asshole.

And now here was this G.I. type, hobbling over to the BMW, getting in. He looked like a million other lifers out on a weekend pass, wearing jeans that never quite got broken in.

Then Naull thought, no, not quite. This one was different. His back was too straight, his shoulders were thrown back—boot camp posture. This one had a serious case of gung-ho.

"Buckle up," Naull said to Roy Boy. The BMW was tearing out of the lot. By the time they got out onto Lombard again, Naull trailed him by nearly a block. Then Hays blew through the yellow on Fillmore, into traffic and out of sight.

"All gone," Roy Boy said.

"Maybe."

The light changed, and Naull moved out more slowly now. Up to

Van Ness, right, over the hump and back down, a right on Jackson Street. There was the BMW, in the garage driveway.

"Hey," Roy Boy said.

"Hey, how about that."

Naull went around the block six times before a space opened up in front of the Korean grocery. He wedged the Camaro in and sent Roy Boy into the store for sandwiches and drinks.

The window of 1-B was open again. A sunny day—you had to take them when you could. G. Gibbs was there, reaching to water a basket of petunias hanging from a hook outside. Naull could see right into the living room, the door. He could see G. Gibbs move around the room, watering the fern and the ficus and the oak leaf ivy. She had that unguarded way people have when they think they aren't being watched.

Very pretty. Very very pretty. Something strange about her, though. It took Naull a minute to catch on. She had a little smile. She was happy. She wasn't with Hays—of course she was happy.

Naull thought, So where's Asshole?

Other side, second floor, a window was coming open. It was Gung ho. Hays came over and stood with him.

Naull put down the sun visor to hide his face. After about half a minute he looked again. Gung ho was alone now at the window.

Roy Boy came out with a bag. Naull leaned across the seat and took it from him. He pulled out a chicken-salad sandwich wrapped in cellophane, and popped the tab on a can of Coke. When he looked up, G. Gibbs was going to her door. She was opening it up and Hays was walking in.

She let him kiss her. This was exactly how Naull saw it. She let him. Then they started to have words. Naull got the impression that she wasn't expecting him. He surprised her, she didn't want to be surprised. This was a guess on Naull's part, going on how she stood, how she moved her hands when she talked. The rest of it, what was happening, he had no doubt. Hays had that smarmy grin some men will get when they're trying to wheedle themselves a piece. He wanted some; she didn't. He dropped by for a quick one; she was letting him know it wasn't that easy.

She shook her head. He hit her across the mouth.

Whack, like that—and hard. His expression never changed. They were talking, he hit her, and afterward he still had that wheedling expression. The only difference was that G.'s head was now turned to one side, where the force of his flat hand had snapped it.

She turned from him. Walk out the door, Naull was thinking. You can do it. Easy. You just walk away from him.

But she was crossing over to the window. Putting down the blinds.

"Asshole," Naull said.

"Huh?" said Roy Boy.

"Jerk. I meant jerk. He's a Grade A jerk."

All of a sudden he didn't want to be watching Hays. Not for a while, anyway. He turned the key and got that sweet V-8 burble.

"What is he?" Naull said. "This is a quiz."

"He's a jerk," Roy Boy said right away.

"What kind?"

"Grade A."

"Correct. Very good. And are we ready to go home?"

Roy Boy took a couple of seconds to answer that one.

"Yes?" he said.

"Right again," Naull said. He backed up the car and pulled out onto Jackson, and he was glad to be going.

"Tell you what I had in mind," Hays said to Welcome as they stood at the window. "Few minutes, we'll shoot on over to Tiburon. I'll show you my little place. You can meet the wife. I told her all about you; she demands to see you. Won't let it alone."

"Okay," Welcome said.

"Drink a little grape, try the hot tub. Taste of the good life, huh? Then dinner—we'll go out. See if we can't arrange just the slightest improvement over military chow."

"All right," Welcome said. "That's fine." He didn't mind somebody planning his whole day for him. It felt like the Marines.

"Be just a few minutes before we leave," Hays said. "Got some business here in the building, won't take me too long. Say half an hour."

"Whatever."

"Don't run off."

"I have no place to go," Welcome said, before he realized Hays was joking.

Hays went out, and Welcome was alone in the apartment. Nice place. Nice neighborhood. Something made him uneasy, though, and after he watched traffic on the street for a couple of minutes he realized he had no idea where he was. Somewhere in San Francisco. But damn, it was a big city. If he left right now, took a cab someplace, he'd never find his way back.

He spotted a pay phone across the street, in front of a corner grocery. He went down, crossed over. The leg hurt. He wished he'd brought the cane. At the phone he tried Grace's number. This time it rang and rang, and nobody picked up.

He went into the grocery, hoping that they had a map. He would buy it, study it, get oriented. He hated feeling lost. But the grocery had no maps. He ended up getting cornflakes, some bread and sugar, and a quart of milk for breakfast in the morning.

It came to him, as he stood in the store, that he was not just in a strange place. He was surrounded by strangers, too. He was cut loose. Nobody knew him, nobody had any expectations.

Duty and responsibility were anchors that kept you grounded. As of today he owed nothing to nobody. He could do anything. *Anything.* He knew that he should feel happy, being free that way. But it made him nervous. It was as bad as being lost without a map.

He walked back to the apartment as fast as the leg would let him. He sat up there by the window, and waited. He hoped Hays wouldn't take too long.

Naull and his son got home a couple of hours ahead of Marie. They washed the Camaro out in the driveway, and buffed it with Turtle Wax. Naull went in and was running a vacuum cleaner in the kitchen when Marie came through the front door.

Roy Boy ran up to her and shouted, "Hounds from hell!"

She looked at Naull and said, "Where in the world—?"

"Don't ask me," Naull said. "The things he picks up. I have no idea."

23

On the way home, Hays stopped at a deli on Union Street. Welcome went in with him and watched him order grilled duck breast with black currants, baked eggplant with goat cheese and fresh basil, and an arugula salad. From there the way to Tiburon was past the Presidio, up a highway ramp, and onto the Golden Gate Bridge.

The ocean was to Welcome's left, the bay on his right. The bridge was not golden, but vermillion. Hays said that the Golden Gate was the mouth of the bay. It had the name before there was ever a bridge.

They were halfway across when Welcome swung his head around. He had never been over the Golden Gate before, but he knew what he was about to see. Wasn't it in movies and dozens of TV shows and commercials? He looked over his right shoulder and got this knockout vista of the San Francisco skyline, the white office buildings downtown, wharves jutting into the bay.

"The Streets of San Francisco," the old TV series, used that shot all the time. Not to mention every Dirty Harry flick Welcome had ever seen.

Up to his left, across the span, was a high bluff that seemed to be covered in nappy green felt. From up there you would get a view of the city above the bridge cables. Arnold Palmer once knocked a drive off that bluff, lofting it toward the city. He was selling pocket dictation machines. At about the same spot, some geek once jumped in the air and clicked his heels because he was so happy about his Toyota.

Sure. Welcome knew the place right away.

"Not bad, huh?" Hays said.

"To say the least."

"The city, what do you think? Bearing in mind that you haven't seen a tenth of it."

"I'm not much of an expert on cities. Special Forces are boonie rats."

"I would have thought you traveled quite a bit."

"I did. I saw a lot of swamps. Deserts, jungles. You want to rate jungles, I'm your man. I've seen a few cities. Beirut, I was there for a while. Riyadh, Panama City. Tegucigalpa. San Salvador. Oh, yeah, early 'eighty-seven, I was in and out of Tripoli. Libya."

"Tripoli. In 'eighty-seven. Sure you were." Hays glanced over at Welcome to give him this don't-shit-a-shitter look.

"Just the harbor, though. Does that count? With scuba gear. We rode in on this two-man submersible, launched off a submarine. It wasn't like I had much time for sightseeing."

Hays's disbelief gradually vanished, like rain washing a chalk mark off a wall.

"I guess San Francisco would look pretty good after that," he said.

"No question about it."

MARIN COUNTY, said a highway department sign on the other side of the bridge. SAUSALITO, said an exit marker off the freeway. To the right, beyond the freeway guardrail, gingerbread houses nestled into a steep hillside that fell away to the bay. Spectacular. Welcome knew plenty of places that jangled you, made you jumpy or depressed. This was the opposite. You felt good right away. It was the arrangement of things, hills and sky and water, a perfect accident.

After a few miles they turned off the freeway. TIBURON, said the exit marker. Now they were on a two-lane road where pocket tracts of homes peeked out from screens of pine and poplar. The lawns were landscaped, and just big enough—in Marin County, even suburbia looked good. The grass was trimmed, and the flower beds were weeded. Apparently paint never peeled here. The streets never got potholes.

They were turning left. Altamonte Drive. The BMW surged up through the curves. Five, six switchbacks. As they climbed, the bay came into view below them, San Francisco across the water. They went through a couple more turns, still climbing, and Welcome said, "So where are we headed?"

"Home," Hays said.

I see, Welcome thought.

Now it was getting to be unreal. It was almost a joke. These houses. Welcome always knew that somewhere people lived in splendor and glorious comfort, but it was an arcane phenomenon. Driving up Altamonte was like watching Saint Elmo's Fire dance around your bed.

And when he thought that it couldn't get any better, Hays steered through two more curves and pulled into the driveway at the top of the hill.

Home. My little place. Right.

They got out. Welcome expected Hays to gloat a little, let a strut seep into his walk. At least check out his guest's reaction. It would be natural. But the way Hays walked up to the front door, they could have been in the parking lot of a Kwik Mart.

That in itself was arrogance, Welcome thought. To take all this as your natural due.

Inside it was like the hayloft of a very large barn. Limestone posts, redwood beams. You found yourself in a brief entryway that was a sort of shelf above the main floor.

Somebody was playing music, loud. If you could call it music. An eerie chorus, wailing, no instruments.

Welcome followed Hays down a flight of stairs, smooth slabs of redwood. Welcome could see the layout. The house rested along the south slope of the hill. This floor, the main living area, was actually a level below the front entrance. The whole south wall was glass, from the floor on up. Along the west wall was a big fieldstone fireplace, with a stone chimney that shot straight through the ceiling two stories above.

Hays went over to a console with stacks of tape players and stereo receivers and two big TVs. He punched a couple of buttons, and the wailing stopped.

"*Spare* me," he said.

A pair of sliding glass doors led out onto a plank deck. The sun was warm, and a rising breeze carried the scent of oak and laurel. Hays went to the rail of the deck, looked down, and said, "Hey, babe."

Welcome went to the rail, too. Below was a terrace that held a small lagoon. Directly beneath him was a ledge where a small waterfall cascaded down into the pond. At first he thought it must be a miracle spring here on the top of the hill, incredible. He looked again and saw that the pond was artificial. It was painted the color of granite. Shrubs and boulders disguised its concrete apron.

At about the same moment Welcome noticed a woman in the water, stroking a languid crawl to the edge of the pool. She pulled herself up on a flat rock. She was naked.

Why not? Welcome thought. By now nothing would surprise him.

She stood and stretched, and waved. Slender, good-looking. Live, real, and naked. It had been months.

"That's Caitlin," Hays said.

"Your wife."

117

"The one and only. If you don't count my ex." He didn't seem to mind another man watching his naked wife.

She was still waving.

"Come on in," she said.

"Sorry, sweetie, no can do," Hays said. "We're ravenous up here—gotta eat."

Welcome pulled his eyes away and followed Hays inside. Hays was digging through the refrigerator when Caitlin came in. She was wearing a gauzy white robe that her wet body dampened in spots.

Hays began spooning the food out of paper cartons.

She said, "You're Merle." Before Welcome could answer she said, "You're my first Merle. That's such a sincere name. Do you know what I mean? Direct and unassuming."

"Thank you." Welcome didn't know what to say.

"I've been excited to meet you. A genuine hero." She looked directly at him when she talked. Welcome knew this was supposed to be polite, but the way she did it made him nervous. She wouldn't let go. "You were actually over there. I try to picture you. Over there. And now you're here. Standing in my kitchen. I find it very difficult to grasp."

"I was thinking the same thing," Welcome said.

"The dissonance!" she said.

They were at the table, eating, when she said, "I must tell you, speaking frankly, at first I was against this conflict on principle. No blood for oil. I meant it. Don't hold it against me."

"That's okay, everybody's entitled to their opinion."

She said, "Then I started to understand what a complete and utter asshole we were fighting. That got me hooked. I couldn't stop watching CNN. It was irresistible, this primal drama. The polarity, you know what I mean?"

"Positive and negative," Welcome said. He was looking at her, too. It wasn't just the damp places on the gauze, knowing what was underneath. Something about her was reckless and a little crazy. It was like she was juggling knives. She made you watch.

"Exactly!" she said. "And of course there was the spectacle. Life and death, the real thing. The very real thing. I was entranced."

"War is hell," Hays said.

"Absolutely," she said. "That's what makes it so interesting."

Hays opened a bottle of champagne with lunch. Dom Perignon. They asked Welcome for war stories. He had plenty of those, even if he left out the ones that were gruesome or classified. The champagne loosened him up. He wanted Hays and Caitlin to like him. He needed that job. And they were eating it up.

The first bottle was empty. Another Dom, Caitlin told Hays. Welcome was giving them the one about Grenada, the night before the invasion. How he climbed a cliff outside St. George's, crawled half a mile to the perimeter of a Cuban ammunition dump, disabled a pair of trip wires, and planted a set of satchel charges. Caitlin was staring at him. Hays had stopped trying to wrestle the cork out of the bottle.

At that moment it occurred to Welcome that this was not the image he wanted to get across.

"Look," he said, "I don't want you to think that this was all blood-and-guts stuff. People have that impression. Special Ops, these super commandos. Snake-eaters. But it's just a job. See, it's all in the training. Special Forces aren't born, they're made. They're trained." He was reaching for words. He wanted to get this point across. "I was trained to perform a variety of tasks. Okay, maybe they're specific to the military, these tasks. But I can be trained—that's what I'm trying to say. I have the discipline to be trained."

"I'm sure you do," Caitlin said.

"I'm speaking as a would-be employee," Welcome said. "So you know what you're getting."

"Put it out of your mind," Caitlin said.

"I know what I'm getting," Hays said.

"You're perfect," Caitlin said. "Absolutely."

They made a good dent in the second bottle. Caitlin said she'd show Welcome the rest of the house. Their first stop was the stereo cabinet, where she punched a couple of buttons, and the crazy wailing started again. *Le Mystère des Voix Bulgares* was the title on the CD cover. "*The Mystery of the Bulgarian Voices*," Caitlin said. It was, no fooling, the Bulgarian State Radio and Television Female Choir. Caitlin loved choral music. She devoured anything ethnic and indigenous. These were the phrases she used.

There were two more levels in the house. Below the main floor were the bedrooms. Hays and Caitlin slept in a room that was about half the size of a basketball court, decorated in shades of cream and tan. Sitting on a pedestal was the biggest brass bed Welcome ever saw, flanked at the head by two huge beige vases that held stalks of dry pampas grass.

The foot of the bed faced out to a glass door and another deck. The view was of the bay and San Francisco and the Golden Gate. They would see it every morning when they woke up.

He went to the door. Caitlin came in behind him and stood close to his elbow. Welcome thought that if she got any closer, he would feel her breasts through the gauze. The house had views everywhere, but they were slightly different from one room to the next. Welcome knew that they would change with the time of day and the weather, the shifts of light and clouds and shadows. You would never get tired of looking outside. Welcome imagined Hays and Caitlin together in the big bed. It made him wonder about Hays and Grace. Would you want a mistress if you were married to Caitlin? She would keep you interested, for sure. It would be like living in this house, with all the changing views demanding your attention.

Down on the last floor was a single large room that was full of exercise equipment. Nautilus machines, weight benches, stationary bikes. There was a sauna and a whirlpool bath. Hays and Caitlin weren't fat, but they didn't look like exercise fiends. It was probably too much work. You would feel wholesome as hell, though, having your personal health club in the basement.

A door from the exercise room took them out to the lagoon. Hays was up on the deck above the waterfall.

"Let's swim," Caitlin said. Jesus, she was taking off the robe.

"I don't have any trunks," Welcome said. To Hays he said, "Got some trunks?" But Hays couldn't hear him. The splashing water was too loud.

"Come on," Caitlin said. She was talking to Welcome.

"Trunks," Welcome shouted to Hays. "Can I borrow some trunks?"

Hays was amused. As his naked wife tugged at Welcome's T-shirt.

"There hasn't been a bathing suit in this pool since the day it was built," Caitlin said.

"Sorry about that," Hays said.

All right, Welcome thought. Fine. He could feel the sun on his head. He could feel the champagne. He pulled off his shirt, sat on the nearest big rock, and took off his shoes and his socks and his Levi's. Caitlin dived into the lagoon. Hays came down from the deck, bringing a cordless phone and more champagne. He took off his polo shirt and unbuckled the belt of his khaki slacks. Caitlin was gliding underwater, and before she could surface Welcome stripped off his shorts and slipped into the pool.

They were in the water for maybe an hour, swimming, splashing, laughing. Welcome wasn't sure about the time. They took turns drinking from the new bottle. After a while Welcome swam off by himself and watched the sky. He hauled himself up on a rock and went to the edge of the terrace.

From here you could look almost straight down. At the foot of the hill, beside the bay, was a village that Welcome figured was Tiburon. The cars, the houses and stores, the boats looked tiny and perfect.

Welcome wondered how it felt to live this way all the time. Swimming tadpole naked in your own lagoon, high above a model railroad town. Laying in bed and looking at Clint Eastwood's favorite bridge. Listening to the Bulgarian Mystery Voices.

The cordless phone was chiming. Hays got out of the water and answered it. From the way he was talking, playing with the antenna, Welcome knew that the reception down here must be poor. Hays took the phone up to the deck.

Caitlin said, "Hey, Merle. You have to see this."

She was hip deep in the water, beside the waterfall. Welcome started to walk around the lagoon, then got self-conscious and swam over the rest of the way. He was almost there when she ducked through the cascade and was out of sight.

Welcome walked through the falling water, too. On the other side was a small grotto. Along the back wall a long flat rock formed a bench at about water level. The falling water was a curtain outside.

She touched the bicep of his right arm.

"Love the tattoo," she said.

"That. I was nineteen. Young and dumb."

"I still can't get over it, your being here. I inhabit this certain sphere, and you have your own sphere, and they're so different, nobody would ever expect them to intersect. Only somehow they did, and now our spheres share some of the same space."

"I guess that's right," Welcome said. He was thinking about Hays up on the deck. What Hays would say if he found them together down here. Would that be the end of the job? Hays was about as broad-minded a husband as Welcome had known. But there had to be a limit.

"Up here," she said. It sounded like an order, and Welcome was sitting on the bench before he even thought about it.

She said, "You're the real thing, aren't you?"

Welcome didn't know how to answer.

"Did you kill anybody over there?" she said.

121

Welcome thought that was the most intimate question anybody could ask. He thought she was way out of line, and that he ought to tell her so.

But she was standing right in front of him now, her hips against his knees. She was touching his thighs. His chest.

"No," he said.

"You have, though."

"Yeah. I have."

"What does it feel like?"

Wrong, Welcome thought. *That* was the most intimate question anybody could ask.

He said, "You don't think about it. If you have to do it, you do it. Training. You sure don't think about it afterward."

She laid a hand lightly on his chest, let it rest there a second, and then moved it slowly down. Down. She grasped him. Right there. He was bursting. He wanted to get up and leave, now. He wanted to sit right here and let her do anything she wanted.

If Hays should come down now . . . good-bye apartment. Good-bye job.

"We're going to be good friends, aren't we?" she said.

He didn't get a chance to speak. She bent and took him. All of him, was how it felt.

Welcome looked at her head in his lap, the most amazing sight yet. He tried to figure how many months it had been. He left Bragg for the Middle East in October. This was July. Nine months.

He was barely able to make this calculation. He didn't think about Hays or the job or the apartment. He knew he ought to think about the right or wrong of it, too. But it was moot. She was drawing him out, she knew exactly what to do, she was finishing him. Nine months off the board in about ten seconds.

He nearly blacked out. He had to put his head back against the wall. That, or slide right off the bench. When he opened his eyes again Caitlin was kicking away from him, back-stroking through the waterfall and out of sight.

Welcome caught his breath. He swam out into the sunlight. Caitlin was up on the edge of the pond, rubbing her hair with a towel. Hays stood beside her.

She said, "I was just asking Merle if we were going to be friends."

"Are we?" Hays said.

"I don't know," Welcome said.

"Yes we are," Caitlin said. "Trust me. We are. I have an instinct for these things."

On the way back to Jackson Street Hays and Welcome stopped for dinner in a Japanese restaurant. Caitlin stayed home. Hays insisted that Welcome try a piece of raw tuna fish.

It was purple.

Welcome tried it, though. He thought it was the least he could do. And it wasn't so bad.

Hays said, "In the service, you used computers, right?"

"Not computers per se," Welcome said. "Not PCs. But devices with microprocessors, sure, all the time."

"Good enough, good enough," Hays said. "What I was thinking, was starting you in the warehouse. Fulfillment Monitoring. No lifting, none of that; it's an office job, all keyboards and video screens."

"That would be great," Welcome said.

"Start you at six fifty a week, plus the normal menu of benefits."

"Goddamn, that's great," Welcome said. It sounded like a lot of money, and he did quick multiplication in his head. Thirty thousand-some a year. "That's *great*."

"It isn't as much as it sounds. You won't believe your expenses. Take it from me. But the apartment's yours for a couple of months, give you a running start."

"I can't tell you how much I appreciate this," Welcome said. He felt awful. He couldn't stop seeing Caitlin touch him, hold him, bend over him.

"Warehouse's here in the city, Howard Street, south of Market Street. Somebody'll be by, pick you up, noon on Monday. It's arranged. I've got you down for half days, Monday and Tuesday, until you get in the swing of things."

"Thank you," Welcome said. "Really. I don't know how I can thank you enough."

A modest shrug from Hays. He said, "In the Marines, did you ever build a bomb?"

"No," Welcome said. "That's one thing I never did."

"No bombs? You never blew up a bridge? You never set a booby trap?"

"You mean an explosive device," Welcome said. "A bomb is something you drop out of an airplane."

"What do I know? It goes boom, it's a bomb."

"I improvised some devices in action. I did a lot of them in training."

Hays popped a purple slice of tuna into his mouth.

He said, "You want to do one for me?"

He did it in the same tone that some men will come on to a girl. Like he was ready to make it a joke, retreat behind a laugh, if he got turned down.

But Welcome knew it was no joke.

"No thanks," Welcome said.

"Big money in it. One day's work could bring you what you'll make in a year. More. And no payroll deductions."

"Is that what it's all about?" Welcome said. "The big hustle, wine and dine, so I'll blow something up for you? And if I don't, I lose the job, I lose the apartment and all the rest, is that how it goes?"

"Did I say that? We're talking about two different things here. The job is yours. The apartment, I told you, couple of months. You mentioned gratitude, I thought about this unusual problem I have—not involving people, strictly an inanimate object—and I thought, what the hell. Throw it out on the table."

"I'll have to come up with another way to thank you."

"Whatever," Hays said.

Grace was looking out the window when the BMW pulled in with Hays and Welcome. It was night, around ten, and she was thinking about getting to sleep early.

Another surprise visit, she thought. The idea of facing him knotted her stomach.

She went into the bathroom and checked the cheek. No bruise, but there was still a red mark. A little powder, a little blush, it didn't look so bad. Or did she want him to see it? She sat on the couch and waited. She kept running over what she would say to him, how she would handle it this time. She heard a car door slamming outside, an engine turning. She looked out to see the BMW driving away.

She found that she was disappointed. This amazed her. Tonight she detested the SOB. Yet she was sorry to see him go. She wanted him to want her, this was the perverse thing. As long as he wanted her, she was okay. Now she wondered what it meant, that he would leave without seeing her.

She took the stairs to 2-A and knocked.

Welcome came right to the door.

"Grace," he said. He leaned closer, looked at the bruise.

"What happened to you?"

"A domestic accident," she said.

"You want to come in?"

"It's late," she said. "I'm being a neighbor. See if you needed anything."

"No, I'm all set. For tonight, anyway."

"Fine."

"But thanks."

She said, "You spent the day with him, huh?"

"Their house. What a place."

"Both of 'em."

"Uh-huh. Him and her. Caitlin."

I've heard the name, Grace thought.

"Did he happen to mention me?" she said.

"Not that I remember," Welcome said.

"How do they treat you?" she said.

"Real good. The red carpet."

She said, "What does he want from you?"

Welcome looked like he might take offense, but he changed his mind.

"I'm not sure yet," he said.

"You better find out," she said. "And when you do, you better know how much it's worth. Otherwise he'll eat you alive. You better believe, he knows what he wants out of you and what he'll pay. That's what he does, he buys and sells, he's good at it."

"You sound like an expert," he said.

"I'm here under the same arrangement you are," she said. There, let him have it.

Not much reaction. Nothing obvious.

But he seemed to draw up inside.

She said, "Anyway, good night. Welcome to the building. Anything you need, let me know."

Welcome stood in his doorway and watched her walk down the steps. A vision.

He knew he should get out now. Pack his bags, walk out and flag a taxi, go away and never come back.

Guy buys you dinner and asks you to blow up something.

He had his mustering-out pay, he had his disability coming in. And he had himself. He always thought that was worth a lot. In the Marines it was. Could it be so different here?

But there was Grace. One good reason not to leave. Grace and all the places where he wanted to glide his fingers. And something even more tender, something she touched in him that made him want to give her everything, all that he had and all that he was.

Hays had her, and that should be it. But Hays was occupied, Hays was sitting in his house on the hill. While he himself was here, one floor above her. There was a lot to be said for proximity.

If he left, he was another face in the crowd, another panting hound among what had to be a multitude.

He stood in the doorway. She was nearly at the bottom of the stairs.

He said, "I was wondering if you'd want to go out with me tomorrow. Drive around, show me the city. Is that against the rules?"

She turned around.

"There are no rules," she said.

24

That night Hays and Caitlin and Naull popped a town house in Foster City, south of the airport. A couple in their forties, no children, Naull judged when he was inside.

It was a fair haul. On the walls Naull found four Disney cels, animation drawings on celluloid. Prime ones: Mickey as the Sorcerer's Apprentice, Dumbo soaring above the clouds, Snow White with Sneezy and Goofy. Naull knew that Andy Pops would be nervous about them—cels were unique, thereby identifiable—but he would take them after some haggling. They were too good to pass up.

Hays and Caitlin left the BMW in the parking lot of a La Quinta Inn, in a long strip of motels in San Mateo, a couple of miles from the airport. They had Naull drop them off along the strip, and when he was gone they walked to the car.

He was paying attention to traffic, getting ready to turn out of the lot, when Caitlin beside him said, "Hey, limp dick."

He turned. She was pointing a gun at him, a chrome automatic.

"What the . . . Where . . . What are you doing?" Hays said.

"Dear, you're babbling," she said.

"Put it down."

She lowered the gun. She passed it over to him.

He had never handled a gun before. It was heavier than he expected.

"In one of the kitchen drawers," she said. "Isn't it great?"

It was garish. Mother-of-pearl handles.

"Gimme," she said, and he gave it back to her.

"A hot forty-five," she said. "Your classic untraceable firearm. Think about it."

25

Welcome woke up early. He did six blocks up Jackson Street, six back. The leg hurt, but it held up. He showered and dressed, and Grace came to his door. She asked him what he wanted to do with the day.

He told her he wanted to be a tourist. Easy, she said.

He was hungry, too. He wanted a late breakfast. This narrowed it down some.

The Cliff House, Grace said.

She wanted him to wear a jacket. A jacket in July, he thought, got to be kidding. He brought along a red sweatshirt with a USMC emblem. They drove in her Ford, out Geary Boulevard. It was a long straight reach across the city, nearly from the bay to the ocean. She knew what she was doing, where she was going. Welcome sat back and relaxed with the window open on the passenger side. It was a sunny morning.

Geary was busy at first, but traffic began to drop off as they approached the ocean. He smelled brine, and the air became chilly. He rolled up the window.

On outer Geary, all the intersecting streets were numbered avenues. A little past Fortieth, Geary made a slight jog and became Point Lobos. Point Lobos crested a rise, and Welcome could see the water ahead, gray and blue and choppy.

Point Lobos passed through a strip of parkland studded with wind-bent cypress trees. Now they were on a high bluff, and the ocean was ahead of them, down at the base of the bluff.

Point Lobos swept into a wide left-hand turn. Grace braked and pulled out of the curve, into an asphalt parking lot at the top of the bluff. The lot was nearly full, several tourist coaches, dozens of cars. Beyond the asphalt, rooted at the lip of the bluff, jutting over the ocean, was a building the size of a very large family home. It was mostly wood and glass and concrete. It reminded Welcome of an ammunition bunker.

This was the Cliff House.

A low stone wall bordered the parking lot, almost at the brink of the bluff. Some coin-operated binoculars stood on pipes at intervals along the wall.

Grace and Welcome walked over to the stone wall. Welcome thought about it for a few seconds, then reached and took her hand.

She squeezed it and they kept walking.

Since they left the car Welcome had been hearing the bark—*yarp, yarp, yarp*—of seals. Now he could see them, a hundred or more, on a couple of craggy high rocks out in the ocean, about as far as Welcome could chuck a baseball. The rocks were brown, and white splashed with guano. The seals crawled over them like fleas on a dog.

Grace had a dime for the binoculars. But Welcome didn't care to see the seals up close. They reminded him of crows in a field. Like crows, they were dark, dirty, and noisy. He had seen plenty of crows in his time.

Instead he took in the wide spread of the view. Ahead was the ocean. It rocked in from the horizon and slammed into the base of the cliff beneath him. To his right, and below, were concrete ruins. SUTRO BATHS, said a sign nearby. Destroyed by fire. To his left, beyond the Cliff House, was a long beach where white curls of surf broke against a sandy esplanade. From the elevation of the bluff he could see more than a mile, south along the beach.

Behind him Point Lobos Avenue swept through its long curve, down the side of the bluff and straight along the esplanade. Past the Cliff House, once it dropped off the bluff, the road had a new name. The Great Highway, it was called. You could follow it into the distant haze.

Welcome and Grace went in to eat in the Cliff House restaurant. It was full, and they had to stand in line for a table. Welcome didn't mind. The line was tight and they had to stand close. He liked that, feeling that they were a couple.

When they got to the table, he pushed aside the ashtray and the candlestick, so he could hold her hand. He could look straight at her now.

The meal came way too soon. The busboy cleared the table way too fast.

They went out. To the north side of the building, a sign pointed down a concrete walkway to something called the Musée Mechanique. They followed the walkway. It led to the west side of the Cliff House, above the ocean.

The Musée Mechanique turned out to be an old-fashioned penny arcade. It was closed. The door was locked. They stood and watched the gulls and the seals and the spume that flew when breakers bashed the bottom of the cliff.

They were alone. The wind was blowing through Welcome's sweat-shirt, and the air was so damp you could feel it on your skin. Run a finger along your chin, it would come up wet and salty.

Welcome put an arm around Grace, drew her in close. She let herself come to him. They were still watching the ocean. Somehow the closeness, surrendering space, was easier without eye contact.

Ahead was the ocean. To his right was the parking lot and the low stone wall at the edge of the cliff. To his left, down below and stretching far to the south, was the long beach, the surf, the Great Highway. It was a memorable arrangement, forever imprinted in his mind when he took her in his arms, and held her, and kissed her for the first time.

A Marine. Naull knew that wearing a USMC sweatshirt did not automatically make you a Marine. But when he saw the shirt, the globe-and-anchor emblem, it clicked into place with his all-around gung ho appearance. The shirt was no affectation. Welcome, M—the way he had it on his mailbox—was a Marine.

With nothing better to do, Naull had parked outside the Jackson Street apartments, ready to sacrifice a couple of hours to the cause of unraveling Hays and Caitlin. He had followed Welcome and Grace up Geary to the Cliff House.

Welcome, M was a Marine, and he was holding hands with Hays's sideshow, G. Gibbs.

It solved no mysteries, and actually deepened a few. But it did firm up one idea. Welcome, M was somebody to watch, Naull thought. Somebody, maybe, he should get to know.

Monday morning, Welcome did ten blocks up Jackson, ten blocks back. Took him almost an hour. He was dragging, the last few blocks. This was a good way to do it, out and back like this. Near the end, when he was really hurting, he had to keep pushing if he wanted to get home.

He was back by seven-thirty. Around eight, Grace was at his door, asking him if he wanted breakfast. That was how he saw her apartment for the first time, when she asked him down for coffee and fruit and muffins.

Unlike his own, Grace's place actually looked like a home. You ran into the occasional military wife who could do this, take a generic one-bedroom, and with work and a very few dollars turn it into something that was bright and warm and pretty.

She had a scrapbook of clippings and tear sheets, her modeling work, back to when she was eighteen and new in town. If anything, she was even more succulent then. But he liked her better now, completely a woman, with a woman's bearing and gravity. And still wholly succulent.

He looked at the clips and the dates that she had written in the margin of each one—she was organized. He thought of himself on those dates. What was he doing, 9-22-88? He couldn't remember, exactly. He was probably engaged in something that meant a lot to him then, and not so much now. In any case he had been apart from her, unaware of her.

And if there was the past there was the future. That brought him pangs, too. He might be apart from her—probably would, it would have to happen that way—but he would never again be unaware of her.

Later she drove him to a mall, a men's clothing store. He spent almost a thousand dollars of his mustering-out pay on what he hoped was management-track apparel.

Grace helped him pick it out. She also pressed what he was going to wear today. Not to make a habit of it, she told him.

Tweed slacks, blue blazer, beige button-down, paisley necktie, cordovan wing tips.

At noon he was in the hall, looking out the door, standing straight with his hands by his side, not in his pockets—he was a U.S. Marine, he knew how to stay spruce—when a pale little man named Beauregard came up the walk, and said it was time to go to work.

"How's he doing?" Hays said. He was buttoning his shirt, getting ready to leave her apartment that afternoon.

"He's okay. He's been walking. For exercise."

"Seeing much of him?"

"We went to the Cliff House yesterday. Spend time with him—you said."

"That's what I wanted. Don't be defensive. The Cliff House, anything else?"

"Breakfast this morning. I took him to Serramonte so he could buy some clothes."

"He must like you."

"I guess he does."

"Come on, come on, it's all right."

"He likes me," she said. And, "I'm starting to feel like your tease mare."

He was knotting his tie. He turned from the mirror to her, and said, "A what mare?"

"Tease mare. You wouldn't know, you've never been on a farm. A tease mare—for artificial insemination, you have to take the dose from your stallion. Take what he's not interested in giving. So you make him interested. You get a mare, mare in heat, tie her outside his stall, he's real interested. His nostrils are wide open, he lets you take what you need, because he has that tease mare on the brain."

"What an idea," he said. He finished the tie, slipped into his jacket. He was at the door.

"There's nothing between us," she said. Adding, "Him and me."

He looked back at her, over his shoulder.

"Sweetheart," he said, "I don't demand fidelity."

You should, she thought, you pay for it.

She went to the window, watched him walk to his car. Easy, comfortable, and satisfied.

But if that's the way it is, she thought.

Fulfillment Monitoring was a windowless office space that occupied a corner of a warehouse at Second and Howard streets. The office had white walls, oak veneer work stations, and fluorescent lights that gave Welcome a headache. On each of the three work stations, and on the supervisor's desk, stood a computer video screen and a keyboard.

The orders were punched in elsewhere, at sales desks and processing offices. They came in over phone lines. Warehouse pickers tore a copy of the shipping order off a printer. They pulled the items off shelves, and dollied them to Packing and Shipping, which checked the list and boxed the shipment for UPS.

This process was called order fulfillment. Fulfillment Monitoring sat on top of the process. Using keyboard and video screen, the staff—known as monitors—in Fulfillment Monitoring checked lists against actual shipments, as recorded by bar-code scanning in Packing and Shipping. On occasion a monitor actually left the office and walked out into the warehouse to physically verify an order or the shelf inventory of a certain item.

But that was unusual. Most of the time it was white walls, video screens, fluorescent lights.

No wonder Beauregard was pale, Welcome thought.

Beauregard resented Welcome. He resented having to pick him up during his lunch hour, he resented the infringement. The office had room, literally, for a supervisor and three monitors. Welcome was not the supervisor and he was not a monitor. Beauregard had to search the warehouse for a metal chair so Welcome would have a place to sit.

Welcome thought he also resented the blazer and the paisley tie. Nobody in the warehouse wore a sport coat. Only Beauregard wore a tie, and his was a clip-on bow.

Four and a half hours in the windowless room. Welcome needed about fifteen minutes to catch on to what happened here. The monitors watched the pickers and packers for screw-ups; Beauregard watched the monitors.

At five, when they knocked off, Welcome left the office, walked out into the warehouse with the light and air from the open bays of the loading dock. Felt like the first day of spring after a long winter.

Beauregard gave him a ride back to the apartment, and showed him how to catch the bus next time. Walk to Van Ness. Catch the bus down Van Ness to Mission Street. Transfer to a Mission Street bus, get off on Second, walk one more block to Howard.

It was slow going home. They had to cross downtown. The buildings were disgorging people. Welcome imagined the workers swarming out of their rooms, away from their video screens and fluorescent lights, fleeing home.

He thought of them doing this five times a week, fifty weeks a year, all their lives. He admired them, he was amazed, he was truly in awe.

Grace caught Welcome in the hall.

"First day, how was it?" she said.

"Beats getting shot at."

"Really?"

"Not necessarily," he said. "But it sounds like it should be true."

"You can tell me about it. Want to have dinner?"

"Where?"

"Someplace cheap. Seven, can you make it?"

"I can handle it," Welcome said.

"Ask him," Caitlin said. "Stop farting around. Put it to him, if he says no, he's out of the apartment, out of a job. Give him something to think about."

"Too soon," Hays said. "I want him to have some time."

"Time for what?"

"To get interested. Let him think about it, something he likes. Let him really want it. Then, when he's hooked, he'll know the only way he can have it is to do things our way."

"What's he supposed to want so much?"

"What everybody wants," Hays said. "The good things in life. What else?"

27

"No," Naull said. "I don't think so."

"You haven't even seen it," Hays said.

"This is the mark of a small mind," Caitlin said. "Resistance to anything new or different."

They were sitting on the top row of stone benches in the amphitheater on Mount Tamalpais. Midmorning, a Tuesday, it was deserted. Good place for a meet.

"Okay, I'm small-minded," Naull said. "But I know one thing. In this business, when you find something that works, you better stick with it. Get out of the groove, you're in trouble real fast."

"We're still following the game plan," Hays said.

"No we're not. This is different. What you have going for you is the line you get on prospects. How you do it, I haven't figured it out yet, but it's good. This one doesn't come that route, though. You tell me he has a safe in the basement."

"People don't have safes for nothing," Caitlin said.

"I realize that. But the only way you'd know about it is if you've been there and seen it, or if somebody you know has been there and seen it. Either way, I don't care, it's too close to home."

"At least look at the place."

"Furthermore," Naull said, "I know zero about safes. You get me up here, this hot opportunity, it turns out to be a safe. A complete waste of time. It might as well be in Afghanistan, all the good it does us."

"We're working on that," Hays said.

"An outside expert," Caitlin said.

"That's all we need, another hand in the pot."

"*Negativity!*" Caitlin screeched.

"Look at the place," Hays said.

"Before you kick prosperity out of bed," Caitlin said.

"What's in the safe?" Naull said. "If you know so much."

"Negotiable securities," Hays said after a beat.

"Jewels," Caitlin said.

"Which is it?"

"Both," Hays said. "He keeps jewels, he keeps negotiable securities. Minimum of a million and a half."

"He's a very wealthy individual," Caitlin said.

"What the hell," Naull said. "I'll look."

"Jewels?" Hays said when they were alone. *"Jewels?"*

"Better than you. Negotiable securities."

"I can see it. Ruark. With jewels. The guy wears a Casio watch. Black plastic strap."

"Ralph doesn't know that," she said. "What you don't realize, a barney needs something concrete to hold on to. A mental picture to keep him going. That's the state of mind we're dealing with. What does he know about negotiable securities? Jewels, that's different. That'll stick, he won't be able to get it out of his head. He'll have to pop the place, or it'll drive him crazy."

"You've always got an answer," he said.

"Just watch."

You caught Tomales Road out of the city of Novato, up Highway 101 in northern Marin. First thing Naull noticed, the area had a real rural feel. All those trees, the county road's lazy looping and curving through the hills, in no special hurry. It was quiet and very green out here. The air had a moist, earthy smell.

Very few houses. Most of those were secluded in the woods. This was a place for people who wanted their privacy.

And who didn't mind the fog. Today was clear—clear at the moment—but here on the ocean side of the hills you would have plenty of fog. Between the fog and the redwoods you might never get enough sun to burn the damp out of your bones.

The house in question was one of those stuck in the trees, farther back than most. Naull found the gravel entrance road. He drove past it a couple of times, on Tomales Road. All he could see of the house was a brick chimney and wooden shakes on the roof, little peeks that he got through the foliage.

The next time past, he turned onto the gravel. The drive dropped away from the road, and near the bottom of the grade he spotted the steel gate. And the surveillance camera. Whoa. He stopped short and backed to the road again.

A gate, he thought, there had to be a fence. The fence would have to enclose the house.

He rolled slowly up Tomales Road. A thick border of shrubs, madrone and buck brush, heavy chaparral, grew up against the shoulder. You would need a machete. Beyond it were the trees.

He pulled onto the shoulder. Here was a gap in the brush. Not much, maybe a deer trail, but it headed straight to the trees. At this point he was two hundred, three hundred yards from where the gravel entryway struck the road.

Naull locked the truck and started down the trail. It took him through the waist-high brush and into the trees. Second-growth fir and pine, planted too thick but still with room to walk.

And there was the fence, standing up straight and tall and dark in the middle of the forest.

The upright steel shafts were close to eight feet high. They came to a point—it looked like a good sharp point—at the top. At the bottom, each was set in concrete in the ground. They were about six inches apart, reinforced by horizontal runners near top and bottom.

The house had to be across the fence, somewhere on the other side of the trees. You couldn't see it from here. And here you could not be seen from the house.

He started to follow the fence. It looked out of place in the softness of the forest. Where you would expect a split-rail fence, maybe white pickets, here was this steel barrier that you might find containing grizzly bears in a zoo.

The trees started to thin. The forest cleared, and Naull followed the fence out into the edge of a meadow. He stopped. The fence crossed twenty or thirty yards of clearing before it ran into the forest again.

Now he could see the house. Big rambling country place, shake roof and unpainted wood shingle siding. Another video cam under the front-porch eaves. Another near a back corner pointed toward a small orchard at the rear of the house.

Naull retreated back into the forest. He followed the trail through the brush, back to the truck.

He started slowly up Tomales Road again. A couple of hundred yards along, he noticed a power pole beside the road, and a transformer, and a line that ran off the pole and through the woods, in the direction of the house. A little farther, at the intersection of Larkspur Road, he spotted the knee-high PacTel junction box.

He kept thinking about the fence. How many thousands it must have cost, a fence like that. Why would somebody do that? He could think of any number of reasons. But the obvious one did stick in his mind.

"You didn't tell me about the fence," Naull said, back in the amphitheater again. "A minor detail you neglected to mention."

"What fence?" Caitlin said.

"Don't give me that."

"There was never a fence, last time I saw it."

"That's right," Hays said.

"When was that?"

"It would be a couple of years," she said.

Naull described the fence, in detail.

"I never knew," she said.

"You're looking at the fence, you're looking at the security system, you got to be looking at motion detectors, circuits on the doors and windows, probably an alert line to the sheriff."

"What are you telling me?" Caitlin said. "This is a no-go?"

"Not necessarily," Naull said. "But first I want to get this right. One man in a house that size. No roommates. You haven't been there for two years, but you can guarantee when he's out of the house."

"Absolutely," Hays and Caitlin said together.

"The fence can be overcome," Naull said. "The alarms, everything, can be defeated. If he didn't have electricity, didn't have a phone. But you've still got the safe."

"We're working on it," Hays said.

"You get it worked out, let me know."

"You want to do it," Caitlin said.

She looked awful eager. Both of them did. Ordinarily that alone would be enough to put him off it, if it was something they wanted that much. But that fence, the cameras. They weren't there for nothing. Nobody spent forty, fifty thousand dollars to protect the wedding silver and the Yule plates.

"Against my better judgment," Naull said.

137

28

Tuesday morning, Welcome did twelve blocks each way on Jackson.

Went to work. Buses packed, his shirt got wrinkled. Eight hours under the fluorescents, longest eight hours of his life. Buses packed on return. Dinner with Grace, burgers at the Hippo on Van Ness.

Wednesday, fifteen blocks each way. Buses packed. Beauregard snotty. Dinner with Grace, late picnic in Golden Gate Park.

Thursday, fifteen blocks and he still felt good. He tried the five blocks from Jackson to Union, down to the bottom of Pacific Heights. Down was easy. Up, it was a killer. But he made it. Work, he got through, he didn't know how. Quarter after five, he couldn't remember a thing he had done all day.

How did people live like this?

Another thing. That morning he learned from Grace that his one-bedroom rented for fifteen hundred a month. A nice place, he liked it. But when Hays's goodwill ran out—if it hadn't already—he'd have to move. He could never swing the rent on thirty-two thousand a year, less taxes.

Thirty-two a year got you nowhere. Taxes, car payments, clothes and food, the telephone—you were treading deep water on thirty-two a year.

When he walked into the building he was doing arithmetic in his head. He almost didn't notice Grace open her door.

"What about dinner?" she said.

"Where?"

"Here," she said.

Welcome was patient. As much as he wanted it, he let her carry it along. It was her call.

If she had any leftover doubts, his patience chased them.

They finished dinner, Welcome knowing what was about to happen, but not pushing it. They stacked the dishes, didn't wash them. Bottle of wine, lights down. He reached and held her. His touch was light but not at all tentative.

He brought her to the bed.

She knew how it would be. He was a quiet man and was comfortable with himself. He could be hurt, but for a good reason he would endure a lot. All this being true, she knew that when he took her she would feel loved, and protected, and wanted.

And she did.

Welcome lay in her bed, looked around her dark room.

He couldn't help it; he kept thinking about Hays. Here, beside her this way, in this bed. You couldn't get away from him. Welcome was here, Grace was here, because of Hays.

Say what you wanted about money, it got things done. It moved people around.

"I want you," he said.

She was drowsy, nuzzling.

"Here I am," she said.

"This is just the start."

"Don't push. Please? We're here, this is tonight, it has to be good enough."

He kissed her. Money moved her in, he thought. Money would move her out.

Hays was on the deck, with the sun rising in front of him over the bay, when Caitlin beeped him from inside. Welcome was on the phone.

"I'm not working anymore," Welcome said. "I can't hack it, it's not for me. I wanted you to know."

"I'm sorry about that," Hays said.

"What about the apartment?" Caitlin said. She was on an extension.

"That's right," Hays said, "I need to put that apartment on a paying basis."

"You mentioned another situation," Welcome said. "Is that for real?"

"It is," Hays said.

"Say no more," Caitlin told him. "We're on our way."

Welcome sat on the front step and waited for them. Keep Hays and Grace apart; keep Caitlin and Grace apart, for that matter. The BMW pulled up and Welcome got in the back. Hays and Caitlin were up front.

They drove over the bridge, into Marin. Some small chat, nothing else. Every couple of minutes Caitlin would half-turn in her seat and slip Welcome a buttery look.

He knew he had seen the look before, but at first he couldn't place it. Then he remembered. The grotto. Him and her.

Hays took the Mount Tamalpais turnoff.

"We want to get into a safe," Caitlin said.

Rich people, Welcome thought.

"I gather it's not your safe," Welcome said.

"That's a fact."

"I don't crack safes."

"You blow up bridges and ammunition dumps," Caitlin said. "*Allegedly.* Are you telling me you can't blow the door off a safe?"

"I guess I could. But I'm not a burglar."

"Who's mentioned burglary?" Hays said.

Caitlin turned full around in the seat. She clamped her eyes on Welcome, ratcheted the look up to full force.

"Make the bomb," Caitlin said, "we'll handle the rest."

"What's in it for me?" Welcome said.

"Friendship," she said. The look was supposed to be soulful, Welcome thought, and back in the grotto it did seem that way. But today it made him want to laugh.

She kept her eyes on him. Hays was driving the car, oblivious.

"That doesn't work anymore," Welcome said. He could have been answering Hays, but he wasn't. He was speaking directly at Caitlin. He wanted her to know how much things could change in a few days.

The look curdled on her face. She swiveled back in her seat.

"Ten percent of what's in the safe," Hays said.

"What would that be?" Welcome said.

"Minimum of a million and a half in jewels and negotiable securities."

In his head Welcome lopped a zero off a million and a half dollars.

Welcome knew that right here, right now, he was stepping into forbidden territory. Hays and Caitlin were outlaws, and he was about to become one, too.

Funny, though, it didn't feel all that different from what he had done so often before. Crossing borders without a passport, being where you were not supposed to be, doing things that would get you in serious trouble if you got caught. He knew all the rules of that little game. He had to admit, a lot of the attraction of Special Ops was in possessing secret knowledge, getting trained and paid and encouraged to do jobs that would put other people in prison for a long time.

This was just another op. Probably less dangerous than most.

Put it that way, he knew how to deal with it. He was right back home.

"I could probably put together something that would get you into a safe."

"I knew you could," Hays said.

Naull was at the amphitheater on Mount Tamalpais, sitting in the top tier. He watched Hays and Caitlin walk in with Welcome, M.

141

"Before we get started," Caitlin said. "Don't utter a word until we get this straight. For security purposes we are not using real names. Mike, this is Ike, Ike, meet Mike, that's good enough."

"Hey, Mike," Naull said.

"I'm Ike," Welcome said. "You're Mike. I think that's how it went." Giving the needle to Hays and Caitlin. This guy was all right.

"I don't think so," Naull said. "I'm Ike, you must be Mike."

"Cut it out," Hays said.

"Mike and Ike," Welcome said. "Can you believe it?"

"Why not Amos and Andy?"

"Mutt and Jeff."

"Curly, Moe, and Larry is more like it."

"Harpo, Groucho, and Chico."

"Manny, Moe, and Jack, the Pep Boys," Naull said.

"*Please,*" Caitlin said.

"I'm trying to place the accent," Welcome said, as if he never heard her.

"Northern Oklahoma."

"How far north?"

"About as far as you can get, little town called Lenapah, northeast of Bartlesville, right up by the Kansas state line."

"Man, I'm from Coffeyville," Welcome said.

"No kidding. Thirty miles up the road. Saturday nights, when we didn't have nothing else to do, we used to drive up and whip y'alls' butts for entertainment."

"Not when I was around," Welcome said.

"That's it, end of old-home week." Hays was shouting. "Forget Mike and Ike, okay? You're Kansas, you're Oklahoma, can you keep that straight?"

"Fine by me," Naull said.

"You want to get into a safe," Welcome said.

"I want to know if it can be done," Naull said.

"It can be done, sure. The way I'd handle it, shear off the locking lug where it seats in the wall, do you follow me?"

"So far," Naull said. Welcome was talking like he had done this before.

"Eliminate the locking mechanism so you can tap the lug arm back out of the way. That's it, you're in."

"You know about this shit?" Caitlin said.

"I took a flaps-and-seals course at Fort Bragg. Locks and such."

The U.S. government, Naull thought. Giving courses in Basic Burglary and Advanced Safecracking. Incredible. Your Tax Dollars at Work.

"I know what you're saying," Naull said, "but I don't know how to do it. You say shear off the locking lug. Like it's as easy as biting the end off a carrot."

"Shaped charge," Welcome said. "Vaporize a hole big enough to stick that carrot in."

"Oh," was all Naull could say.

"Have you ever made one before?" Caitlin said. "That charge thingee?"

"Three, four hundred times."

"What about it, Oklahoma?" she said to Naull. "Are you in?"

"I'm in if Kansas is."

"He's in," Hays said.

"Sounds like a deal to me," Caitlin said.

31

"Let's talk money," Welcome said. He was with Caitlin and Hays in the Mercedes again, headed back to San Francisco.

"Ten percent, we agreed," Hays said.

"I have no idea what's in the safe. I want some kind of guarantee. A flat fee against the percentage, so I know I don't come out of it with nothing. Twenty-five thousand. And six months in the apartment, a paid receipt. It'll give me some time to think about what direction I want to go next. That way I don't rush into something that isn't right for me."

"I can't pay twenty-five thousand," Hays said.

"I think you can," Welcome said. He was feeling cocky. It was childish, but he liked being the one with the answers, the guy everybody else looked to. He didn't know how criminals were supposed to act, but he figured he could pass. He knew how to be tough, hardheaded—he knew how to be threatening, if it came to that.

Funny, Hays and Caitlin had the idea about the safe, but nothing else. They needed him to get into it. They needed Oklahoma to be their burglar. Everybody knew that rich people hired other people to do the shitty jobs they themselves couldn't be bothered with. But farming out your crime, that had to be the ultimate luxury.

How did it feel, to be so dumb and hapless? And to be able to afford it?

"I don't have twenty-five K to throw around," Hays said.

"You ought to know. I'm not going to sit around all night arguing about how much money you have. But that's the price, twenty-five."

"Pay it," Caitlin said. She was talking to Hays. She sounded firm.

"All right," Hays said, "all right, twenty-five."

"Upon delivery."

"All right."

"Anything else?" Hays said.

"For shaped charges I'll need plastic explosive, C-4. You don't walk into a hardware store and buy it. The military uses a lot of it. I happen to have an old battle buddy, he's out of Recon now, he's a platoon sergeant down at Camp Pendleton. He might help. It won't be cheap, though."

"How much?"

"I'd figure on ten thousand."

"Ten!"

"This is serious contraband. He'd be risking Leavenworth, you can't expect him to do it for nothing."

"God, ten. See if you can't get him down to five. It's a lot of money for an enlisted man."

"It ought to be ten."

"Darling," Caitlin said, "stop trying to chisel, it's unbecoming."

"All right."

"And I'll need to borrow one of your cars to go down there. A long trip, I think the Mercedes would be great. Give me room to stretch my leg. I'd fly, but I wouldn't want to check C-4 in the baggage. I couldn't carry it on."

"Fine, fine, the car, overnight."

"I thank you, my bum leg thanks you."

"Twenty-five thousand, ten for the material," Hays said, "ten percent of the proceeds, and a Mercedes to drive. You're a big-league negotiator."

"Know what you've got that the other guy wants, and know how

144

much it's worth. Somebody told me that once, and the more I think about it, the more it makes sense."

They brought Welcome back to the apartment. He had missed his walk this morning. He changed into a sweatsuit and sneakers, and went out and started down Jackson. He was about to cross Divisadero Street, four or five blocks along and going strong, when a car cut sharp in front of him as he stepped off the curb.

It stopped in the crosswalk. A blue Camaro.

"You want a beer?" Oklahoma said.

"They're not like you and me," Naull said. "They think different. They're different inside. Even when they talk. You recognize the words, but the words don't mean the same."

They were in Naull's living room, two cans into their second six-pack of Budweiser. Eight cans into what looked like friendship.

"Zombies," Welcome said. "Like this movie I saw once, when I was a kid. Zombies of the stratosphere, that's them."

"They're no good," Naull said. "They're snakes."

"So long as you know that going in," Welcome said.

"But you're never sure how no-good they can be. You think you've seen it all, then they'll throw you something new. That's what scares me about this proposition. I'm afraid I haven't hit bottom with them yet."

Welcome felt good here. Naull's house felt like home. Welcome couldn't remember ever knowing an ex-con. Naull didn't seem like a criminal, though. He seemed normal. Lot more normal than Hays and Caitlin.

"The money is right," Welcome said. "If it's there."

"Something is there," Naull said.

Million and a half. Naull and Welcome sat with beers in hand and considered it.

You could not ignore it. A million and a half dollars, even the chance of 10 percent, commanded your respectful attention.

"How would you spend it?" Naull said. "Your share?"

"I want to find something to do that doesn't grind me down. I don't want to suck hind tit till the day I die."

"That's not very specific," Naull said.

"It's the best I can do. I'm at loose ends, and it bugs me."

"I want to go home," Naull said. "I've been fighting it, but I keep losing."

"A place gets in you," Welcome said. "You think you're rid of it, but it sneaks up on you."

"I could farm," Naull said. "It's a good living. Do you have any idea how much farm half a million will buy, back home? You got to be talking a thousand acres or more."

"Great money," Welcome said. "If you can get it out of them."

"I need a plan," Naull said.

"Better watch your back," Welcome said.

"I've got a better idea. You watch my back," Naull said, "and I'll watch yours."

Next evening Hays and Caitlin dropped off the Mercedes. The Benz, Hays kept calling it. They also gave him the ten thousand.

Welcome spent the night with Grace. Before they slept she said, "Are you going to tell what this is about?"

"No," he said. "I don't want to get you involved. It's illegal, but it's not especially wrong. Rich people farting around, doing what gets them off, I think that's what it comes down to. And I need the money."

"Not for me."

"Everybody needs money."

"There's a limit to needing it."

"I'm not there yet."

"What do you want so bad?" she said.

"You."

"Me."

"Will you be mine?" he said.

"What's that supposed to mean?"

"You know what it means. Be mine. Nobody else's."

"Please don't push me," she said.

"There you go. See—I still need the money."

"What a way to talk."

"I see the way things are. That's all."

"I don't want to see you hurt," she said.

"I'm just doing what I know how to do," he said.

The Mercedes, what a car. Welcome left San Francisco at daybreak. He caught Interstate 5, pegged the cruise control at seventy, and let the car haul him down the Central Valley. Even with a break every couple of hours to walk around, keep the leg from cramping, he still breezed through Los Angeles around mid-afternoon.

He had an early dinner in San Clemente, and didn't hurry. He drove down I-5 to Oceanside, and into the town. It was a long time since he'd been stationed at Pendleton, but he was sure he could find what he was looking for.

A couple of miles from the post gates. The Fox Hole, a sign in rippling red bulbs and neon. The parking lot had rows of Blazers and Trans-Ams and Wranglers, all with base parking permits and globe-and-anchor stickers on the rear bumpers.

Inside: strobe lights, cloud of cigarette smoke, smell of beer, and music so loud it hurt your ears. Tables and tables full of brush-cut heads, watching a girl on a runway, girl in a G-string twitching her hips.

An unpleasant memory. Something about it made Welcome bleak and unhappy, all the nights he had spent, this bar and a dozen like it.

Now he felt out of place. That was not all bad, he thought.

"Welcome."

Somebody was bellowing his name. Welcome could hardly hear it over the music. In a corner, there, alone at a table, waving his hand. Littlejohn.

He was a couple of years older than Welcome, short and straight. Slim and agile and black. A Sammy Davis Marine.

147

It had been a few years. Back then, if you were his friend, the handshake would be a three-way soul shake, grabbing thumbs and fingers before you settled on a palm clasp.

Now he held the hand out, steady. Welcome shook it once. Still all muscle in the wiry arms. It had been more than a few years, Welcome thought. It had been since Beirut.

Welcome ordered a pitcher to go with the one that was half-finished on the table. They talked for a while, old times and war stories and the First Brigade. Welcome told him about the little bastard in the hole. Littlejohn wanted to know about getting discharged, civilian life. His twenty was up soon, and he wondered whether he ought to take the money and run.

"It's a different world out there," Welcome said. He didn't know how else to put it. A lot of it, he couldn't find the words for. "You can look at it and see it, but you never know until you're in it, you never know how different it is."

"Different good or bad?" Littlejohn said.

"Different. That's all. Good or bad, I guess it depends what you're looking for."

Littlejohn wasn't satisfied, but he changed the subject.

"This ordnance . . ." he said.

"I hope I didn't put you in a bind."

"It's out in the car. Ain't no big thing. But you don't mind my asking."

"I need it for a job," Welcome said.

"Some job."

"One rich guy wants to get into a safe that belongs to another rich guy." Hays had whipped up an alternative story in case Littlejohn asked, something about an insurance scam, blow up a vacant building. But it sounded phony, and the truth felt safe. Littlejohn wasn't going anywhere with it. "I figure, a couple of one-pound shaped charges, shear off the locking lugs."

"That would work," Littlejohn said.

"I said I'd do the devices. The money was right. I needed the work."

"Nobody gets hurt?"

"Nobody gets hurt, I'm not blowing up any airliners or recruiting offices. I just want to make a few bucks."

Littlejohn told Welcome to follow him out to the car. He had a white Pontiac, a Grand Prix. The stuff was in the trunk.

Welcome brought the Mercedes up beside the Grand Prix.

"Damn, boy," Littlejohn said, "it didn't take you long to move up in the world."

"Strictly an overnight loaner."

"Nobody ever loaned me one."

They opened the trunks, the Pontiac and the Mercedes. In Littlejohn's was a wooden crate.

CHARGE, DEMOLITION BLOCK, M I A I

"Because it's you," Littlejohn said. He was hefting the crate out of his car, into the trunk of the Mercedes.

"How many in there?" Welcome said.

"Half full."

Twenty-four blocks to a case. One kilogram per block, two point two pounds.

"More than I need," Welcome said.

"Keep it. Sneaking it in is harder than bringing it out. Oh yeah, blasting caps. I threw in a couple dozen. You didn't say."

"Blasting caps, I forgot. That's the way it is in the world. You don't think about details like blasting caps. You've got other things on your mind."

He closed the trunk.

"Use it well," Littlejohn said.

"This is worth money," Welcome said.

"Keep it."

"It's not my money. There's plenty to go around."

"I could use a set of speakers. New rubber for the car. Make it five hundred."

"Think big," Welcome said.

"Okay, a thousand. Two thousand. What do you want me to say, five thousand dollars?"

"Say it."

"Five thousand. You're not serious."

"In the car," Welcome said.

They sat in the Mercedes. Welcome had some of the money in his pockets, the rest locked in the glove compartment. He counted it out, five thousand, in fifties and hundreds.

"Use it well," Welcome said.

"You're doing all right, I can tell."

"So far so good."

149

"I've been worried, you know, I get out, I'll end up living in a house trailer somewhere, spend all day watching 'Wheel of Fortune.'"

"That could happen," Welcome said. "But you and me, we have skills. There's a market for what we do, if you can find it. Hook up in the right situation, you can make out good."

"I see what you mean," Littlejohn said.

"Go for what you can get. You see it, grab it. If you don't, somebody else will. That's how it works out there."

"I'll keep that in mind," Littlejohn said.

Welcome drove away from Oceanside. His original idea was to find a room for the night, head back in the morning.

But he was thinking about Grace. The Fox Hole had something to do with it, remembering all the nights at the bars. Full of juice and jizz, but hollow in the part of you that fighting did not fill up. Drunk and howling with all the other burr-headed Marines, dogs in a pack sniffing up every female around, knowing that it was dumb, a waste, but doing it anyway. And in the morning, feeling even more hollow, whether you had got lucky made no difference.

When all along, all he wanted was her.

Not even eight o'clock yet. He wasn't tired. The car felt like it could run a hundred years. Be there before she woke up. He turned up I-5, the northbound ramp, and he set the cruise control at seventy-five.

34

"His name is Sonny, she's Marie, their kid is Roy," Welcome said. Grace was driving; he was pointing her through San Pablo, to Naull's house. "Nice little family, good folks. Nothing fancy, though. They're real people."

"You make it sound like I'm too uppity for them."

"Just so you'll know."

"I'm real people, too."

"I didn't say you weren't."

"I was born on the farm. I came here straight out of Hick Central."

"And you've been trying to improve yourself ever since."

It was banter, but with the barb of truth on it. Welcome believed that self-improvement, taken far enough, was another form of flight.

She said nothing. The barb apparently stuck.

He showed her the right turn off San Pablo Avenue, then the left, then the bungalow. She pulled into the curb.

He said, "Tampering with perfection, you can't win, that's all I'm telling you."

"I know what's in me," she said. "It's still the same. I can mess around all I want with the rest, it doesn't change what's inside."

Roy was kicking a football out front. Marie was on the porch, waving hello. Naull was in the backyard, jabbing a fork at a piece of meat on a barbecue grill.

Welcome said, "One other thing. Sonny knows Hays. Kind of the same way I know Hays."

"But don't ask, is that it?"

"If you don't mind. And Hays, see, Hays doesn't know I know Sonny, and it would be just as well if Hays didn't find out. Do you follow me?"

"You'd rather I didn't mention it to Hays."

"Can I trust you?"

Now she was truly frosted. The way she turned on Welcome, he knew he'd gone one line too far.

"You want it in writing?" she said.

Grace didn't need long to understand why Welcome liked them, Marie and Sonny and Roy Boy. Like he said, real people, good folks. That aspect of Welcome wasn't obvious, the folksy side. But it was there, and Sonny and Marie drew it out.

It looked good on him.

She had to admit, too, that he might have been right, wanting to warn her ahead of time. Being single, in San Francisco, you could forget that people still lived this way. Daddies burning chicken on the barbecue, mothers harping on kids to brush their teeth, checking their face and hands for grime before putting them to bed. Kissing them good night.

Women washing the dishes while their men puttered out in the workshop.

Nothing wrong with it. She could do it, she thought, under the right circumstances. Not that she was drawing any conclusions. But it was something to file away.

She was drying the dishes, Marie was washing. From the kitchen window they could see Merle and Sonny, their heads and shoulders, out in the garage.

"He's good with his hands," Marie said. "He can do things."

Grace wondered which of them she meant. Probably didn't matter, she thought. It probably applied to them both.

"Some people would call it faint praise," Marie said, "but I disagree. It isn't just the hands. You have to be able to think a thing through. I always liked that about Sonny. He can make things work. Maybe it's silly, I don't know, but I feel like whatever happens, it'll never be so bad that he can't find a way."

"That's good."

"It helps you sleep nights, let me tell you."

Merle and Sonny were tinkering. She couldn't see what. It was in front of them, out of her sight. They would bend to look at it. The way their heads bobbed, their thoughtful faces, they looked like a couple of birds pecking at a feeder.

"How much do you like Merle?" Marie said.

"I like him quite a bit."

"Is it serious? Now that I've started to pry."

"I don't know. Serious is what you do something about."

"In the service it's different," Marie said. "They live with men, they're with men ninety-nine percent, marriage doesn't have to enter into it. Now he's out, he's on the table, somebody's going to snap him up."

"I don't know. It's too soon to think like that."

"You have no problem finding men. They find you. But the good ones don't come along often. The odds are against it, I don't care who you are. That's the thought for today."

"This is the stuff?" Naull said.

"That's it. Go ahead, tear off the wrapper."

It was a rectangular block, about two by two by twelve, wrapped in plastic. It came from a green canvas satchel that Welcome brought from the Ford out front.

"Use your knife," Welcome said.

"A knife is safe?"

"You can bend it, break it, stick it with a knife, pound it with a hammer—it doesn't mind. You can also mold it into Frosty the Snowman, if that's what turns you on."

Under the wrapper it was a pale white. It looked like bread dough. But it was more solid than that. It felt like clay.

Welcome was removing other items from the satchel. Wooden dowel rods, some Rubbermaid containers for leftover food, half a dozen Budweiser empties, small funnels with the spouts removed.

"You going to make bombs with that?" Naull said.

"I don't make bombs. I'm going to improvise some shaped charges."

"Will they blow up?" Naull said.

"Under the right conditions."

"That's all I want to know."

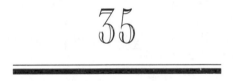

Hays and Caitlin picked him up outside the apartment. The green satchel was slung over his shoulder. They opened to let him in, and Caitlin reached for the satchel.

"You finished it?" Caitlin said. "Let me see, I want to see."

Welcome held on to the satchel. He wouldn't get in the car.

"The money, you don't mind my asking."

"Pay him," Caitlin said. She wanted to get her hands on the satchel.

Hays passed a tin box out the window. Amaretto cookies. Welcome pulled off the top of the tin, saw the cash inside. He replaced the top on the tin, handed the satchel to Caitlin, and climbed into the car.

He said, "Down on Polk, there's a Wells Fargo, I've got a deposit box, let me get rid of this."

"These don't look very impressive," Caitlin said. She was into the satchel already.

"They'll do the job," Welcome said.

Hays said, "What will you do with it, may I ask?"

"The plastic?"

"The money," Hays said.

"I've got plans," Welcome said. "I'm in for the long haul."

The BMW was alone in the parking lot when Naull drove up to the amphitheater on Mount Tam. Hays, Caitlin, and Welcome were sitting near the top steps. The green satchel sat beside Welcome.

"Hey, Kansas," Naull said.

"Oklahoma."

"Guys, please, business only," Hays said.

"Sit down, let me show you," Welcome said. He unzipped the satchel.

It was full of Rubbermaid containers, marked with black ink. Welcome held up one. TC, the lid was marked.

"Thermite charge," Welcome said. "For the transformer. Fifteen-minute fuse, set it and forget it. I put a couple of feet of one-inch PVC pipe into the bottom of the bag. The fuse will make some sparks at night. You want to run it down the pipe, it'll burn, nobody can see it."

"That's smart," Naull said.

"He's a pro," Caitlin said.

"Thank you," Welcome said.

He was holding another container, peeling off the cover to reveal one of the Budweiser cans cushioned in shredded newsprint. He pulled it out. Three pieces of dowel rod, each several inches long, were taped outside the can, making stubby legs. The can was full of C-4.

Welcome sat it, on its legs, on one of the stone benches.

"Shaped charge, the principle is, you form the charge in such a way that you concentrate the explosive energy on a certain point. Like you hold a magnifying glass up to the sun, focus it on a piece of paper, you burn a hole in the paper. That's what the legs are for, get the correct stand-off distance. The funnel gives you a concave shape, a lens. Basically, you sit this thing on a piece of steel where you want to bore a hole. That's what it'll do.

"You've got six charges here. Three different sizes, marked one, two, and three. This is a number three, a heavyweight. This charge will put a three-inch hole in tank armor.

"You don't know anything about the safe, right, so you want to be careful how you use these. A safe has an outer wall, a layer of insulation, and an inner liner. You want to use a number three to eliminate the locking lug, where it seats. You point this down the sidewall, so you shear off the lug but the inner liner will contain the blast. Otherwise, you punch all the way through, you're going to vaporize anything that's inside.

"The little hole on top, that's for the blasting cap. I taped a cap under each cover, see? You put the cap in when you're ready to use it, not before. An electric cap, very simple. You wire the two ends, you find a place to duck behind, you make a circuit with a battery."

"Will a nine-volt do it?" Naull asked.

"A nine-volt is golden," Welcome said.

Naull picked up the charge. The top end of the can was packed to the lip. At the bottom, the explosive formed a conical cavity around one of the funnels.

"I never blew up a bomb before," Naull said. "Hand grenades, that's all."

"Don't think of it as a bomb," Welcome said. "Imagine it's a drill. The loudest, fastest drill you ever used. Get that in your head, you'll be okay."

"I'm impressed."

"You should be," Caitlin said. "He didn't come cheap."

Welcome was putting away the charge, zipping up the satchel. He handed it to Naull.

"You get what you pay for," he said.

36

Welcome told Grace he wanted to take her out to dinner. Nice place, money is no object.

"Money is always an object," she said.

"Not tonight. Tonight I've got it to spend. And more on the way."

She drove him to a Thai restaurant out on Clement Street, nice but not especially expensive.

Over dinner he said, "Would you be mine if I was rich?"

"Money doesn't enter into it," she said.

"Doesn't it?"

"I said it didn't. All right?"

"Whatever you say."

"That's it, that's the truth."

He gave her a minute or so to cool down. She didn't need long.

When she was calm again he said, "But you wouldn't hold it against me."

"Merle," she said, "you're not going to be rich."

"But if I were?"

"No," she said. "I wouldn't hold it against you."

Half an hour later, on the way out, she tugged at his arm.

She said, "Not too rich, okay?"

"I'll try to hold it down," he said.

37

In the afternoon Sonny asked her if she'd fix Swiss steak for dinner. His favorite meal, Swiss steak smothered in onions, mashed potatoes, sautéed green beans. Sure, she said. And chocolate cake, he asked, from scratch? Okay, she said, chocolate cake from scratch, so she ended up spending most of the afternoon in the kitchen.

Which she didn't mind, in and of itself. What bothered her was the restless way he passed the afternoon, staring out windows, slouching on the sofa, finally going out back to vacantly flip a rubber ball against the side of the house. Again and again. *Thump, thump, thump* for an hour or more, his face somber.

Like he was facing the gallows. And if he were, he would want Swiss steak with onions, mashed potatoes, and green beans and chocolate cake, for his last meal.

At dinner he kept telling her how good it was, but he left most of it on his plate. Roy wanted to play Nintendo, but Sonny said no, they ought to do something together. So he and Roy spent a couple of hours building skyscrapers with Legos. Then Sonny took him in for a bath, brought him to bed, tucked him in and kissed him.

Marie was in the living room. She had "Cheers" on the TV. Sonny stood beside the sofa, watched for a minute, and sort of laughed at a couple of jokes. Then he bent close and kissed her on the neck, below one ear . . . right there. It started a shudder that shot down her spine.

"Sonny," she said. "It isn't bedtime."

"It is if we pretend it is."

He took her to the bedroom, and he was soft and slow and careful. He was pretty wonderful. Even if he wasn't all there. Afterward he held her, stroked her. He kept looking at her in the darkness, running his eyes up and down her body.

"You're something," he said. "You're really something."

"We aim to please."

They fell asleep. Sonny nodded off first, and she thought that whatever was grating on him, he had put away until morning, and maybe for good. And she slept, too.

Next thing she knew, the alarm clock was jangling.

He turned it off. Right away he sat on the edge of the bed and started to dress.

"Where are you going?" she said.

"Going to work."

"You're not."

" 'Fraid so."

He was pulling on his pants, buttoning his shirt.

"I wish you wouldn't," she said.

"I wish I didn't have to. But I do."

He jammed his feet into his boots. From the foot of the bed he said, "If this works out the way I want tonight, I'm calling it quits tomorrow."

"What's special about tonight?"

"A good one."

"But not easy."

"The good ones never are."

So that was it. The gallows meal. Doing everything like he might never be able to do it again. Even the last roll in the hay. With his alarm already set.

The clock beside the bed said almost one.

"You promised," she said. "You promised you wouldn't take chances, and now that's what you're doing."

157

He didn't bother to argue, just stood above the bed and looked down at her.

"Goddamn you," she said. Even in the dark she could tell it hurt him, and she reached out, reached up, and he bent to hold her. He held her a good long time, long enough that she thought maybe he'd changed his mind about leaving.

But then he kissed her, and took his arms away, and he walked out of the room.

He went out the back door. She watched him through the bedroom window as he went into the garage and came out with a canvas satchel hanging from one shoulder. He carried it out to the van and put it in the back. He got in, the van started on the first try, and he was gone.

Caitlin had the pistol. She held it out at arm's length and sighted down the barrel.

"Ka-pow," she said, and she jerked it back, like a recoil. She sighted down the barrel again. They were in the BMW, parked off Blithedale Avenue in Mill Valley, waiting for Naull and the van.

"Put it away," Hays said.

Caitlin ignored him.

"Ka-pow."

"Somebody'll see," Hays said. Sitting in a car in Mill Valley and aiming a chrome-plated .45 out the window.

"Nobody'll see it," she said. The streets were quiet. It was almost quarter to two—Naull was supposed to pick them up in a few minutes.

One more time she squinted down the barrel.

She squeezed the trigger.

"Ka-*pow*!" she said.

"Don't do that. It might go off."

"Don't be lame. The hammer isn't cocked, it isn't even loaded. If you want to shoot it, you have to have a bullet in the chamber and the hammer has to be back."

"Have you done this before?"

"Have I ever killed somebody?"

"Fired a gun."

"No," she said.

"You know how?"

"It isn't exactly astrophysics," she said.

"But do you know?"

"Yes," she said. "I know how."

"You know how to load it?"

She touched a button on the side of the pistol. A metal ammunition clip popped out. She shoved it back in.

"Insert the clip. Pull back the slide." She was doing it as she said it. "When you let go, it loads one in the chamber and cocks the hammer."

The slide snapped back.

"Just like in the movies," she said. "Or if there's one in the chamber already, you can cock the hammer with your thumb."

She pointed it at Hays's face.

"Then aim it at something you don't like."

"Put it down," Hays said.

"Pull the trigger and blow the shit out of it."

"Put it down," Hays said.

She slowly lowered the pistol.

"Is the safety on?" Hays said. "Don't forget the safety."

"All of a sudden you're an expert," she said. "Maybe you ought to do him."

She put the gun between them on the seat. Hays looked at it but didn't make a move.

She picked it up again.

"I thought not," she said.

She straightened her arms and sighted down the barrel.

"Ka-*pow*!" she said.

Naull picked them up in Mill Valley, then took 101 up to San Rafael and the county road over toward the ocean. They were on the west side of the coastal hills when they hit fog. Thick, misty fog—Naull was counting on it.

Hays and Caitlin changed into their black jumpsuits. Naull steered through the fog, too busy to look back when he heard noisy, exaggerated breathing in the back. Sounded like somebody was in labor.

"What's that?" he said. "What's going on?"

"Deep-breathing exercises," Hays said. Caitlin kept drawing in and huffing out.

"What does that do for you?" Naull said. He wanted to hear this.

"It helps you concentrate," Hays said. "It clarifies."

"Clarifies," Naull said. "Clarifies what?"

"Aims, needs, desires."

"It centers," Caitlin said at the end of a long exhale.

"Maybe I ought to try that. Getting centered."

"You should but you won't," Caitlin said. "The ones who need it most never do."

Fuck you very much, Naull wanted to say. But he kept silent, and steered through the fog. He reminded himself that if it went right tonight, he'd never have to see them again.

Yeah. That was better. The idea of just kissing them off—it made him feel good. Clarified and centered.

The Larkspur Road intersection and the Blue Goose sign swung past on the right. Naull pulled off to the side. He got out and took a tool kit with him from the foot well of the front passenger seat. Hays and Caitlin stayed in the truck. Anything that might involve screwdrivers and wrenches was beyond their interest.

Naull started walking toward where the telephone junction box ought to be. The old line about fog so thick you couldn't see your hand at the end of your arm—it was almost true tonight. He knew about where the box should be, but he didn't see it until he almost stumbled on it.

It was a muted lime green, a few inches wide and a couple of feet high. PacTel decal on the front. Naull knelt close. The face plate was fastened with a couple of hex-head screws. Naull tried a seven-sixteenths socket, and it fit. He ratcheted out the screws and pulled away the plate. Inside was a nest of thin wires, some in bundles, various colors, making intricate connections on a board. Naull would cut just one, if he knew the right one. But who could tell?

He got a pair of wire cutters and snipped the wires in bunches. Took him about ten seconds to do them all, and he replaced the plate.

Back in the truck. He pulled out onto the asphalt again and started following the curve of the yellow dividing lines, a right and a left. When the second curve straightened, he slowed and pulled across onto the little gravel turnout at the base of the power pole.

He cut the lights and turned off the engine, went around and opened the back doors of the van. He put on a headlamp with a battery pack that slipped into his pocket.

"Hey, Mr. Miner," Hays said. "The Miner Forty-niner."

"Right," Naull said.

"You load sixteen tons, huh?"

Actually it was a coon hunter's lamp. You hunt coons at night, you want light and you want your hands free while you run after your dogs. Naull had done some coon hunting in his time. But he wasn't going to admit it. The fun they'd have with that. He buckled on the climbing cleats and tightened the lineman's harness and slung the canvas satchel over one shoulder. He walked over to the pole, snapped the wide leather climbing strap around the wood, and started up. He leaned away and let his legs and the strap take his weight.

He went up. He had practiced this on the power pole in front of the bungalow, looking like a fool in front of Marie and half the neighborhood. Here was easier. Here it was just Hays and Caitlin, and he didn't give a shit what they thought about him.

The wires were humming. He could feel it in the pole, up through his spikes.

He looked up and saw nothing but misty white. He raked himself up another foot or so and looked up again, and there was the transformer, right in his face.

He inched up closer. The transformer was a metal canister. The feed from the high-voltage trunk came in on top. Out one side came the 220, two 110-volt wires and a ground cable bound in a single black triplex cable that pointed through the fog in the direction of the woods and the house.

Naull crabbed sideways and came up beside the transformer. He kept his movements small and careful, aware that thousands of volts—what would it be? Ten thousand? Fifteen? Plenty, anyway—were very much within reach.

He reached in the satchel and came out with Welcome's thermite charge. It was a cardboard Bon Ami can with the top cut off, weighed four or five pounds. The fuse cord trailed out of the top, about a foot and a half long. Inside the can he could see a top layer of Welcome's fire fudge, which Welcome said was a mixture of sugar and potassium chlorate. It looked like the white glaze on a Pop-Tart. The fuse ignited the fire fudge, was the idea. The fire fudge ignited the subigniter beneath it. The subigniter ignited the thermite on the bottom.

Naull placed the Bon Ami can on top of the transformer. The fuse cord trailed down. Naull didn't think there was much chance of anybody spotting it as it burned. He hadn't seen another car since San Rafael. And this fog. But what the hell, Welcome had him all set up. Naull took out the piece of half-inch plastic pipe, about as long as his forearm. He pushed the fuse cord through until about half an inch peeked out at the end. Then he duct-taped the pipe to the side of the transformer.

He looked at everything. Looked good. He took out a Bic lighter.

Right away, touching the Bic, he wanted a cigarette. He wanted one bad. Welcome had told him it would be all right to smoke around the explosives, no problem. But it made him nervous to think of puffing on a Camel while he worked with thermite and fire fudge and C-4–shaped charges, so he left the Camels at home. Now he was sorry he had.

He rasped the lighter and held the flame at the end of the fuse, and when the cord started to sizzle and glow, he came down the pole fast. He put away the harness and the cleats, kept the headlamp, and sat the satchel on the seat beside him. He had about fifteen minutes of fuse, and he didn't want to waste any of it. When the thermite caught, it would fume for a few seconds. Then it would flare and burn white hot. It would burn through the cover of the transformer, drop into the innards—the sparks would fly!—and keep on burning. This fist-sized blob of liquid burning metal would sizzle through the transformer and fall to earth approximately where the van was parked right now. Be a hell of a show, but he'd rather miss it, thanks.

Back inside, Caitlin was doing the breathing number again, but faster, shallower. Naull drove back onto the highway for a couple hundred yards, then pulled back onto the shoulder and crawled forward until he stopped beside the gap in the brush.

He said, "Okay. Let's do it to it," and he got out again. He gave Hays the satchel, and went around back for the twin tanks of the cutting torch. They sat in a rack that he hefted onto his back. Even the minitanks were heavy.

He turned on the headlamp and started picking his way through the brush, then into the trees. His clothes quickly got soaked from the mist on the leaves. The beam of the lamp poked a few feet ahead and then seemed to get swallowed up.

For once Caitlin had nothing to say. Naull wondered what was wrong with her.

They kept walking through the trees and almost walked into the steel fence. Naull put the tanks down and took the satchel from Hays. He got out the torch head and screwed it into the tanks, put on a pair of welder's glasses, pulled a heavy rawhide glove over his right hand, dug out a welder's sparking tool. All this came out of the satchel. He opened the valves on the tanks, and there was a throaty hiss when he turned the petcock on the torch head. He held the sparker in that invisible stream of gas near the mouth of the torch.

The sparker was like a long wire nutcracker, with a striking plate at the end. He pressed it once, and the plate scratched a spark, and the flame came on with a good healthy thump. It was cobalt blue with a yellow rim. Naull slowly turned the valve on the oxygen until the yellow disappeared.

The upright shafts of the fence were about half an inch thick, set in longitudinal steel braces. Naull figured he would cut out two of the shafts. That would give them a couple of feet to slip through.

He laid the tip of the blue flame against the first shaft, where it joined the upper brace. In a few seconds the shaft under the flame turned orange, then cherry red. Then it started jumping away in a spray of molten flecks. It was fair-quality steel, it didn't just dissolve, but it didn't stand up to the torch, either. Within half a minute Naull had cut a smooth gap all the way through.

Then he started in on the bottom, and in another half a minute the shaft was teetering and falling to the wet turf. Up to the top of the next one, down at the bottom, and the second shaft clanged down on top of the first.

Naull shut off the flame at the torch head and turned off the valves of the two tanks. He put away the sparker and the welding glasses and the glove.

Now wait for the transformer. Couldn't be long.

Hays said, "Mister Fix-It. The ultimate handyman."

You could say that in a way that would sound friendly, even respectful. But from Hays it came out an insult.

"That's right," Naull said. "I know what I'm doing."

"Where would we ever be without you?"

"You'd be nowhere."

"Somehow I think we'd make out," Hays said.

Naull was wondering whether he ought to take him on after this was over. Get him down in the wet grass, go at it. Minute or two would be all that you'd need. Naull couldn't remember the last time he threw a punch. He *liked* people. Even in Vacaville he got along with almost everybody. But this smart-ass little prick, Naull wanted to grind his face in the mud.

"Hey, pal," Naull said, "your kind would be shit out of luck without my kind. Think you can build a house out of balance sheets? Without us you'd be living in a tree and eating grubs for dinner. But with style, no doubt."

Finally Caitlin jumped in.

"Ralph," she said. "All that time you spend getting your fingernails dirty, aren't you afraid you'll miss something important?"

"I don't miss much," Naull said.

"You sure of that?" she said, in a way that made Naull nervous. He wondered what she was getting at.

Then the charge kicked in beyond the trees.

The sky lit up behind them, a silent bloom of white light that made the fog glow. That would be the thermite getting hot. It flared and ebbed, and the transformer blew with another surge of light and a muffled *whump.*

Quickly the light fell off to almost nothing, a faint creamy smudge above the trees. Naull watched it die. He held the satchel but didn't pick it up. All of a sudden he felt immensely depressed about having to go through the fence with Hays and Caitlin, about being a part of this with them, about ever letting them draw him in. He was surprised, how strong he felt about it.

"Well come on, come on, let's *go,*" Caitlin said.

It was depressing, okay, but here he was. And for the last time.

He stood, he poked the satchel through the opening in the fence. He turned sideways and pushed himself through to the other side.

Evan was clicking right along when the power went out. At the time, all the lights in the room were on. His video cam was set on top of a tripod, and the reels were turning on the cassette in the recorder.

Evan was pumping away. He could sure do that, Kristal Starr thought. Keep at it from start to finish of a two-hour tape, never draw a deep breath. Take the tape out, pop in a new one, pick right up again. Most girls at the escort service wouldn't go with him a second time. Who wanted to run a marathon? An Olympic quarter-miler was what you looked for, quick lap of the track in under a minute.

Kristal didn't care. She could zone out so deep, it was like an out-of-body experience. Float above the bed watching some unknown slut thrash and moan as if she really meant it. And Ruark wasn't as bad as some—he had his points. He paid the cab fare both ways from San Francisco, and always added a hundred-dollar tip to the four hundred that the service billed for an all-nighter. He was clean, he didn't bitch when you pulled a Trojan-Enz out of your purse, and he wasn't fancy or perverted (if you don't count the camera and recorder, and she didn't).

He had one quirk. His first time with Kristal, he wanted to know her real name. She almost told him the truth, that her real name was Kristal Starr. A hookshop handle if there ever was one. Talk about being born to the game. But she thought quick and said, Brenda Jo Sperling. It was the name of her best friend in high school. *Brenda Jo*—Evan liked that. When he got near the end, finally, he would clutch her and start yelling it. *Brenda Jo, yes, Brenda baby yes, Brenda Brenda Brenda Jo.*

Whatever worked was okay with her. It was his five hundred and cab fare. She didn't understand why anybody would want to get it on for two hours straight, much less watch a tape of it. But she knew that you could go dippy trying to figure the logic of lust.

When the power went, Ruark was going at it regular as an oarsman. She herself was sighing deeply and compiling a grocery list. The lights dimmed, came on hard, then blacked out.

The darkness seemed final.

At first Evan didn't seem to notice. He zones out too, Kristal thought. Then he broke his rhythm, slowed, and stopped. It was like a toy soldier winding down. Apparently it wasn't the same without a recorder rolling.

He padded over to the bathroom, took a leak.

In the meantime she went to the nearest window and saw that the fog had come in.

Evan finished in the bathroom, came back and sat on the edge of the bed.

He picked up a telephone receiver on the nightstand. Put it to his ear, listened, clicked the button a couple of times. He went over to the window and parted the blinds. He saw the fog.

He didn't like it. He went to the door, stopped, came back to the nightstand. He opened it and took out a flashlight. And a revolver.

He said, "Stay here." He was different now. He was alert, taut. He went naked out the door, down the stairs without a sound.

Naull thought there was something strange after they walked out of the woods, crossing the wet grass to the house. Caitlin bolted ahead of him and went up on the front porch. She told Hays to come, too. Hays followed her and turned off his flashlight when he got to the front porch.

Something's happening, Naull thought. He thought he ought to turn around and get out now. Except if he did, whatever it was, it would be totally out of his control.

Cut the light, Caitlin said to Naull. Naull thought he wasn't going to do anything she told him to do; this was his job. Take charge. But at that moment he saw the flashlight inside, moving around the room.

Naull hit his switch quick.

Caitlin flattened out against the side of the house and edged right up to the front door. It looked like something out of a TV cop show, and somehow Naull knew that's where she got it. A teenage Caitlin seeing Angie Dickinson do the same thing in "Police Woman," salting it away all these years until she finally had the chance to use it.

Hays stood on the other side of the door. Caitlin was holding . . . no. No. Not a pistol? Yes. An automatic. Her with a gun, Jesus, Naull could feel things getting way out of hand.

A lock turned on the door. The doorknob squeaked, and the door swung in. Somebody with a flashlight took one step out on the porch. Pale and naked, a plucked chicken.

Caitlin stuck the automatic in his ear and said, "Evan. I don't want any problems, I don't want any kung fu shit. Drop the Goddamn gun or I drop you."

"That would be Caitlin," he said. Whoever he was, Evan knew her.

"The gun," Caitlin said.

A pause while Evan considered the situation.

"Bitch. Worthless, crazy bitch," Evan said. He knew her, all right. "Hays, shit, my man, what are you *doing* here?"

"The gun," Caitlin said. A few more beats, and something thumped down on the boards of the porch.

"Get it," Caitlin said to Hays, and Hays bent down to pick up the other pistol. "Let's all go in, it's chilly out here, don't you think, Evan?"

Like she'd been rehearsing it for weeks.

And Naull realized, she probably had.

Kristal Starr listened for a while, and heard nothing. She wondered what Evan was doing. Naked, with a revolver.

Downstairs—was that a door opening? Front door? She heard a voice. Evan. No, *voices.* Another man, and a woman, too.

Kristal made her way across the dark room, to the foot of the stairs outside. From here you could see most of the living room. Or you could when you had light.

There was movement. People were coming in the front door, two bright spots from flashlights jiggling ahead of them. She could make out a man and a woman, plus Evan. They stood inside the front door. The second man was holding another flashlight. He held it straight into Evan's eyes. Evan held his own light down to the floor.

The lights were bright in the darkness, but they shone only in certain spots. You could see Evan's face bright and white, you could see where Evan's flash pointed at the ratty carpet. Everything else was dim outline.

"Come on in, Ralph," the woman said. "Don't be bashful."

Apparently Ralph didn't move.

"Ralph, don't you know? You're in, Ralph. You're in all the way now."

This struck Kristal as a crazy thing to say. Ralph was still outside.

"You can't stop it," the woman said, out the door to him. "You can walk away, that's up to you. But it doesn't get you anywhere. You can't stop us, and you're still in up to your eyebrows. We go, you go."

She told the second guy, the one with her, to take Evan's flashlight, and he did. He gave it to the woman; she held it in Evan's face. That made two in Evan's eyes. And now Ralph was coming in, standing in the doorway.

"Ralph, I want you to meet Evan," the woman said. "Evan, this is Ralph."

She swung her light over on Ralph, and Kristal got a quick hit of a fellow who—except for the lamp around his head—looked like he might have showed up to fix the furnace.

"Ralph," the woman said, "this has nothing to do with you. I suggest you go get down there and do your thing, fast, 'cause we won't be staying for dinner."

Ralph said, "Evan, I don't suppose you'd want to give me the combination to the box?"

Evan, at first without an answer, finally said, "Up yours, Ralph."

"Goddamn you assholes," Ralph said. But he turned on his head-light, and the spot bounced as he looked around. He found the door to the kitchen and went through.

"You're completely whacked," Evan said.

"Hey, coming from you . . ." said the second man.

The woman said, "Back up. Turn around. Hands on the wall."

Evan did what she said. When he turned, Kristal noticed that he didn't have a gun anymore.

Somebody did, though. She heard a sound.

Certain things, when you heard them, you knew what they were even if it was the first time. Like the sound of a rattlesnake, a rattlesnake getting mad. Even in the darkness, you knew what it was.

Kristal heard a sound like that, down in the living room. Crisp, mechanical, certain.

The sound that came up to Kristal from the living room was the unmistakable sound of a pistol being cocked.

41

Naull went down the basement stairs. He was out of choices. Caitlin had it right, she had him dead on. Whatever he did, he was in.

He tried to make sense of it, grasp what was going on.

Evan had seen him. Evan had seen them, too.

Evan could name them. And they knew that, going in. They knew he'd be here.

Naull stepped down into the basement. He realized that once he had told them yes—and it might go as far back as Ghirardelli Square—nothing he did made any difference. They would have things their way. They had wanted Evan to be here. Knowing that he could name them.

Evan was a dead man.

Naull went over to the washing machine and pushed it aside. He looked down and the burnished bright finish of the safe shone back at him. It gave him a thrill, even with all the rest that was happening.

He got closer to look at it. He thought about crazy Caitlin with the gun upstairs, pointing it at naked Evan who had to be a dead man.

Naull told himself that killing wasn't what he signed on for, it wasn't what he wanted; he would stop it if he could. But he could do nothing about it. He couldn't stop what was started.

He reached inside his jacket, to the pocket of his shirt. Where he usually kept his Camels, an automatic move.

The pocket was empty. He went through all his pockets, looking for anything, a butt, a pinch of loose tobacco he could stick in his cheek.

Nothing.

He made himself concentrate on the safe. Dial here, handle here. The hinge would be to the left side, so the locking lugs would be on the right, recessed into the frame.

Just for the hell of it he checked the handle.

Nope.

Okay, the lugs. If there was only one, it would be off to the side, about parallel with the handle. Try that first.

Welcome's Rubbermaid containers were in the bottom of the satchel. Naull found a Three and a reel of two-strand bell wire. He opened the Rubbermaid, took out the charge. The ends of the wire were already stripped. He twisted them together with the end of the blasting cap.

He stood the charge on its dowel legs, near the right edge of the safe, about parallel to the handle. Upstairs he heard nothing. No gunshots. He wondered what that meant.

He pulled wire off the reel, all the way across the basement. The stairs, near the bottom, made a ninety-degree turn around a concrete retaining wall. Naull took shelter around that corner. He sat on the steps, cut the wire, stripped the ends. He fished out a nine-volt battery and connected one of the two ends to the negative.

The battery was in his left hand. The other wire was in his right. He crouched lower behind the wall and touched the bare wire to the second terminal.

She wasn't ready to do it. Not right away. Hays could tell. What she really wanted was to *talk* about it for a long time. Evan, no dummy, picked up on this.

"I want to ask you a question," he said. He was spread-eagled with his hands against the wall, leaning forward, legs spread, talking over his shoulder. He was several feet from a corner of the room. To his left, a few feet away, was a large bay window that on clear days offered a view of green lawn and an orchard. He said, "You have to tell me. Come on, hell, you owe me this much."

"Sure, sure," Caitlin said. "What do you want to know?"

"What's going on here?"

"That's it? God. Is that the best you can do? *What's going on here?* That's lame. That's unworthy of you, Evan. No shit, I expected better. I give you one last question, you sound like some old feeb watching a couple of punks rip off his Social Security check."

"What would you suggest?"

"It doesn't matter anyway," Hays said.

"Shut up!" she said to Hays. To Ruark she said, "A much more intelligent, a much more *perceptive* question might be, 'How do you'— meaning me—'find yourself in such an extreme, such an arcane, situation?' That would be a good one."

"You're right," Ruark said. "That is better."

"And the answer would be, I have never taken the well-trodden path. Never. I have never shied away from the dark or the forbidden. Above all I have *never* feared to confront the extreme ramifications of my choices. Some time ago I took a path, I followed my inclination, my intuition and instinct, and I have followed it as far as it would take me. And that is here. The extreme fucking here and now. I won't say that this is the last station on the journey, far from it, but as of tonight I have entered some pretty exotic territory."

"That's true," Ruark said.

"You might also ask, 'Why me?'—meaning you."

Kill him if that's what you want, Hays wanted to yell. He wished it were finished. Waiting didn't make it any easier—not for him.

"And the answer is," she said, "that you're out there, Evan. You're like this juicy apple at the edge of the limb, hanging over the wrong side of the fence, and you can't be small, you can't be insignificant, no, not you, you've got to be special. You're out there asking for somebody to take you off, *demand*—"

The blast was like a huge hand coming up from the basement, slamming into the floor. It shook them and the house and everything in it. It shattered windows and shot lightning-bolt fissures up and down the old plaster walls. For an amazing slice of a second the carpet got elastic under Hays's feet, and he felt it try to launch him.

He kept his balance. Caitlin didn't. It dumped her. Ruark went to his knees. When he looked around, Caitlin was getting up and had the automatic pointed at him again.

The walls were still up, the roof was still over their heads. But when Hays swung the light around, everything in the room seemed slightly ajar.

"Goddamn," she said. "We have to get on the stick here. We have to get *focused.*" She was jabbing the automatic toward Ruark. "Hays, honey, go down there and tell him to cut out that shit. Enough. Couple minutes, we're out of here."

So she was going to do it after all, Hays thought. He stuck Ruark's pistol in his waistband and went through the kitchen, down the stairs. He saw the battery, and followed the bell wire across the basement to where Naull was kneeling at the safe.

The air was thick with dust and particles, like a fish tank when the water is stirred.

"You almost blew us up," Hays said.

"Air pressure. You get a concussion like that in a confined space, you're going to move some air."

Hays looked around. The basement was not in bad shape, not what he would've expected. It looked as if anything that could move had been picked up and put down again slightly out of place. The skirts of the washer and dryer were dented, scorched. But that was all.

"Well, don't do it again. Come on up. We're leaving."

"Is that right?" Naull looked at the floor overhead. Ruark would be standing right about there.

"Don't worry about him," Hays said. "It's out of your hands. Let's go."

"One more," Naull said. "Almost through—look."

In the door of the safe, near the edge, was a hole about an inch across, three or four inches deep.

"A one-lug model," Naull said. "I almost got it—see? One more, a light charge, vaporize the rest of that lug out, that's all."

What would it look like, Hays thought, if they left with the job nearly done? It would look like they really didn't care about getting into the safe. That wasn't what they wanted.

"Will it take long?" Hays said.

"Half a minute, if you let me stop talking."

"Don't blow us up," Hays said.

"It'll be a small one," Naull said. "Nothing to it."

"Fast," Hays said, and he turned and left. He went up the stairs, expecting to hear the shot, come up and find it all finished. But when he got to the living room, Ruark was still spread-eagled against the wall. Caitlin was pacing behind him—stalking—panting again, waving the automatic.

Come on.

"Are we going to do this?" Hays said.

"Yes," she said. "Yes, we are going to do this, yes. I don't know how, is the only thing. I should've thought about it, well I thought about it but I didn't have an answer, I thought I'd get inspired when the situation presented itself."

"Point the gun at him and pull the trigger, how's that for inspiration?"

"You don't get it. You have no sense of these things. It has to be done right. I don't want it to be banal. I want to do it with *panache*."

Downstairs Naull's charge blew, but this time it was only thunder-clap loud, and the house's shudder was almost imaginary.

"I thought I told him—"

"Last one. He wanted one more."

"That's all."

"Why not? Long as we keep screwing around—"

Ruark was standing straight, turning, putting his back to the wall. He said, "We can work this out."

"Turn around." Caitlin leveled the automatic at him.

"You think you're beyond the point of no return," Ruark said. "But you're not. Look, what have we got so far? Few broken windows. Who cares? No blood, no foul."

"Turn your ass around."

"No," Hays said. His voice was urgent. "Shoot him like that."

"Banal, hackneyed—"

"Talk to me," Ruark said.

Hays said, "*Shoot him.* I just thought. It has to be like he's surprised. Right? He comes down, he runs into a burglar, he's surprised. If you shoot him in the back while he stands against the wall, that's not realistic. That's suspicious."

Ruark caught on fast, while Caitlin was still thinking about it. He turned to the wall. He bent his knees. He squatted. He wrapped his arms around his head and held his head between his knees.

"Like this?" Ruark said. "Go on, put one in me now. See how realistic it looks."

Down in the basement Naull was pounding away, a blacksmith's sound, the ring of a hammer, steel on steel.

"Damn it," Caitlin said. "It's getting all fucked up. I wanted it to be right."

The ringing stopped down below.

"To really make it look good, you should have done it right away, out by the front door. That would have been realistic."

"Good idea," Ruark said from his tangled crouch. "You want to try it now? You want to try dragging me to the front door? Idiots."

Right then Caitlin lost it.

"Shit, this is the end, I don't care, I don't *care*"—she was suddenly screeching, wild—"I'm killing him."

"All right."

"Kill the fucker, that's what I came here to do."

She started toward Ruark.

"Not too close," Hays said. "Powder burns, it wouldn't look right."

"Fucking powder burns, to hell with them, I don't care."

She stopped a couple of paces away. She straightened her right arm, the pistol in her hand, she pointed it at his head.

Hays thought the house seemed to hold its breath. Or maybe that was just him, his heart suspended, waiting.

She said, "Ready to die?"

Her finger squeezed the trigger.

Nothing happened.

She squeezed the trigger again. Hays, moving his light to the gun, could see muscles tense in her wrist.

Nothing.

Hays said, "Dummy, the safety."

Ruark sprang from his crouch. On his feet, he looked once at them, at Caitlin fanning her thumb near the safety and Hays with his free hand going for the pistol at his waist. Ruark leaped and kicked, caught Caitlin on the wrist of her extended hand, and the gun cartwheeled into the darkness.

Hays had his hand on the gun. He was four, five steps away.

The bay window was right beside Ruark. It was broken now, but big wedges of glass still stuck in the frame.

Hays had the pistol out.

Ruark took a running step and covered his face and leaped at the window. Caitlin scrambled for her automatic. Hays fired and Ruark dove through the shards and kept going.

He disappeared.

Hays pulled the trigger and kept on pulling, firing wild, the gunshots insanely loud, clattering inside the house. Finally he clicked on empty chambers, and he ran to the window.

Ruark had slipped, and for a moment Hays thought he was down. But then he got up and kept running, his bare ass disappearing into the fog. Caitlin was at Hays's shoulder now, with the automatic, and she snapped off a couple of booming shots into the fog.

Ruark's bare feet pounded outside, the sound diminishing as he ran.

"This is great," Hays said. "This is just super."

"I don't want to hear it."

"We are completely fucked." Hays wasn't hysterical, but he thought that maybe he ought to be. He was considering Ruark, remembering incidents over the years, how Ruark had reacted in certain situations, a sudden cascade of recollection.

"Shut up, shut up, I do not want to hear it."

Ruark could be a cold mother. He could cut you off at the knees. Hays supposed that he had always known this about Ruark, but until now it never seemed crucial.

"We are in huge trouble," Hays said.

"Shut up or I'll kill you," she said. "I will."

Naull came through the kitchen, carrying his satchel. He stood in the doorway. The beam of his headlamp jabbed into corners and swept around the floor. Looking for Ruark.

"He isn't here," Hays said. "He got away."

"Outside?" Fog was spilling through the window. "Never find him."

"Thanks," Caitlin said. She put the gun into a pocket of her jumpsuit. "We appreciate that."

"Is there a reason why we're standing around here?" Hays said. "Waiting for trouble to show up?"

"We don't have to wait for it," Naull said. "It'll be waiting for us. I hope you all are ready for a knock on the door in the next couple hours. Dozen or so boys in blue. Be about as long as it takes your friend to get to a phone, dial nine-one-one, and say your names. That's a good one, doing somebody who knows you, that's brilliant. Sure do wish you'd checked with me on that one."

"*Don't,*" Caitlin said.

"Let's move on," Hays said, "get going, we'll take it from there."

"Whatever you want. I guess you all are in charge."

Outside the fog was swirling. They walked into the woods, along the fence until they found the gap and slid through.

Hays kept thinking about Ruark. It occurred to him that he didn't know Ruark very well, considering what they had done together, what they had been. But what Hays did know made him uneasy. He could imagine the anger, the fury, that would have been in Ruark as he crouched on the floor to save his life.

He got a stray thought: he wondered whether calling the police would be enough for Ruark. Quirky Ruark—would he be satisfied to let the law take care of it?

Come on. What more could he do?

They reached the van. Naull put the gas tanks and his tools in back, and the satchel up front. Hays and Caitlin got into the second row of seats, behind Naull.

Naull drove through the fog. Hays kept thinking about Ruark. He kept seeing Caitlin's finger tighten on the trigger, and hearing the silence in the house.

Then, like it was an afterthought—which it was—Caitlin said, "Ralphie boy. What about the safe?"

"What about it?" Naull said.

"What'd you take?"

"Nothing," Naull said.

"Hold on," Hays said. "I went down, you told me you needed one more shot to get in."

"I did. I got in. There wasn't nothing in there."

"Nothing?" Caitlin said.

"A few papers."

It sat out there for a few seconds, the idea that Ruark would have a safe hidden in his basement for the protection of a few papers.

Hays reached over the seat. He wanted the satchel. Naull went for it too, and Caitlin was out with the gun, quick, cocking it, putting it to Naull's head.

"Yeah, oh yeah," she said, "that's great, fucking hick, just give me a reason, I'm ready."

Her voice had that wild edge that made you pay attention. Naull let go of the satchel, and Hays pulled it into his lap.

Hays put it on the seat between them. He unzipped it and started to go through the jumble. Caitlin held a flashlight and peered in with him. Tools, goggles, gloves. The explosives—Hays opened every Rubbermaid box and looked in.

Nothing.

Caitlin put the gun to Naull's head again.

"Pull over," she said, and he did.

"Out," she said. Naull got out of the truck and stood in the gravel beside the road.

"Search him," she said to Hays, and Hays started to pat him down, unzipping his jacket to feel his chest and his back, down his legs, pulling up the trouser cuffs to check inside his boots.

Nothing.

"Shit," she said.

"You want to get going," Naull said, "or would you rather wait to watch the cops go by?"

They climbed back into the van and drove out of the fog.

As usual they made Naull drop them a block away from the Bimmer. They were getting out when Naull said, "If I was you, I'd put together all the money I could between now and about noon. You'd have about half a day. After that, you'll have to figure they're watching your accounts. I'd leave the state and start over someplace else. You don't know much about being on the run, but that's your best shot. Ordinarily I wouldn't give a shit what happened. But like you said. They find you, they find me."

"Fucking-A right," Caitlin said.

"So my advice is, get the hell out of Dodge City soon as you can."

Hays was already thinking about it. He was telling himself that they could put together maybe thirty thousand when the banks opened. Unfortunately, most of his money was at work here and there, real estate, equipment leases. He could get maybe another seventy thousand if he closed out his brokerage accounts. That would be a risk. He couldn't get the checks until the end of the day.

Sell the cars at a discount, some broker—take a big loss.

In the end, within a couple of days, they might have three hundred and fifty thousand to run away on. Tops, four hundred thousand.

The way they lived, spent money, it was nothing. That would stop. Have to cut way down on spending. Have to live like real people.

They would buy a small business. Settle down, low profile. He could see it now. He and Caitlin running a Subway shop or a Kwik-Print franchise in Real America. Living in a three-bedroom tract home, driving a used Buick . . .

He opened the door of the van and stepped out into the street. Caitlin got out behind him, and Hays was about to close the door when Naull said, "Hey, guys?"

"Yeah?" Hays said.

"You ain't just two of the creepiest mothers I ever met. You're two of the dumbest, too."

Tires squealed, the van shot away with the door still open. It was gone, certainly out of earshot, before Caitlin could answer. She stood beside Hays on the sidewalk, fumbling for the automatic, sputtering, for once denied the last word.

Kristal Starr hid for a while in a bedroom closet. At first she was at the top of the stairs, wondering what she ought to do. They were going to kill Evan, and she thought she ought to do something. Not that she owed him, but it did seem awful cold, shooting somebody, and first *talking* about it.

Then there was the big blast. It chased her into the closet. She didn't know what they were doing, but she wanted no part of it.

She heard the smaller boom, she heard the gunshots. Afterward she caught a short conversation downstairs, the sound of it, but not the exact words, two men and a woman.

Then silence. And darkness. Was she going to wait up here all night?

She tried it for a few minutes with the closet door open. The house sounded empty. She put on her clothes and waited at the top of the stairs. Nothing moved except her.

She went down into the living room. Place was a mess. She went around the room, he must be dead. But all she found was broken glass and raw fog pouring through the windows.

At the window—something moving.

"Brenda Jo," it whispered. Evan! "Anybody here?"

"No . . . don't think so . . . no."

He said he'd come around the front, and she met him at the door. There was just enough moonlight, she could see what a mess he was. Bloody face, blood in a dark stream along his right arm, making a *pat pat* sound where it dripped onto the floor.

He was ticked off, no mistake, but trying not to show it.

She said, "Oh my God."

"I'm all right," he said. He went into the kitchen and got a couple of candles, put them in saucers. They seemed bright when he lit them. In the light Evan looked like one of the living dead. There had to be six or seven cuts that she could see, all of them weeping blood. But none of them were gushing, she noticed. He might not be in such bad shape if he stopped the bleeding.

She thought that's what he'd do first, at least get the blood stopped. But he took one of the candles, told her to stay where she was, and he went downstairs, into the basement.

He wasn't down long. When he came back he was even more p.o.'ed than before, and trying even harder not to show it. He was looking around, at the fog outside the windows, nervous. She hadn't thought of that, the possibility that they might come back.

He told her again to stay there, and she did. He went back upstairs. When he came back, before long, he was wearing pants and leather sandals. He was carrying a briefcase, and he had an armload of towels.

He told her to wet a couple of the towels. He opened the briefcase on the kitchen counter. Inside was what looked like a change of clothes, a shaving kit, a cellular telephone, a stack of cash—hundreds, if they were all like the first bill in the pile—and a gun.

He took out the gun, a little machine pistol, like an Uzi, the kind you saw all the time in movies about drug lords. Evan was still upset and watchful, but with the gun in his hand he didn't look nervous anymore.

He was pulling himself together, tough and brisk. He put down the gun on the counter, took out the telephone, got a kitchen chair and pulled it up next to the counter. He sat down. He punched up one number, and while he waited for an answer he told her to get one of the towels, and he held his free arm out for her to clean.

Somebody came on the line, and Evan asked for a Gerald. Before long Evan was telling Gerald that he wanted him at the house right away.

Kristal could see that several of the cuts would have to be stitched up. He said good-bye to Gerald—actually he just clicked off—and when he had both hands free he tore a couple of the towels into strips, and told her to pretend they were bandages.

He wiped the blood out of his face and punched another number on the phone. This was a Harmon. Evan wanted Harmon here, right away.

He clicked off on Harmon and let her start on the other arm. After a minute she said, "You sure you don't want to call an ambulance?"

"No," he said, end of discussion.

He let her clean up the rest of the cuts and tie the scraps of towel the best she could.

He was still alert, but he was tired, she could tell. He told her to get him the money out of the briefcase, and she gave it to him. He told her to get a chair and sit down beside him, and she did.

He said, "Brenda Jo. You're a nice girl, Brenda Jo, sorry this had to happen."

Like they were talking about a run in her stocking, a broken heel on her shoe.

"Well, it was interesting." She tried to be light and cool.

"We'll get you out of here as soon as we can," he said. That was when she remembered, the gate. No electricity, the gate wouldn't work.

He counted out some bills. Five hundred as usual, he said, another five for her troubles, and he gave her the money.

"You going to call the police?" she said.

"Why?"

"On account of all this."

"You really want to get involved with the police?"

"Not especially," she said.

"Okay then."

"But my goodness—"

"Don't blow it out of proportion. Couple of my friends, a misunderstanding. It was nothing."

"Nothing!"

"Nothing I can't handle myself," he said. The little machine gun was on the counter. He reached down, picked it up, put it in his lap so it would be close at hand. The last part, about what he could handle—she believed him.

43

Naull stopped at a 7-Eleven just off the highway in San Rafael. He went in, bought a pack of Camels, and took them out to the pay phone outside. All the time he kept an eye on the van. He lit one of the Camels before he tried Marie.

She got testy with him. She was already awake, waiting for him to show up, that wasn't the problem. It was hearing that she had to pack up herself and Roy Boy, leave home within the hour, bringing only what she could put into the backseat and trunk of a Camaro—she wasn't happy about that.

He told her, It's either run or go to prison.

Naull wished he didn't have to put them through this, but he didn't have a choice. He was good only as long as it took Evan to get to the police, and the police to find Hays and Caitlin. It might be days. Might be only hours if Hays and Caitlin sat waiting to get caught.

He went back into the 7-Eleven and got a cup of coffee, all the time keeping the van in sight. He brought the coffee with him to the back of the van. He unlocked the rear doors, and started pawing through the tools behind the backseat. He lifted the tanks of the cutting torch. Underneath was the black velvet pouch, tied with a ribbon.

Stick it in his jacket pocket, carry it out of the house, that was the chancy part. Hope that Caitlin and Hays had other things to think about. And they did. Once he got to the truck, slipped it into the jumble in back, it was as safe as in a vault. They'd never get near it—Hays and Caitlin with their chemical aversion to the tools of a working man.

Now he wanted it with him. He wanted to see it again. A few seconds down in the basement, he could tell that he had something special. But he wanted a better look.

He closed the back door and went up to the driver's seat. He sipped some more coffee, lit another Camel. He made sure all the doors were locked.

The velvet roll was on his lap. Nobody else was in the parking lot. The 7-Eleven clerk was paging through a skin magazine.

Naull untied the ribbon and opened the pouch. He looked in, reached in and dug through the stones. They fell against each other with soft clicks. Time paused. Naull thought he might live this way forever, suspended in euphoria, the stones ticking as he sifted them through his fingers. Many delicious handfuls of jewels. Half a million dollars? Had to be more, even at a fence's discount.

Naull closed the pouch and tied it. He stuck it under the seat, and got out and locked the door, and went to the pay phone. He owed Welcome a call.

Welcome picked up on the second ring. He was waiting, Naull thought, to find out how rich he was.

"I got something to tell you," Naull said, and he gave it to him in about three minutes. Welcome listened, didn't interrupt.

"Couple of creeps," Welcome said when Naull was finished.

"Yeah, well. You swim in the sewer, you're going to run into your share of rats."

"You in trouble?"

"I'd say we have a chance of making it. See if we can't cash out, take the money and run. Ten percent is yours, you know. It's a lot of money, the way it's looking."

"That was my deal with them, not you."

"It's still the deal. Let me see how it shakes down, we'll get together, see that you get what's yours, huh?"

"Okay," Welcome said. That was all. Naull liked that.

"I'll be in touch."

"Sure," Welcome said. "Anything else?"

"Not right now. But later, yeah, maybe."

"Okay, later," Welcome said. "You all right?"

"I'll tell you, I've been worse."

Naull drove out of the 7-Eleven. He drove back across the bridge to Richmond, and up Interstate 80 to the Union truck stop near Vallejo.

In Vallejo you were just half an hour from San Francisco, still hard by the bay. But in a truck stop you could be anywhere. You smelled diesel smoke, you heard truckers' accents of South Dakota and Alabama and West Virginia, you listened to truckers' country music and ordered from a menu of truckers' food.

Naull parked the van outside the restaurant. Near a window, so he could watch it from his booth. Naull liked this, the feeling that he was already on the road: gone, gone, gone.

Naull ordered biscuits and gravy, grits, ham, and scrambled eggs. He was still eating when morning started to break, and Marie and Roy Boy walked through the door.

Welcome put down the phone. Grace was beside him, awake, up on one elbow.

"That was Sonny," he said.

"I gathered."

"He's all right," Welcome said. "He had a bad night, but he's okay now."

She was waiting for him to say more. But he thought of her and Hays, past and maybe future. So much he didn't know: how it had been, what was between them, how it would be.

What she might say to Hays.

"I'll tell you about it sometime," he said, and he turned over and went back to sleep.

The phone was ringing down in the big room when Hays and Caitlin came home. It kept ringing when they walked down the stairs from the landing. Hays ignored it. Caitlin didn't seem to hear it. She was distraught.

"We're going to *leave?*" she said.

"We have to."

"My God, we're going to leave our house, leave our things, our beautiful house, our beautiful things?" It was starting to sink in.

"Got to be done."

"My clothes, my furniture, my house . . . We have to think about this."

"ASAP. No time to fart around."

"Oh God, God, God, what have we *done?*"

"You screwed up," Hays said. "Not me—you."

"Blame me," she said, "right, dump on Caitlin, that's fine, that's perfect."

The phone quit. Hays went into his office to the desk drawer where he kept his electronic Rolodex. He started a pile of things he would need later in the morning when he started to cash in.

Caitlin was standing by the glass wall, looking out at the deck and the pool. Hays took her by the shoulders, not gently, and pointed her toward her dressing room. He told her to pack. A couple of minutes later, when he looked in, she was heaping clothes on the floor.

The phone started again. Hays didn't answer—it could only be bad. He tried to shut out the ringing and think what he would need. Pink slips for the cars. Certificates of deposit. The phone kept hammering. Passports? he thought.

The phone quit. In the dressing room Caitlin was filling suitcases.

"Jewelry," he said.

"You don't have to remind me to bring my jewelry."

"I mean give it to me. We'll get what we can for it."

"Not my jewelry."

"Won't need it where we're going."

"Where *are* we going?"

"Any place far away from here. East Buttfuck, Arkansas, how's that sound?"

"You're enjoying this!" she screeched.

"Two suitcases, max."

"Two—I can't, it's not possible."

"Two. We're traveling light." She was right. He enjoyed it, seeing her brought down this way. Before long the grimness of it would grind him to desperation, too. But she was there first, and it was something to behold.

"Which cars are we taking?" she said.

"Car. One. We'll get what we can out of these, buy a used one."

"My cars," she wailed, and the telephone started again.

Hays wanted to be out of there inside an hour, but there was no way. Things just didn't work that fast. It was like two hours, and off to the east the sun was starting to show when he loaded the suitcases into the BMW.

Sell the Bimmer—now he was starting to feel pangs.

They were going to take the BMW and the Land Rover first. His idea was to get a motel room not far away, come back and get the other two cars one by one. Then when the banks and brokerage houses and car lots opened, begin painful divestiture.

He carried out the last suitcase. Caitlin was standing at the front door, looking numb. He was ready to get her, hustle her down to the car, when the phone chimed inside the Bimmer.

He went over and picked it up. They were almost gone, they were out of here, what could go wrong now?

"Yeah," he said.

"Hello, partner," said Evan Ruark.

The power crews worked fast. They were on the scene and had the transformer replaced just about the time that Gerald showed up. Ruark buzzed him in. Harmon came along a couple of minutes later.

Ruark told Harmon to take him to a hospital, Marin General. They would drop off Kristal in San Rafael. Gerald, he had other plans for Gerald.

All the while Ruark kept trying Hays and Caitlin on his cellular phone. The house number, the car number—they had to be hearing one of them. Nobody answered but he kept trying, letting it ring, thinking that it would rattle them.

Even in the emergency room he kept trying. He got a long look from the admitting clerk. Tapping in phone numbers while he bled through bandages of towel scraps.

Got drunk and fell through a window, he told the clerk. As he cradled the phone against his shoulder.

A nurse came and cleaned the wounds. Ruark kept tapping the phone numbers, listening to them ring. The doctor came to stitch the wounds. Ruark switched the phone from one hand to the next as the doctor worked on one arm and then the other.

The doctor started on his face, his forehead, and told Ruark to put down the phone. Ruark was going to, until he heard the thock in his earpiece of a connection being made.

"Yeah," Hays said.

"Hello, partner," Ruark said.

A good long breathless pause. Ruark pushed away a nurse who started to swab one of the cuts along his hairline.

"You must be upset," Hays said.

"Upset, yeah, that's a word for it. I'm upset. But this will pass. You know what I mean? Diamonds are forever, though—do you follow me?"

At first Hays said nothing. Ruark wished he could see his face.

"I guess maybe I don't," Hays said.

Ruark was sitting at the edge of an exam table. Now he hopped off and brushed past the doctor and the nurse, and stood alone against the wall.

Keeping his voice low, he said, "I want what's mine. Give me back the damn stones and maybe you save your life. Everything else is negotiable. But I want those stones."

Ruark knew something about Hays. When he was in a tight spot Hays would purse his lips, make a thoughtful little smacking sound.

For cellular, it was a good, clear connection. Ruark heard a noise on the other end that he thought might be Hays pursing his lips.

"Are we talking about jewels?" Hays said.

"Don't be cute," Ruark said.

"Evan, on the level, we took nothing out of that house."

"Hey, pal, let me tell you the alternative." Ruark had to work to keep his voice down. "It's the jewels or this. I string you up like a hog—alive, I mean—and cut you a good long slit down your abdomen, from your throat to your balls. You can watch your own guts fall out on the floor, how about that? Do you doubt me?"

"We didn't take anything." Hays was getting shrill now.

"Do you doubt me?"

The doctor and the nurse were staring.

"No. No. I don't doubt you. But we didn't take anything."

"I went down and *looked.* The safe is open, there's about two cubic feet of air where my stones used to be."

"Aw no. Aw no. I know what happened."

"I know what happened, too—you stole my stones."

"I need an hour," Hays said. "An hour, I'll get your stones."

"What are you going to do, run away? Leave all you've got, run away so you can keep the stones? You have to be crazy, they aren't worth *that* much."

"I'm not running."

"You better run if you want to keep those stones. Because if you don't, you're dead."

"The guy with us, the one that did the safe—he took the jewels."

"He's your man, it was your gig."

"Took them and didn't tell us."

"Listen, slick, you cannot talk your way out of this one."

"I'm not, I won't, I wouldn't try. An hour, that's all I ask."

"It's the stones or piggy-on-a-string. Do you believe me?"

"Yes," said Hays, with the fervor of a new convert.

"I want those stones before I finish my second cup of coffee this morning."

"I'll call you."

"Don't worry. I'll be in touch."

"Right," Hays said. "One question."

"I have one answer. The stones or else."

"What about the law, that's all I want to know."

"Partner, I've got a switchblade injunction and I pay a retainer to the law firm of Smith and Wesson. Do you follow me?"

He clicked off right away. Let Hays try to finesse a dial tone.

He walked back to the exam table and hoisted himself back on the edge.

"Business. Never ends," he said. "Can I get out of here sometime before the end of the millennium?"

The Bimmer was packed, so they took the Corvette over to San Pablo. They'd been past the bungalow once, before the first time they called Naull, when they wanted to see what kind of a character they were getting involved with. Caitlin thought the bungalow was dreary, depressing. Hays thought it looked like the home of somebody who was ready for a proposition.

Now it looked empty. Dark, when all the other houses on the block were lit up and lively. The van was missing.

Caitlin went up to the front door, Hays walked around to the back. He could hear her up front, banging on the door and yelling for Naull.

Hays looked in a window. It was a bedroom. Dresser drawers were open, clothes were scattered on the bed and the floor. It looked like their room in Tiburon.

Hays tried the kitchen door—locked—and started around to the front again.

"Ralph, you can't do it, Ralph, come on out, Ralph," Caitlin was yelling.

She kicked the door.

"Hey," said a man leaning out the window of the bungalow next door.

"Go to hell," Caitlin said.

"I think they're gone," Hays said.

"Ralph!" Caitlin said. "Give it up, man, it's all over."

"*Hey*," said the guy next door. He was wearing a blue work shirt. Hays could see an embroidered Chevy emblem and the name Hank above one pocket, the houses were that close together.

"Are they here?" Hays said to Hank.

"Let me see. Cars're gone, nobody answers the door, I don't see anybody moving inside—I'd say they're not here."

"Prick," Caitlin said.

"You expect them back?" Hays said.

"They don't keep track of me, I don't keep track of them."

There was a toy on the front porch, a Ninja Turtle doll. Caitlin picked it up, and before Hays could stop her she threw it through a front window.

Hays pulled her to the car.

"Okie asshole!" she yelled from the Vette as Hays drove away.

They got on the bridge, across to San Rafael.

"What can he do to us?" she said.

She meant Ruark.

"You ought to know," Hays said.

"Why? We did a little of the old in-and-out for a while, so what? Is that supposed to imply some kind of *intimacy*? Some miraculous *insight*?"

"You think he's normal?" Hays said.

"Normal—what's that?"

"He scares me."

The car's tires made a ripping, whirring noise over the metal grate of the bridge. Down below was the northern neck of the bay, green and blue and choppy white.

"Yeah," she said. All of a sudden she was quiet. "Ruark can do that."

Traffic moved along until they got to the Marin side. Then they hit 101, what looked like all the world's commuters funneling into two lanes southbound for San Francisco.

It was awful, creeping, stopping, lurching and stopping again. This was the middle of morning rush, past eight now. The hour Ruark gave them was long spent. Hays wondered if Ruark was trying to call them. Should've taken the Bimmer, he thought, the car phone.

The deal with the knife. Guts on the floor. He wouldn't, would he?

Gerald Moon drove up Altamonte about the time the sun started to come up. He parked in the cul-de-sac opposite the big redwood house, top of the hill. The east side of the house was glowing orange, sunrise color.

Scare the shit out of them, Mr. Ruark said. And don't let them leave. Whatever it takes.

Gerald figured he would do both at the same time. He took the tire iron out of the Isuzu. It was a long wrench that doubled as a jack handle. He walked up the driveway. They will not call the cops, Mr. Ruark had said, sounding sure of it.

Gerald didn't imagine they were gone already, three cars in the carport. Didn't look like they were awake yet. But it wouldn't be long now.

He rapped the wrench on the front door fifteen or twenty times. The sound boomed inside, he could hear it.

No other houses around. Everything else was down the hill, that was good.

He left the front door and went back down to the carport. The wrench was sharpened at the handle, like a screwdriver, for prying hubcaps. Gerald bent down near the BMW and grasped the wrench and punched the sharpened end right into the sidewall of one tire. The tire collapsed with a rush of air. Gerald went around to the other three tires, punched holes in them, and watched them go flat. He went around to the other vehicles, and flattened their tires, too.

Now where were they going to go?

He expected something from the house by this time. He went up to the front door and banged the wrench on it again. The wood was now pitted with a couple dozen deep ruts.

He listened inside. Quiet. What, hiding under the bed? He walked back out to the cul-de-sac and looked at the house again, get some distance on it. The place looked like nobody was home.

They didn't have three cars, Gerald realized. They must have four. They were already gone.

Gerald got upset. Not that he hadn't followed Mr. Ruark's directions, driven over as fast as he could. Not that the people who were supposed to be inside had driven off to spite him personally. He was still upset.

He decided to take it out on one of the vehicles. He went back up the drive, swung the tire iron to bash out all the BMW's windows. He dug long furrows in the paint, he even kicked in some of the panels, the metal giving way under his feet. The BMW had suitcases in the backseat; he pulled them out, tore them open, threw the clothes around.

There was still the Land Rover and the Mercedes. But now he felt a little sheepish, the way he always did when he lost his temper. The wreck of the BMW did look impressive. If only someone were there, to be impressed.

He went back to the Isuzu and hunkered down to wait. He wondered if Mr. Ruark would understand that it wasn't his fault. He decided he would wait all day. The man at least had to give him credit for effort.

San Rafael to the Tiburon off-ramp was something over an hour. Turned out, there was an accident just north of the exit. Eighteen-wheeler ran right up the back of a 944 Porsche. Twisted red sheet metal, bits of chrome and glass. A fire truck was washing blood and gasoline off the asphalt.

It was not what Hays needed to see at this particular time, this particular day.

Hays blasted the Vette along Tiburon Boulevard and up Altamonte. He was convincing himself that Ruark was still his partner, his friend. They went back too far to let something like this come between them: they would work it out. He would have to make good on the jewels. All right, borrow some money, cut back on expenses, bite the bullet for a couple of years.

He would explain it all to Ruark. About how this started with Caitlin, how Naull got involved. Ruark knew her, Ruark would understand. Maybe it would mean ditching Caitlin. A show of good faith. So be it.

The idea felt good. Talk to Ruark, make him understand. Get things back to the way they were before the craziness started. Yes, after a long nightmare night, the end of his troubles.

Yeah. Felt *good.*

Then, when he was about to turn into his driveway, Hays saw the big slope-eye out front, standing beside a white compact car parked in the cul-de-sac. The slope looked as huge and solid and imperturbable as an Easter Island statue. His eyes locked onto Hays and followed the Vette up the drive.

Hays pulled into the carport and found that something, an earthquake, a crazy tornado, had destroyed the Bimmer. Its tires were flat, most of the doors and panels were dented. The paint, some great claw had dug deep scratches right down to the primer. The windows were broken out, and their clothes were strewn outside.

Hays parked the Vette and got out. He looked back down the drive. The Easter Island head was watching him. Only now, showing a little bit of a smile. And Hays got a bad feeling that he was wrong, his troubles weren't over, they hadn't even started yet.

Welcome was out for a walk. This morning he went all the way down to the hill, to the yacht harbor on Marina Boulevard. Then back up, the tough part.

This morning he took Webster Street. It was straight up the high flank of Pacific Heights. At his back was the bay, big and blue, the view widening as he climbed.

Welcome didn't look back. He stayed focused on the grade ahead of him, so sheer that the city had provided concrete stairs instead of a sidewalk. Welcome honestly thought that he had seen mountains less steep.

He kept climbing. The leg hurt, but it was more an ache than anything sharp or urgent. It was manageable. He pushed himself. At the top of the hill, he was soaked. It felt good, being able to work up a sweat, make demands on his body. He was starting to feel whole again.

Now it was a couple of easy blocks to the apartment. He let himself cool off. When he walked in the front door, five minutes past ten, Grace was there.

She said, "Hays has been calling. My place and yours both."

"Is that so?"

"He wants you over there, Tiburon."

This was interesting, Welcome thought. In light of Naull's story, Hays wanting him in Tiburon.

Grace said, "He claims somebody's trying to kill him."

Real interesting.

"Did he mention who?"

"He didn't say, I didn't ask."

"Hays the Daze," he said. "Why would anybody want to kill him? Besides general principles?"

"He didn't say. But he was shook up, it wasn't any act."

"You didn't mention Sonny?"

"Why would I mention Sonny?" she said.

The phone kept ringing. Welcome thought if it was Hays, he'd keep trying.

"You could mess me up real bad, telling him about me and Sonny knowing each other. Up until now it would've just been embarrassing, you know, getting caught in a lie. Now it's serious. You could put people's heads on the block."

"Yours too?"

"It could come to that."

"I wouldn't let anything happen to you."

"I wish I knew whose side you were on. I wish it was my side."

"I'm doing the best I can."

He walked over to the phone. He held the receiver without picking it up. It rang again, he could feel the jangling under his hand.

"One of these days," he said, "you have to choose. Him or me."

"Is it such a bad deal now?"

"It can't last. If you don't decide, something decides for you. Things shake down. Suppose you ended up on his side. Where does that leave me?"

He picked up the phone.

"Merle, Merle, hey, how you doin' buddy?"

Welcome thought that he had never heard anything so phony as Hays Teale being a good old boy.

"I need a favor," Hays said.

Welcome didn't say anything.

"Some people are after me." In three sentences Hays went from false-cheery to pitiful. "I need your help, Merle."

"Call the police," Welcome said. "That's what they get paid for."

"I would rather not do that."

Welcome wanted to prod him. Ask him, Who would want to hurt you? And why?

But he decided he'd just shut up. Hays was already in agony. Something or somebody had already done a thorough job of rubbing the starch out of him.

"I'm in a tight spot," Hays said. "There's somebody across the street—a very threatening individual—I know he wants to hurt me. You can deal with him, Merle. I wouldn't ask, but I don't know anybody else who can. Merle. You're living in my apartment. Merle, I need you."

Welcome was about to tell him that he'd already gotten plenty of mileage out of the apartment. That account was already overdrawn, he wanted to say.

Something made him stop, though. The fright in Hays's voice—it was the sound of opportunity.

"I'll be there," Welcome said.

The cab driver gave a long hard thought and told Welcome that he didn't know of any place between Jackson Street and Tiburon where a fellow could buy a shotgun.

And, anyway, there was a waiting period. Background check. Waiting period, Welcome couldn't believe it. Waiting period for a gun.

Welcome didn't want to actually shoot somebody. He was mainly looking for psychological effect. Of all the common household implements, nothing beat a shotgun for sheer fear-of-God deterrent value. Just shucking the action on a 12-gauge pump, the pure unmistakable sight and sound of it, halted even brave and foolish men. It was like a cold hand grabbing your testicles in the middle of the night.

Welcome got another idea. A cutlery shop. The driver found one in Sausalito, on Blithedale Avenue right along the waterfront.

Four-hundred-dollar carving sets. Swiss Army knives with little scissors for cutting fingernails. Jackknives with scrimshaw handles.

What Welcome wanted was gathering dust up on the top shelf behind the cash register. It was a Ka-Bar, dark steel, a broad and thick blade, nearly as long as Welcome's forearm.

The Ka-Bar had been Marine Corps issue for more than forty years. **Guadalcanal, Inchon, Khe Sanh,** said the advertising blurb on the box.

Welcome bought it and took it out of the box. He tried it in his pocket, but the handle stuck out. He pulled up the cuff of one pants leg, and slid the knife between his calf and the sock. The sock was tight. It held.

He walked out to the cab. He looked natural. The leg didn't bother him. Not the knife, not the wound.

"No luck?" The driver saw his hands empty.

"Sometimes you win, sometimes you lose," Welcome said, and he told the driver to take him to Tiburon.

Gerald was standing by the Isuzu, stretching his legs, when the yellow Corvette came up the hill. Gerald could see it down below, taking one turn after another. He thought it would stop somewhere short of the top—he didn't dare hope that it would come all the way.

But it did. The dorkus inside was grinning at the world. He lost his grin as he saw Gerald. The man and the woman hurried inside the house, like they were trying to get out of the rain.

Gerald walked slowly up the drive, milking it. He wondered what window they were peeking out of, but he didn't search. He knew they were there someplace.

One by one, he did the tires on the Vette. Doosh, doosh. Gerald going from one to the next with great dignity until the Corvette sat on four flats. It looked ridiculous, all those swoopy sculpted lines anchored in place, like an airplane bolted to a runway.

And the windows. *Bam!* A thousand square bits of safety glass, scattered across the pavement.

The body was mostly fiberglass and plastic. Instead of scratching, Gerald started putting holes in it. He punctured it with the wrench, sinking the shank deep into hood, trunk, door handles. When he finished, it looked like The Last Ride of Bonnie and Clyde.

He felt much better when he went back to the Isuzu. Scare them and keep them there. Mission accomplished. He sat down to wait.

The taxi showed maybe an hour later. It turned up the driveway and a guy got out. He was in his thirties. He had a lousy haircut and he carried himself straight up and down, almost like he was wearing a back brace under his shirt. Otherwise he was Joe Ordinary, as far as Gerald could tell.

Mr. Ruark said nobody leaves. He didn't mention about anybody coming. Gerald decided it was just one more to keep inside the house. He made sure that nobody sprinted for the cab. They didn't. The front door opened to let in the new arrival, the cab backed out and drove down the hill.

In a few minutes Harmon showed up. He was driving his Toyota, which belonged to him in the same way the Isuzu belonged to Gerald—apparently Mr. Ruark had a thing for big men in small cars.

Harmon strolled over to Gerald, nonchalant. Like he was John Wayne, and just rode up with the Seventh Cavalry. He carried a shopping bag. The Nature Company.

"They still inside?" he said.

"Three of 'em," Gerald said.

"Three?"

"Guy and lady and a new guy."

"Who's the new guy?"

"Just a guy."

"We're supposed to go in," Harmon said.

"And do what?"

"Didn't he tell you?" Harmon said. "Oh, man, you are out of it. Jewels, dude. Diamonds, excetera."

"They're going to give us jewels?"

"When I get done, they'll be begging to give us jewels."

"Fair enough," Gerald said.

"Here," Harmon said. He opened the shopping bag. "Take your pick. The magnum's lighter, the Uzi's meaner."

Two guns in the bag. A blue steel revolver, a small black machine gun.

"What's that for?" Gerald said.

"Equalizers. Supposedly they have guns inside."

"No thanks." The truth was, Gerald had never held a gun in his life. Never saw the need.

Harmon thought about it for a few seconds. He stuck the pistol in his belt and picked up the Uzi.

"Here's what I figure," he said. "You go knock on the front door. Get them thinking that way. I'll go around the back. Surprise the motherfuckers."

"If that's what you want."

"That's just what I want. Give me a couple minutes, I have a ways to go."

Gerald watched him cross the road and creep among the green shrubs that grew around the base of the lot. A machine gun in his hands, a pistol in his pants. Gerald thought it was pretty funny: this big pinheaded hunk of muscles toting guns, slinking around like a kid playing soldier. Maybe it was just his crazy, Samoan-Korean sense of humor, but the whole scene made him want to laugh.

How long would Harmon need to creep around the back? It was a big house. Gerald gave him a little extra time on top of the two minutes, and then he started up the driveway again.

Welcome watched it all from the brush. From the house itself you could see very little of the street. But outside, if you looked out from the little bluff where the house sat, the view was much better. You could hide in the brush and see everything that went on down in the cul-de-sac.

Now the new beefcake was playing Natty Bumppo in the bushes. The route he was taking, he would come out on the back deck, maybe the pool. He would come through the sliding doors in the back.

Welcome wanted to keep track of the big brown one. Korean, if you only looked at his face. But bigger than any Korean Welcome ever saw. The way he moved, he was the one to watch.

The giant Korean started up the driveway. As he came on, in the space of about five steps, he was transformed. He hunched his shoulders, his stride became shorter, more direct, balanced. He somehow seemed to coil inside. It was your ultimate one-fist-of-iron-another-of-steel walk.

And he was headed this way.

Welcome scurried back to the house, screened by brush, keeping his head down. He went in through a window on the side. Hays and Caitlin were in the big open room downstairs.

"They're on the way," Welcome said.

"Both?" Hays said.

"Yeah."

"We have a gun."

"They have guns. If it comes to shooting, we're overmatched."

"What do we do?" Caitlin said.

"We don't let it come to shooting, that's all."

He told them to keep the pistol, stay in the bedroom. A stranger came in, they should feel free to cap a couple of rounds.

They hurried, they *ran* to the bedroom and shut themselves in.

Welcome walked over to the sliding glass door. That entire wall was glass, with the door in the middle. But there were curtains down both sides. He drew the curtains as far as the edge of the door. Outside was the wide deck, with a peek of the fake lagoon below. He waited. Now, beyond the deck, a big clump of manzanita was rustling.

Welcome opened the door a couple of inches. Just enough to let Beefcake know he could use it. He stepped out of sight, behind the curtains, and he waited.

47

Ruark sent Harmon up the hill to do the job with Gerald. Ruark thought that while he waited, he would have a drink at one of the waterfront restaurants in Tiburon village.

He ordered a mimosa and took his glass out on the dock. He was alone out there, too early for lunch. He sipped the drink and collected himself. Champagne in orange juice, gulls tipping their wings beyond the dock, sunshine on the water.

He felt rumpled nerves become smooth. The alcohol and the sunshine helped, but mostly it was knowing that the stones were his again. He imagined Gerald handing him the velvet pouch. He thought of Hays and Caitlin, he imagined Gerald forcing his way into their house, pinning them in a corner.

He saw only one possible outcome. He figured it would take as much time as drinking one mimosa. Not sipping it, either.

The smooth nap of the velvet pouch, he could feel it under his fingers. The wonderful weight of the stones, he could feel it in his hands. Ruark finished the mimosa. He went inside, dropped a quarter in the pay phone.

Gerald came up the driveway. He worked himself up by thinking about people inside with a gun. Maybe somebody very scared at the front door, finger getting tight on the trigger as this huge mother approached.

From the driveway a set of six stone steps tiered up to the front door. Gerald took the steps without stopping, quick but not in a hurry, feeling bouncy, poised.

He took the last step and didn't slow down. Knock on the door,

Harmon said. *Knock* on the door? I don't think so. Gerald took the last step and kept coming. He had momentum. In front of the door, still moving, he gave a juke, a sidestep; he coiled and swung his right foot up and around, waist high, and he slammed it into the door right above the dead-bolt lock.

The door was solid wood, almost three inches thick. A leaf in the wind. It flew away as the jamb tore apart with a crack loud as a shot. The door swung back on the hinges, banged against the wall, and swung back toward Gerald.

He put out a hand to stop it, and stepped through. The door frame was in jagged pieces. Gerald looked around and found himself in the elevated entryway, empty. He walked to the railing and looked down.

He took it in. No movement, nobody. What a house. Everything was down below, a living room and more, spilling away from the bottom of the stairs. Glass and light. Stone fireplace like something out of King Arthur's castle. Near the center of the room a tan sectional sofa, looked like calfskin suede, faced out toward sliding doors and a deck and a view that took in half of California . . .

He saw Harmon. Actually it was the legs of Harmon's Gitanos, and Harmon's Pumas and his white socks. The rest of Harmon was hidden by a leather hassock. He was down, just inside the sliding doors, and he wasn't moving. Gerald started slowly down the stairs, wondering if Harmon for some reason was hiding behind the hassock.

But as he came down the stairs, Gerald saw that Harmon wasn't hiding. He was out. Face down, quiet as a stump—Gerald wondered if he was dead.

He stopped at the bottom of the stairs. Waited and looked around and listened. Movement, a sound, anything. But the place was absolutely still, until a groan came from the other side of the hassock.

Harmon was alive. To some degree.

Gerald didn't go to him right away. He waited, and listened and watched some more. He was in no hurry.

Gerald wondered if he could have missed a gunshot. No. So whoever got Harmon surprised him, hand to hand. And was probably still out there. Gerald picked out a path toward Harmon that would keep him in the open, give him a chance to react if somebody jumped out at him.

He moved. Gerald wasn't scared, but he was damn sure alert. He made it across the room in a half crouch, and looked around, and finally glanced down at Harmon.

Harmon. His nose mashed flat and bleeding, his lips swollen, purple, one eye puffed shut by a throbbing welt. It would be a while before Harmon reminded anyone of Elvis.

Gerald didn't see any guns. He rolled Harmon on his side. No guns under Harmon.

Now Gerald knew they had to get out. He briefly considered leaving Harmon. Ruark wouldn't like that, though. Okay, bring him out. The sliding door was behind them, quick and easy. But it went nowhere. The deck, the side of the hill—Gerald couldn't see himself carting big groaning Harmon through the trees, the brush, trying to make his way back to the road.

Out the front door, the only way. Get across the room, they'd be scat free. Upstairs and out the door.

Gerald didn't bother asking Harmon if he could walk. Harmon was someplace else. Gerald put his arms under the thick body, and lifted him, and started across the floor with him. Harmon's nostrils bubbled blood. Gerald skirted the suede sectional. They were almost halfway across the room now.

When something swung out from behind the sofa.

It was the color of brass, moving fast—a fireplace poker—whipping toward Gerald's legs. Gerald thought that was impossible, nobody could be behind the sofa, he just looked back there five or ten seconds ago.

But somebody was there. Rising up and swinging the poker in a flat arc. The bad haircut was popping out from behind the sofa where nobody was supposed to be.

The poker's head caught Gerald square in the right kneecap. Pain shot up Gerald's leg, up his spine, up into his brain and along his arms to his fingertips. It made him go buttery. He couldn't hold Harmon anymore. Gerald reached for the kneecap. He knew he shouldn't be doing that, he should be defending himself instead, but he couldn't beat the impulse to squeeze his knee and make it stop hurting.

Gerald grabbed his knee. The poker jerked up and caught him in the neck, and Gerald's vision turned to pulsing red.

Joe Ordinary with the shitty haircut was coming right behind the poker. His knee sank into Gerald's groin, his forearm took Gerald under the jaw and threw Gerald's head back farther than Gerald would have imagined possible.

Gerald was off his feet. Falling across Harmon. When Gerald blinked and looked again, he was on the floor. Somebody was straddling his spine, pulling Gerald's head by the hair, pulling it back, exposing his neck.

"Don't move," Joe said. He was straddling Gerald, holding a knife to Gerald's bare neck. Knife as mean and ugly as a shark, the keen edge of it resting against his skin.

Gerald was young and strong. His head was recovering fast now, and he still had power in his arms and legs. Joe Ordinary gave away maybe a hundred and twenty pounds to Gerald. But he did have that knife.

Gerald thought two kinds of people would carry a knife like that. There were those who flashed it to distract you from what they lacked inside. And there was the minority who lacked nothing inside and knew exactly what to do with the knife.

Gerald put Joe in Category Two. It was an easy call, a no-brainer.

"I'm going to let you up," Joe said. "I don't want you anywhere near this house again. I want you to leave these people alone. Do we understand each other?"

"Yes," Gerald said.

"You're going to take this sack of shit up the stairs, out the door, am I right?"

"Yes," Gerald said.

"Stay out of here, stay out of my face."

It wasn't a question, and Gerald didn't think it needed a response. Joe stood up, but he kept the point of the knife about a quarter of an inch behind Gerald's right ear. Gerald got up carefully, picked up Harmon again, and started across the room and up the stairs. Joe matched him step for step, and kept the point of the knife lodged behind Gerald's ear.

At the entryway, almost out the door, Gerald couldn't help himself. He said, "Damn. This is all I was trying to do in the first place, get him and me out of here. I didn't want to come back anymore."

"But you could have been talked into it."

Gerald thought that was probably true. Mr. Ruark might have been able to make him try again. Not now, though.

They got outside the door, and a high trill started in Harmon's pants. Joe made Gerald put him down, and he reached into one of Harmon's pockets and came up with a small portable telephone, a cellular phone.

Joe hit a button, the buzzing stopped, and he put the phone to his ear.

"No," he said after a few seconds, "no, I'm not Harmon. My name is

Merle. Merle Welcome." He looked at Gerald. "Is one of you Harmon?"

"Him," Gerald said.

"Maybe you better handle this," Joe—no, Merle Welcome—said, and he gave the phone to Gerald.

It was Ruark.

"This is me, Gerald," Gerald said.

"Who was that? What's he doing there?"

"I think he said his name was Merle," Gerald said. "I believe he's a friend of the people in the house."

"Not their friend," Welcome said.

"He says he's not their friend. But he did all right by them."

"Where is Harmon?"

"Harmon can't talk at the moment."

Mr. Ruark wanted to know if they were in the house. Gerald said no, not anymore, they were outside now.

"Did you get what I want?" Ruark said.

"No sir, we didn't."

"Go back in and get it."

"To be honest, I hate to say this, but I don't think that's going to happen."

Ruark told Gerald to wait for him, and he hung up.

"He wants me to wait," Gerald said.

"Out by your car, don't come any closer."

"Right," Gerald said.

"He told you to go for it again."

"Yeah," Gerald said. "Some people have no concept. They pay you money, they want a job done, they don't want to hear if, and, or but. You're supposed to do it, and it's your ass if you don't, no matter what. Know what I mean?"

"Do I ever," Welcome said. "You think that's bad, you ought to try the U.S. military."

Hays and Caitlin cautiously ventured out of the bedroom, up the stairs, and outside. Picked up the Uzi and the pistol that Welcome left outside the room, and now they were a little braver.

They walked through the broken front door and found Welcome outside. Down at the cul-de-sac the big slope was bending over a muscleman, shaking him by the collar of his shirt. The muscleman was laid out on the pavement like a corpse on a slab.

"What's going on?" Hays said.

"Nothing," Welcome said. "It's all over."

"That's it?" Caitlin said. "Just like that?"

"They had second thoughts."

"Wow," Hays said. "Wow." He was trying to adjust to the idea that it could be finished, that you could go from terror to security, from sure death to a reprieve, like flipping a light switch.

But there you go, Hays thought. Have an eye for talent, get the right people on your team. All things were possible.

They were free, he thought. What could Ruark do, hire another crew of goons? Let him try—it really was finished this time.

Finished, he thought.

And then Ruark's beautiful old Shelby racketed up to the top of the hill, into the cul-de-sac. As Ruark downshifted it made a throaty burble, a growl, a real sports car sound that you didn't hear on modern automobiles.

Ruark slowed where Gerald had Harmon laid out on the pavement. But he didn't stop. He cranked the wheel hard right and accelerated up the drive.

48

Naull drove down to Santa Cruz in the van. Marie and Roy Boy followed him in the Camaro. He kept checking his mirrors to make sure that she was still there, not dropping out of sight. By accident or otherwise.

Outside Santa Cruz he saw a sign for housekeeping units, vacation rentals. He followed the sign and took a cabin for a week. Fully furnished, two bedrooms, cable TV, block and a half from the beach. Four-fifty for a week. He wanted to do something nice for them.

He was in the room now, watching the noon news from San Francisco while he shaved. In a few minutes he'd be headed back to the Bay Area. Marie was taking clothes out of suitcases and putting them into dresser drawers. She had nothing to say. Since his phone call from the 7-Eleven she had spoken maybe twenty words to him. He could count them.

An ad came on Channel Four, and he switched over to Seven. He didn't know much about the news business. But he thought that by now there ought to be something on TV or the radio. Especially San Francisco TV news, with its taste for the bizarre and sensational. Three killer bandits stealing jewels from a farmhouse in Marin, naked man crashing through a window to save his life—you'd think it would be their meat.

And the radio, as he twirled the dial on the way down. Not a word.

Marie shoved the drawer closed, with more force than necessary. She said, "By the way, our son is five years old? Starting kindergarten in the fall? Or did that slip your mind?"

Thereby doubling her output of the entire morning.

"I know how old he is," Naull said. "I thought we would look around, find a nice town somewhere out of state where they have a good school system. Buy a little place and get him enrolled."

"Buy a little place," she said.

"A big place, whatever you want."

Naull buttoned up a clean shirt. He checked the part of his hair. Doing business, you wanted to look good.

Roy Boy caught on that he was leaving. He grabbed his sneakers, and Naull told him no, not this time.

"Oh, a big place," she said. "Anything we want. Just like that. There *is* the question of money."

"No," Naull said. "I don't believe so. Not anymore."

49

Ruark braked hard at the top of the drive and climbed out of the Shelby. He looked like hell, stitches and bandaged cuts, blood staining the bandages.

Caitlin leveled the Uzi at him.

"Don't come near me," she said. She meant it. She was scared. Hays was nervous too, and wasn't even trying to hide it.

Welcome was impressed. Skinny little ponytail dink having that kind of effect.

"Now think about it," Ruark said. Of the three of them, he was the steadiest. In fact he seemed to find some humor in the situation. And he was the one with a machine gun pointed at him. "You can kill me in my place, four in the morning, you might get away with it. But in your driveway, middle of the day, uh-uh."

He took a couple of steps toward Hays and Caitlin. His arms were spread, showing his open hands.

Caitlin said, "Don't let him get us, Merle."

"Give me a break," Welcome said.

"Who's this?" Ruark said.

Caitlin said, "This is Merle, Merle is bad, he's *bad,* he took care of your two hatchet men, he can take care of you."

"That was you?" Ruark said to Welcome. He looked down the driveway. Harmon now was sitting on the curb, holding his head. "All by yourself? You must've had some hand-to-hand training."

"Some."

"Send your two bad boys to kill us," Caitlin said, "Merle put a Goddamn hurt on 'em."

"They weren't going to kill you," Ruark said. "They just wanted my stones."

"We don't have the stones," Caitlin said. "We never did have the stones, we didn't take the stones, we've never even seen the stones."

"It was your little gig," Ruark said.

"We can work this out," Hays said. "Pay for damages to the house—"

"I'm not bitching about the house."

"—Put together a figure, what you think the stones were worth, we'll make it good."

"I doubt it."

"Whatever it costs. Tap into my credit, write you a check."

"I don't want a check," Ruark said. "I want my stones."

He was looking at Welcome now. Back and forth from Hays to Welcome, like he was saying too much in front of a stranger.

Hays picked up on it. He said, "Evan. Maybe we ought to discuss it. You and me. When did things ever get so bad, we couldn't work it out between us?"

"All right," Ruark said after a second or two.

"Out by the pool. Get down to it. Like old times, huh? Work it out."

"This better be good," Ruark said.

"Yeah," Hays said. "Like old times. Uh-huh. Work the mother out."

Gerald watched the Marine with the friendly name, Welcome, come toward him down the driveway. Gerald was sitting on the curb beside Harmon, who was just starting to come around. But it was slow. His head still wasn't in the proper zip code.

Gerald stood and took a couple of steps out toward Welcome. He wondered what he should do if Welcome hassled him, told him to move on. Could the guy take him again? One thing Gerald had going for him, he had a good idea what Welcome could do. But Welcome hadn't seen a move out of him yet.

Gerald told himself that he wasn't going to let Welcome push him around. If Welcome wanted another piece of him, Gerald would give him plenty.

And then just when Gerald decided to get tough, he took another look at Welcome and changed his mind. Welcome was now crossing the road. He didn't especially appear to be a bad-ass. But something about him, his eyes. Even while the rest of his face was neutral, he still had this hardness around his eyes, toughness carved with a fine chisel. Suddenly Gerald knew that Welcome had done things that Gerald couldn't even imagine.

"What's the problem?" Gerald said to Welcome.

"No problem," Welcome said. "The beautiful people decided they don't want to kill each other after all. I'm out of the picture. Just hanging out with the rest of the hired guns."

"Be my guest," Gerald said.

There was an oak tree beside the curb, not far from the Isuzu. Welcome walked over like he couldn't wait to get a load off his feet. He sat in the oak tree's dark pool of shade.

He looked at Gerald. More curious than hostile. Gerald noticed that Welcome didn't mention what happened in the house. No apologies, no gloating. To him it was probably nothing, Gerald thought. He wouldn't even remember it tomorrow.

While he, Gerald, would never forget it. Falling like he was shot, the pain lancing through his body, the feel of the blade on his neck.

Welcome was still looking at Gerald.

"Something the matter with me?" Gerald said.

"No. Hell no. I was just trying to get a fix on you. I'm usually pretty good with Asians, but you, I don't know."

"Maybe I'm Chinese," Gerald said. "Fat Jap, a sumo wrestler."

"Get serious. I'm thinking Korean. You've got the looks. You've got the intensity. I've known Korean special forces, ROK Tigers, Republic of Korea. They were tough, they were smart. Real fighting men. You've got some of that in you. So that, and the face, I'm thinking Korean. But I never saw so much Korean in one package."

"Nobody ever guesses Korean," Gerald said.

"Korean, but with a twist. Something more laid back. An island attitude. Sleep on the beach, catch a few waves, pop a beer or two. Maybe Polynesian."

"Samoan." Gerald was amazed.

"Samoan-Korean, is that it?"

"You got it."

"A great combination. No kidding." Welcome sounded sincere. Not like he was doing a snow job. He didn't have to.

"Thank you," Gerald said.

"Korean-Samoan, if I'd known that, I might not've been so quick to take you on."

"You did all right."

"Sure. With your arms full."

"Harmon didn't have his arms full," Gerald said.

"Him. The glass door, I leave it open, I step around the side. He waltzes in, I swear, like he's walking into McDonald's for a Big Mac."

"What'd you hit him with?"

"You know any tae kwon do?"

"Fourth-degree black belt."

"Okay. I let him get through the door. Front kick to the wrist, so he'd lose the Uzi. Elbow to the kidneys, side kick to the stomach, kick-in-stride to the face."

"How's your kick-in-stride?" Gerald said.

"I'm a little rusty. But I used to be good for a four-board break."

Four-board break, four one-inch pine boards.

"That would do it," Gerald said.

"We never saw any jewels. We never knew they were there," Hays said to Ruark. They were out on the deck above the pool. "The third guy, Ralph Naull, he did the safe, he has to have the stones."

"Who is Naull?"

"A burglar we found. A numb-nuts."

"Apparently not."

"We wanted to do some breaking and entering. Don't ask me to explain this. Shit happens."

"Shit happens to shitheads. Where is Naull?"

"I don't know."

"Jesus."

Hays watched Ruark. Keep talking, Hays thought. Ruark might not like what he heard, but he was still listening.

Ruark said, "What I don't get, if it's not the jewels, what do you gain from killing me?"

"Oh, insurance. The key man. Remember? But that's just an excuse. She decided she wanted to kill somebody. She had to have it, it had to be you."

Ruark was looking out over the bay. Hays tried to read his face, see where to go next.

"This all started with her," Hays said. "She's never satisfied. It's something in her, she's always got to have more, she's got to keep pushing, pushing. You know how she is."

Ruark turned away from the bay and looked at Hays.

"I know."

"Goddamn, it drives me crazy."

"I knew you were making a mistake when you married her. I wanted to tell you, you were signing on for trouble."

"You should've said something."

"You weren't in the mood to hear it. Getting out of one marriage, going straight into another, it's a wild time. A man loses his perspective. His judgment goes out the window."

"You're right," Hays said. "*Mea culpa.* For everything. Right down the line."

Ruark was noncommittal, almost bland, looking back at Hays.

"*Mea culpa* does not cover the stones," Ruark said.

"The stones," Hays said, "what can I do? All I can tell you is, we'll pay."

"You don't even know the price. You ready to lay out three million, minimum, to replace the stones?"

Hays watched him. He wondered if Ruark was serious.

Hays said, "You laid out three million for jewels?"

"I didn't say that. I said if you want to replace them. Three million minimum. Upwards to four. You ready to write the check?"

No, Hays thought. Ruark couldn't be serious. Ruark was trying to test him, throw out some ridiculous figure, wait for them to argue. Because if they really hadn't seen the stones, how would they know what was ridiculous?

Ruark waited. If he was playing games, he was doing it with a poker face.

"Let's not get into specific figures," Hays said. "Let's just say we're friends, we'll work it out."

Was this good enough? Ruark's face was impassive. Hays caught flickers of . . . what? Impatience? Contempt? Anger?

No. Better than that. A smile was forming now, a dry grin. Ruark was amused.

"Yes we will," Ruark said.

It was hot and dry on top of the hill. Gerald and Welcome got thirsty. They walked up to the house together, found a garden hose, and took long drinks.

Harmon stayed down in the cul-de-sac. He didn't want to go near the house, he didn't want to be anywhere near Welcome.

"One thing I want to know," Gerald said. "If you don't mind."

"Sure," Welcome said.

"You could've killed me," Gerald said.

"Maybe."

"The knife was there. I felt it. I don't even shave that close. You could've done it."

"Why would I want to? I mean, if I can stop you short of hurting you, that's the way to go. I've got nothing against you."

"I'm glad," Gerald said. "I've known plenty that wouldn't feel that way. In a situation like that, they're going to take it personal."

"I don't see why. It's not my house. And you're in there because whoever pays you tells you to go in. Am I right?"

"That's right," Gerald said.

"The one on the phone—in there now—you work for him, huh?"

"Yeah," Gerald said.

"Money any good?"

"I can't complain. The only drawback is, you start to be sucked in. It gets hard to say no."

"Money will do that to you," Welcome said.

"It isn't just money. You have to choose sides. The way the world is, nobody can go it alone. You try it, you're gonna lose, I don't care who you are. You got to have somebody to watch your back. He takes care of you, you take care of him."

"The question to ask yourself," Welcome said, "is who's taking care of you. And why."

"Those two, him and her—they're not your friends?" Gerald said.

"Not even close," Welcome said.

"So what brings you here?"

"Actually," Welcome said, "it kind of comes down to the bucks."

"Doesn't it always?" Gerald said.

Ruark said he'd like to speak with Caitlin. Hays went out and told her it was fine, he and Ruark had smoothed it out. He made her leave the Uzi while she went down to the deck.

She was wary. She stood out of his reach.

He said, "You. When I saw it was you. Holding a gun on me, in my own home. You. What a kick in the ass. You were the last person I'd expect it from."

"Get off it, Evan."

"We had something between us. Don't deny it."

"Why deny it?" she said. "But give me a little credit."

Ruark was starting to grin.

He said, "I never thought you were run-of-the-mill, if that's what you want to hear."

"I was always ready to go the route. How many people can you say that about?"

"Goddamn, though, you tried to kill me. Me!"

"Hey, I figure, start with the best." She was grinning too, getting into it. "I'd take it as a compliment."

"You're warped."

"Tell me that isn't why you liked me in the first place."

"It entered into the equation."

"Myself, personally," she said, "I always thought we made a great couple in that respect."

There it was, sitting there between them. Neither of them spoke. Evan moved in closer, very much within arm's length now.

He said, "Why did you ever leave me?"

"Sweetie, it wasn't what I wanted, you have to know. But you were impossible. You build these walls, I could never get close, I would wait for a sign, any little thing to show me that one day you would let me in. But it never came. I got tired of looking in from the outside."

"You hurt me bad."

"I never knew."

"Nobody ever hurt me that way."

She said, "I never would've imagined."

"And seeing you with Hays. I mean, Hays."

"Hays gave me the sign. He wanted me."

"But Hays. Really."

"I didn't say I was happy. I didn't say he was anywhere close to you."

"I hope not. Hays has his uses. But for somebody like you . . ."

"This is amazing," she said. "This is predestination, it's psychic confluence, I don't know how else to explain it."

"Yeah?"

"All this morning, I've been thinking along these same lines. Almost the exact words. About you and me and Hays. I've been thinking, the reason I didn't kill you is because I didn't *want* to kill you."

"I'm glad to hear it."

"I don't want to kill you, baby. I just want you."

"It's about time," he said.

"I do want to kill somebody, though. I've got it in me to do it," she said. She was jabbering, okay, trying to connect with Ruark, saying whatever sounded good. But this was real, and it was connecting with Ruark, she could tell. She said, "Can you get behind that? You can, I know you can. A long strange trip out to the extremes. You've been there, baby, you know the territory. Uh-huh. Seeing your muscle, what's been going down this morning. You're *out there*, baby."

"Maybe I am."

"Now let me tell you, along those lines. I have been thinking. The key man insurance—look, if you're going to kill somebody, it might as well be worth your while, am I right?"

Ruark didn't flinch. She knew he wouldn't.

"Might as well," he said.

"Doing you, it would have been worth about three million to the company. Pay losses, it's a mill to Hays and me if we took it out in dividends. But I'm thinking—how could I miss this?—Hays is covered too, same policy. If Hays goes, it's the same payout, only it's a mill to you, another mill direct to me because I get his shares. Not to mention the house, the cars, the investments."

"All this is true," he said. He wasn't stopping her.

"I could do it now, no shit, I'm primed, I could walk out there and do it to him."

"Hold on."

"Then it would be me and you again. I'm ready. I want you now. I've been wanting you a long time, sweetie."

"That would be dumb," Ruark said. "If we're going to do Hays, the last thing we want is you leaving him for me."

He was talking about it like it was something real.

"But I'm ready for it," she said. "You and me."

"Do it smart. You're going out there, you'll be the greatest little hausfrau he ever saw. Smart."

"All right, shit, smart. But we are going to do it. Am I right?"

"It's something to keep in mind," Ruark said.

Hays and Caitlin and Ruark, the three of them, walked down the driveway together. They stood around and chatted with Welcome and Gerald and Harmon. War could get weird at times, but Welcome thought this was truly bizarre, go so fast from guns and mayhem to small talk.

Ruark started ragging Gerald and Harmon, riding them hard.

"My big boys, my beef trust," he said. "Couple of humpties. All show, no go."

Harmon looked down at the asphalt. Gerald pretended not to hear. He had borrowed the Ka-Bar, and was shaving even, precise curls off an oak twig. Welcome wondered what Ruark paid them, how much it would have to be, to make them put up with this.

"Harmon," Ruark said, "what'd he drop you with?"

"I don't know," Harmon said.

"He put you on the floor, you don't know how?"

"I never saw him," Harmon said.

"Harmon, my man. What a piece of work. If brains were muscles, you couldn't lift a teacup."

Harmon looked at him through puffy eyes, but didn't answer.

"And Gerald, Ger', Doctor Death. My ace. What the hell happened to you?"

Ruark's voice made Welcome think of a little kid pulling the legs off insects.

"He surprised me," Gerald said without looking up. "He turned out to be someplace I didn't think he could be."

"What'd he hit you with?"

"A fireplace poker," Gerald said. "In the knee."

The knife peeled off a shaving that was as thin as paper. You could read through it.

"Did it hurt?" Ruark said. "As if I have to ask."

Gerald looked up from the knife and the twig. He looked straight at Ruark. Welcome thought of how Gerald had broken the door with one kick. He wondered if Ruark knew what he was doing, pushing Gerald like this.

"For a little while," Gerald said.

"Did that put you down? A poker in the knee?" Ruark seemed to know how far he could go.

"Yes it did," Gerald said.

"And the earth shook. I should've been there. It would've been something to see. My two big whales flopping around on the beach."

"They split up, was their only mistake," Welcome said. "Take them one at a time, I had a chance. I wouldn't want to go around with them again."

Ruark turned to Welcome now. He had a tautness about him. When he went from Gerald to Welcome, it was like moving a spotlight. He bored in on Welcome now. Gerald and Harmon didn't even exist anymore.

"Marines," Ruark said.

"That's right," Welcome said tightly. He wasn't going to take any lip about the Marines.

"But not just Marines," Ruark said. "Marine Recon."

"That's right."

"Best of the best."

"We like to think so."

"You're a warrior," Ruark said. "Partner, I don't know how you did it, but when you found this one you glommed onto the real thing."

He was talking to Hays and Caitlin now, but still looking at Welcome.

"We know," Caitlin said.

"Hand-to-hand, special weapons, airborne, underwater operations, demolitions . . . Did I miss anything?"

"That's about it," Welcome said.

"And improvised shaped charges. It had to be you, rigged the charges for my safe."

"Wasn't much," Welcome said.

"I could find a use for you," Ruark said.

"I'm more or less retired."

"I don't think so," Ruark said. "You whip up some bombs for my safe, you take my two big boys and hand them their butts, you don't act like you're out of business."

"I'm looking for a real job."

"Are they signing your checks?" Ruark said. He meant Hays and Caitlin.

"In a manner of speaking."

He turned to them.

"What do you think? You don't need him now. Can we work out some lend-lease deal here?"

"He's all yours," Hays said. "Least we could do."

Listen to them, Welcome thought. Shuffling him back and forth like an old lamp at a flea market.

"I make my own arrangements," Welcome said.

"Well, what about it?"

"I'm wondering what you had in mind."

"Let's say I'll keep you busy doing what you do best."

Gerald spoke up.

"Mr. Ruark operates in many spheres," he said. Welcome thought he caught some sarcasm. But maybe not. Nobody else seemed to notice.

"Indeed I do," Ruark said.

Gerald was watching Welcome. Everybody was watching Welcome, waiting for his answer. But Gerald especially.

"I'm a free agent," Welcome said. "I guess I'm open to offers."

Hays and Caitlin turned the two guns over to Ruark, and when Welcome said he'd like to keep the pistol, Ruark let him have it.

It was a Colt Python, .357 magnum, a nice weapon. Until now Welcome had no desire for a gun. He assumed that he could buy one any time he wanted. But to find he couldn't, to learn of waiting periods and background checks, that changed everything. The Python suddenly looked real desirable.

Gerald and Harmon left, drove their cars down the hill. Ruark got Welcome's number, and told him he'd be in touch.

Hays said, "Evan—those two are yours?"

"All mine."

"What for? If I may ask."

"Never know when I might need them," Ruark said.

Then he drove away.

Welcome walked into the octagon with Hays and Caitlin. They didn't invite him, but he walked in anyway, following them through the splintered door frame.

Down in the living room he said, "About my ten percent . . ."

"There is no ten percent," Hays said.

"There was supposed to be a million and a half."

"It was there," Hays said. "You want your cut, you'd better talk to Oklahoma."

"How do I find him?"

"Good luck."

"Well, shit."

"We have no money, Merle," Caitlin said. "We did the job, we got nothing. I give it all to you. You have a hundred percent of nothing. What else can I do for you?"

Welcome watched the view out the glass door. He did his best to look like one pissed-off Leatherneck who was trying to stay cool.

"You can get me something to carry my pistol in," he said finally. "I guess you can call me a cab."

50

"Holmes," Naull said to the guard inside the fence.

The guard went into his shack, picked up the phone. Few seconds, the gate was opening. Naull drove through and parked and went on back through the warehouse.

Andy Pops was waiting.

Naull didn't speak. He drew a plastic bag out of the pocket of his jacket, and he emptied it onto the blotter on Andy Pops's desk.

It was the butterfly, and about thirty assorted gems.

"Oh my," said Andy Pops.

He picked up the piece.

"I want you to notice," Naull said, "that's Tiffany."

"Noted."

"Late Twenties, maybe early Thirties. I haven't had a chance to look it up, but I doubt that you'd find a reference. My guess, it's a one-off, custom."

"Beautiful," Andy Pops said.

"I knew you'd appreciate it."

"And loose stones. Where did you get this?"

"I had a good night."

"So I see."

"More where that came from."

"Really."

"You could fill that coffee cup on your desk and have plenty left over. And I don't think it's been reported. If it hasn't been by now, I doubt it will be."

"Is it known?"

"It's known, all right. But people have their reasons."

Andy Pops wouldn't put down the butterfly. He kept holding it, admiring it.

"You're selling this?" he said. "I can cover this. Give me a few minutes, let me grade the stones."

"Go ahead."

"And there's more?"

"Knock your eyes out."

"Did you bring them?"

"Come on. You think I'm running around with a couple million in stones rattling around in the van? Sure I am."

"But you are selling."

"I didn't steal them so I could hang on to them."

"I would like to see them," Andy Pops said.

"Pick and choose?"

"I may be interested in the lot."

"Hundreds of stones, Andy."

"At a very deep discount, naturally. To be buying in such quantity."

"Not too damn deep, I hope. You have that kind of money?"

"I have access to it."

"It would solve some problems for me. That's no lie."

"The time is"—Andy Pops was looking at his watch—"a little after three. Can you have the stones here by eight?"

"Eight? Tonight? You work late."

"This is worth a little overtime."

"Eight, fine, no problem. And you want the whole bunch?"

"Unless you'd rather wear them."

"I'd rather feel the cash in my pocket."

"A good choice," Andy Pops said. He gathered up the gems, dropped them into the plastic. He gave the butterfly another look, front and back, before he slipped it in.

He held out the bag. Naull was nearly out the door.

"Hold on to it," Naull said. "What am I going to do with it?"

"You'll let me keep it for you?"

"Sure," Naull said. "I trust you."

Naull made his way to the front of the warehouse. He looked back once, before he got to the door. Andy Pops was on the telephone.

Naull went straight out to the van and waited for the guard to open the gate. He drove out, and kept driving.

His radio was tuned to KSAN. They were reading the local news update. Nothing about an attempted murder, stolen jewels.

It was one thing to possess a fortune in stones. In some ways this was the easy part. Getting money out of them, that was a challenge. Naull had brought Andy Pops what he figured was the limit that Andy could handle. The butterfly first—that was identifiable, unique, therefore the most dan-

216

gerous. The rest, he hadn't been sure what he would do. He wanted to go out of state. But out of state he had no outlets. Take the stones out of California, he was looking at a federal charge with all the rest.

Now Andy Pops was offering to cash him out. Solve all his problems. Easy.

Naull knew he needed help, somebody on the outside.

Not Marie. Keep Marie out of it. Where would Roy Boy be if they both went to jail?

He thought about Welcome. Naull liked Welcome a lot. Naull never got close to people very quickly, but right away he'd felt close to Welcome.

Why not? They were about the same age, they grew up the same way. Kansas and Oklahoma, that was part of it. When you and another guy ate the same dust and sweated under the same sun and froze in the same bitter north wind, you felt you had an inkling of what was in him.

He was in downtown Hayward now, Winton Avenue. It was a thriving city, Hayward. Winton Avenue was busy.

Here was a Federal Express booth on the corner. Drive-up service.

Naull pulled in front of the booth.

The attendant was polite and efficient. Naull showed her what he wanted to send, and she said probably he ought to go with a FedEx box instead of an envelope—it was sturdier.

He filled out the airbill. It wanted to know the declared value of the shipment.

Maximum Declared Value $100, it added.

"$25," Naull wrote.

The attendant was waiting with the box. Naull took the black velvet pouch out of his jacket. He put the pouch in the box. It left lots of room, which he filled with crumpled newspaper from the floor of the van.

The attendant gave Naull a copy of the airbill. She attached the airbill to the box, and sealed the box with tape.

Naull paid her in cash. Cross-country or crosstown, it was the same price. She gave him his change and stuck the box into a tray full of envelopes and boxes behind her.

It looked just like all the other boxes and envelopes.

If you only knew, he thought, and he drove off to find a phone.

Sonny Naull was a good source. But good sources came and went, Andy Pops told himself, and when they went away, others always appeared.

While a good customer could never be replaced. A good customer was something to be cultivated, looked after. You never turned down a chance to do a favor for a good customer, especially if the favor cost you nothing.

So the decision was easy, from a business point of view.

Which was the one that mattered.

Andy Pops knew the number without looking it up.

"Mr. Emerson," he said, "you know who I am, yes?"

Grace Gibbs was expecting Welcome at any time. While she waited for him, she stretched out on the batik print on her sofa and listened to her French tapes. When the knock came she took off the earphones, turned off the Walkman, and went to the door.

She expected to find Welcome.

It was Hays.

"Come on," he said. "Let's go for a ride."

"Duty calls," Ruark said to Welcome on the phone.

"Already?"

"I told you I'd keep you busy. Five hundred a day, how does that sound?"

"What would that buy, five hundred?"

"Your undivided loyalty," Ruark said. "It buys me *Semper Fi.*"

Hays was driving a car Grace hadn't seen before, a Land Rover. He took her across the Golden Gate. He wouldn't tell her where they were going. When they took the exit for Tiburon, she thought they were getting kind of close to home.

Hays didn't say much. But he seemed to be in a good mood. Even better than that—almost bubbly, but trying to keep it under control.

They turned up Altamonte Drive.

"What are you doing to me?" she said. She knew the address.

"Trust me."

The Land Rover kept climbing.

"This isn't funny," she said.

He thought so, though. He was enjoying it.

Up the driveway and into the carport. The house.

The house. She couldn't help it, it came over her, it surprised her, to feel it this strong and sudden—the envy. She envied them. Him and her, living like this. Especially Caitlin. She envied Caitlin and didn't like her very much, Caitlin whom she had never met.

"You're going to make trouble for everybody," she said.

"She isn't here. She's gone for the day. Couldn't take the noise."

She heard it now. Hammer-and-nails sound, up at the house. A couple of workmen were pounding at the frame of the open front door.

"What am I supposed to do?" she said. "Walk into your home?"

Her home, she thought.

"That's it. Walk in, look around."

"I don't want to."

"Part of you doesn't. Part of you does."

He was right. It was there.

She followed him inside. God, the house, the house. She wondered what Caitlin felt when she walked in this door and stood at this landing and looked down into this place of hers.

They went down into the big central room. Even better here. The glass, the deck, the view . . . Did it make Caitlin happy? Did it fill her up, the way Grace herself was full right now?

Hays always said she was never happy, never satisfied. But he would not be an authority.

He went out on the deck, and she did, too. Over to the rail. Sun and a breeze, and the feeling of being free and light and untouchable.

"I've been a real shit," Hays said beside her. He waited. He said, "You can always disagree."

"Why would I disagree?"

"You and the Marine, it eats me up. I did it, I know. I threw you together. I told myself that I had reasons, but damn. As soon as it happened, I was sorry."

Grace kept quiet. She didn't see that she had anything to add.

He said, "Do you forgive me?"

"I probably ought to thank you. He would."

He said, "It's all over."

Wait a minute, she was about to tell him. *You can start it. You can't stop it.*

But he was going on.

"I've had it with her," he was saying. "Parting of the ways. Enough is enough."

She was watching him.

"Split the sheets, it'll cost plenty. She won't get this place, though. I'm holding on to it. It's too good for her. This is for you and me."

You and me, he was saying.

"Oh hell," she said. "Oh hell."

It was almost five when Hays dropped her off. He didn't come in, and good thing. In front of her door was a rose in a jelly jar. Under it a note.

Dearest G:
Missed you.
Gone for a while. ETA Unknown.
Be mine, be mine.
M.

52

Five minutes to eight, Naull drove up to the warehouse fence. The gate opened before he could stop.

The loading dock was closed. Naull went in the only other way, the door beside the dock.

He was two steps in when an arm closed around his throat. A gun barrel stuck in his ribs.

"Don't fight it, just move," Merle Welcome said.

"Damn right," Evan Ruark said.

*   *   *

After Ruark searched him, they sat Naull in Andy Pops's chair. Hays and Caitlin were there, too, along with a couple of walking mountains whom Ruark sent out to search the van.

Gang's all here.

After a few minutes one of the two haystacks, the one showing some wear, came back and told Ruark that the jewels were not in the van.

"I told you so," Naull said.

"You said you would bring them," Andy Pops said.

"I know. But I decided against it. I thought something like this might happen."

Ruark said, "Where are the stones, Ralph?"

"I gave them to my partner."

"Your partner!" Caitlin said.

"Uh-huh. That's right, Miz Hames. Mister Teale. Mister and Miz Tiburon, Altamonte Drive, top of the hill."

You could see their surprise. There was no hiding it.

"It was kind of funny at first," he said, "you thinking I was that dumb. I put up with it for a while, okay. But it gets tiresome."

"You're so smart," said Ruark, "why'd you come back here, knowing this might happen?"

Naull sat back in the chair. He hooked his thumbs over his belt.

"Same reason I came the first time," Naull said. "I want to sell the stones."

"What I know about them stones—" Naull started to say. He stopped. To Ruark he said, "But maybe we want to discuss this in private."

"Maybe we should," Ruark said.

Ruark told them all to leave. Then it was just him and Naull in the office, the others outside in the dark warehouse, looking in through the glass partitions.

"About my stones," Ruark said.

"You can call them yours. But I don't know. They're out of your hands. I doubt that you ever had any receipt. No insurance—otherwise you'd want a police report to back up your claim. My guess would be, you had some dirty money you wanted to do something with. Buying from

Andy, the price would've been right. So you had them once, and now I have them. But you can call them yours if it makes you feel better."

"I could kill you," Ruark said.

"Then you lose the stones. What did it take you, couple of years, a few here and there, to put together a mess of jewels like that? You'd be starting from Square One again."

"And you'd be dead."

"Uh-huh. But I go out knowing that my wife and my kid are set up. See? It means a hell of a lot more to me than it does to you. If you had to, you could flush those stones, it would hurt but it wouldn't make any difference. For me, they're worth dying for. It's the hunger factor. You think about it, it gives me a hell of an edge."

"What do you want?"

"I counted two thousand, one hundred and nineteen pieces. Five hundred each would be a million, million one."

"Three hundred apiece, it's a little over six hundred thousand. Call it six-fifty K. That's the price. I don't haggle."

"You can do better than that."

"I don't have to. It's already more money than you ever thought you'd see. And the alternative is a bullet in the brain. You can't say no to six-fifty. It looks too good."

The idea of it, six-fifty in cash, hung in the air between them.

"Yes it does," Naull said.

"There's the phone," Ruark said. "You want to call your partner, set it up."

"Maybe not tonight. He's hard to find. Tomorrow."

"Up to you. Your ass is mine until we do the swap."

"Hey. By the way," Naull said. "Before we do it, I want to know you've got the money."

"Hey. Before we do it, I want to see you've got the Goddamn stones, how about that?"

Andy Pops went away. He didn't want to see any more. This left Hays and Caitlin standing with Welcome and Gerald and Harmon, watching through the glass.

Ruark came out of the room. To Welcome he said, "He doesn't leave the room till we're ready to go. Got that?"

"Sure," Welcome said.

"What about it?" Hays said.

"We have a deal."

"What is this going to cost us?" Hays said. He was anxious—he had promised to make good. It was one thing, to give promises when matters were up in the air. But now they were out of the clouds, getting down to concrete.

"Start with fifty K for the Greek. He saved your bacon."

"Fifty? For a phone call? I'm not sure I can lay my hands on fifty, short notice."

"Find it," Ruark said.

"Right."

"Aside from that, the price is six and a half large. I accepted."

"That's a lot of money."

"Good price, for what's involved."

"A lot to pay for what belongs to you."

"We'll see about that," Ruark said.

53

They let Naull call his wife. Hung up on business, he told her, be back tomorrow night. Then they brought him out. Until the swap, Ruark was going to hold Naull at his place.

Ruark told Gerald and Harmon to take Naull there in the Isuzu. Still riding them hard. He wouldn't let it alone, what happened this morning. *Think you can handle him? Sure you don't want him in handcuffs? In cuffs and leg irons? Cuffs and irons and a straitjacket, how's that?*

He was braying this in front of the others, Hays and Caitlin and Welcome. Hays and Caitlin ate it up, like this was dinner theater and they had a table in the front row.

Gerald wouldn't look at Ruark, or at anyone else. He was taking it to heart, Welcome thought.

Hays and Caitlin went home. This left Ruark and Welcome, and Naull's Econoline. Ruark rode along while Welcome drove the van.

They were on the Nimitz, heading north, in swarming traffic.

"The way you handled him, coming through the door," Ruark said. "I was watching. I wanted to see. You were smooth. You were silk."

"He's a burglar, that's all. Not a fighter."

"I don't care. Smooth as you moved, you'd have handled anybody."

"I was an easy five hundred."

"You'll make it up tomorrow."

"Tomorrow," Welcome said. "Let me see. Tomorrow you're doing the buy. You want the stones but you don't want to spend the money. You're looking for somebody to take down the whole show. Maybe me."

"Definitely you."

"That one is worth a bunch more than five hundred bucks. Who knows what the setup'll be? Ralph says one partner. But suppose it's three or four, and they have the same idea, rip off the whole deal, the money and the stones both. It gets complicated."

"What is it worth to you?" Ruark said.

"Actually, I think the question is, what's it worth to you? You're asking me to save you six-fifty. That's a pile of money. I would say ten percent isn't out of line."

"Sixty-five thousand for a few minutes' work."

"It's not unreasonable."

"It is to me."

"You could always use Gerald and Harmon."

But he wouldn't, Welcome thought. The luster was off Gerald and Harmon. Welcome thought he was learning about these people, rich and restless. They saw something they wanted, they had to have it. Then they got tired of that, got distracted, and moved on to something else. Something else they just had to have.

Oh, and it had to be new and different, and it had to be quality. If it was the best, or they believed it was, they'd pay anything for it.

Welcome thought that Ruark, ratty as he appeared, was not immune to the disease. You could tell, the way he soured on Gerald. Just because Gerald got whacked in the knee while carrying Harmon through the living room.

Welcome told himself that at the moment he was new and different, he was the hot item on the market.

"That must've been plastic you used on my safe," Ruark said. "You'd have to mold it to make the shaped charge."

He was trying to avoid the sixty-five thousand, Welcome thought.

Changing the subject. Okay, no problem—they'd get back to it eventually.

"C-4," Welcome said.

"Nice piece of work."

"Pretty elementary," Welcome said.

"You know your way around explosives, huh?"

"It comes with the territory."

"What about remote charges? Radio actuated?"

Traffic was heavy and crazy, dicing in and out on the three-lane. Welcome was driving down the middle lane, concentrating on the highway. Ruark was becoming hard to follow.

"I've done a few. I know the basics."

Ruark shifted in his seat, a quarter turn to his left, so he was looking directly at Welcome.

Welcome took his eyes off the road long enough to see that Ruark was staring. He was intent.

"Build one for me," Ruark said. "Tomorrow."

"Why?" Welcome said.

"Build one for me. You want your sixty-five. Build me the bomb, take care of business tomorrow night, sixty five thousand, it's all yours."

"What did you have in mind?" Welcome said. "Specifically."

"What's it to you?"

"Excuse me. Pay no attention. All I had was seventeen years of booby traps and ambush tactics, that's all."

A Chevette whipped in front of Welcome, not a foot from the bumper of the van. It slid into the right-hand lane, and down an exit ramp. Never even touched the brake light.

They were nuts out here in California.

"I know where I want to get to," Ruark said. "I know the desired outcome. But I'm not sure how to get there yet. You got any ideas?"

"Try me," Welcome said.

Ruark's house was cold. At least half the windows were broken. Ruark found some plastic trash bags that they cut and taped over the holes.

Naull didn't help. It was their job, to hell with them. He watched them work. He watched Welcome working beside them.

Welcome, like he belonged there. When they finished, Ruark told Welcome to go home, get some sleep. Reminding him that he had work to do tomorrow.

What was that supposed to mean?

Naull, when he walked into the warehouse, truly thought he had it figured. He thought he was ready for anything. Then he heard Welcome's voice—*Don't fight it, just move*—and he realized that he was ready for nothing.

His pitch was prepared. About being willing to die for the jewels. It sounded convincing. And it worked. But when Ruark asked him to call his partner, what was he supposed to do? Shout?

Welcome left the house. He got into the van. *My van,* Naull thought. *My stones, my van, my plan.*

As Welcome drove away without even a backward glance.

Eleven o'clock, and Merle wasn't home yet. Gone all evening. A rosebud, Grace thought, cute note—and he vanishes.

It was his business, she thought. But supposedly he knew nothing about San Francisco, supposedly he knew nobody. So what was he doing, out past eleven?

She spent the evening on the sofa. She could hear the front door of the building, the sound of the lock. Whenever somebody came in, she went to her own front door and looked down the hall, to see if it was him.

Which made no sense, she thought. When Merle came in, he would stop first to see her. Wouldn't he?

The door. She looked at her wall clock, 11:17. Forget it, she thought, and half a second later changed her mind.

She opened her door. Welcome was standing there, ready to knock.

"I want to talk to you," he said.

"I want to talk to *you*."

"I also want to go to the Cliff House."

"The Cliff House is closed. You wanted to go to the Cliff House so bad, you should've been here five hours ago."

"Will you bear with me on this?" he said.

They took Grace's Ford out Geary Boulevard. The Cliff House was closed. It was dark. Furthermore, there was nothing else nearby to give light, or to draw people. The parking lot was empty. So was the Great Highway. If you looked around you had the ocean, the beach, the rocks, and the forest park. The air was cold, and it had a rough salty edge. This was the way Welcome remembered it, but he wanted to be sure.

He walked around the edge of the parking lot, the side closest to the ocean. That low stone wall with the ten-cent telescopes and a couple of garbage cans beside it.

The seals barked and barked. They were worse than crows. Welcome wondered how it would be to work in the Cliff House, waiting tables or peddling souvenirs, hearing the seals all day, every day. They would remain charming for about half an hour.

Welcome was trying to remember something that Gerald Moon had said this morning. About life, trying to go it alone.

You have to choose sides, was what Gerald had said.

You have to trust somebody, was how Welcome would put it.

Grace was beside the car, arms crossed, watching him. They had said nothing since the apartment.

Welcome stood in front of her, close enough to reach her.

"You want to hear a story?" he said.

He told it all. She kept listening, once in a while shaking her head—exasperated, amazed, disapproving—but letting him go on.

"There must be something wrong with you," she said when he was finished.

"No, I'm fine. There's something wrong with *them,*" Welcome said. "Hays and his bunch. The way they think and act. I'm on the outside, Sonny's on the outside. We're involved, but we don't belong." *And neither do you,* he wanted to say.

"No," she said. "You're just a wild man."

"I think we can do it," he said. "I've been thinking about it, the right and wrong. Anything that happens to them, anything, it's not more than they deserve. But I want to know. Are you with me?"

"Maybe you ought to hear *my* story," she said. "In a nutshell. Hays is finished with his wife. He's dumping her, any day now. He's in love with me. He always was but now he knows for sure. He'll do anything to keep me. Everything he has is mine. That's what he said."

"What did you say?"

He held her arms. She looked up at him. For some time she looked up at him, while the seals barked.

She said, "What do you think?"

56

Naull started calling Welcome at seven in the morning. He listened for the sound of an extension breaking in, somebody eavesdropping from another phone in the house. But it didn't matter. He got no answer at the apartment, no answer at Grace's number.

He tried every ten or fifteen minutes. Around eight-thirty Ruark made a crack about how funny it would be if Naull's partner had skipped with the stones. A little before nine, Ruark amended that. It would not be funny at all. He reminded Naull that the stones were keeping him alive.

Naull tried the numbers again, one and then the other. He looked at his watch—9:14—and at the sweep hand moving around the dial, while the phones rang and rang.

57

After they left the Cliff House, Grace and Welcome checked into a motel on Lombard Street. Her request. She didn't want to spend another night in Hays's apartment. And wherever she was, there Welcome also was expected to be.

This was unspoken but understood. Somehow, in the space of a few hours—maybe within a few heartbeats, Welcome thought—she had passed from uncertainty to bedrock solidness. She was with him now, she would be with him for as far as they both could see. Even Welcome sensed this.

They woke early and ate light in the motel coffee shop. Welcome borrowed a Yellow Pages from the cashier. Toys and Hobbies was the heading he searched.

At nine, they were waiting outside when the Serramonte Center, big shopping mall, opened for business. Welcome went to the toy store, to the section of radio-controlled model planes and cars. "Largest Selection in the Bay Area," claimed the ad in the phone book.

Welcome was the first customer in the store. The clerk had plenty of time to spend with him, going over the merchandise.

The goodies that were available, Welcome had no idea. For a few hundred dollars you could buy a quarter-scale Cessna with a six-foot wingspan. You could buy kits for a B-17 bomber or a Beech Starship. All the controls were the same as a real plane—ailerons, rudder, elevator, throttle.

You commanded all this with a radio transmitter about the size of a hardcover book. It had joysticks and buttons and a telescoping antenna. In the plane your receiving unit actuated small electric motors, servos, that moved the plane's control surfaces. The receiver was no bigger than a pack of cigarettes.

At a flying field you might have eight or ten planes operating at the same time. Then you would attach a small colored banner, a frequency flag, to your antenna. This way you did not duplicate a frequency already in use. Otherwise when you banked your plane left, for example, you would also be banking somebody else's plane to the left.

Welcome considered that. One transmitter, one frequency, two planes.

The clerk tried to sell Welcome a complete setup, plane and engine and transmitter and receiver.

Welcome said he was not that interested. Mainly he cared about the radio gear. He told the clerk what he wanted, and the clerk pulled it off the shelves.

On his way to the checkout register Welcome passed a wall full of toy guns. Some were so realistic that he had to touch them, lift them, to know they were plastic.

He picked out one, a sawed-off double-barrel shotgun, and brought it to the register. He wondered what Naull would say about a plastic shotgun. But it couldn't be helped. In a world of waiting periods and background checks, sometimes you had to compromise.

Grace went into her apartment to pack. Welcome took the stairs to his own place. The phone was ringing when he walked in. Naull.

"There you are," Naull said. "I've been trying all morning."

230

"I've been out."

"I'm going to want the stones," Naull said. "We're selling the stones."

"Good."

"But there are special circumstances," Naull said.

"Somebody's with you."

"Yes indeed."

"Anybody else on the line?"

"I don't think so. Listen. The people who are buying, they want to inspect the goods. We have to set up a meet, so they can look it over. You still have it, right?"

"Not yet."

"Good, good, that's fine," Naull said heartily.

"By noon at the latest, isn't that what it's supposed to be?"

"So they say."

"We'll assume it'll be here. Is Ruark with you?"

"Yes."

"Tell him to send one man, sidewalk in front of Perry's on Union Street, San Francisco, half past noon."

Welcome heard him relaying this to Ruark.

To the telephone Naull said, "You should look for a very large Oriental gentleman with a Polaroid camera."

"Damn," Welcome said. "I was hoping he'd send me. But he knows I'm busy. It's okay, I'll finesse it."

"Yeah, your new job," Naull said. "What a surprise."

"This isn't the time to talk about it," Welcome said. "But I'll tell you this. I don't think you want to let go of the stones."

"Yes I do," Naull said. "The price is right."

"Take the money, sure, but keep the stones. Do you trust me?"

Naull said nothing. Welcome heard only Ruark's voice, indistinct.

Naull said, "He also wants to set up the buy. It should be today."

"Tonight. Tell him, I set it up, at this end. I'll call, let him know when and where. That's how it has to be."

Another exchange between Naull and Ruark.

To Welcome Naull said, "Call this number when you know."

Welcome jotted it down.

Ruark spoke again, louder.

"I can't talk anymore," Naull said. He did not sound happy.

"Do you trust me?" Welcome said.

"Do I have a choice?" Naull said.

58

"Perry's, San Francisco," Ruark said to Gerald. They were in Ruark's living room, Gerald ready to leave. "On Union Street, Cow Hollow. Want me to draw you a map?"

"I know where it is," Gerald said. "I lived all my life in San Francisco."

"From now on, where you're concerned, I take nothing for granted."

"Get off my back," Gerald said.

Ruark slapped him across the face, hard.

"You don't talk to me like that," Ruark said. "You know better."

Gerald looked down at him. No-account little Anglo. Break his skinny neck.

Ruark glared up at Gerald. So sure of himself.

Easy. Snap it like a chicken neck.

"Call home, Gerald," Ruark said.

Gerald stared and tried to get what he meant.

"Call your mother, call home," Ruark said. He was holding out his little pocket-sized cellular phone.

Gerald took it and tapped his mother's number.

A man answered.

"Who is this?" Gerald said.

"Gerald, is that you?" the man said.

The man was Harmon. Gerald had noticed this morning that Harmon was gone, and was wondering where he went.

"Is my mother all right?" Gerald said. "My sister?"

"Better let me talk to Evan," Harmon said.

"Where's my mother?" Gerald shouted.

"It's okay," Ruark said. "Put her on."

"Gerald?" his mother said a few moments later. "Gerald? Where are you, Gerald?"

"I'm working, Ma," Gerald said. "Are you all right? Is Jinky all right?"

"We're all right. Gerald, who is this jerk? Is he really with Mr. Ruark?"

"Yes he is, Ma."

"Gerald, what is going on here?"

"Don't give him any trouble," Gerald said. "Do what he wants, it'll be okay."

"Say bye-bye," Ruark said.

"Ma, I got to go," Gerald said.

Ruark reached in and shut off the phone.

"Once an hour, on the hour," Ruark said. "I call in to tell him we're cool. Using the correct words, so he knows you're not twisting my arm. If he doesn't get the call . . . One thing about Harmon. He may not be the smartest cock on the row, but he follows orders. And he's a mean one. You've never seen him in action, but take my word."

"You shouldn't have done that," Gerald said.

"Look at it from where I stand. I've got a huge deal going down, my main man turns out to be an unreliable fuck. In a few hours you and I will be driving around with a bag full of money, and I can't trust you from here to the door. What do you want me to do?"

Gerald started to speak —*You shouldn't have done that*, he was going to say again—but Ruark put up a hand to cut him off.

"Don't answer," he said. "All that's asked of you is to get over the bridge, find your way to Union Street, and stand on the sidewalk. Look at the stones, take some pictures. *Comprendez?*"

Gerald turned to leave.

"Think of it as incentive," Ruark said. "An attention-getter, something to sharpen the wits. Get you out of this rut you're in."

Gerald kept going, out the front door to his car.

Shouldn't have done that, was all he could think.

The lunch crowd filled Perry's. Perry's, Union Street, in Cow Hollow at the foot of Pacific Heights. Where the elite meet to eat and greet. Gerald watched them through the plate glass, banging dice cups and drinking beer at the polished bar, four and five to a table over blue-checked tablecloths. They were mostly suits, business types. Plenty of Hart Schaffners and Nino Ceruttis.

The clock in Perry's said 12:45. But that would be bar time, help to hustle the drunks out at closing. Gerald's wristwatch was exactly ten minutes slower. He looked up and down the street.

233

Though he didn't know who he was waiting for, or how they would arrive. He assumed it would be by car. But for all he knew, somebody would walk out of Perry's and tap him on the shoulder.

Across the street he saw Welcome.

Seeing Welcome, he got steamed again. Ruark had sent Welcome to check up on him.

Welcome crossed the street.

"I'm fine, I'm fine, go away, I'm handling it," Gerald said.

"Don't get upset," Welcome said.

"It's not you. But Ruark. Goddamn. The man is all over me."

"I hope you don't blame me," Welcome said.

"You're all right," Gerald said. "You seemed pretty neat, till you hired on. Then I started to have my doubts. You're making a mistake."

"I don't see you quitting."

"Stick around and watch."

Gerald looked up and down the street.

He said, "But I still have to get through today. You better move on. It's supposed to be just me. They see two, they might get nervous."

"They aren't coming," Welcome said.

"Is that why he sent you?"

"He didn't send me," Welcome said. "He doesn't know I'm here."

Gerald hated to feel dumb. But something was wrong with this picture. Welcome touched him on the arm.

"Gerald," Welcome said. "You want to see some stones?"

Welcome brought Gerald up to his apartment, then went downstairs alone. Grace said, "This came for you . . ."

The FedEx.

He kissed her and went upstairs. Gerald was examining the work on the kitchen table, but he asked no questions. Welcome brought the FedEx box into the bedroom. He told Gerald to come in.

Welcome opened the box. Took out the black velvet pouch. Unrolled it. Spread the jewels on it.

For a little while they both stared.

"You better take your pictures," Welcome said.

"Right."

Gerald shot a whole pack of film, some close up and others from a few feet away, the jewels blazing in the burst of flash. The camera kept rolling out prints.

"You," Gerald kept saying. "You're the partner. Oh wow. You."

When he was finished Gerald squared the prints in a neat stack and put them in his front pocket. Welcome gathered the stones, rolled them up. He left Gerald alone while he went down to Grace again.

She was almost packed. He put the velvet pouch in her last open bag.

"Tonight," he said, and he kissed her.

Upstairs Gerald was once more looking over the work on the kitchen table.

"What do you think?" Welcome said.

"This is a radio. This stuff is—it couldn't be clay, could it? Kiddie clay?"

"It could be, but it's not."

"You're making a bomb," Gerald said.

"An explosive device."

"Did he order that up?"

"You're a very sharp kid, Gerald."

"You got the man turned around but good," Gerald said. "You going to do a number on him?"

"I'm going to try. Does that bother you?"

"Not anymore," Gerald said.

"I could use your help. I was going to go it alone, but you'd make it that much easier. There'd be money in it. Lot of money. You want in?"

"Yes," Gerald said. "I'm not doing it for the money. You want to come up with some afterward, that's okay. But it's not why I'm doing it."

"You have a few minutes?"

"I'm supposed to call him when I'm done."

"Call him."

"Then I have another errand to run."

"Would this involve buying a couple of suitcases?"

"How did you know?" Gerald said. "You know the plan?"

"I should," Welcome said. "It's my plan."

"Then you know," Gerald said. "I'm supposed to buy two suitcases, completely identical. He gave me fifty bucks. For two suitcases."

"We can do it on the way to the Cliff House," Welcome said.

"Cliff House?" Gerald said.

Gerald drove the Isuzu out Geary Boulevard to the ocean. It was a straight shot heading west. You got the feeling that you were in a neighborhood more than in a city. Geary was commercial, but there were neighborhood businesses, shops and restaurants and taverns.

On 15th Avenue, a few doors from Geary, was a shoemaker and luggage store. In the front window was a display of Louis Vuitton luggage—fake Vuitton, Gerald noticed right away. The overnight bags were forty dollars. They came with small brass padlocks to lock the zippers.

Welcome told Gerald his idea as they drove to the ocean. They got to the Cliff House as Welcome was finishing.

"What do you think?" Welcome said.

Gerald parked in the middle of the lot. He got out and looked around. The Cliff House, the rocks and trees and the beach, Geary Boulevard and the Great Highway.

"I see what you mean," Gerald said. A grin was starting to form on his face. He was showing white teeth. "Yes. Yes." The grin was spreading across his broad brown face. He said, "Yes indeed."

59

"You have to be there," Ruark said to Hays.

Hays was at work, at the office.

"We do?" Hays said.

"Goddamn, we're supposed to be partners. One of the biggest days of my life, you don't want to be there."

"I do," Hays said. "But I didn't think you wanted us interfering."

"I didn't say interfere. I said be there."

"I don't know," Hays said. He didn't want to be anywhere near Ruark and the stones.

"I'm sensing some resistance here," Ruark said. "Now I'm getting the stones back, you act like you owe me nothing, trying to weasel out. You trying to avoid me?"

Yes I am, Hays thought. You scare me.

"No," Hays said. "Not at all."

"For one thing, it's symbolic. You lost the stones, you should be there to help me get 'em back."

"If you say so."

"And to be practical, I could use another set of hands. After the Marine makes his entrance—who knows how it might go down? I'd want you two to leave with the money, get it out of there as fast as you can."

Hays said nothing.

"I consider it a sign of good faith," Ruark said. "Or not. We're at a crossroads. Where we go from here is pretty much up to you."

"Whatever you want," Hays said. "I'm all yours."

"You and Hays will leave with the money," Ruark said to Caitlin. She was at his place. Ruark had asked her to come. With Harmon and Gerald gone, he wanted help watching Naull. She agreed right away. This was too exciting to ignore. Naull held captive, a big-bucks swap for a fortune in jewels. And now armed robbery, getting back the money and the jewels both. Too much!

Naull was out on the porch now. Said he wanted some air. Ruark and Caitlin both watched him through the living room window. Ruark knew, though, that Naull wasn't going to run away. Run out on his life's jackpot.

Ruark kept his voice low.

He said, "I don't know where it'll be yet. But wherever it is, we'll improvise. The Marine comes in, takes the money, he gives it to me and I give it to you. I want it out of there. It'll be confusion. Who knows what might go down?"

"You'd let me carry the money?" Caitlin said.

"Why not?" Ruark said.

"That's an act of trust."

"It's an act of love."

"Of commitment," she said. "Of trust and love and commitment."

"You have to watch Hays," he said. "When I told him, I could hear him thinking. You and him alone with my six and a half big ones."

"I'll handle Hays," she said. "Won't be long, Hays will be handled for good."

"That's right," Ruark said.

"Going to be you and me."

"Until the end," he said.

Ruark went out onto the front porch. Naull was sitting beside the porch railing.

"Rec period is over," Ruark said, and Naull went inside.

Ruark had tried to hate Naull. Naull, after all, invaded his life. Naull stole his stones, and was holding them ransom—it amounted to that.

But Ruark couldn't make it stick. He could feel nothing for Naull; Naull betrayed no trust. Naull didn't even know him. Naull would receive his exact due. Which was nothing.

Hays and Caitlin, that was different.

Let people into your life, this is what they do to you.

Hays and Caitlin, he could feel plenty.

Ruark looked out across grass and trees. He could see it. Night. Down a road, a highway. He is driving. Hays and Caitlin are driving too, up ahead. Hays and Caitlin, betrayers of his trust, violators of his life. Hays and Caitlin with their knowledge of him, their intimacy, their special insight.

He drives, he watches them up ahead. He draws closer, closer. Too close, maybe, but still closer: he wants to see it happen. In his hands he holds a magic box with a magic button.

Hays and Caitlin, rolling merrily along with larceny and betrayal in their hearts. His finger is on the button. He watches them. They are powerless now, their lives completely his, and he deigns to grant them these last heartbeats, these final moments of perfidy. And their unconcern gives him some pleasure, too. If they only knew.

He presses the button. And witnesses the last instant of their existence, the first instant of their absence.

Talk about intimacy.

Hays told his secretary he'd be having a long lunch. He left the building, drove out and onto Highway 101, and across the bridge to the Jackson Street building.

Two calls in the middle of the night, a dozen through the morning, he got no answer from Grace. He couldn't believe that she would spurn him. Yesterday at the house, her refusal, he knew that had to be a gambit. She couldn't possibly refuse him.

Welcome must be complicating things. If she wasn't at home, she had to be with Welcome.

Okay, get her back, he thought, steal her back if that's what it takes.

At the building, he tried her door first, just in case. No. Then up the stairs to Welcome's. Hays told himself not to think of Welcome as a trained killer. That would be intimidating. No, Welcome was out of work. He was aimless and rootless, he was adrift. He was a loser.

That was better. Grace would see it that way, too.

He thumped on Welcome's door. No answer.

Hays had keys. Just in case. He let himself into Welcome's door. Walked through. There was nobody. The apartment was neat. No sign of Grace.

Hays left and closed the door behind him. He went downstairs, and let himself into 1-B.

She was out. She was gone. He went through the room. Closets empty, dresser drawers half open and empty.

Little bitch. Little bitch blew her chance. Talk about dumb . . . you almost had to feel sorry for her.

In the middle of the empty apartment, Hays suddenly wanted to be with Caitlin. They had been through so much together, he thought: a whole lifetime in the last couple of days. Caitlin, let's face it, Caitlin was irritating. She could be annoying, yes.

But she had spirit, she had vision. God knows, things were never dull around Caitlin. There was a hell of a lot to be said for it.

Grace, Grace was a first-class cupcake, have to give her that. But dull as dishwater, when you were past the frosting. Vision, she couldn't see past her nose. A lifetime with Miss Congeniality, what could he have been thinking of?

He hurried out of the apartment. He wanted to go home.

Caitlin made Naull lay on the living room couch. He didn't want to lay down. She stuck the gun in his face, the chrome automatic, and he lay down.

She didn't want to have to worry about him. She wanted to close her eyes and visualize the scene.

They are driving away from the setup. Ruark is somewhere behind her, trailing her by a few minutes more or less.

She has the money.

She parks at the rendezvous. She waits for Ruark.

Caitlin opened her eyes. Naull was still on the couch, but she didn't see Naull. What she saw was Ruark, in the night, coming up to her car and asking for his money.

She brought the gun up, held it in both hands, sighted down the barrel.

Ka-POW!

Ruark went through the stack of Polaroids. He gave each a long look before he put it down and went to the next. Some of them he put down quicker than others. The shots that showed the whole pile weren't worth much. It could have been a pile of rhinestones and junk crystal, for all he could tell.

But some of the close-ups were convincing. They had the look. He thought he recognized a few of his favorites, certain stones that you didn't easily forget.

"Tell me about it," Ruark said. He was standing at the living room window with Gerald, looking at the pictures in the light. Naull and Caitlin were at the other side of the room.

"Not much to tell," Gerald said. "A man and a woman, both of them in their thirties. She's driving. An old Dodge Polara, I'm not sure what year. He's in the backseat. They pull up, he opens the back door—it's a four-door—and he tells me to get in. The pouch is on the seat between us. I get in, he shows me the gun."

"What kind of gun?" Ruark said.

"Sawed-off double barrel. Bad news. She drives down the street, Union Street. He says I have half a minute to take my snapshots. I finish, he drops me off, corner of Union and Fillmore."

"What did they look like?"

"The woman, I'd say early thirties, black hair. I didn't see much of her. The man, he's a face in the crowd. Joe Ordinary."

"What about it?" Naull shouted from across the room.

"They pass," Ruark said.

"All right now, the money. No money, I told you, if I don't see the money first, I don't do the meet."

"Shut up!" Caitlin said.

"The money," Naull said.

Ruark checked the Casio on his wrist.

"Gerald, let's get the damn money," he said.

They took Gerald's Isuzu west toward the ocean.

"Mr. Ruark?" Gerald said. "How is my mother? How about my sister?"

"They're in great shape," Ruark said. "You haven't tripped over your dick yet today, have you? Long as you don't screw up, they're fine."

"I know I let you down," Gerald said. "I feel bad about it. I want to make it up to you, give me a chance."

"It'll be a long day," Ruark said. "You never know."

The little town of Tomales, on the coast, had a branch office of the Bank of America. It was on the main street, in a building roughly the dimensions of a three-car garage. One teller and one desk suit, both of whom recognized Ruark when he came in carrying one of the two fake Vuittons.

The second fake Vuitton was still in the trunk of the Isuzu. Caitlin and Naull knew nothing about it.

Gerald came into the bank, too, but stayed up front while Ruark and the desk suit went back to the safe-deposit boxes. It was a small room in a small bank. Gerald couldn't see everything, but he could tell that Ruark gave the suit two different keys, and that the suit used the keys, and one of his own, to open two different deposit boxes and pull them out, put them on a table.

Big boxes, big as drawers.

The suit left and closed the door behind him. Minute or so later, Ruark came out. The Vuitton was locked, and it didn't look empty anymore. The suit shoved the drawers back and locked them and returned the two keys to Ruark.

Tomales Road, the way back to Ruark's place, was north of the town. But Ruark told Gerald to drive south on Highway One, the Coast Highway.

Actually you were not along the coast here. To your right, beside the road, was the narrow inlet called Tomales Bay, and beyond that the humped green hills of Point Reyes Park. The ocean was on the other side of the hills.

They drove. Tomales Bay was flat and calm. The farther they drove, the narrower it got.

Pull over, Ruark said. There was a wide gravel apron to the right. WILDLIFE REFUGE, said a sign. VIEWING AREA.

Hundreds of shorebirds—Gerald tried to think of the names: terns? Plovers? Rails?—waded in the marsh at the bay's edge, delicately strutting on legs thin as wires.

Only one other vehicle was in the lot. The Econoline. Gerald parked next to it, and Welcome got out.

He was carrying a box, cardboard box.

He brought it to a picnic table beside the marsh. Ruark and Gerald locked the Isuzu, with the money bag on the front seat. Ruark got the second fake Vuitton, the empty one, and brought it with him to the picnic table.

Welcome opened the carton. "Life Savers Assorted Display Pack 36 Count," it said. Inside—Gerald got a good look to make sure—was the radio, the transmitter. And a device. One device. Also a few used paperback books.

Electronics was not Gerald's strong hand. The device, as far as he could see, was basically a few electronic bits wired to a nine-volt battery and a block of the stuff that looked like kiddie clay. It was all mounted on a piece of plastic, thin green plastic like a circuit board. It was hand rigged, you could tell. But done with care. You would expect it to work.

Ruark opened the empty Vuitton. Welcome was supposed to put the device inside.

"It's not very heavy," Welcome said. "I would add a few books for weight. Verisimilitude."

Ruark seemed amused, a word like that coming out of a Marine. But he put in the books, Gerald noticed. Then the device, carefully.

He zipped the bag and snapped on the small brass padlock.

Now Welcome was showing Ruark the transmitter. The on-off switch, telescoping antenna.

"Radio devices," Welcome said, "the problem is premature detonation because of stray signals. Especially in a populated area, you've got electrical fields everywhere, commercial radio, CB, God knows what all. You don't want this puppy going off early."

"No," Ruark said.

"So I've got it wired, a sequence of three circuits before you get to the cap. They have to be opened, in correct order, before the device is armed. Like this. Ailerons." He touched a small silver joystick. "Rudder." Another silver joystick. "Throttle, this slide. You push the first one, that'll open that particular circuit. Then you can open the next one. The last is this button." Small red button to the side of the case. "Auxiliary One, that's the one makes the big noise."

He pressed the red button. The power switch was off.

"Nice," Ruark said. He took hold of the radio. But Welcome wasn't letting go.

"What about my money?" Welcome said.

"When you're finished," Ruark said. "A little piece of work tonight, you didn't forget, did you?"

Welcome still wasn't letting go.

"The money will be with me," Ruark said. "Ride with me when we're finished, we'll get out of there together. We'll make sure this little beauty works. Then you get your money."

Welcome still looked reluctant.

"Seventy-five," Ruark said. "It all comes off, you've earned a bonus."

Welcome let go of the radio.

"You hear from him yet?" Welcome said.

"Not yet. We'll hear. They want the cash more than the stones."

Back at the Isuzu, with Welcome driving off in the van, Ruark told Gerald to hold the money bag. Gerald did. Ruark stuck the second Vuitton, the device, behind Gerald's seat. Took off a jacket, a scruffy nylon windbreaker, and draped it over the bag, to hide it.

"We get back," Ruark said, "I want you to park away from the house. I don't want anybody looking in."

"Yes sir," Gerald said.

"Here," Ruark said, and he made a gimme motion with his hand. He wanted Gerald's suitcase, the money. He was holding a small strip of paper . . . no. It was an adhesive label, the kind that comes with blank videotapes. Ruark peeled the backing off the label and wrapped it around the handle of the suitcase. It looked like an airline baggage check.

It was small. In the excitement Naull would never notice.

"Don't want to mix 'em up," Ruark said.

"No sir."

"That would put us in a world of hurt."

"It sure would."

"Now, just for the record," Ruark said, "the one with the label contains the money."

"Right."

"The one with the label stays in the car. The money does not leave the car."

"Right," Gerald said. "Got it."

"The one you take out is . . ."

"The one without the label," Gerald said. "The device."

"Very good," Ruark said.

Let's get back to the house, he told Gerald, and Gerald turned north up the Coast Highway, beside Tomales Bay again.

"You want a second chance with the Marine?" Ruark said.

"Yes sir, I sure do," Gerald said.

"Think you can handle him next time?"

"If I don't have my hands full."

"You won't. Near the end, when we're all leaving, he'll try to leave with me."

"He wants his money," Gerald said.

"Yes. Don't let him in the car. Him and me alone with the money and the jewels, he'll get ideas."

"His mind would work that way," Gerald said.

"Whatever it takes, keep him out of the car with me."

"I won't let him near you," Gerald said. "Believe me."

"Your second chance, chance for redemption, how often does that happen?"

"Not very often," Gerald said.

"Don't fuck it up," Ruark said.

"I appreciate it," Gerald said. "I really do."

61

"Another beer," Harmon said.

Right away the girl, Jinky, went to the fridge and brought him a Coors. Poured it into a clean glass and gave it to him.

He watched her walk away. A sweet little thing like her, coming from the same parents who gave the world great big Gerald. Believe it or not, Ripley.

He was sitting in an easy chair, beside the door. The telephone was beside him. From here he could block the door, catch the phone, and watch TV. They had cable, HBO and Showtime, but no remote.

And the beer was cold.

Harmon caught Mama in the kitchen door, watching him watch the girl.

"Old lady," he said. "Don't let it break your cookies."

62

In Ruark's house they waited. Hays showed up after dark, with take-out meals from a vegetarian restaurant in Mill Valley.

They finished the food, and waited.

"Your partner is playing games," Caitlin said.

"He doesn't play games," Naull said.

"Jerking our chain."

"He wants the money. It's half his, he wants it as much as I do."

"Then why doesn't he call?"

"He'll call," Naull said, and tried to sound convinced.

Welcome took Grace out to a late dinner. Italian, North Beach. It was nearly nine-thirty when they ordered.

Grace knew Italian food. She rattled it off without a menu. Antipasto, *bracciole,* ziti, tortellini, zabaglione, zuppa inglese.

Welcome was expecting spaghetti.

Trust me, she said.

Welcome asked the waiter where he could find a telephone. The pay phone was on the wall outside the rest rooms.

"Yes," said Ruark after half a ring.

"Naull," Welcome said. His hand muffled the mouthpiece.

He could hear the phone being passed.

"Yeah," Naull said.

"Is this private?" Welcome said.

"Close enough."

"Cliff House, midnight," Welcome said. "Parking lot out front."

"The Cliff House?" Naull said.

"Ideal."

"You'll be there."

"You won't see me at first."

"Repeat that."

"Look for an orange trash can. You'll know it when you see it. Stones'll be there. And you'll want a gun, too. Everything you need will there."

"Are you sure?" Naull said. He sounded very unhappy.

"Gun, stones, everything. Trust me, I'm going to take care of you. Oh yeah, and you want to frisk everybody. Don't worry, they'll go for it."

Naull, or somebody, hung up the phone.

The meal was a feast. They ate for almost an hour. Welcome felt stuffed and happy, with the food in his stomach and Grace across the table from him.

He spooned out the last of his zuppa inglese, which turned out to be a soupy custard. But nice. He went back to the phone again.

"Yes," Ruark said after half a ring.

"Got anything?" Welcome said.

"Jesus, where you been, we're running out of time."

"Late meal," Welcome said.

"Midnight, the Cliff House parking lot, you know where it is?"

"I've been there."

"Cliff House, what do you think? Does it work?"

"Ideal," Welcome said.

They had her Ford. She drove him across town to Mission Street, and down Mission.

He watched the street signs, then the addresses.

"This is the place," he said. The only parking space on the street was a red zone, no parking at any time, eighty-dollar ticket.

But he told her to pull in.

"I won't be long," he said.

64

Harmon watched the Giants blow one to the Padres in the ninth. After the game was the eleven o'clock news. Forget it. He got up and twirled the cable selector until he found a "Mork and Mindy" rerun.

He was almost back at the chair when somebody knocked at the door.

"Harmon," somebody said outside.

Harmon opened it but kept the chain on. Looked through the crack. It was the Marine. Ruark's Marine, now.

Official business, Harmon thought. He hoped the Marine wasn't coming to relieve him. This wasn't bad, beer and the tube and Jinky.

He slipped the chain and opened the door.

65

Gerald concluded that the Okie, Ralph Naull, was no fool. The five of them—Naull and Gerald, Caitlin and Hays, Ruark with the money bag—were crossing the front yard of Ruark's house, ready to get into the vehicles. It was quarter past eleven, the Cliff House at least forty minutes away, when Naull stopped and said, "I want to see the money again."

Waiting until the last second, so he would know if they were playing games with him. That afternoon he had seen it, counted it. But they took it away, and anything could have happened to it.

"What for?" Ruark said.

"I want to know it's there. I don't see it, you got no deal."

"Shut up," Caitlin said, "screw you, get your ass in the car."

She was a sleek-looking woman, Gerald thought. She certainly knew how to put herself together. Tonight she was wearing a pants suit— Shantung silk, Gerald was willing to bet—and a long suede duster. But it was like unwrapping a beautiful package and finding a ferret, hissing and spitting and ready to chew off your arm.

"The money," Naull said.

"Who are you to be making demands?" she said. "You're nobody, you're nowhere. Hick piece of shit."

"I'm the guy who can put his hands on what you want," Naull said. "I don't go near it till I know what you're bringing."

Ruark stepped in. Literally, right between them.

"No, no, that's reasonable," Ruark said. "That's prudent."

It sure is, Gerald thought.

Gerald was walking directly behind them.

Ruark said, "Gerald."

Gerald handed Ruark the fake Vuitton overnighter.

"I wouldn't mind seeing it in the light," Naull said.

"Next you'll want to count it again," Caitlin said.

"No," Naull said. "Just get a good look at it."

So they went back into the house. Ruark laid the suitcase flat on his coffee table. He popped off the small padlock and opened the zipper.

Wham, right there in your face. It was solid Franklins. Packets and packets of Franklins, hundred to a packet. Sixty-five packets at ten thousand each. Thirteen stacks of five packets apiece.

Naull shuffled through some of the stacks, riffled through some of the packets. A careful man. And he was enjoying this, too, the cash in his hands.

"Ralph," said Ruark, "we *are* on a schedule."

"That oughta do it," Naull said. He replaced the packets in their stacks and zipped up the suitcase.

"Can we go now?" Caitlin said.

"Good idea," Naull said.

Gerald picked up the suitcase and they all went out again, Gerald with the suitcase to the Isuzu, Ruark and Naull to the Shelby, Hays and Caitlin to the Mercedes.

Then Ruark left Naull standing alone. He walked over to Gerald. The Isuzu was parked apart from the others, where Ruark wanted it.

Gerald was outside the car, the money bag in his hand. He had the driver's-side door open. Ruark went over to him, looked inside.

There was the second suitcase, behind the driver's seat.

"Just one more time," Ruark said quietly. "The white label is what?"

"White label's the money," Gerald said. "It stays in the car."

"And just for the record, the one you take out is . . ."

"The one without the label," Gerald said. "The device."

"You're my man," Ruark said.

Oh, yeah.

"I appreciate that," Gerald said.

Ruark went over and got in the Mustang, with Naull. In a few seconds, they were all up and running, headlights on. Gerald reached down and got the second fake Vuitton, and he put it on the seat beside the other one. Two suitcases, identically fake. Except for the white label nobody could tell them apart.

Ruark had the gate opener. He went out first. Gerald followed him, and Hays and Caitlin in the Mercedes pulled in behind Gerald, and they got out on the two-lane and started rolling toward San Francisco.

Grace and Welcome drove to the end of the boulevard. The road crested a rise and dropped downhill. There were no more houses. For about a block the dark battered forms of cypress trees lined both sides of the road. Once more the boulevard dipped, and they were out of the trees, and the ocean and the rocks were straight ahead. Grace pulled into the empty parking lot in front of the Cliff House.

The seals were yapping when Welcome stood outside. The air was still and clear. It smelled of brine. And cold—early July felt like a Kansas November, but damp on top of it. The dampness cut right down to bone. Welcome wore a pair of Levi's and a cotton sweater. He wished he'd brought a jacket.

Grace's Ford faced the Cliff House and the ocean. It was near the building's north side, the entrance for the Musée Mechanique. The low stone wall marked the end of the parking lot. Drive any farther and you'd be over the edge, down with the seals in the surf.

Welcome walked over to the stone wall. He was carrying a camera bag over one shoulder. He went over to one of the two trash cans along the wall.

The can had a fold-up lid, hinged at the top. Welcome folded back the top of the trash can. He unzipped the camera bag and took out the rolled velvet pouch.

Tonight the sea wasn't pounding. Welcome could hear it lap and wash down below in the darkness. That and the seals' yelping.

The trash can was almost full. Welcome laid the velvet pouch inside, on top of a red-and-white box from Kentucky Fried Chicken. He went into the camera bag again and took out the sawed-off toy shotgun, and he placed it in the can, beside the velvet pouch.

One more time Welcome put his hand in the camera bag. He got a can of spray paint, and started spraying the trash can. The paint was fluorescent orange, lurid in the car's headlights. Welcome sprayed a big runny orange splotch on the side of the trash can. Then he capped the paint and threw it into the trash can, and he closed the lid.

He walked over to the car, driver's side. Grace's window was down.

"I guess this is it," she said.

"It'll be over before you know it."

"Please be careful. Please."

"Sweetie, this is nothing."

"Nothing can kill you. People die of nothing all the time. Yesterday in San Ramon, I saw it on the news, a man fell off a chair changing a light bulb, he broke his neck and he died before anybody found him. Do you get my drift?"

"I get it."

"I care about you. You make somebody care about you, practically against their will, then you expect them to turn it off and stop caring— uh-uh, it doesn't work that way. You have to take it as it comes, hassles and all."

"I love you, too," Welcome said. He leaned in and kissed her, and when he was standing straight again he told her good-bye.

She pulled a slow U-turn and waved good-bye in the mirror, and drove up toward Geary again. The Ford was the only car in sight on the boulevard, and it was going away fast. Down the other side of the curve, the Great Highway showed no headlights for as far as he could see. It had to be nearly two miles, straight along the ocean.

Welcome walked to the stone wall, and he went over. He started along the narrow margin between the wall and the cliff's edge. He passed the trash can with the orange splotch, and he kept walking. In front of him a big brown rat scrabbled up the wall and over and across the empty parking lot.

The wall turned almost ninety degrees to follow the hill's contour. Now it was the Sutro ruins, not the ocean, down below. Welcome was maybe twenty, thirty paces past the trash can with the orange blotch. He had it in sight. His view up to Geary was blocked now, but he could still see through the wide curve and down the Great Highway.

He stopped, kicked aside a used condom and an empty pint bottle of Canadian Club, and he crouched against the wall. Far down the beach, a bonfire winked red in the darkness, feeble and distant as a star. Welcome could see the ocean, too. A low creamy wall of fog was sliding over the water, a few hundred yards out, scudding toward the beach.

Welcome took the camera bag from his shoulder and put it beside him on the sandy ground. One more time, he went into the bag. He pulled out the Colt. He flipped out the cylinder. The gun was loaded. Welcome shook out the bullets. He slid one of them back in, put the rest in his pocket, and he replaced the cylinder so that the live round would be the next one under the hammer. He stuck the pistol under his belt at the small of his back, and he waited.

Harmon woke up in the bottom of a closet. Darkness, the smell of mothballs, the spike heel of a woman's shoe digging into his side. He tried his hands. Hands were tied behind his back. His legs were flexed, his feet were tied. His ankles were tied together, and somehow were also attached to his wrists: when he straightened his legs he almost pulled his shoulders out of joint.

He shifted his body to take some pressure off the high heel. It was a small closet, and the movement wedged one shoulder against the wall.

It gave him an idea. He put some weight against the shoulder and pushed with his legs. He started to inch up. Once his shoulder slipped, and he fell—onto the high heel again—but he started up once more.

This time he got to his feet. The way he was tied, wrists and ankles somehow connected by a short cord, he could hardly stand. He had to bend backward to straighten his legs.

He turned around to get his hands on the doorknob. His fingertips reached it, barely. He wondered which way the door swung. He turned the knob.

The latch clicked, the door fell open, and Harmon with all his weight tumbled out into the bedroom of Jinky Moon.

The bedroom was dark, but some light shone from up the hall. He saw that he was tied with sash cord from Venetian blinds. Never break it. He crawled out of the bedroom, down the hall, through the living room. Up to the front door. He turned and pressed his right shoulder to the door, and slowly started sliding himself up. This was easier than the closet. The door was painted with high-gloss enamel, smooth, and he pushed himself to his feet on the first try.

The front door was hinged to swing inward. This was a problem. He could turn the knob, pull the door open a few inches. But he kept losing his balance when he tried to swing the door. He kept falling against the door, slamming it shut again.

He tried one more time. He opened the door, pulled it toward him, and fell out of the way.

He hit the floor. The door swung wide open.

He crawled out onto the landing at the top of the stairs. Two other apartments up here on the third floor. He heard nothing from either of them. He saw no light under their doors.

He wondered if he should yell. Call for help. What would that get you, after eleven o'clock, in a Mission District apartment house? It would get you attention, for sure. Would it get people to open their doors? Probably not. A quick call to the cops was more likely.

But if he could get down to the street. Find somebody walking by. A man tied up like a salami would have a certain sympathy factor going for him. Establish some eye contact. People were more helpful if you looked them in the eye, and didn't have to wake them up first to do it.

No elevator. He could not walk down the stairs. Never. Crawl down. Maybe.

He went on hands and knees to the top of the stairs. It looked like a long way down. He tried to remember why he was going to all this trouble.

It came back to him. The Marine. Harmon wasn't totally sure what Evan had going tonight, but he knew it was important, and he decided that the Marine was trying to screw it up. Evan would want to know. Gerald, pain-in-the-ass Gerald, had to be involved, too. It would be worth plenty to Evan.

Harmon tried crawling down, headfirst. This was a mistake. He began to slide, then tumble, and he ended up at the bottom of the stairs.

He lay still long enough that anybody watching might have thought that he was unconscious. But he started to move again. Feet first this time, he wriggled down the next flight of stairs.

Northbound was free on the Golden Gate Bridge. Southbound, you stopped at the toll plaza to pay your money.

Ruark guided the Shelby into a line at one of the toll booths. It gave Naull a chance to make sure that the other two cars were still behind them. The Isuzu, the Mercedes.

He saw them both. From the toll plaza Ruark gunned the Shelby down straight Park Presidio Drive. It was a fast road, concrete walls and fences down both sides, no intersections for the first mile and a half.

Naull looked back. He wanted to keep the other cars in sight. Especially the Isuzu, the money.

Now they hit the first light, California Street. It was green, and Ruark went through without slowing.

The Isuzu was a couple of hundred yards behind. Naull couldn't see the Mercedes.

"They aren't back there," Naull said.

"Who?"

"Hays and Caitlin."

"This morning you didn't want 'em to come along," Ruark said. "Now you can't see 'em, you're all upset."

"I'm trying to stay on top of things," Naull said.

"Don't bust your chops. You have to loosen up if you want to play with the heavy hitters."

The next light was Sacramento Street. Ruark hit it on the red. The Isuzu pulled in a few cars behind them.

No Mercedes. What happened to them?

Naull caught himself. Worrying about Hays and Caitlin—get off it. Seven months they'd been bugging him. Losing them now, it would be like losing a hernia.

The next light was Geary. Ruark turned right on the boulevard, westbound toward the ocean. Naull glanced back one more time.

There was the Isuzu, turning right under a yellow. The money.

"Well?" Ruark said.

"Forget it," Naull said.

"Right-hand lane," Caitlin said near the south end of the bridge. "Booth on the right."

There were three lanes open southbound.

"The other one's shorter," Hays said.

"Booth on the right," she said, and Hays steered the Mercedes right.

Five cars ahead of them. It was almost half a minute before Hays pulled up at the booth. The attendant was giving him change for a ten when Caitlin said, "Turn right."

"What?"

"Turn right, I want you to turn right. We'll take Lincoln, it's quicker."

"We're going straight—"

"Will you hang a Goddamn right?"

Immediately past the toll plaza was the turn for a service road. It cut through a highway department maintenance yard, then ran up into the hills and bluffs of the ocean headlands. Hays knew the road. It connected to Lincoln Drive, which eventually brought you to Geary Boulevard. But it wasn't the fastest way to get there.

Hays followed the winding road. Dark, deserted. No houses; this was public land, the Presidio post. Trees grew in close to the edge of the road.

Across the seat Caitlin looked thoughtful, almost placid.

"Here," she said. A sign for Baker Beach, down a dirt road.

"Come on," Hays said.

She reached for the steering wheel and wrenched it right. Hays hit the brakes and grabbed the wheel. By the time he got the wheel back, they were turning down to the beach.

"I want to go to the beach," she said.

It was a short road. Hays followed it down and stopped the Mercedes against a parking bumper. Beyond was the sand and the water.

Caitlin got out of the car and started walking toward the water. Not a word, nothing.

She got about halfway across the sand and stopped.

Hays wondered if she had lost her nerve. Maybe she'd been thinking about what was going to come down at the Cliff House. Maybe she had changed her mind.

Maybe changed her mind about all of it. Wanted to be normal, live like everybody else. Maybe reached her limit with it—it had to happen eventually.

Hays got out of the car and started over to her. She was bundled in the suede duster, hands in her pockets. She looked small and cold. To their right the lights of the bridge made a long, graceful reach across the water to Marin.

He decided he would put his arms around her. Them and the water and the bridge and the night. Tell her it was all right, they would start over together.

She heard him coming. She turned to face him, a few steps away.

She was holding a gun, the silver .45. She was pulling the trigger.

Hays went down. It was like walking into a wall, the bellow of the gun, the astonishing crackle of flame that leaped out of the barrel.

He was on his back, writhing in the sand. His stomach burned. His stomach, his right hip, Jesus it hurt. He couldn't move his right leg. Jesus.

She was walking over to him. Standing over him, putting the gun to his forehead.

Hays couldn't speak.

Happy Trails, she said.

68

Gerald tried to let out some distance between him and Ruark as he followed the Shelby up Geary Boulevard. He dropped back discreetly, a few more car lengths every block.

At 29th Avenue Ruark made the light, Gerald didn't. The Shelby kept going and was out of sight by the time Gerald got the green.

This took a little pressure off. Gerald drove up Geary, clicking through greens again. At 37th he slowed. Parking lot of the Cala Foods, Welcome had said, northwest corner of the intersection. Blue Ford Tempo, good-looking blonde.

There she was. Gerald drove into the lot and pulled up beside the Ford.

She was standing beside the car. Good-looking? No. A fox.

Gerald got out of the Isuzu.

"Grace," he said. "I'm Gerald."

"You certainly are," she said.

She was holding a fake Vuitton, number three. Gerald pulled the money bag out of the Isuzu.

"A little complication," he said, and he showed her. The white sticker. He tried to pull the sticker apart, but the paper started to tear.

She tried. Her fingers were small and deft. She peeled the sticker apart, and stuck it on the handle of number three.

"You get this," Gerald said. The money bag. "And the key."

She opened the money bag.

"Holy moley!" she said.

Gerald liked that. It sounded like a line from a corny old movie. Mickey Rooney, maybe, squawking in an Andy Hardy flick. People didn't talk that way anymore, if they ever did.

But didn't he just hear it? Now, of all times?

She gave him number three.

"Here," she said, "it's all yours. That thing"—*thang*, she said—"makes me nervous."

He took number three, now with the sticker, and put it on the front seat of the Isuzu.

"Got to run," he said.

"I know."

"It's been real."

"Not hardly," she said. "But thanks."

Harmon told himself that he didn't actually have to make it out to the street. Any old asshole on the stairs would do.

But nobody used the stairs. Harmon crawled down all three flights, and through the entry hall. He managed to open the front door, and when it was open he teetered and fell down the front steps.

He found himself on the sidewalk. An empty sidewalk. He wondered if any part of his body did not hurt.

No. Probably not.

This would be worth plenty to Evan. Harmon promised himself that he would make sure Evan knew how much it was worth.

257

Mission Street was half a block down, bright and busy. Harmon could make out the sign, a storefront restaurant on the corner. TAQUERIA SANCHEZ.

He started to crawl again.

Ruark pulled over and stopped across from the Seal Rock Inn. It was the last building on Geary. The Cliff House was a couple of blocks farther on, visible through the gap in the black cypress trees.

The Isuzu, the money car, was not behind them. Naull didn't like this, and neither did Ruark.

Maybe a minute later, maybe two, the Isuzu glided in behind them and parked. Ruark started walking toward the car, and huge Gerald got out to meet him halfway.

Naull could hear the conversation. Ruark wanted to know what held him up, and Gerald said it was the traffic lights, he must've hit every red light on Geary.

Ruark sat in the Shelby again. Sat, said nothing, didn't make a move.

"What are we waiting for?" Naull said.

"My friends."

"Do we need 'em? I'm ready to move."

"When I say so."

This was more than a minute or two. More like ten, before the Mercedes finally rolled up Geary.

It pulled up abreast of them. Down slid the window on the passenger side. Ruark cranked his down.

It was Caitlin, alone.

"Where's my partner?" Ruark said.

"Hays has totally lost interest in the proceedings."

Ruark took this in. Naull could see him digesting it.

"What do you say?" she yelled. "Let's do it."

The others followed as Ruark drove the Shelby slowly down Geary, then straight into the parking lot of the Cliff House.

Halfway across the parking lot, Naull told Ruark to stop. He wanted a cushion, leave himself some space. Ruark stopped. The Isuzu swung around right and stopped beside the Shelby. The Mercedes swung left and parked on the other side.

Naull could see the can, the orange splotch.

"I got to pat you down," he said. "Everybody."

"I'm clean," Ruark said.

"You want the stones? Because you're not there yet."

They both got out of the Shelby. Naull patted Ruark, and Ruark made Gerald and Caitlin stand still for it, too.

All clean.

Naull started to walk across the pavement. Their headlights were bright, the three cars lined up in the lot. Naull felt like a butterfly pinned to the wall.

And where was Welcome? Naull looked over the wall. What he saw was fog. It was already in along the beach. It was churning around Seal Rock and clawing to get up the cliff.

He opened the lid of the trash can, and looked in.

Welcome was behind the wall, far enough from the trash can that he was out of the lights. Nobody saw him as he watched Naull reach into the trash can.

Naull picked up the plastic shotgun. His back was to the cars, so his face was in shadow. Welcome couldn't see his expression. But imagine.

Naull put down the shotgun. He picked up the velvet pouch. Untied the string and looked inside and even put his hand in to make sure.

Welcome saw his shoulders slump. You could read it in his body, what he found inside the pouch.

Ruark was out of the car now, standing beside the Shelby, yelling something at Naull.

Naull tied up the velvet pouch. He picked up the plastic shotgun, and squared his shoulders, and he turned to face the lights.

And behind the wall, Welcome put his hand on the Colt.

Ruark noticed that there were no other cars in sight. How was Naull supposed to get away with the money? And Naull's buddy—where was he?

But these were Naull's problems, Ruark thought. More to the point, Naull was taking too much time at the trash can, standing with his back turned toward them, illuminated in their headlights. Way too much time.

Ruark stepped out of the Shelby.

He yelled, "What you got for me?"

Naull turned. In his right hand was a sawed-off shotgun, double-barrel. In his left was the pouch.

He held up the pouch.

"Got it," he said.

Carmen Galario Sanchez was alone behind the cash register of her taqueria. The place was quiet, and the chairs were turned over on most of the tables.

The large gringo came through the open front door. Flopped through.

He was tied up, scraped and bloody, and winded. Big as he was, she felt no danger. Not in his condition. She picked up a kitchen knife, went around the counter, and cut the cords at his feet and hands.

"I will call the police," she said. "An ambulance also."

"Fuck that shit," he said. "Where's the phone?"

69

Naull looked into the velvet pouch and found pea gravel, pebbles. A toy shotgun and pebbles.

He had to hand it to Welcome. Welcome delivered exactly what he promised. *Stones,* Welcome had said. *And you'll want a gun, too.*

Here they were. Stones and a gun.

I'm going to take care of you, Welcome had said.

You've done that, Naull thought. You have damn sure taken care of me.

"What have you got for me?" Ruark yelled behind Naull.

Naull lifted the velvet pouch.

"Got it," he said.

"The stones," Ruark said.

"The money," Naull said.

"Gerald, the money," Ruark said, and Gerald pulled a suitcase out of the front seat of the Isuzu. He showed the suitcase to Ruark, and brought it toward Naull.

Naull figured maybe eighty or ninety feet between him and the cars. Gerald carried the suitcase about halfway, and put it down.

"Back off," Naull said. He waved the plastic shotgun, and Gerald stepped part of the way back toward the cars.

"The stones," Ruark said. "Now."

Naull kept his eyes on them as he walked toward the suitcase. He put the velvet pouch on the asphalt and pulled the suitcase back with him.

Gerald walked out and picked up the pouch. He untied the ribbon. He looked inside the pouch.

Naull watched Gerald's big hands, and thought how it would be to have those hands on his throat. He felt naked and alone. He felt cold, not just on his skin, but cold and dark and hopeless deep in the center of himself.

Gerald kept peering into the pouch. Naull leveled the plastic shotgun. Ready for the bluff of his life.

"Okay," Gerald said over his shoulder to Ruark. "Looks good."

Looks good? Naull thought. *Looks good?*

Gerald rolled up the pouch. Naull grabbed the suitcase and started to take it back to the wall. He didn't know what was going to happen next. Whatever, by God, he wanted the money with him.

Gerald tied a knot in the pouch's ribbon.

Was he blind? Naull wondered. Was it possible, he really didn't know?

Ruark put out his hands, inviting Gerald to toss him the pouch.

Welcome stood up behind the wall. Pistol in hand.

He vaulted over.

"Relax, take it easy," Welcome said. "Like the wise man says. You can be a hero, you can live to a ripe old age, but you can't have it both ways."

The phone rang and rang at Ruark's house. Whatever was going down, Harmon thought, was going down soon.

He hung up, picked up again, punched in the operator.

"I want to make a call," he said. "Car phone, I don't know how to do it, I have a name, no number, do not give me any shit, this is a real-life emergency."

Silence on the other end. Harmon knew that she was deciding whether to flush him.

"The party's name," she said finally.

"Ruark," he said, "comma Evan. Want me to spell it?"

Welcome walked out until he was in the lights, standing about in the middle of them all.

Old buddy, Naull thought. Thanks. But actually, I was doing all right by myself. Me and my pebbles and my toy shotgun.

"Put down the gun," Welcome said. He was looking at Naull.

Naull considered bluffing him. With a toy shotgun that Welcome knew was plastic.

Naull put the shotgun at his feet.

"The money," Welcome said.

"No," Naull said.

"Give me the money," Welcome said.

"No."

Welcome fired once. Something kicked up asphalt about a foot to Naull's left. Naull could see the mark that the bullet made, he could hear the ricochet singing over the ocean.

"I'm going to get that bag," Welcome said. "If I have to pry it out of your dead fingers."

"Bastard," Naull said. Fellow hick, brother redneck, comrade of the plains. *"Bastard."*

He gave the suitcase a hard shove across the asphalt.

Welcome came over and put his hand on the suitcase. For a moment he looked straight at Naull. What he saw made him glad the shotgun was plastic. Maybe waiting periods and background checks were not such a shabby idea after all.

He started to carry the suitcase past Gerald, to Ruark. Here was something else to think about: How did you carry more than half a million dollars? What were you supposed to look like? Should you cradle it in your arms? Six hundred and fifty thousand dollars. It had to be different from carrying a six-pack out of the PX.

Then he thought: you should carry it about the way you would carry an improvised explosive device. With respect and tenderness.

That worked. Ruark bought it, anyway. Welcome carried the bag past Gerald, to where Ruark was. He put it in Ruark's hands, and Ruark passed it over to Caitlin.

"You did him?" Ruark said to her.

"I sure did."

"By yourself."

"The way it had to be."

"It's you and me now," Ruark said.

"Uh-huh, yes baby, you and me," Caitlin said.

"Sloat Boulevard, entrance to the zoo," he said. "Be there or be square."

"I'll be there," she said. "Count on me."

"I do," he said. "Now and forever."

Naull watched him give Caitlin the money.

Her, Naull thought. With his money.

He was watching his money disappear forever. With *her*.

Now Caitlin was bringing the bag into the Mercedes with her, slamming the door, turning south onto the Great Highway. Naull watched his money drive away. He realized he didn't even have a ride to Santa Cruz. He didn't have cab fare across town.

Gerald was at the Isuzu now. He took out a bag—*the* bag, Naull thought, and then thought no, couldn't be, *the* bag was with Caitlin in the Mercedes, it had to be a bag just like *the* bag—took it out of the Isuzu and gave it to Ruark.

Ruark put it into the old Shelby, the passenger seat.

"Gerald, stones," Ruark said, like he was in a hurry, and Gerald handed him the pouch.

Ruark placed the velvet pouch beside the suitcase. He ran around and slid behind the wheel. Welcome too was getting into the Shelby, on the other side.

He was halfway in when Gerald grabbed him.

Gerald lifted him right out of the car. Welcome swung at Gerald, and Gerald tossed Welcome down to the pavement.

Welcome pulled out his revolver. Gerald wrenched it out of Welcome's hand, and it skittered across the asphalt, out of the light.

Welcome lunged to get away. Gerald caught him by an ankle and dragged him in. He flipped Welcome on his stomach, easy as turning over a pancake. He put a knee in Welcome's back and threw an armlock around Welcome's neck.

He was trying to break Welcome's spine. He could do it, too. You could see it happening.

Naull found himself running. He was running toward Gerald and Welcome, holding the plastic shotgun.

Let him go, let him go, Naull was yelling. Let him go or lose your head.

Naull jammed the two plastic barrels into the side of Gerald's skull. "Let him go," Naull said.

Nobody moved.

Ruark, in the Shelby, was no more than ten feet away from Gerald and Naull and Welcome. He looked Gerald right in the eyes, Gerald with both barrels of a 12-gauge caressing his cranium.

Ruark gunned the Shelby and put it in gear, and dumped the clutch.

The Shelby shot past them, so close that Naull could feel the breeze, the hot pulse of the exhaust. Ruark turned hard left, accelerated past the Cliff House and out of the lot, south onto the Great Highway.

Gerald let go of Welcome's neck. He was watching the Shelby as it sped down the hill.

Naull kept the plastic shotgun jammed in Gerald's hair.

"What are you going to do?" Welcome said. "Blow his brains out with a toy?"

Naull pulled the gun away from Gerald's head. Gerald didn't seem to notice. He kept watching the Shelby.

"No good," Gerald said. The way he stared at the Shelby, there was no doubt that he was talking about Ruark. "No good. Never been any good, never be any good."

The operator had to be at a keyboard. Harmon could hear her typing. Tickety tickety.

"I have a Ruark in Marin," she said. "Initial E."
"That's the dude."
Pop snap click went the connections in Harmon's ear.
A pause. Beat. Beat.
The number was ringing.

Focus, Ruark told himself. It was the ultimate lesson of martial arts, the mental discipline to refine life down to a single task, a single crucial movement of hand or foot, shutting out all else.

He was in the Shelby, headed down the hill from the Cliff House, following Caitlin. She was near the bottom of the hill, where the Great Highway ran straight and unvarying behind surf and sand. The distance between the cars was less than a quarter of a mile.

Focus. He tried to concentrate on the red taillights of the Mercedes, reel them in.

But it was hard. The stones were nagging him. They wanted him to look at them, feel them in his fingers.

Caitlin drove straight into the fog and kept going.

The pouch was in the passenger seat, against the suitcase. Ruark leaned over and reached, driving with his left hand. The pouch was maybe six, eight inches beyond his fingertips. He backed off the accelerator, leaned hard, and snagged the pouch. The Shelby swerved. It headed off the road, and Ruark had to straighten it out quick.

He sat back in his seat. Up ahead the taillights were murky in fog. Ruark hit the gas again, and the Shelby shot on down the hill.

Focus, he thought again.

The pouch was in his right hand, but just then the Shelby hit the bottom of the hill and punched into fog. All of a sudden Ruark didn't have any choice. He stuck the pouch between his legs, deep down between his legs, nestling up against his scrotum.

They felt just right.

He had both hands on the wheel now; he was concentrating on the road, gaining on the Mercedes. Yes. The taillights were closer, getting bigger as he drove.

Ruark steered with his left hand again. With his right he pulled the airplane radio from behind the passenger seat. He put it on his lap, facing him. He extended the chrome antenna.

He turned on the power.

Ailerons, rudder, throttle, Aux 1, he thought. In that order.

Ailerons, rudder, throttle. He pushed them, one after the other. Aux 1 was the red button off to the side.

Now he was closing fast on her. Less than a hundred yards. Now fifty. He wanted to be close when it went. He imagined it, the Mercedes coming apart, disintegrating, consumed. He wondered how close was safe. Should've asked Welcome.

He would take his chances.

Ruark put his thumb on the red button, but he didn't press it. Sloat Boulevard and the zoo were two miles down the highway. He had time.

He wanted to think of Caitlin. He wanted to remember her standing behind him with a gun, chattering about his death. He wanted to remember quailing on the floor, in a coward's posture, to save his own life. While she held the gun on him and talked about how to murder him.

He wanted to feel her under his thumb.

His telephone chirped.

It was like having a beautiful dream interrupted by a kick in the head. Ruark looked away from the taillights, briefly down to the phone and then back up to the lights.

The phone chirped again.

Ruark tried to concentrate. The lights, the red button, the vision of the Mercedes, and Caitlin inside, shattering in the blast.

Focus.

The phone chirped a third time.

He reached down and picked up the receiver. He brought it up in front of his face. The face of the receiver was softly lit, the buttons and numerals and switches.

Ruark's thumb slid the on-off switch. Disconnect. Ruark thought he could hear a voice begin to say his name, and get strangled in mid-word. "*Ev—*" the voice seemed to say. Or maybe it was just his imagination.

The phone went dark. Ruark tossed down the receiver, put both hands on the wheel again, and locked in on the car ahead of him, focused at last.

*   *   *

The three of them got to their feet in the parking lot of the Cliff House.
Welcome and Gerald didn't take their eyes off the lights on the two cars, the
Mustang and the Mercedes down in the fog on the Great Highway, so Naull
watched too without knowing exactly what he was supposed to see.

"You almost let me get in that car," Welcome said to Gerald. He spoke
without turning his head from the highway. "I thought I was going for a
ride."

"It had to seem like you wanted to be there," Gerald said. "The man
was supposed to give you seventy-five K, you should've been *jumping* in
that car."

"Then you about broke my back."

"Verisimilitude," Gerald said.

They both kept looking at the taillights in the fog.

The way they were standing, like they had just finished a tough job,
Naull knew that somehow it had all shaken out.

He said, "That isn't the money."

"Correct," Welcome said.

"So what's in the bag? My bag?"

"Same thing that's in the other one," Welcome said.

"The man got what he asked for," Gerald said. "In spades."

Caitlin drove through the fog.

You and me baby. Well, yes. In a manner of speaking.

What would the police say, when they found her husband and his
business partner both dead—Hays at Baker Beach, Ruark at Sloat
Boulevard—each killed by the same gun?

They would say plenty, she supposed. But she didn't think they
would have much for proof.

Anyway, this was secondary. Two nights ago she had learned that
you could think think *think* about it, but thinking didn't get it done.
Eventually you would think all the life out of it. Sometimes you had to act,
you had to *do*. Follow the impulse out to the Goddamn extremes, to the
extremities of the extremes. Into the abyss, if that was where it led.

Think about it later, if you had to.

She would park at the zoo entrance on Sloat, sit there with the
window down. Ruark would walk over to the Mercedes, wanting his
money. He would bend close to speak, to ask for the bag.

She put the pistol in her lap.

267

Welcome watched both cars enter the fog. First the Mercedes, then the Shelby. Ruark was closing in on her.

The taillights made red blurs. They were the only lights on the Great Highway. It should be anytime now, Welcome thought. Ruark should have the radio out. Throw three switches, hit a button, that was all.

The cars kept receding. The red lights were indistinct, just smudges. In a few seconds the fog would swallow them.

A pair of headlights appeared to his left, up on Geary and moving closer. It was the Ford. Grace.

The radio? The radio had to be good, Welcome thought. The devices, jury-rigged that way, one of them might go bad. But not both.

Ruark must have changed his mind.

Grace stopped beside them. The two pairs of red taillights faded below.

Changed his mind.

"Are you coming?" Grace said.

"Coming," Welcome said.

The red smudges were gone, lost in the night.

"I'll be damned," Welcome said, and he turned to leave.

He had his eyes on Grace when the two cars blew. The sound came to him as a single bellowing rupture, but when he looked down the highway he saw two distinct balls of flame, distant twin infernos that burned and kept burning through the fog.

72

Gerald drove the Isuzu through Mill Valley, then up Highway One. Welcome sat beside him. They passed Stinson Beach, up to where the road climbed and followed the lip of high cliffs that were as straight and sheer as stockade walls. Around some of the curves the edge was fenced off with a single steel guardrail, but otherwise there was just the road and then a fringe of grass or dirt, then abrupt turquoise sky that yawned above water.

Gerald followed the curves for a couple of miles, until he found a gravel shoulder along the ocean side of the road. He pulled in there, and they walked out to the edge. It dropped straight. Down below was the ocean. Far below. The white surf tore a thin ragged line at the base of the cliffs where wrinkled waves ran against the rock. The sound was a near-silent hiss that rose up and faded, and rose and faded.

"This'll do," Welcome said. Gerald pulled a big cardboard carton out of the backseat and brought it to the edge.

Inside the carton were two or three dozen of what seemed to be balls of cookie dough, about apple sized. Welcome reached in and took one of the balls. He stepped back a pace, then stepped forward again and heaved the ball into the sky. It seemed to hang there for a moment and then fell, fell, fell toward the ocean. The water dimpled for a moment and swallowed it.

Gerald took one of the balls. He gave an easy sidearm flip that shot it out toward the western horizon. It was out of sight before it started to drop, and then Welcome heaved another.

Felt funny at first, throwing it away. Like a magnum pistol, plastic explosive was one of those things you took for granted until you realized you couldn't go out and requisition it. You at least wanted to hang on to a kilo or two, never knew when you might need it.

But Welcome realized, there comes a time in life when you have to give up your goodies and move on.

Near the bottom of the box they started throwing them out rapid-fire, heaving one and grabbing another and heaving that one, seven or eight in the air at once, some still arching upward and others in a fall, until the box was empty and every one dropped into the water, pock pock pock and gone.

"Do they have cable in Oklahoma?" Roy Boy said.

"No cable on a farm," Marie said.

"No cable!"

"No cable, nothing. Eighty miles from Tulsa, you don't even get local TV unless the weather's right."

They were back at the house in San Pablo, Marie in the kitchen packing cartons, midmorning. Naull came in pushing a hand dolly.

"To heck with cable, we're getting a dish," Naull said. He started stacking cartons on the dolly.

"What kinda dish?" Roy Boy said.

"Satellite TV, a dish, *the* dish."

"Does it have HBO? Does it have the Braves and the Cubs?"

"It has HBO, it has the Braves and the Cubs and everybody else; it has world news from Moscow, if you want to get fancy."

"Neat," Roy Boy said.

Naull wheeled the dolly out, through the house, down the front steps to a U-Haul trailer hitched to the back of the Econoline. He loaded the cartons inside—it was almost full now—and he pulled the dolly up the steps behind him.

He was back in the kitchen again when the horn bratted outside, three times.

"That's them," he said.

"Go ahead," Marie said. "I'll finish up."

"Pack the boxes, I'll load 'em when I get back."

"I'll do it. You get back, we'll be set to go."

"You sure?"

"I'm ready to get on the road," she said.

"I've been ready," Naull said.

"On the road!" Roy Boy said.

"Damn straight."

He kissed them both, Roy first and then Marie.

"Won't be long," he said.

She said, "Sonny, you really want that satellite TV?"

"What's the matter, you got something against the dish?"

"We watch too much as it is. I was thinking, since we won't have cable, we wouldn't have to spend so much time in front of the tube. Kind of turn over a new leaf."

He walked up to her. Took her head in his hands. Looked her in the eyes as he gently brushed his thumbs across her brow. In no hurry. Kissed her and held her and kissed her again.

"Oh, we're doing that," he said. "A new leaf, you got it. For sure."

"When's the last time you were in Samoa?" Welcome said. He was beside Gerald in the Isuzu, waiting for Naull outside the bungalow.

"The year I turned eighteen," Gerald said. "We went back for Christmas."

"Nice?"

"Samoa isn't nice," Gerald said. "Samoa is fabulous."

"I figured."

"You want to go to Samoa?"

"I've been thinking, I need to log a little island time."

"That's always a good idea."

"Sit on a beach, watch the waves come in, think about life. Figure out where I go from here."

"You'll enjoy it," Gerald said. "Kick back for a couple of weeks, no pressure."

"Actually," Welcome said, "I was thinking in terms of eight or nine months."

Gerald considered this.

He said, "You going to sit on a beach for eight or nine months by yourself?"

"No," Welcome said. "It wouldn't be just me."

The fox, Gerald thought. Eight or nine months on a beach with the fox out of the Andy Hardy movie.

Holy moley.

"In that case," Gerald said, "you'll definitely enjoy yourself."

Naull came out the front door and down the walk. Welcome let him in the backseat. With the three of them crowded in, Gerald drove off, to the freeway and east to the town of Walnut Creek.

He turned into the parking lot of the Crocker Bank, couple of blocks off the interchange. Nice suburban bank, big lot, plenty of parking. Gerald pulled in beside a new white Continental, where Andy Pops sat behind the wheel, with a briefcase on his lap.

They all got out and stood in the sunshine. Andy Pops was holding the briefcase.

"Here we are again," Welcome said.

"Getting bored?" said Andy Pops.

"Not even close," Welcome said.

Unloading the stones was no problem in theory. Andy Pops was a buyer. But he was unwilling to do business outside the security of his warehouse, while Naull and Welcome and Gerald refused to walk into his turf with the stones and no guarantees.

Gerald got an idea, which he had conceived after watching Ruark at the B of A in Tomales. A security deposit vault was neutral ground, with bank clerks and guards and customers and security cameras outside to keep all parties honest. For added peace of mind they broke the stones into

271

six parcels, to be sold on consecutive days. Each parcel was cached in a different bank; Andy Pops had stashed money at each of the same banks.

Today was day six of six.

They walked into the bank together. The assistant manager brought them into the vault. Naull gave her a key, slid out the box, and cradled it in his arms. He brought it to a small privacy room in the vault. The room had a counter and two chairs, and the four of them filled up the rest of the space. Naull sat in one of the chairs, and Andy Pops took the other.

Andy Pops unsnapped the briefcase and took out his scales and his magnifier and a pair of pincers; Naull opened the box and extracted a cloth pouch.

He tumbled the jewels out into his cupped left hand, and carefully spilled them into a neat pile on the counter.

Andy Pops used the pincers to pick a diamond out of the pile. He held the diamond under the lens, and dropped it onto the scale. Little over a carat and a half.

"Six and a quarter," he said. Andy Pops also had a pocket calculator. He tapped 6–2–5 into the calculator, and dropped the diamond into the cloth bag.

They knew that Andy Pops must be writing himself a sweet deal. But the numbers kept mounting on the calculator. Andy Pops's finger jumped on the keypad.

They worked through the pile that way. Each day for six days there were more than three hundred stones in the pile; needed more than an hour to get through them.

Last one was an emerald nearly as big as a thumbnail. Andy Pops punched in 8–7–5.

He held up the calculator for them. The display read 119,800.

"Fair enough," Naull said.

Andy Pops went out with his key, found the assistant manager, and came back with his own box. Stacks of cash inside. Fifties, hundreds. He counted them out into piles. Filled the counter, piles of twenty bills each, and then he started again, laying stacks crossways over the first piles.

Naull watched the money, the stacks growing, Andy Pops's fingers flicking bills off a wad. Naull couldn't keep his eyes off it. You did not get used to it in a week or two, he thought. Maybe never, but for sure not in a week or two, after a lifetime of never having enough.

Andy Pops peeled off the last few bills.

"You want to count it?" Andy Pops said.

"You?" Naull said to Gerald and Welcome.

"No, that's it," Welcome said.

"That's it," Gerald said.

They knew. They were watching, too.

Right away Naull started to gather the stacks, whisking them up, binding them with a thick rubber band and putting it away in the metal deposit box. Andy Pops dropped the cloth bag into his own box, which he took out of the room, and when he came back a few seconds later his hands were empty, the stones locked away.

Naull was gathering a second thick pile of bills.

"Lot of money," Andy Pops said.

"A good day's work," Gerald said.

"For the week you got to be over seven. Seven of the extra-large variety."

"Seven hundred eighteen thousand, three hundred," Gerald said.

"Be careful," Andy Pops said. "That kind of money can sit up and bite you."

"How's that?" Naull said, without looking up.

"Money will agitate the mind," Andy Pops said. "It doesn't like sitting quietly. It wants to get out and do things, and one feels compelled to let it stretch its legs. But that's like putting a leash on a lion and going for a walk. You must be strong. You must know where you want to go. Or else you will end up going where the lion wants you to go. You may even become lunch. I've seen it happen."

Now Naull looked up. He looked at Welcome. Welcome was relaxed and happy. But he also stood alert and straight and ready. Welcome was always ready. Naull looked at Gerald. Big Gerald, solid, immovable, imperturbable.

Welcome was beginning to grin. A smile broadened on Gerald's face, too, pushing out the sides of his cheeks. Naull caught it, a happy light that glowed inside and brightened and worked its way out, a glee that he had to contain, or else laugh out loud.

Andy Pops seemed puzzled. He was trying to get the joke.

"You know," Naull told him, "I wouldn't worry about it, if I were you."

ABOUT THE AUTHOR

Phillip Finch has been a reporter for the Washington *Daily News* and the San Francisco *Examiner*. He now lives in Howard, Kansas, and is the author of ten books, including *The Reckoning, In a Place Dark and Secret, Trespass,* and *Sugarland,* which was cited by the *New York Times Book Review* as one of the notable thrillers of 1991.